CHRONICLES OF THE CROSSGUARD

THE BELT OF TRUTH

JEREMIAH LASALLE

HOUSE OF LORE BOOKS

For my wife, my parents, both little
brothers and the one who I saw as my
older brother. The one who gave my
baby boy a name to inherit-
Kylor.

Published by House of Lore Press

ISBN:
Cover Design: Micah & Tyler Millard
Interior Design: Created by Author

Printed in the United States of America

1 3 5 7 9   10 8 6 4 2
First Edition.

*"Put on all of God's armor so that you
will be able to stand firm...
For we are not fighting against
flesh-and-blood enemies,
but against evil rulers in the unseen
world..."*
– Ephesians 6:11-12

CONTENTS

CHAPTER ONE
SILENCE AND ECHOES

H ave you ever noticed?

An echo, just out of reach? Or the darkness, an unknown illness of the mind, seeping into society's veins?

While everyone else keeps going through their day as if nothing happened. Your shadow is on a delay, the mirror lagging ever so slightly, hiding a secret you're not supposed to know.

You're not going crazy. You've just woken up, as I did.

My name's Kayson Cavalier, and my origin doesn't begin with prophecy or stormy nights.

No, it starts with the one thing everyone once dreaded. The first day back to school. The alarm never got the chance. Silence beat it there.

Not the peaceful kind you can roll over and sink back into. This was sharp, like the air had swallowed its own breath and was holding it to see what I'd do. I stayed on my back, hoodie twisted around me from the night before, listening for a reason to feel stupid.

Same cracked ceiling. Same Sonorah High jersey hanging off the chair. Same half-finished stack of comics and paperbacks like they knew I'd lied about finishing them.

Everything looked normal. It just didn't sound normal.

My eyes landed on the mirror over the dresser. I don't really use it. It's just there. Today it felt pointed, like a question I didn't remember asking.

I slid out of bed and padded closer across the floorboard. I let out a breath. Cold air followed.

For a second, the glass struggled to hold me. Pale light lifted off my shoulders, a thin outline forming smoke shaped like armor. The hint of wings folded tight behind my back. It was gone before I could flinch.

I stared hard. Messy dark hair, sleep-crease across my cheek, eyes carrying a question I couldn't phrase. I tipped my head left; the other me followed on time. I tipped right; the lag didn't repeat.

"Great," I muttered. "Now my mirror's lagging."

My palm met the cold glass. The air pressed against my skin. Light but focused, the way a storm tests a windowpane before breaking it.

A normal person would stop there. I stayed and breathed once, then again. My breath fogged a perfect circle as if something on the other side had exhaled back.

The temperature dipped. Not by much. A thread of cool that slid along my wrists and under the hoodie like water. Sound thinned, allowing the room's normal hum to take over; plumbing, a neighbor's truck, the house's old bones flattened out until it felt like I was listening through cotton.

I don't scare easily. But I recognize when something sees me first.

Somewhere in the wall, a low hum started. Then stopped, like the house clearing its throat.

Footsteps creaked down the hall, followed by a gentle knock. "Breakfast in five, boys," Mrs. Miles called.

"Got it," I croaked, voice rougher than I meant.

"Don't be late on the first day!"

From the bathroom across the hall, Cody: "He's always late!"

The moment cracked. I stepped back from the mirror fast, like staying meant I'd let whatever-that-was finish blinking.

Backpack slumped by the closet, zipper half-open like it had been rifled through. I didn't remember touching it the night before. I closed it, then grabbed my phone off the dresser. It lit up in my palm.

Cody: Shoes. Pancake Mountain is real.

Cody: Also, you snore like a dying vacuum.

I thumbed back: Lies and slander. Then: Be there in a sec.

A few minutes later, hoodie on and heartbeat finally slowing, I took the stairs two at a time.

Downstairs smelled like cinnamon and ambition.

Mrs. Miles ran the kitchen like a general. Her pan in one hand, spatula in the other, syrup streaming over a stack tall enough to apply for statehood. She glanced over, smile soft but steel-backed. The kind that raised me better than blood ever tried.

"Big day, Kayson. You ready?"

"As I'll ever be," I said, dropping into my usual chair.

Cody was mid-devour, shirtless, hair inexplicably perfect as always. He grinned through a mouthful. "You look like you saw a ghost."

"Just your face," I said.

"Rude. Accurate. But rude."

Mrs. Miles set a plate of three pancakes in front of me. Syrup bleeding from them like a delicious crime scene. She rested a hand on my shoulder. "Prayed for you both this morning. Just covering."

The word landed like sunlight filtered through glass. Warm, but with the outline of the pane still there.

Usually, covering felt warm. Today it felt heavy, like someone lowering armor over my shoulders piece by piece.

"Thanks," I said, and meant it.

I cut a piece and took a bite. Cinnamon hit first, then vanilla. They tasted like comfort. The syrup landed like a pebble in a pond that didn't ripple.

"First day," Cody said around another bite. "Place your bets. How many freshmen cry before lunch?"

"Wow," I said. "Starting the year with compassion."

"Realism. My money's on at least three. Bonus point if one's a football player who can't find the locker rooms."

Mrs. Miles slid an extra pancake onto his plate without asking.

"You boys will be kind," she said, and didn't look at him when she said it. She looked at me.

"We're kind," Cody said, offended for no reason. "We're pillars of kindness."

"You're pillars of something," I said.

We spiraled through the normal stuff, returning seniors with invented personalities, worst-case lockers, that one vending machine that eats singles and faith.

Cody brought up Judah's girlfriend, who swears there are fifty-one states, and somehow it made the coffee taste stronger.

Under the chatter, I kept listening for the house's normal singsong. The tick of the hallway clock, the old fridge's low whirr, the water heater clearing its throat.

They were there. They just sounded farther away, like the house had stepped into another room and forgot to invite me.

"Eat," Mrs. Miles said when she noticed I'd only moved the pancakes around to make it look like I'd eaten half. She wasn't the pressuring type.

She radiated suggestion.

"I am," I said, then took an actual bite to make it true.

I didn't mention the dream. Not a nightmare exactly. There was a voice that knew my name like it had been practicing for years.

Along with flashes of gray streets, light that wasn't light, all stitched together by silence.

People think fear is all about shouting and sprinting. Mine shows up quieter. It loosens the world's grip and lets it slide a little.

Cody paused long enough to squint at me. "You sure you're good?"

"Yeah." The lie was automatic, gentle. "You know, nerves. First day back and all."

"You? Nervous? You do deadlifts for fun."

"Deadlifts make sense."

"So does school."

"That's a rumor."

"Fine. On a scale of one to existential dread..."

"Cody," Mrs. Miles said without looking up.

He smirked at me instead. "He's fine."

"I'm fine," I echoed, and took a sip of water that felt heavier than it should.

My hands were steady when I reached for the syrup, but the fork rattled once against the plate. A small, almost polite shake, nothing dramatic. If you weren't looking, you'd miss it.

Mrs. Miles never misses anything. She came back around and set a napkin down near my elbow like she always does, an excuse to be close. The faintest pressure of her palm warmed the center of my back.

"First days are weird," she said, voice low enough to make it ours. "But you're covered."

I nodded once. The word pressed against my chest again, protective maybe, or a warning. She didn't sermonize. She never did. She just carried light around like it was part of her groceries.

"Question," Cody said. "If I tell Coach I'm experiencing spiritual burnout, do I get out of the mile?"

"Absolutely not," Mrs. Miles said, like she'd been waiting.

I chewed and tried on a smile. "Try it after roll call."

"See? He supports my growth."

"I support watching what happens."

"Betrayal."

I let the normal talk of schedules and rumors wash over me. Outside, a car door shut. Somewhere upstairs, the old pipes ticked like teeth. Life was doing its part. The quiet in my ribs didn't move.

My eyes drifted to the hallway. The first time I'd walked it, eight years ago, my whole life fit in a black garbage bag. I'd rehearsed not-crying for two days. Cody was smaller and louder then; he asked if I liked superheroes and if I wanted the last popsicle. Mrs. Miles hugged me like she'd been saving the spot, not just filling it.

That was it. I never left.

Sometimes I listen for the sound that first night made. How the air changed when someone decided I could stay. The house remembers it; maybe that's why the silence feels heavier now. Maybe being covered means the silence reaches me first.

I still check the door, though, half expecting the world might change its mind.

"Yo," Cody said suddenly, waving his phone. "Judah says they're enforcing the no-hood rule hard this year. You ready to reveal your face to the public?"

"No."

"He thinks the vice principal carries scissors."

"She does," Mrs. Miles said, unbothered. "But for paper. And paper only."

I tugged the hood anyway, as it could argue for me. Not as a fashion statement. It was a portable wall.

"Besides," Cody said, "you look good without it. It's a service to the community."

"Your community has low standards."

"True," he said cheerfully, and shoveled in more pancake.

I tried another bite. The flavors still rang true, but the sweetness hit my stomach with the weight of a yes I hadn't actually said.

What would I even tell them? Hey, the silence upstairs watched me first. Too weird for breakfast. Too weird for this house that had saved me on the day I needed saving.

"Eat," Mrs. Miles said again, softer. I listened. Mostly because it was easier than explaining why the milk tasted faintly metallic for one second and then didn't.

Cody leaned back, finally full. "Alright. Prediction two." He held up two fingers. "Three hallway fights by Friday."

"Zero," I said.

"You underestimate this institution."

"I believe in growth."

He narrowed his eyes. "You okay for real? Your hands..."

"They're fine," I said, and lifted them to show steady fingers. He accepted it because the alternative was digging where he didn't like to dig.

Mrs. Miles squeezed my shoulder once more and started loading plates in the sink. "Shoes," she said, not looking at anyone in particular, and meaning both.

"On it," Cody said, bolting toward the stairs as if they'd move without him.

I stayed a second longer. The kitchen light hit the syrup, making it look like prehistoric amber. I set the fork down, let my breath out slowly, and listened.

The refrigerator's hum. The faint chatter of the TV two houses over. A car easing by outside. All normal. All present. But underneath, the same thin, expectant quiet I'd woken to, like a held note that hadn't decided if it was music or a warning.

I scraped my chair back and stood. The room breathed with me. I told myself it was nothing. The kind of nothing you can step around if you don't name it.

As I crossed the threshold, the air changed by a hair. Warmer near the hallway, cooler when I stepped under the house's other mirror, its silent twin, waiting on the wall like it knew its turn was coming. Usually, you don't think about these things unless you have to. I think about them all the time.

At the bottom of the stairs, I paused and glanced up. Shadows lay where they always lay. No shapes. No glow. Just the house that became home because someone decided I belonged.

"Let's go, laggy mirror," Cody called, already at the front door, shoes half-tied and confidence fully laced. "If I'm late on Day One, I'm blaming you in writing."

"Please learn to write first," I said, grabbing my bag.

He clicked his tongue and opened the door. Morning slid in, chill and bright. The world outside felt louder than inside, which should've made me relax. It didn't.

Mrs. Miles pressed two granola bars into my hand in passing, as a magician and a mom had collaborated. "Lunch is on me if you forget yours," she said. "And if anything feels off, text. Doesn't matter what, just text."

"Okay," I said.

She studied me for a beat longer than usual. "Covered," she repeated, like she was pinning the word to my chest.

I nodded. It settled there, protective maybe. Or a thin line drawn in chalk that something else would try to step across.

Cody hopped out to the porch and yelled back, "Are we getting a ride or jogging to enlightenment?"

"Headed towards enlightenment," Mrs. Miles said, kissing his temple in a move he pretended to hate and always leaned into.

I slung the backpack on. The strap bit into my shoulder; I adjusted it and told myself that's why my chest felt tight.

We moved toward the door. The house exhaled. I would've blamed it on the draft, or the change in pressure, or old wood being dramatic. I wanted to blame it. I really did.

But the hum in my ears faded back into that earlier silence.

It hadn't left.

We cut through the back street behind the baseball fields. The one where the sidewalk cracked like puzzle pieces, and the chain-link fence leaned inward as if it had secrets to tell.

If you slowed down, you could almost hear it whisper. The air smelled like damp concrete and faded grass, like summer hanging on by its fingernails.

Somewhere underneath lingered the faint sting of something burnt, like August not ready to give up.

Cody filled the silence with noise because that's what Cody does.

"First thing I'm doing in gym is faking an injury," he announced, limping like he'd been drafted into war. "The second I hear *endurance,* I'm going down. Full collapse. Maybe one heroic tear. Really sell it."

"You'd better bring your Oscar performance," I muttered.

"Pain is temporary. Gym grades are forever."

He grinned. I half-smiled. The morning light felt staged, the breeze timed to an invisible metronome. Even the birds overhead repeated the same three-note loop every fifteen seconds. Not that I was counting.

But I was.

"Yo, ghost boy," Cody said, snapping his fingers in front of my face. "Earth to Kayson."

"Yeah. Sorry. Thinking."

"About?"

"Stuff."

"Ancient rituals, maybe," he said solemnly. "Vague answers until death."

I kicked a rock into the gutter. It bounced, then landed with a click that sounded like it was edited. I think the reality show's producer had gotten lazy.

Cody didn't press. He never does. That's his mercy, he asks, but never chases.

Sonorah High rose ahead, glass and steel catching the sun like a mirror angled at heaven. A temple pretending to be a school. It gleamed too clean, like it hadn't earned its scuffs yet.

Scarlet-and-silver banners flapped from every light pole. Each bore a symbol: a sword, point down, circled by fire.

"New crest?" I asked.

"New principal," Cody said. "New branding. Next up, mandatory pep-chanting."

He laughed. I didn't.

Because the symbol didn't feel *new.*

It felt remembered.

Something wordless shifted behind my ribs, like a name I'd forgotten but the air still knew.

We passed under the front gate. The sound of normal chaos hit like a wave; lockers slamming, shoes squeaking, laughter ricocheting off glass.

But underneath, where the world keeps its secrets, everything went quiet.

Clusters of students scrolling, laughing, and shoving filled the courtyard. But some weren't moving. They stood too still, heads tilted, faces slack, as if they were mannequins waiting for permission.

One girl near the steps moved her hand from her forehead to her heart,

Her fingers trembled like she was trying to remember the order. Her lips moved soundlessly.

It wasn't a prayer.

It was a defense.

"Is it just me," I said, "or is everything a little off today?"

Cody looked around. "Feels normal. You're just allergic to school spirit."

"Right."

His joke landed softly, like he didn't quite believe it either.

We reached the flyer board. Pinholes layered like fossils; tape crusted over older tape.

Most flyers were the usual suspects: theater auditions, chess club, lost-dog pleas.

One wasn't.

Parchment-colored paper. Torn edges. Red ink that shimmered when the sun hit it too deeply, almost alive. The kind of red you remember later without knowing why.

THE SPIRIT OF OBEDIENCE: ORDER BRINGS SAFETY.

No club name. No contact info.

Just the sword-and-fire emblem stamped at the bottom, like a seal of approval from something ancient.

The air thickened.

The edges of the world twitched, half a frame behind.

Mrs. Miles's voice surfaced in my head, *covered.* But the air around the board didn't feel like shelter.

It felt like testing.

Cody kept walking. I didn't.

I stared, heart thudding in my throat. The smell of burnt summer crept back.

Covering from what?

I reached toward the flyer.

It didn't feel like I moved.

It felt like it did.

A static hum, sharp, brushed the hair on my arms, then was gone.

Somewhere behind me, a PA speaker crackled, hissed, and went dead.

The silence after wasn't empty. It listened.

"You coming or what?" Cody called, holding the main door with his foot. "Sacred halls of teen misery await!"

I blinked hard. The world snapped back.

He grinned the same bright grin he always had, stupidly human.

Behind him, the still students hadn't shifted an inch.

My fingers hovered inches from the flyer.

A whisper, *not sound but thought,* passed through me: Don't touch it.

I yanked my hand back. "Yeah," I said, voice uneven. "Coming."

Cody's grin softened. "You good?"

"Yeah. Just... déjà vu."

He nodded once, accepting the lie.

I managed half a smile. "That's it."

We pushed through the doors.

The inside of Sonorah High smelled like bleach and too-fresh paint. Maybe someone had tried to scrub history off the walls.

Fluorescent lights hummed overhead in uneven rhythm: *bzz-bzz ... pause ... bzz.* Every pause felt a beat too long.

Posters lined the hall: *Courage Week. Safety First. Obedience Is Strength.* Each carried the same sword-and-fire crest stamped in red.

Cody whistled low. "Wow. Nothing says school pride like dictator décor."

"Guess rebellion's out this year."

He smirked. "Good thing I've always been an underachiever."

A group of sophomores passed, eyes glassy. Their laughter arrived half a second behind their mouths.

I tried to tell myself I imagined it.

We hit the main atrium where sunlight poured through the skylight. For a heartbeat, everything in the lively crowd looked normal again.

Then I caught the reflection in the polished floor.

Everyone's shadows moved with them. Except mine.

Mine lingered.

Half a breath behind.

"Great," I muttered. "Now my shadow's lagging too."

"What?" Cody asked.

"Nothing."

The bell rang before he could push.

Only it didn't *ring.*

It warped.

The tone stretched, fluttered, doubled back on itself, like someone dragging a finger across a record. Students didn't notice.

They kept moving, heads down, screens up, conversations intact.

The sound bent again, lower this time. Then snapped back into the regular chime.

Cody groaned. "First bell. I was really hoping summer would last forever."

"Yeah," I said softly. "Forever's shorter than it used to be."

He gave me a look. "You sure you're not writing poetry in your sleep?"

"Wouldn't sell."

"Depends on the font."

He clapped my shoulder. The touch grounded me. It was warm, human, loud enough to push back against the quiet humming at the edges of everything.

Outside, sunlight burned against the glass, as if it were trying to see in.

For a moment, I wondered which side of it I was really on.

The hallway swallowed me, buzzing with chaos; shoulder-to-shoulder traffic, lockers slamming, sneakers shrieking on tile. But underneath it all was quiet.

Not less noise. Less *life* inside the noise.

Like we were listening to the memory of a hallway instead of the real thing.

Cody didn't notice. He was already drifting toward the varsity crowd, fist-bumping two seniors and launching into his ritual complaint about Coach Marcus's back hair being a fire hazard.

I tried to smile. Tried harder to care.

Something crawled up my spine. A pulse behind my ears that refused to fade.

Everything looked right. That was the worst part.

The trophy case still gleamed with crooked rows of fake gold.

Pine-Sol, AC, and teenager still mingled in the air.

Flyers still clung to corkboards like overstayed guests.

And under it all, the same rhythm beat again.

A low vibration gathered under my ribs, faint as a second heartbeat trying to sync with mine.

Judah Walker leaned against his locker, two clones boasting the same cheesy grin and flexed, skinny arms.

"Yo, Cavalier," he called. "Back to bless us with your holy weirdness?"

He and his minions barked a laugh, pleased with themselves.

Shaking my head, I spun my lock. Click—clink.

Something metal dropped inside. Not from my books.

A black pen rolled out, sleek and heavy, tapping the floor.

The sound echoed too far. As if it hit something deeper than tile.

I crouched. My fingertips buzzed before they even touched it.

Not from fear. From certainty.

That wasn't an accident.

Across the hall, a locker slammed.

A girl froze, hand still on the metal. Her chest barely moved. Then she lifted her right hand to her forehead, then to her heart.

That same gesture as before.

Her lips moved, silent.

Not a prayer.

A response.

The air rippled once, subtle as a shiver.

That shape again. It was following me.

I looked toward Cody. He was mid-story, alive, oblivious.

He didn't see any of it.

Then the bell rang.

Only, it didn't ring.

It *bent*.

The tone dragged low, then high, like someone stretching the sound in slow motion.

It echoed through more than one hallway, bouncing between layers I couldn't see.

Every light flickered once, proof enough for me.

My pulse tripped.

I needed to move.

Mr. Sterling's classroom sat at the far end of the west wing, past the trophy cases and the vending machine that hadn't worked since spring.

With every step, the air thickened, pressing against my ribs like the building was trying to keep me out.

By the time I reached his door, my palms were slick.

I grabbed the handle anyway.

Inside wasn't silent. It was *still*.

The noise of the hallway didn't follow me in.

This room felt protected or quarantined.

Mr. Sterling looked up from his desk.

"You're early."

"Just needed to breathe."

He studied me for a heartbeat too long, like a guard checking for cracks after a storm.

"Then you picked the right room."

I slid into my seat, third row, right by the window.

Outside, the football field looked printed.

The grass was unnaturally green. The flag, barely moving. Light hovering instead of shining.

This class used to be my quiet spot. Mr. Sterling let me think.

Today, the quiet listened back.

He rose slowly and wrote on the board in neat block letters:

THE INVISIBLE WAR

The scratch of the chalk cut straight through me.

My stomach knew that phrase before my brain did.

It wasn't a topic.

It was a warning.

Mrs. Miles's voice flickered through my head, *covered. B*ut this didn't feel like shelter.

It felt like being drafted.

Mr. Sterling turned toward the window, and his gaze fixed somewhere past the horizon. As if watching something approach.

Without turning, he said quietly,

"Pay attention today, Kayson."

The words slid into me as a blade sheathed in calm.

My heart jolted once, hard.

Not fear. Recognition.

He knew.

Mr. Sterling faced the class again, eyes steady, expression unreadable.

He started talking about history, probably wars or civilizations. But the words blurred behind the hum in my ears.

The hum wasn't electrical. It was alive.

I tried to ground myself.

Posters lined the walls with justice quotes, ancient ruins, and a Latin phrase carved above the chalkboard: *Veritas Libera Vos.*

The truth will set you free.

A Roman gladius hung above the board. And above that, a shield.

Midnight blue iron. No shine. Just weight.

The light from the window slid across it.

For a heartbeat, it breathed.

Not a glare. A pulse.

My breath caught. Then stillness.

Mr. Sterling's chalk kept scratching.

The sound doubled. Once in real time, once a half-beat later.

I looked up. He was already watching me.

The kind of look that had seen something crawl out of eternity and recognized its scent.

Then he blinked. The moment died.

The bell shrilled, thin and sharp. It skipped like a scratched record, then continued as if nothing happened.

For a second, no one moved.

The sound hung between us as a string pulled too tight.

I exhaled. The pressure in the room eased.

Behind him, Mr. Sterling put the chalk down, turned back to the board, and underlined the title once slowly and deliberately.

THE INVISIBLE WAR

The line rang louder than the bell.

Its surface was blank now.

But faintly, just enough for doubt, my reflection stared back a half-second late.

The world exhaled.

The bell's echo lingered, whispering my name.

It didn't sound like fear anymore. It sounded like a reminder to stay awake.

The bell quit shouting, but the building didn't relax.

Noise drained down the corridor in waves. Chairs were scraping, voices rising, doors slamming. Underneath it ran a thinner sound, almost not a sound at all. A held breath stretched across the hall like plastic.

I stayed behind in Mr. Sterling's room, pretending to stack handouts. The paper felt cool, edged. The fluorescent lights hummed their steady *bzz-bzz...pause...bzz,* except the pause lasted a fraction too long, like something was counting my heartbeats to see if I'd miss one.

Figures, my brain's haunted now.

The door clicked open.

"Did he forget his soul?" a voice asked lightly.

I looked up. Sarah Storm stood in the doorway, one hand curled around a library copy of *The Republic.* Dark hair in a loose braid, eyes too awake for the first period. A small cross on a thin chain rested against her collarbone, the metal slightly askew.

"Probably Cody?" I said. "He never had one to begin with."

Her mouth tipped at one corner. "Fair. Mr. Sterling asked if anyone had grabbed the extra syllabi. I said I would." She lifted the folder in her other hand. "Heroics."

"You're saving lives out there."

She stepped in and let the door shut behind her. The room cooled a degree, no, not cold-cold; a thread of winter braided into September.

"You feel that?" she asked, voice almost casual.

"What?"

She glanced at the lights, then at me. "The air. Not broken. Like the temp is off."

I could've lied. I almost did.

"Yeah," I said. "I feel it."

A breath of relief moved through her shoulders like she'd been holding a question since she woke up. "Thought I was crazy."

"Congratulations," I said. "Guess I'm not the only one wondering if I'm awake."

She laughed softly, set the syllabi on Mr. Sterling's desk, and dust motes hung in the pale window light, suspended as if they'd forgotten how to fall.

Outside, the field still looked printed. The flag twitched without moving the pole. Far past the bleachers, a thin cloud unraveled without going anywhere.

"Do you know Mr. Sterling well?" she asked.

"Starting to," I said. "He lets me think."

"Nice," she said. "Most people are allergic to that."

The room exhaled a little warmth back into my hands. I shuffled the stack again for no reason and caught my reflection in the window. There and then, a beat late. I looked away before the second I could finish the movement.

"Bell's about to ring again," Sarah said. "Want a head start on the stampede?"

"Maybe give them something to trample," I said. "I hear it builds community."

She smiled, but the corner of her mouth held a warning that didn't belong to the joke. The cross at her collar tilted farther, as if the chain had twisted itself.

The temperature dropped again.

Not dramatically. Just enough that the breath I let out made a thin ghost in front of me. The lights didn't flicker. They dulled, colors washing out to hospital white.

Sarah's hand drifted to the chain like she was steadying it. "Okay," she said under her breath. "There it is."

I didn't ask what. The answer arrived first.

It wasn't a sound in the room. It was a thought wearing my voice, confident in the wrong direction.

You don't belong, it said pleasantly, like giving good advice. *They saved you as a project. You're work, not family. Walk away before they notice the mistake.*

I stiffened. The room hadn't changed. Only the suggestion of winter had crept behind my ribs, blowing inward.

Sarah's eyes narrowed, searching the corners the way you look for a draft that keeps moving your paper. "Do you..." she started, then shook her head. "Never mind."

The voice returned, helpful. *You don't have to fight it. Quit before you're asked to. Slip out early. Leave the weight for people who were born for it.*

The sentence slotted so neatly into the groove of old fears that for a second, I forgot to separate mine from *not-mine.* Pressure gathered at my temples like I'd sprinted up a mountain by mistake. Fingers tingled.

I put the papers down.

Sarah's braid lifted a hair with the same unseen draft; she rubbed one forearm with the other hand, quick and practical, like warming muscle for a run.

"It's colder," she said, eyes on the far wall. "But not... here." She pressed a palm to her chest. "Out here." She gestured at the space between us.

It wasn't inside either of us. It pressed from the gap, the way patient water presses on a window underwater not yet breaking anything while promising it could.

The thought-voice gentled, almost kind. *You can rest. Tell the truth later. There's no prize for being early.*

I almost agreed. It would be so easy to do nothing. Doing nothing tasted like syrup and sleep. Doing nothing felt like sitting down on the exact step where you ran out of breath.

"Hey," Sarah said softly.

I met her eyes.

Something steadied.

Warmth bloomed in my chest, small as a matchhead and just as complete as heat without burn. It spread along the lattice of breath and settled like a belt fastened from the inside.

It tightened, not choking, but exact. Like the air itself had decided which parts of me were still mine.

Maybe this was what Mrs. Miles meant by *covered.* Warmth that pushes back. No glow. No spectacle. Just the space where thoughts move, growing firm.

A faint gold thread of sunlight broke through the blinds, thin but steady. The room remembering what warmth looked like.

The cold retreated a step.

Sarah blinked. "It passed through, didn't it?" she whispered. "Like... a draft with opinions."

"That's one way to put it." My voice came out steadier than my hands felt. *You don't belong,* the not-voice tried again, softer now, annoyed it had missed. *Quit later,* it amended, as if bargaining. *Later's responsible.*

"Rude," Sarah said, almost smiling, as if she'd heard her own version. "It sounds like me when it talks."

"Same."

Color slid back into the posters by degrees. The dust remembered gravity. The cross unclenched and leveled.

I didn't realize I'd said it out loud until the sound reached my own ears. "No."

Sarah glanced at me like I'd tossed a pebble into a pond. "No," she echoed the same word, the same weight. Like a password.

The door opened without sound. Mr. Sterling was already there.

He didn't fill the doorway; he steadied it.

"Hallway's enthusiastic," he said mildly, as if remarking on the weather.

"It got cold," Sarah said. "But not a draft kind of cold."

"A false presence," Mr. Sterling said. His gaze flicked to the window, then to me. "They send chills ahead of themselves. See who shivers."

"They can't... be here," Sarah said, hearing the doubt in her own voice.

"Not in the way you're imagining," Mr. Sterling said. "Not yet. Not without help. But they can lean on the wall and whisper."

"Through?" Sarah asked.

"Against," he said. "Enough to see if anyone listens."

His eyes softened, and for a moment the room learned how to be warm at the corners. "You didn't."

It wasn't a question, and I didn't want to tell him how close I'd been to sitting down on that step that felt like rest.

"What if someone does?" Sarah asked. "Listen."

"They won't think that's what they did," Mr. Sterling said. "They'll call it common sense, or maturity." He stepped inside, and the temperature climbed a notch, like the thermostat answered to his voice. "You two need to get to your next class."

The second bell wasn't due yet, but the building seemed to remember it, because the hum shifted to anticipation, a chorus of clocks clearing their throats.

"Mr. Sterling," I said.

He turned back.

"The words on your board," I said. "That wasn't... random."

"No," he said simply.

"*The Invisible War,*" Sarah read softly from behind me, like testing the shape of it.

Mr. Sterling's mouth tipped at one side, not quite a smile. "Learning the names of things gives you an advantage over them."

"Like when you label the mystery meat," I said before I could stop myself.

"Exactly," he said, deadpan. "Now, both of you, shoes in motion. There's a schedule to pretend we trust."

He stepped aside. Sarah moved past him, and I followed. In the doorway, she slowed and glanced up at me. "You okay?"

"I am now," I said, surprised by how true it felt.

"Good," she said. "Because..." She hesitated, then shrugged the sentence away. "See you."

"See you."

We stepped into the corridor together. The air out here had warmed, but the warmth was thin, like sunlight through cheap blinds. Students flowed around us, laughing, complaining. The vending machine clicked mournfully and failed to vend.

A cold feather slid along the back of my neck.

It wasn't the same as before. Not an invasion. A reminder.

Later, the not-voice offered, polite again, from just beyond hearing. *Later's wiser.*

I kept walking. The warmth at my core held. It wasn't dramatic. It was stubborn.

"Do you hear it?" Sarah asked under the crowd noise.

"Not with my ears," I said.

"Same." She touched the cross, felt it steady under her fingertips. "It's going to get worse, isn't it?"

"Probably," I said. Honesty didn't feel brave; it felt like balancing on something narrow and right. "But we're not crazy."

"We're just awake," she said, and met my eyes like we'd rehearsed the line in another life.

The fire alarm chirped once, a glitch that made four people jump and everyone else ignore it. The chirp didn't become a wail. It just hung there, a small red dot of possibility, then went out. I heard two tones inside that dot, one honest and one hollow, braided like they were practicing being the same sound.

We hit the junction where the west wing split: stairs down to the science hall, stairs up to the library, and the old art rooms with the smeared windows. The crowd thinned enough to hear separate conversations. Someone was breaking up with someone. Someone else was selling energy bars two dollars above cost. A teacher scolded a cluster of sophomores for treating the stairwell like a photoshoot.

"I've got English," Sarah said, nodding left.

"History," I said, nodding right.

"Just..." She paused again, puzzling something. "If it does that again, don't pretend it didn't."

Truth didn't crackle. It settled. "Okay."

She half smiled. "Okay."

We separated. The hallway absorbed it like it absorbs everything.

Halfway to history, I passed a bulletin board covered in new posters. **Courtesy is Courage. Order Brings Safety.** The sword-in-fire crest stamped red in each corner, as if the paper had been sealed by a ring on a hand I couldn't see. I reached out, not touching. Just close enough to feel the temperature. The space in front of the ink was cooler than the space around it. A quiet place for a lie to sit.

"Keep moving, Cavalier," someone said behind me. Judah, probably. I didn't turn. Not today.

When I stepped into the classroom, the hum that had followed me since morning slipped sideways and waited near the ceiling like a spider testing a web. Mr. Gale droned on about attendance. My desk felt like the exact size of the life I'd been handed. I took a breath and sat in it anyway.

Somewhere, two halls over, the bell that wasn't scheduled rang once. Clean, correct, like it had remembered its job and wanted credit. No one reacted. Maybe no one heard it.

Except the sound wasn't a ring. It was the shadow of a ring. The suggestion of metal making a promise.

I felt the warm belt of not-light fasten again, quiet as prayer. Not armor you wear; armor you are.

The chill retreated. Not gone, never gone.

But farther from the center than it had been a minute ago.

I wrote my name on the slip with a black pen that felt heavier than it should. The click when I capped it traveled deeper than the desk.

"Kayson," Mr. Gale said, not looking up. "Present?"

"Present," I said.

The word felt truer than it had yesterday. Not safe, not easy. Just here.

At the edge of hearing, something tested the wall again, polite as a salesman. *Later,* it was offered.

"No," I said in my head, and the warmth answered like a hand pressing back. Somewhere beyond the walls, winter waited for permission to speak again. For now, this was enough.

Apparently, honesty counts as disrespect now.

Technically, Mr. Gale wrote "detention for inappropriate tone," which is teacher for *you made a joke I couldn't grade.* I didn't argue. After the morning I'd had, a quiet room sounded like mercy.

Detention lived in Room 217. One of those end-cap classrooms that smelled like dry-erase markers, chalk dust, and ozone—the scent classrooms get right before a storm. The blinds cut the late-afternoon sun into neat bars across scuffed tile. The clock above the door ticked like a metronome that didn't believe in music.

Tick.

...half a breath...

Tick.

The space between ticks felt wider than the ticks themselves.

I dropped into a desk near the back and made a show of getting out a notebook. I wrote my name on the top corner like I was about to repent in cursive.

The door slid open without a squeak. Mr. Sterling stepped in with a thin stack of forms, nodded at me like I was a regular, and set the stack on the front table. No lecture. No, *why are you here?* He took the teacher's chair, angled toward the window, as if he meant to give the sun a chance to explain itself.

We let the room breathe.

Outside, Sonorah's field turned that late-day green that looks lit from the inside. The flag climbed and drifted back down the exact inch it had gained. The sky was a clean sheet with one lazy contrail trying to write a sentence and failing.

"Assignment?" he asked after a minute, like the word was optional.

"Reflect on my choices," I said.

He almost smiled. "That could take a while."

I considered saying, *I've been doing it all day.* Instead, I stretched my legs until my heel hit the desk's bottom bar and tried to make the metal ping quietly.

Ping.

The sound fell short, as if the air had padding.

I glanced at the clock again. Tick...tick. The second tick arrived on time, but I heard it a heartbeat later, like the room was practicing lag for sport.

"Do you remember," Mr. Sterling said, still watching the window, "what you felt this morning?"

Which thing? The mirror lag, the warped bell, the breathing shield, the draft with opinions.

"All of it," I said. Honesty isn't brave. It just weighs more at first. "The air listened. The bell bent. There was a chill that talked like me when it wanted me to quit."

"And did you?" he asked. "Quit."

"No."

"Why not?"

The question was too simple, which meant it wasn't. I thought of Sarah's steady eyes. Of warmth stitching around my ribs. Mrs. Miles pinned a word to my chest like a badge.

"Because the lie sounded... intentional," I said slowly, "but not true."

He nodded once, satisfied, and finally turned toward me. In the slanted light, his face looked carved, not stern, just patient. "You think you're hearing something new," he said. "You're hearing what didn't work on you."

"That's what an echo is?" I asked. "Garbage day for lies?"

"Residue," he said. "Temptations leave an imprint when they fail. Sometimes it's light, sometimes sound. Sometimes the mind keeps the shape."

"Feels like punishment."

"No," Mr. Sterling said. "Proof."

The word landed like a weight that didn't crush.

"So the echo is... an after-image."

"After-sound," he corrected gently. "People imprint what they believe; walls just echo it. Sonorah feels heavier than it should. Too many hearts listening to the wrong voices."

"Why here?" I asked. "Why our school?"

"Because schools gather people who haven't decided what they are yet," he said. "And because someone is helping."

The blinds made slow shadows across the chalkboard. One shadow moved the wrong direction for a heartbeat, backward up the board, then corrected. I blinked and decided not to dignify it with a comment.

"If truth pushes them back," I said, "why do they keep coming?"

"Because they want it silenced." He said it like the weather. "Truth isn't opinion. Its alignment. It doesn't move when you do."

"So truth hurts on purpose."

"Only to break bones that healed wrong." His voice softened. "You've had a few of those."

I didn't ask how he knew. The air thinned a little, the way it does when someone opens a box you've kept taped for years.

"Mrs. Miles would say I've had covering," I muttered.

"She's right," he said. "Covering isn't quarantine. Its presence. It doesn't remove the weather; it puts a roof over a mind."

I pictured the warmth from earlier fastening like a belt I hadn't earned and couldn't put on myself. The room answered with a small drop in temperature, as if to test the thought.

"I don't want to be dramatic," I said, "but I'm one weird noise away from stapling my hoodie to my skull."

"Don't," he said dryly. "Ruins the stapler."

The clock ticked again. Tick...

Then a second tick arrived that wasn't the clock's. It came from the same corner, half a second late, like the minute hand clearing its throat. The hairs on my arms rose and then pretended they hadn't.

We both heard it.

"Echoes," Mr. Sterling said. "Do your best not to feed them."

"How would I even do that?"

"Repeat them. Name them as if they're you. Argue with them as if they're reasonable. That's feeding."

"And starving them?"

"Name truth out loud." He said it like telling someone to drink water. "Not *your* truth...*the* truth."

"Seems inconvenient."

"Truth is rarely on time for what you planned," he said. "But it's always on time for what you need."

"That's a poster?"

"It will be," he said. "Someone will misuse it at a conference."

A laugh escaped before I could stop it. The room liked the sound. It warmed a degree, like the HVAC registered delight.

The door cracked. A kid I didn't know slid in a hall pass, got a signature, and vanished without dignifying us with eye contact. The door sighed shut.

The quiet inside the sigh held a mirror of the sentence we'd just said, as the room repeated it to make sure it understood. A whisper followed, low and almost polite:

"...always on time for what you need."

Not my voice. Not Mr. Sterling's. The hallway is making an impression.

The temperature dipped a thumb's width.

"That's new," I said.

"That's old," Mr. Sterling said. "You're new to hearing it."

"Is this where you tell me I'm not crazy?"

"No," he said. "This is where I tell you to practice being sane on purpose."

He pulled a thin, battered notebook from his satchel and set it on the table, half-turned so I could see without getting up. The leather was cracked where hands had gripped it too hard for too long. A sigil stamped the cover. Not the school's sword-in-fire crest, but a woven belt circling a shield, tiny windows in the weave.

"This is a copy," he said. "The original is older than anyone here."

"What is it?"

"Listening exercises," he said. "Breath. Attention. Naming. It's what the Crossguard taught before they taught anything else. Not weapons. Not courage. Hearing."

"Because you can't fight what you can't hear," I said.

"Because you shouldn't fight everything you hear," he corrected, gently. "Some things require standing still."

The clock ticked. No echo. Progress.

"Try one," he said, sliding the notebook a fraction closer. "Breathe in on four. Hold for four. Out on six. While you breathe, list three things in the room that are undeniable. Not opinions. Not feelings. Facts."

I rolled my eyes, the correct response to being assigned to inhale.

"Humor me."

"Fine," I said, and did the count silently. In. Two. Three. Four. Out. Two. Three. Four. My brain tried to be clever; I ignored it.

"Three facts."

"The window has dust on the inside. The second hand's on the nine. Your notebook's leather, five by seven, stamped with a belt and shield."

"Better," he said. "Again."

We did another cycle. The room cooled and warmed in tiny ways, like a cat testing laps. Somewhere in the hall, a locker slammed and didn't echo. Someone laughed twice; the room refused to imitate it.

"Now," Mr. Sterling said, "name one truth about you that isn't a feeling."

There were plenty of sentences that felt true for five minutes and poisoned the hour.

"I'm here," I said finally.

He nodded. "Say it again."

"I'm here."

"Again."

"I'm here," I said, and on the third time, the sentence stopped being proof and became a place. The warmth along my ribs found the buckle and clicked in without asking.

"What if the truth seems small?" I asked.

"Then you found the right size to stand on."

The clock ticked. No echo. The room felt like a classroom again.

"Someone is going to ask you to choose easy over true," he said. "Soon."

"Mrs. Miles says easy's expensive."

"She's right."

He reached into the satchel again and laid a photocopy next to the half-torn notebook. Lined, worn, three-hole-punched. At the top, a neat hand from another decade: Resonance Notes — Intro. Below it, a list in bullets:

Notice: Where does the cold sit?

Name: Which lie is asking for rent?

Breathe: Count until the first answer stops shouting.

Repeat: Out loud, the truth that doesn't move.

Refuse: "Later" is a lie's favorite word.

I tapped the last line. "Seems personal."

"Lies don't mind being late," he said. "They plan to live in the space you give them."

I ran a finger along the edge of the page, careful not to tear the holes further. "Who wrote this?"

"A friend," he said. The way he said *friend* sounded like a name he didn't want to set loose in this room. "A long time ago."

"Is this where you tell me there's a club and dues are due?"

"This is where I tell you to do the homework," he said, but his mouth tipped. "And to stop earning detentions you don't have time for."

"Noted."

We sat in good silence for a minute. Outside, the light turned honey. The bars from the blinds shifted a little left. The clock said 3:41 and meant it.

"If I can hear what fails," I asked, "does that mean it'll try more?"

"Yes," he said simply. "Because you're worth the effort."

The room didn't applaud. It didn't need to. The sentence was too heavy to throw far.

He stood, slid the notebook and the copy nearer. "Borrow them," he said. "Return them when they feel lighter."

"That a thing?"

"It will be," he said, and I couldn't tell if he was joking.

He opened the detention log, scribbled a note that probably said *served without incident,* and closed it with a soft *thap.* "You're free to go when the bell..."

The bell rang.

Clean. Correct. No warp. No double. My body tensed anyway, like a dog who's learned the shape of thunder.

The sound faded. For one second, very clear, another voice arrived, quiet, and delayed:

Later.

Not my mouth. Not Mr. Sterling's. A cousin of the not-voice from earlier. It was cleaner, more patient. It landed at the base of my skull like an index finger tapped twice.

I didn't look at Mr. Sterling. I didn't have to. We both breathed as we'd trained it.

"No," I said softly, and the warmth around my ribs answered, fastened.

The air declined to echo me.

Mr. Sterling capped his pen. "Good," he said, almost to himself. "You're learning to answer the right person."

"Who's that?"

"You," he said. "And the One who knows your name when you forget it."

He didn't explain, and I didn't push. Some truths go brittle if you handle them too early.

I stood, slid the copy into my notebook, and palmed the old leather. It felt heavier than a book should be and exactly as heavy as a promise.

"Thanks," I said.

"Walk the long way," he said, nodding toward the opposite hall. "It'll be louder there. Practice."

I put a hand on the door and hesitated. "Why help me?"

"Because the Order can't watch every corner," he said quietly. "Someone has to notice when the truth starts going quiet."

"Terrifying."

"Accurate," he said, and waved me out.

The corridor greeted me with normal volume. Fluorescents hummed, feet shuffled, after-school plans collided. I walked the long way anyway. It did get louder. At the far stairwell, a teacher argued with a thermostat. The vending machine decided to vend for once and then changed its mind.

Twice, something tested the air beside me. Polite taps against glass. *Later,* it suggested, with the confidence of a calendar.

"No," I said in my head each time, and the belt of not-light held unshowy, stubborn.

At the doors, the evening came in gold. I stepped into it and didn't look back. The day wasn't over. It was just finally telling the truth about itself.

The gold light caught in the window glass and held there, patient-like, as if it planned to wait for morning.

If motivation had a smell, it would be Gatorade and lies.

Coach Marcus herded us onto the football field with the same tenderness he used on tackling dummies. He called it a "unity assembly," which is adult for *we don't have a plan, but we have a microphone.* The bleachers rattled beneath Sonorah High's idea of togetherness: half-hearted clapping, restless feet, contraband snacks rustling in backpacks that "definitely don't have food, Coach."

Late afternoon painted the field in movie-trailer gold. The grass had that too-green I'd seen from Mr. Sterling's window, like someone turned the saturation up and forgot to put it back. Warm metal and cut turf mingled in the air; it smelled like pep talk and ozone. Flags along the track flinched without committing to the wind. A Bluetooth speaker near the concession stand coughed out half a chorus, then silence, then another chorus, as if the playlist were arguing with itself.

Cody wove through clusters like he owned stock in them. "Prediction," he said, falling into step. "Two speeches, one chant, a raffle for closet T-shirts, and Tyler tries to crowd-surf."

"Unity," I said. "Truly, we are one."

"You're welcome." He pointed at my hood. "Coach'll make you take that off."

"He can try." It wasn't fashion. It was a door I could carry.

Students marbled across the turf. Tiny planets with their own gravity. Bumping, orbiting, pretending they'd chosen their place. Teachers lined the track, whistles ready, referees for a game nobody scheduled. At midfield, a portable stage sulked: two metal risers, a podium, and a scarlet-and-silver banner. The sword-inside-fire symbol hung from the bottom hem in glossy ink like a seal that approved itself.

The principal climbed the steps with a smile that didn't reach her eyes. Two assistants flanked her, trying to look both approachable and necessary. Coach paced the fifty, clapping at random. "Phones down," he barked. "We're unifying, not livestreaming!"

Three dozen phones rose to film him as he said exactly that.

We found a spot near the thirty where we could pretend to care without getting picked for spirit duty. Sarah stood two pods over. Her hands tucked into her jacket, braid over one shoulder, a thin silver chain catching the light. She wasn't with anyone I recognized. She didn't look like she wanted to be.

The principal tapped the mic. "Good afternoon, Sonorah," she said, voice amplified enough to make the bleachers hum. "We are so excited to start the year with intention. We are..."

Every phone in the stadium vibrated.

Not scattered. All at once. A soft, collective *bzzzt* that rose from the turf through our shoes and out of our pockets, like the field had become a speaker.

The sound landed under my ribs like a marble in a bowl.

Students laughed, nervously, then really. Heads dipped. Thumbs twitched. Teachers hissed like sprinkler heads. "Phones down," Coach barked again, a sentence with the same success rate as "Volcano, stop."

Cody checked his anyway. "Group text," he said, brow up. "Whole school. 'Signal Challenge.'"

"What's the challenge?"

"Post your location. Keep a streak going. Attendance points, filters... Coach Marcus is about to be an influencer."

A second all-at-once vibration rolled the field.

The principal blinked, then tried again. "We are so excited to start the year with intention. We are..."

Her sentence looped. Not all the words. Just the opening, like the mic had taken a bite and decided to chew. "We are so excited...so excited...so excited..."

A group of seniors started chanting *"SO EX-CI-TED."* The chant hopped rows like a skipping record.

The principal's smile tightened. She tapped the mic hard. The feedback didn't screech; it sighed.

Phones hummed a third time. Not louder, lower. The sound figured out how to sit down.

A hush rolled over the crowd that wasn't respect. It was easy. Like the field had turned into a mattress and we'd all climbed on. Voices softened by half, then again. A few kids sat where they stood without deciding to. A teacher's arms dropped. Two freshmen laughed at a joke that didn't exist and stopped mid-breath.

The grass lost a shade; the banner's scarlet dulled; the sky held its blue but wouldn't spend it.

Breathe, I told myself. The air obliged, thinner on return.

Cody pocketed his phone. "I feel like napping," he said.

"Don't," I said. "Unity's a gateway drug."

"Harsh," he said, but the humor slid off the moment.

The principal reset: "We are so excited to start the year with intention. We want to celebrate who we are as a community. Order..." She paused, the words hunting for a chair. "Order brings safety."

A ripple of nods moved through the rows like a rehearsed breeze.

Near the stage, a drumline kid scrolled with surgical focus. His mouth lagged half a syllable behind hers, lip-syncing belief. A vice principal leaned on the rail, expression rinsed blank. Another vibration, shorter, more polite.

A warmthless chill slid along the inside of my chest. Not fear. Suggestion. The feeling of a thought that wasn't mine, trying on my voice to see if it fit.

Relax, it offered, friendly. *You've been strained all day. This is nothing. Don't make it something.*

I rubbed my thumb to the fingertip. No ridges.

Two rows over, Sarah lifted her phone, frowned, and tapped twice. Dead. She turned it over, as if checking for a reset switch, then looked up. She was scanning not for someone, just for real. Her eyes found mine.

Another hush-wave pressed down. Helpful.

Scroll, the not-voice suggested. *Save your strength for later. Later is wiser.*

Coach Marcus stopped pacing. The principal kept talking, safe words strung like pearls: *obedience, responsibility, safety.* The crowd breathed in rhythm.

I heard the sound a lot of people make right before they hand their mind a chair and sit down.

The color under my shoes flickered as it normally did. The warmth at my sternum found its spark and lit without show. It spread along the breath lattice, settling like a belt buckled from the inside.

The hush faltered near me. Kids to my left blinked, one rubbing her arms like she'd walked back into herself. The green beneath my shoes rippled outward, half a circle of permission.

Sarah's head tipped. Not a smile, recognition.

Another pulse tried to pull us lower. It found less to grab.

"Signal Challenge," someone murmured. "Just post and forget."

Forget.

Forget, the voice echoed, tame as a pet. *We'll do hard things tomorrow.*

"Later," I said under my breath, and the warmth hissed at the word, *no.*

A freshman's legs folded; he sat, eyes blank. His friend patted him twice, distracted.

I stepped forward before thinking. Didn't touch him. Just caught his line of sight. "Hey. You here?"

He blinked back into himself. "Yeah," he said, voice cracking. "Yeah."

"Up," I said. "Before Coach decides sitting equals detention."

He snorted and stood. That tiny laugh traveled farther than a shout. A couple of students took real breaths again; the air released an inch of what it had borrowed.

The principal's mic hiccupped. *We are* so and stopped. She blinked, surprised, and motioned to the sound tech. The phones stayed still.

Sarah crossed her arms, keeping her hands from clapping at the wrong time. She held up her dead phone: off-grid. I tapped my chest once, palm open. *Mine's loud in here.*

She nodded, steady. The chain at her throat lay straight. She felt like quiet you can trust; the kind that follows truth, not surrender.

Up in the bleachers, Mr. Sterling leaned forward, elbows on knees. Weather-watcher mode. Measuring, not saving.

Near midfield, that same drumline kid stared at the sky like reading invisible text. His pupils are fine, his irises pale for one beat too long. His lips shaped a line he already knew by heart.

"Order brings safety," he whispered. The sentence didn't need to travel; it stuck like static.

A teacher beside him patted his back. "You, okay?"

"Yeah," he said, and believed it.

The principal wrapped with "student-led initiatives" and "new traditions," which is an email that *we'll get back to you.* Coach Marcus reclaimed the mic and did the Coach thing, yelled *FAMILY* until it lost vowels, threatened cardio, thanked boosters, dismissed us like pardoned citizens.

The crowd exhaled. Bleachers trembled under a thousand bodies remembering motion. The playlist found a full song. Color returned in ways you could blame on lighting if you wanted to stay asleep.

Cody stretched like he could reverse time. "Unity achieved," he said. "I feel one with the turf."

"You're allergic to consciousness," I said.

"Big talk from a guy in a portable cave." He tapped my hood. "You good?"

"I'm here."

He took it as a grade. "Pizza later? Judah's mom's fundraiser. Garlic knots for redemption."

"Your souls are on backorder," I said, which wasn't a no.

He peeled away, orbiting others.

Sarah drifted closer. Not a meet-cute. A meet-honest. She stopped just far enough for either of us to call it a coincidence.

"My signal died," she said, showing the black screen. "Guess I'm off-grid."

"Stay that way," I said, more a prayer than advice.

"Working on it." She looked at the banner, the kids filing out, all of us sure the day had let us off easy. "Whatever that was. It felt like being underwater. But warm. Like it wanted me to float."

"Floating's just drowning without bubbles."

She huffed. "Okay, poet."

"I try not to."

"People will say it was a glitch."

"They'll mean it."

"Tell me if it happens again?" she asked, like we already had a pact.

"Yeah. You?"

She nodded. "Yeah."

We stood long enough for Coach to spot us and somehow not whistle. He turned to yell at a sophomore power-walking like it was religion. We moved anyway, not toward the same exit but not away on purpose.

Up in the bleachers, Mr. Sterling stood. He didn't nod or wave. He watched the field like you watch a friend who finally drank water, wanting to see if they'll keep doing it tomorrow.

At the gate, my phone buzzed once. The notification half-loaded: a broken image, a half-sentence. Run the ... and then nothing. My thumb hovered. The belt-warmth didn't flare; it steadied.

The drumline kid stumbled at the track's edge, caught himself, stared at the sky like it had promised to text back. His lips moved. I didn't need sound to know the words.

"Order brings safety," I murmured. Not a vow, a diagnosis.

A polite tap pressed against the air near my shoulder, like a knuckle on glass. *Later,* it was offered as a calendar invite.

"No," I answered in my head. The warmth buckled with the small, stubborn click I'd learned to trust.

I stepped through the chain-link gate into an evening that looked the right kind of blue. The day hadn't decided to be safe. It had decided to be honest.

The wind shifted, carrying the faint scent of ozone and warm grass back over the field. Proof that silence wasn't finished, just listening.

That would have to do.

CHAPTER TWO
BENEATH THE NOISE

The night hadn't really started. It was as if the world stopped pretending to breathe. My shoulder throbbed, the field's impact fresh—a stray elbow carrying a secret's weight. Each pulse of pain dragged me back, anchoring the mood in what was lost under the stadium lights.

I lay flat on my back, eyes fixed on the ceiling's cracked line where moonlight split it in two. Frustration and unease coursed through me as the clock beside me blinked 12:11 a.m., steady, unbothered. Every few seconds, its red glow pulsed across the room like a heartbeat that didn't belong to me, emphasizing how alone I felt.

Sleep wasn't an option.

It wasn't nerves, or caffeine, or tomorrow's classes.

It was the hum.

A low vibration started faint, beneath the skin, like an air conditioner humming out of reach. I pressed my palms to my chest. The rhythm matched my pulse.

I rolled over, burying my head in the pillow. The noise didn't fade. It followed.

The silence between each thrum stretched until it felt alive, listening back.

"Not tonight," I muttered, half-laughing, half-pleading.

No answer. Just that quiet, electric patience.

For a second, I almost convinced myself it was nothing. Just adrenaline's leftovers from the field, or the house settling. But as the charger cord buzzed, tension prickled up my spine, uneasy and sharp. Instinctively, I unplugged it, hoping to end whatever current was moving through the air. The alarm clock light dipped, defying the silence I tried to impose. Frustration fluttered in my chest, but so did a fleeting sense of rebellion. The sound in the walls, unbothered, joined the hum in my ribs; everything vibrated on a single anxious note.

My breath hitched.

The warmth I'd felt at the field returned. It was soft at first, then growing, threading through my chest like light searching for a door.

I knew it was dangerous. Somehow, in its honesty, it felt deceptively comforting.

Then another voice cut through it.

Not from the room. From underneath it.

It's done. You're safe. Sleep.

Calm. Reasonable. The kind of tone adults use when they're trying to close a conversation.

I sat up fast. The warmth vanished.

My eyes swept the room; the desk, the chair, the mirror that I had absolutely covered with a blanket two hours ago. Relief and dread fought inside me. All normal. All wrong.

I pressed my palms together. "No," I whispered, surprising myself. "Not safe. Just quiet."

The air seemed to lean closer.

That was when my phone lit up.

No vibration, no sound. Just the screen was glowing white on the dresser.

Three words floated in the middle, black text with no sender:

COME TO THE SCHOOL.

I stared until the screen dimmed on its own. When I touched it, the message was gone. Only the lock screen clock remained... 12:12 a.m.

I waited for logic to catch up. It didn't.

Instead, the hum under my ribs shifted key, as if it were answering the command.

My shoes were under the bed. The hoodie was draped on the chair; my backpack slouched by the wall. I didn't remember standing. Now, all three moved. An anxious jolt ran through me as my body chose before my brain could argue.

At the door, I paused. The house slumbered. No pipes, no fridge drone, not even wind outside.

The silence pressed against my ears until it felt heavy enough to break.

I opened the door.

The hallway light flickered once, as if it wanted to say 'go,' then steadied.

Downstairs, the Miles' family photos watched from the walls. Smiles frozen in flashbulb amber. I slipped past them and out the front door. The night air hit sharp, cool, honest.

The street stretched empty, wet from an earlier rain. Sodium lamps lined it like sentries. Each one buzzed faintly, the same note as the hum inside me. When I stepped beneath them, the sound deepened, almost harmonic.

Halfway down the block, I glanced back.

The porch light glowed once, almost golden. Then faded to its usual yellow. Mrs. Miles must've turned in hours ago, but for a heartbeat, it felt like she was still praying, still *covering*.

I whispered a thank-you to the quiet.

The hum answered, steady now, patient.

Not words. Not yet.

Just a rhythm that knew where I was going.

I adjusted the hoodie, hands buried in the pocket.

Each step toward Sonorah High dragged, gravity brooding with every block. The air tasted sharp and metallic. Dread stung my nerves, mirroring the current beneath my skin.

Streetlights flickered in sync with my pulse.

Not at random. Not a glitch. There was a pattern.

The closer I got, the more the town thinned out. The sounds of crickets, gone; distant cars, gone. The world was shrinking to one frequency.

A whisper brushed the back of my mind again:

Turn around. Forget this. Be normal.

The warmth surged in defiance, flooding my chest until the cold retreated.

I exhaled. "Not tonight."

Sonorah's gates came into view. Dark outlines against a sky too still to be real. One light burned above the main doors, faint and steady.

For a second, I thought I saw a figure framed there, motionless, waiting.

Then the light blinked once. Twice.

On the third, it stayed.

The hum in my ribs settled into perfect sync with it.

I kept walking.

The steady hum followed me down the street, patient, waiting to see if I'd really keep walking.

Sonorah at midnight didn't look abandoned; it looked like it had agreed to hold its breath.

The front gates were half-open, the chain looped but not locked—rules for show. I slipped inside. A hum in my chest, steady since the porch, shifted; it found a cleaner pitch. Campus lights were stingy: one above the office, one flickering by the gym walkway, two along the track facing the empty stands. The rest settled for halos that didn't touch ground.

The air cooled. Not winter-cold—decision-cold. Concrete still clung to the day's heat, an old argument. My shoes made soft, deliberate sounds. On this much tile, every step seemed amplified. Somewhere, a night bug tried to sign its name against glass and surrendered.

The message, COME TO THE SCHOOL, didn't repeat. The message didn't need to. The hum did the pointing. It tugged me past the main entrance, past the office windows where the paper cranes the art club had made last spring hung frozen in a mobile that hadn't moved since graduation. As I passed, one of the cranes, however impossibly, twitched its paper wings like a nervous heartbeat. Tension pulled tighter in my chest. My reflection ghosted along the glass with my hood up, hands pocketed. A portable boundary against the mounting uncertainty.

I expected to see a teacher night patrol, or the custodian's cart, or a cop car drifting by to ask questions I couldn't answer. Instead, I got exactly what I'd been walking toward, nothing I could explain and everything I couldn't ignore.

The gym wing took the hum up a half-step. The light over the side door flickered twice in an almost pattern on, on, pause, on like a friend trying to wave without drawing attention. The door itself was propped with a folded square of cardboard, a brand-new violation pretending to be a coincidence.

I stopped with my hand on the push bar and let the quiet speak first.

Footsteps behind me said I wasn't alone.

"You came faster than I expected," said a voice that didn't have to introduce itself.

I turned. Mr. Sterling was twenty feet away; coat collar up against a chill that hadn't arrived. He held a flashlight low, so the beam didn't point at me. More like a circle on the ground between us, like an invitation. He wasn't wearing a teacher—no lanyard, no gradebook, no "let's call your guardian." He wore the kind of attention that doesn't waste words.

"The door was open," I said, because small talk survives everything.

"Only just," he said. "Sometimes the world cooperates when you're heading the right direction."

"Is that a scientific statement?"

"Repeatable, under the strangest conditions." He nodded at the door. "Shall we not hold the evening up?"

I pushed, and the hinge sighed like something glad to be used. We stepped inside, and the building's temperature changed by a whisper. The hallway lights were at their nighttime setting; half alive, half thinking about it. Trophy cases slept with their mouths closed. The sweat smell that usually lived here had faded to polish and old banners. Our footsteps discovered quiet in front of them and left it intact behind.

Mr. Sterling let the door fall shut. The soft thap traveled farther than sound normally does. The hum inside me took it personally and adjusted to match.

"You slept?" he asked.

"Not even a little."

"The field would make the best pillow if it weren't pretending to be a sermon," he said, like it was weather. "Any headaches?"

"Just questions."

He angled his head, pleased. "Good. The wrong things give answers too quickly."

We walked, not toward the main gym but past it, along a narrow corridor lined with storage rooms and the wrestling mat closet that still smelled like defeat. The farther we went, the quieter the hum became, which somehow made it feel louder, as if it had finally stopped fighting to be heard because I had finally chosen to listen.

"I need you to tell me whether this is... in my head or outside of it," I said. The sentence sounded better in my skull than in the air.

"Yes," he said.

"That's not helpful."

"It's honest. What you're hearing is in you, and the world is answering back. You can't separate the two neatly yet."

"Yet," I said.

"You're built to notice," he said. "That's not a punishment. It's a skill you didn't ask for."

We reached a patch of scarred floor where the tile had cracked in a spider line, and someone had glued it back down without bothering to line up the pattern. Mr. Sterling stopped with the precision of a man who always means to put his feet where he puts them.

"Here," he said.

"Because of the crack?"

"Because of the echo."

He knelt, not like an old man, but like someone who was ready to meet the floor sometimes. He set the flashlight so the beam fanned across the tile, then placed his palm flat on the ground. He didn't close his eyes like he was doing a ritual. He opened them a little wider, as if he were reading small print only he could see.

The overhead lights didn't flicker. They breathed, once, subtle enough to deny in court, obvious enough to read if you'd learned the language. The hum in my chest answered like he'd struck a tuning fork against the concrete.

I flinched without meaning to. The warmth found me, sure and sudden.

Mr. Sterling looked up, expression softening in the way of a teacher watching a kid get a math proof right with no work shown. "Your shadow," he said, almost conversational, "hesitates because it's learning to keep up with you."

"You're going to have to translate that into not-poetry," I said, because sarcasm is safe when the world stops being.

"You spend a lot of time checking if the room is still here," he said. "You're not wrong to do it. Rooms lie. People lie more. Truth doesn't move when you do. Your body is learning where truth stands so it can meet you there."

"Truth has a location now."

"Alignment is location," he said. "You decide where you'll stand, and that decision teaches your senses where to stop being fooled."

He took his hand off the floor. The warmth didn't leave. The hallway noticed and kept pretending it hadn't.

"Why me?" I asked, and felt unoriginal the second it left my mouth.

"Because some people hear," he said simply. "The rest of us would enjoy the luxury. We get you instead."

"That sounds like a burden."

"It is," he said, and didn't offer synonyms to make it prettier. "It's also a gift when you stop trying to carry it alone."

We let that sit where it landed. My breath did what it was supposed to. The hum settled into a background kind of alive, a presence that acknowledged my growing curiosity and the fear it replaced.

"Back at the field," I said. "Everyone... together. That wasn't hypnotism." I felt a flicker of fear intertwine with intrigue as I reflected on the experience.

"No," he agreed. "It was an agreement, very carefully coaxed. Temptation doesn't require magic. It needs momentum." The statement nudged curiosity to the forefront.

"And tonight?" I lifted my chin toward the lights, toward the parts of the building that had decided to listen. "What do you call this?"

"An invitation," he said.

"From who?"

"From what stands between people and the harm they call normal," he said, which should've sounded like a riddle but didn't. "From the quiet that insists you pay attention."

"Is this the part where you give me a robe and change my name?"

"Not tonight," he said, mouth tipping. "Names have to agree they belong to you. Robes itch."

He straightened, and the joints in his coat made tiny noises, leather or heavy canvas telling each other old stories. He studied me like I was an equation that had arrived at its own answer. The flashlight's beam cut across the corridor, landing on the double doors at the far end. Past those is the small auxiliary gym. Beyond that, a service hallway that ended at a door most students never noticed.

He didn't point. He didn't have to. The hum inside me did that work.

"You said earlier," I said, "that covering is not quarantine."

"I did."

"Is this... still covering?"

"Not if you go forward," he said. "Covering keeps you when you can't stand. Alignment asks you to stand."

"So we're past keeping," I said.

"We're past pretending your life fits in the shape it had this morning."

A part of me wanted to tell him I liked the shape fine. It had jokes, pancakes, and a hoodie I could hide in. Another part was done being preserved and wanted to be useful, even if it meant admitting I'd been hungry this whole time for something I couldn't name.

"What happens if I say no?" I asked.

"Then you go home," he said without blinking. "You sleep eventually. You tell yourself tomorrow is kinder to people who don't pick fights. You'll be right, some days. On others, you'll hear quiet get heavy and pretend you don't. And two or three times a year, you'll wish you had learned how to answer it before it learned you."

"And if I say yes?"

"You'll say it ten times before breakfast and a hundred before you're old," he said. "You'll get tired. You'll meet people who make you want to keep saying it. You'll make mistakes loud enough to scare you. You'll learn to apologize faster. You'll see more than you ever asked for and less than you think you deserve. And you won't be bored."

"That last one is not the sales pitch you think it is."

"It's the only honest one," he said. "What's it to be?"

I tried to come up with a sentence that would make the choice seem smarter. I had none. My body, traitor that it is, had already moved my weight forward, heel-toe, the way you do when you've decided and would like your mouth to catch up.

"Yes," I said, smaller than I meant to, bigger than it sounded.

The warmth answered as if the word had a switch built into its spine.

Mr. Sterling breathed once in approval. A teacher who will not call it pride because pride rots the fruit. He set the flashlight upright against the wall, so the beam shot up, making a fake pillar out of dust.

"Then we listen," he said.

He walked toward the double doors, pace easy, leaving me the space to stop if I wanted to lie about my decision. I didn't. The handles were metal, cold, and indifferent. He pushed them, and the auxiliary gym presented its polished floor and stacked chairs like a stage after everyone had gone home.

We didn't go to the center court. We cut across the near baseline to a side door with a faded STAFF ONLY sign. He drew a key from his pocket, the old kind that looks like a story, not a fob that looks like debt. He didn't need it. The door clicked open before the key kissed the lock.

"Convenient," I said.

"Polite," he corrected. "Some doors open for the right conversation."

The service hall beyond was a throat of concrete and utility paint, bare bulbs in cages every ten feet. The hum snugged closer, like a sweater someone else had made, wrong size until it wasn't.

"You'll be tempted to narrate this in your head as if it's trying to be a legend," he said, walking. "Resist. Not because it isn't. The most important things are. Just because legends make you forget how ordinary each step is. Ordinary is where your choices are honest."

"What are you?" I asked because if I didn't ask now, I might spend the next five years building worse answers. "You knew the word for what was happening before I did."

"A listener," he said. "A man who was told, years ago, that silence is a kind of battlefield, and he had better learn its terrain."

"And you... work alone?"

"Until I don't," he said. "Until someone arrives who makes it obvious I shouldn't."

We reached the end of the hall, where the school's logic ran out. The door here was painted the same beige as the walls and wore it like camouflage. No sign. No window. A fire alarm pull station sat beside it, the sort of red you notice even when you think you won't.

Mr. Sterling laid his palm flat against the door the way he'd touched the gym floor. He didn't push. He listened. I felt nothing at first. Then, the faintest shift, like the weight of the air decided to put its hand down.

"You know the difference," he said without looking at me, "between a quiet that hides something and a quiet that invites you to say your name out loud?"

"I'm learning," I said.

"Good," he said. "This is the second kind."

The hum in my chest, patient all night, drew itself into a single line, taut as a string between two pegs. It didn't hurt. It asked. The hallway lights dimmed. Not flicker, not drama. Just a softer idea of light, as if brightness had stepped back to let sound speak.

"This is where we listen from," Mr. Sterling said.

He opened the door.

Nothing cinematic awaited. A small, square room with an electrical panel, a stack of folded mats, and a school cart with a broken wheel stared back at us like an apology for not being special. It smelled like dust and old detergent. The hum went silent.

The sudden absence rang louder than the noise.

I swallowed. My ears found my own breath and treated it like a song starting up without instruments.

"You'll want to think nothing is happening," Mr. Sterling said quietly. "Because that's what fear says when it has nothing left to prove."

"What is happening?" I asked.

"You stepped into the place in yourself that doesn't need a parade to tell the truth," he said.

He reached past me, picked up one of the folded mats, and leaned it against the wall. Then he sat on the concrete, back to the beige, as if he'd done it a hundred times. He patted the floor beside him without looking to see if I'd listen.

I sat.

We didn't close our eyes. We didn't stir. We breathed in a room that tried its best to convince us it was only a room.

"People want the world to shove them," he said softly. "They think pressure is what makes decisions real. Sometimes that's true. Mostly, it's quieter than that. You stand somewhere, you call it true, and the rest of your life organizes around the sentence."

"What sentence?" I whispered, because the air asked for whispers.

"I am here," he said. "You said it once already today."

I remembered. The detention room. The way the phrase had gone from proof to place on the third try. The warmth returned. Not a flare, a steady coal.

"I am here," I said.

The room didn't change. I did. The part of me that monitors everything for emergencies left its post, briefly, to check for beauty. It found some in the stupidest places: the scuff on my shoe that looked like a small continent; the way Mr. Sterling's breath kept time with mine without either of us agreeing to it; the faint throb of blood in my thumb where I'd jammed it in ninth-grade shop class and never told anyone.

We sat long enough for my sense of long to complain and then adjust. When Mr. Sterling finally spoke, he didn't raise his voice, but the sentence walked out into the hallway and back.

"There's a war," he said, "between what is and what shouldn't be."

I didn't say. *You said that earlier.* I didn't say *Everybody thinks they're right.* I didn't say anything.

"You've already heard its first note," he went on. "Today, you answered it once by accident. Tonight, you answered it on purpose."

I waited, because the next part felt like something that had to choose its timing too.

"If you keep saying yes," he said, "you'll need to learn to move in the kind of quiet that scares crowds."

"Is there a club," I asked, "or is this a very intentional hobby?"

He almost laughed. "There's an order," he said. "It listens. It teaches the chosen to listen. It doesn't belong to the school, or the town, or any place in this world."

"Do they have a name?" I asked.

"They do," he said. "You don't need it yet. Names have gravity."

"And if I ask anyway?"

"I'd tell you a different thing first," he said, tilting his head. "That you aren't being recruited to fight everything frightening. You're being invited to keep your feet in the right place when the frightening starts, pretending to be reasonable."

"That's what today was," I said. "Reasonable."

"Comfortable," he said. "And comfort is an excellent liar."

He stood, not because the moment was over, but because the moment had found a chair and could wait until tomorrow. He offered me a hand. I took it. He pulled me up with the kind of strength that doesn't impress until you notice how little show it makes.

"Will there be more rooms like this?" I asked.

"Yes," he said. "Some with worse paint. Some with better light. Most of them are in you."

We stepped back into the service hall. The hum returned, quieter than I remembered, like a friend who knew it didn't need to shout anymore.

"Go home," he said. "Sleep now, if you can. If you can't, say true things until you run out of air and then start again."

"And tomorrow?" I asked.

"Tomorrow we find out whether you can hear while other people are talking," he said. He tilted his head, as if listening to the building consider its answer. "Bring shoes you can run in. And don't tell Cody everything yet. He'll try to turn it into a bet."

"That is... accurate," I said.

We retraced our steps: the not-locked door unlocking itself, the beam of the flashlight choosing glass over shadow, the gym presenting its empty floor like a stage it planned to rebuild around you while you practiced. At the side exit, the night greeted us with honest cold. The lamp above the walkway buzzed the same note I'd carried all evening.

At the edge of campus, near the chain, I turned. "Why me?" I asked again, softer, the question less about destiny now and more about math.

"Because you didn't let 'later' decide for you," he said. "And because the quiet found a place to set a lamp."

"I don't feel like a lamp."

"You're not," he said. "You're the table. Lamps are for show. Tables are for work."

"That's the least romantic metaphor you could have chosen."

"It's also the one that keeps a house standing," he said, like a man who had sat at too many tables where no one brought food and still kept his chair ready.

He didn't say goodnight. He didn't say be careful. He let the silence do the work it knew how to do and walked back toward the door that had opened when asked. I slipped through the gates and onto the street that had loaned me its light. The hum kept pace at my ribs, steadier now, less a command than a metronome.

When I reached the corner, my phone vibrated—a real vibration this time, almost rude. I pulled it out. A blank notification sat on the lock screen, sender unknown, text empty except for a time stamp: 12:59 a.m.

I stared at it until it cleared itself. The porch light two blocks down glowed the way a blessing looks when it pretends to be a bulb. I put the phone away and started counting breaths, not because I'd been told to, but because I knew where to stand while I waited for morning.

The night had not decided to be safe. It had settled into clarity. The sky in the distance began to lighten, a soft gradient seeping toward dawn. Each step felt like walking toward that faint promise on the horizon, a new day ready to reveal itself.

CHAPTER THREE
THE DOOR BETWEEN

S leep didn't arrive. Something like sleep lowered over me and waited to see if I'd notice.

I lay on my side, hand under the pillow, listening to the usual nighttime noises: the fridge running, pipes settling, a car passing outside. The hum I brought home from school blended with those sounds and set the pace for my breathing. In. Two. Three. Four. Out. Two. Three. Four. It wasn't noisy, not even really a sound. It felt like pressure. It reminded me of everything unsaid, the weight of big questions. I could have ignored it if I wanted to pretend nothing was wrong.

I blinked at the ceiling. The streetlight slanted in through the blinds and broke my wall into neat gray bars. I told my body we were done for the day. It shrugged. My eyes closed on purpose.

The world didn't open.

It inverted.

There was a sense of tilting, not the bed or the room, but in the feeling of which way was down. My stomach dropped like in a paused elevator. My ears popped. I reached for the mattress edge, which was still there. Still, the falling feeling continued, as if something inside me was descending on its own.

"Okay," I told no one, breathing slower. "We're not panicking."

The hum slipped through the gap between breath and heartbeat and settled at my sternum. Warmth followed it, not a flare. More like someone cupped a hand there to keep a match alive. The pressure in the room rearranged. The sound of the house walked itself out and closed the door.

I closed my eyelids and felt the bed move, rolling under me once. The tilting sensation stopped—not with a jolt, but with a soft clicking sound, as if an idea or puzzle piece had fit into place.

Behind my eyelids, Sonorah High waited.

It wasn't the real school. It was a memory of it, the way things look when you only half remember them. Everything was in shades of gray: the glass trophy case, the tiled floor, the dark doorways. The air felt both light and heavy, like swimming without getting wet.

I stood without deciding to. Found myself at the far end of the main hallway. The clock above the office read 12:12, both hands stacked on the twelve, as they had agreed. A sheet of paper mid-fall hung three inches above the floor, corners curved by a breeze that didn't exist. A spill of pencil shavings lay on the janitor's dustpan. Each shaving casts a shadow, as careful drawings do.

My footsteps made a sensation in my bones and none at all in the air.

"Great," I said, voice quiet out of respect for whatever this was. "Dream me still has anxiety."

Silence didn't answer. It didn't need to. It listened back.

I took a step forward. Each step confirmed there was still floor under me, as if I was learning the depth of a pool by testing each foot before trusting it with my weight. My footsteps made my bones vibrate, but made no sound in the hallway air. The hallway kept those movements secret, as if it chose to keep my intentions private.

The first door I passed was the attendance office. Inside, the swivel chair sat angled toward the window, as if someone had just gotten up and promised to return. A plastic plant stood in the corner. Colorless, and somehow smug about it. On the counter, the sign-in sheet had a pen clipped to it, but the line for Name waited blank, as if it wanted me to admit something I didn't have language for yet.

I kept walking. A flyer board on my right had the usual school notices: chess club, drama tryouts, tutoring signups, all faded gray. Near the bottom, a parchment-colored sheet I saw earlier was pinned up: The Spirit of Obedience: Order Brings Safety. The words weren't ink; they looked like wet condensation, forming over and over like breath on glass. As I read, I remembered rumors about those who ignored the warning and faced strange consequences, like vanishing shadows or dreams that trapped you. The slogan felt heavier now, urging me to go along quietly.

When I looked at the phrase, the warmth under my ribs dimmed, as if a cloud had slid over a sun I couldn't see. When I looked away, toward empty air, it returned.

The hallway is at a distance. In the middle of the stretch leading to the art wing, something shifted. Not movement exactly, more like a part of the gray decided it was tired of gray and considered another option.

Down the corridor, someone stood. Not close, not far. Just present in a way that the walls weren't. A girl, hair to one shoulder, arms loose at her sides. She wasn't lit; she simply wasn't flat. Where the rest of the world looked like a pencil sketch pressed too hard, her outline carried a softer edge, a faint warmth outlines get when they're near a light, even if you can't see the source.

I stayed silent instead of calling out; calling would have declared that I was afraid to be alone with her. She turned her head slightly, making it clear that not answering was a deliberate choice. Her mouth formed words I couldn't hear.

No sound.

I took a step toward her. The floor corrected my weight as if it had always been mine. The air pressed against me. Not a shove, a suggestion. Stop noticing, it offered. You're safe if you stop noticing.

The warmth answered with the smallest refusal. I kept moving.

The girl's outline, the not-gray, the almost-light, flickered once. The way a memory does when you check if it's yours. Then she turned away, not in dismissal, more like you do when you assume someone will follow because you've decided you'd like them to.

I didn't reach her. The hallway had other ideas.

Tension filled the hallway, like a storm about to start, but I stayed polite. The floor felt as if it were gently tilting down, unsettling my steps. The walls seemed to close in, as if reminding me this space belonged to them. Out of the corner of my eye, the poster's words, 'Order Brings Safety,' crept into my thoughts, testing how much they would stick.

Later, something said, gentle as a breeze coaxing a sail. You'll be brave later. You'll think clearly later. For now, let yourself float, it suggested, the words feeling less like advice and more like a siren call, tempting me with the promise of ease.

I kept moving, but the tilt slowed me down, like walking on a stubborn treadmill. I stepped hard, feeling the effort in my legs, yet barely gained ground.

The girl, Sarah, my brain supplied, paused at the next intersection of halls. Her head tipped toward me, listening to something I couldn't hear. Then she lifted her hand, palm out. Not a warning, not a command. Something between wait and listen. Her outline warmed a fraction, and even that tiny difference pulled my attention like a magnet pulls whatever it's promised.

The phrase on the wall, 'Order Brings Safety,' caught the light. Safety now seemed tied to being still and quietly trusting.

The pull tightened. The floor would not slope. My body leaned forward without my permission. The back of my neck felt the suggestion again. A pressure. Without hands.

Later.

The warmth faded when I looked at the words. When I looked at the girl, it came back. The choice was simple but hard: holding onto warmth meant standing out—risking being alone against a rule that promised safety for staying silent. Accepting the warmth pushed me closer to a truth that could set me apart from those who hid in certainty.

"You don't get to pick the time," I said, out loud, voice steady because I had nothing left to make it with except steadiness.

My voice had texture here. It marked the air and stayed a second longer than speech does when it enjoys the room it's in.

The corridor turned left, and the world with it.

The cracked mirror from my bedroom waited there. Tall on the floor. Where no mirror had any business standing. Same fracture that split the right top quadrant into an awkward mosaic. Same bevel on the edge that caught light and pretended to be metal. Same refusal to be necessary. It had followed me into a place where mirrors shouldn't belong and acted as if it had always been invited.

The pull loved the mirror. It pressed me toward it with the enthusiasm of a host who doesn't care whether you're ready for the party.

I stopped an arm's length away. The reflection offered what it always does: my features, reissued in someone else's handwriting. Dark hair, hoodie, the kind of face that helps to tuck under a hood when you don't want to invite conversations you can't finish. No lag this time. No late blink. Just a small, heavy tiredness in the eyes that I didn't want to own and couldn't lie about.

The glass didn't shine. It seemed to breathe, softly fogging and clearing.

My reflection's mouth moved. When it spoke, the sound wore my cadence like it had borrowed a shirt.

'Later,' it said. There was no threat or joke in the voice. It sounded gentle, like calming an anxious animal.

The warmth under my sternum flickered, then steadied as if someone had cupped it.

I didn't try to be heroic. I didn't try to make a speech. I picked the smallest word with the biggest hinge.

"Now," I said.

No drama answered. The glass didn't explode into televised shards. The mirror didn't tilt and swallow me. The hallway didn't clap.

Instead, the surface thinned.

Not visibly. Tactilely. The way ice loses the last texture of hardness right before it starts melting. A layer of whatever-you-are between face and face dissolved without acknowledging me, and the weight behind the word later lost its hand on my neck. The pull didn't give up. It simply looked tired of trying to move someone who had decided to weigh what he weighed tonight and not less.

Color didn't flood back in like a victory. It nudged. The gray of the lockers softened toward blue. The tile admitted it had a warm undertone; it had been saved for guests. The world remembered it had a palette.

Far down the corridor, the girl turned her head fully for the first time. No music heralded it. No spotlight found her. She wasn't glowing. She simply existed a little more in this frame than she had in the frame before. When she spoke, the word found me without crossing the distance.

"Listen," she said.

Not a command that makes your back straighten. Not a plea that makes you guilty. A suggestion you recognize because it's what you were trying to do anyway.

The hum under my ribs declined to be a hum. It became a stillness that made room for other things. Silence, not empty, a table cleared.

I took one breath, and it signed the old agreement between body and air. I took another, and the agreement stopped feeling like survival and started feeling like a choice.

The mirror stood. It didn't vanish. It didn't melt. It simply lost its claim. I looked at it and saw a mirror, not a promise. It would try again another day. Lies are patient. That's not their virtue; it's their hobby.

The hallway let go of its angle. The letters on the flyer squeezed themselves into ink again and looked like they'd been printed by a machine that had never learned the dignity of words. The paper that had been falling finished falling and kissed the ground without apology.

I looked for the girl's outline and didn't find it. She didn't run. She didn't fade. She simply stepped back into whatever degree of present the rest of this place agreed to maintain when I wasn't being asked to make decisions.

A pressure at the base of my skull announced a page turn.

I fell up.

The tilt reversed. The escalator under my blood forgot to exist. My ears cleared. My body, that had stood still the whole time, got around to admitting it had been lying down.

I opened my eyes in my own room. Early light pressed against the blinds with two fingertips. The clock read 6:02 in red, looking like something a human had invented rather than something the world had decided on. The hum, the one that had learned my lungs, had left. But it had left a chair pulled out like it planned to come back for coffee. Down the hallway, the familiar sound of Cody's laughter mixed with the clatter of breakfast dishes, a comfortable echo from yesterday, anchoring me back to the present.

I didn't move right away. The urge to label what happens as just a dream arrived on cue. Wearing the voice of every adult who has ever tucked in a child and wanted to believe that makes them safe. My brain offered a backup story. You were stressed; your mind made pictures. The way browsers offer to save passwords for websites, you don't intend on doing anything more than a free trial.

"No," I said to the ceiling, same voice as before. "Not later. Not that."

My hand drifted to my phone on the nightstand. A hairline crack ran from the top right corner toward the center in a neat, indifferent arc. I didn't remember dropping it. Maybe I had. Maybe I hadn't. The crack lived in a world that insisted on being physical about everything. I let it.

Down the hall, someone turned on the water. Pipes admitted they still had work to do. A car door outside thunked the way doors do when the day is honest enough to be loud again. Birds performed some re-entry sequences, notes airborne and irregular, as if they didn't have to pass inspection.

"I'm here," I said. Not proof this time. A place.

The warmth under my sternum didn't cheer. It took the seat it had been waiting for.

I swung my legs out of bed, stood, and waited for the room to prove it was real. It didn't owe me proof. I said it to myself instead, with a steadiness I could practice:

Now.

Again.

Now.

I crossed to the mirror above the dresser without hurry. My reflection waited, obedient. My eyes looked like they'd spent the night reading things too small for other people to see. Tired, yes. But not emptied. I lifted my hand. The other me did the same, on time.

In the glass, behind my shoulder, where nothing stood, color threaded the line where shadow met the wall. The faintest suggestion that light exists even when rooms refuse to brag about it.

A porch light two doors down flicked on and back off, the way blessings do when they practice, then get serious. Somewhere, an engine tried three times and then lived. My phone buzzed once on the dresser. A calendar reminder I didn't need, a notification with nothing to say, a world determined to be ordinary.

I ignored it, pulled on my hoodie, and opened the window just enough to let the morning in. Cool air walked into the room like it had paid rent. The silence that stayed behind didn't feel like an absence anymore. It felt like a seat at a table where true things go first.

I stood there a while, listening on purpose.

Morning came in careful layers, as if it were afraid to wake the house too fast.

I finished dressing on autopilot: jeans, the shoes that didn't argue with my feet, and stared at the mirror long enough to confirm two things: I looked like

I'd slept five minutes, and I didn't look hunted. Tired didn't scare me. Hunted did. The mirror still showed the same face as before, minus the part where it tried to steal my courage.

Downstairs, Mrs. Miles slid a plate across the counter without a word. Two scrambled eggs, toast, and a banana that had considered spots and decided against them. She pressed my shoulder. The same way she sets a mug close enough to warm your hands.

"You okay?" she asked, like "okay" was a place you could stand, not a test you had to pass.

"I'm here," I said.

"Good." She nodded, satisfied with grammar and philosophy at the same time.

Cody thumped down the stairs like gravity owed him interest. "If you yell unity at me, I'm moving out," he announced. He kissed his mother's cheek and stole half my toast.

He studied me. "You look like a thoughtful raccoon."

"Upgrading from feral," I said. "Big day."

"Every day is big if you shout it," he said, then squinted. "You sure you're good?"

"Yeah." The word didn't feel like a lie. It felt like a chair I planned to sit in properly.

School hallways had color again, the kind that isn't trying to impress anyone. Lockers were just their usual blue, banners returned to their indifferent red, and the cheap beige persisted unchanged. Though the noise was back, the old quiet lingered, subtle and undemanding. Without the skill of listening, one might miss it entirely, but for those attuned, it was unmistakably there.

First period found me before I found it. Mr. Sterling's classroom held the kind of stillness you get in libraries that remember being churches. Students spilled in with their usual inventory of energy drinks and sleep debt.

Mr. Sterling started class like we hadn't met the night before. No secret nod, no welcome to the club. Just a piece of chalk and a board that liked attention. He wrote VERITAS in neat block letters, paused mid-underline as if someone had asked him a question he enjoyed.

"Truth," he said, tapping the word, "is inconvenient for people who love stories. Unfortunately, it's excellent for people who need them."

A few groans. One sir, please whispered into a hoodie.

He didn't smile. He never wasted them. "Today, sources. Where we decide what has the right to argue with us."

He lectured in a way that doesn't feel like a lecture. Questions braided into statements. Examples that act like jokes until they land. Half the room leaned forward. The other half pretended not to. While he spoke, the chalk's squeak interrupted him twice, three times. Then, mid-sentence, the sound folded itself, like a bird tucking its wings.

A one-second hush pressed down, exact and gentle, and then the room exhaled back into normal. Most students didn't notice. I watched his eyes when it happened. He didn't look at me. He looked through me, past the wall, like someone listening to a hallway he'd known for years.

By the time the bell rang, I had six bullet points in my notes and one hummingbird trapped behind my ribs.

Students packed up, choreographing people who believe time works for them. Chairs scraped; zippers practiced scorn.

"Five," Mr. Sterling said, without raising his voice. The class slowed. "Four." They hesitated. "Three." Books reappeared on desks. "Two." Silence, curious. "Dismissed."

Half the room laughed. The other half obeyed.

When the door clicked shut, the air changed temperature by a degree you only notice when you need to.

Mr. Sterling erased the board as if he were taking fingerprints off glass. Then he leaned back against the desk, hands braced as if holding the room in place.

"What did you see?" he asked.

I tried a joke in my mouth and put it back. "Gray halls," I said. "Like the school copied itself in pencil. No sound. A flyer that didn't need ink. A mirror that wanted to be a door."

He didn't blink at the mirror. "And?"

"A word," I said. It tasted like admitting something old. "Later."

He nodded once, as if I'd confirmed the weather.

"It sounded like me," I added. "Not the me that says smart things in trouble. The me that offers compromises."

"People think they argue with strangers," he said. "Mostly we argue with ourselves using borrowed lines."

"I told it now," I said, and felt ridiculous for reporting it. Like a child confessing bravery.

"That's a good line to keep," he said.

He pointed his chin toward the window. "Look."

The field lay where it always did, green enough to sell to hopeful parents. A breeze pressed the flag a polite amount, not enough to turn it dramatic. The glass between us and the outside faintly held our reflections, keeping you honest about your posture.

"What color is the sky?"

"Blue."

"What color was it yesterday?"

"Still blue," I said. "Less sure of itself."

He half-smiled. "Then you don't need me to tell you what you saw."

"Tell me anyway. If I say it out loud and I'm wrong, I'll have to pretend I meant to be."

"You saw the In-Between as it is for people who haven't learned to go there yet," he said. "Not a place you walk into. A realm that already exists between the world you touch and what comes after. Most never notice it. A few do and call it dreams. Fewer still practice listening until listening becomes a kind of sight."

"Not a dream," I said. "It used my weight like it wanted to see what I could carry."

"Good sentence," he said. "Keep that one."

He drew two parallel lines on the board. On the top: WORLD. Below: IN-BETWEEN.

"This," tapping the first, "welcomes your body and its needs. Food, deadlines, weather, and so on."

"This," tapping the second, "welcomes your soul and its needs. Warnings, echoes, agreements. You don't cross with doors. You tune."

"Like a radio," I said.

"Like breath," he said. "Ignore it, and you still live, but worse."

"What about the gray?"

"Places can be starved," he said. "When enough people agree to be numb, their reflection obeys. It loses color first. Then sound. If the agreement hardens, the silence grows proud of itself."

"Like a soulless Zone," I said before I remembered I wasn't supposed to know that word.

He tilted his head. "If you like."

"I don't."

"Good."

"Tell me about the mirror."

I told him. About the crack's neat web, the reflection's patience. The voice wearing my cadence, the word that didn't break anything except permission.

He listened the way carpenters listen to walls before they cut. When I finished, he nodded once.

"Temptation is practical," he said. "It rarely tries to terrify. It wants you to be comfortable."

"I prefer honest."

"That's why you're here," he said.

"I didn't go anywhere."

"You learned to hear a place that doesn't require your feet. That's going somewhere."

He wiped his hands, though there was nothing on them. "We have rules. I dislike them. But I find them necessary."

"The good kind?"

"The kind that keeps people from mistaking panic for bravery."

He counted them off quietly. "We don't speak of this with people who haven't asked the right question. We don't advertise it to those who love answers more than work. We don't make a show. And we never confuse resonance with permission."

"Permission for what?"

"To act where you are not meant to yet. Hearing the In-Between isn't the same as moving in it. That requires responsibility you haven't agreed to, and protection you haven't been given."

"The Soul Bible," I guessed, the word arriving like something remembered rather than learned.

He met my eyes. "You like skipping chapters," he said, not unkindly. "Yes. A Soul Bible isn't a book you pick up. It's the embodiment of your soul. You don't borrow it. You don't steal it. You don't get it because you want it. You get it because you agree to be who you are when it stops being charming."

"How do you know I could?"

"I live with classrooms full of noise. I notice people who hear under it."

We let the room rest. Dust floated in the slice of sun on the floor, each pale speck a tiny planet living out its orbit while we pretended to be still.

"Cody," I said, because saying his name felt like keeping a promise I didn't want to leave behind. "He doesn't... hear what I hear."

"Not yet," Mr. Sterling said. "Different isn't lesser, it's timing. Some doors open for one so another can find the handle."

He looked at me, expression unreadable. "Homework," he said.

"For English?"

"For truth. Bring him when the silence hums again. If he says yes, that's his answer. If he says no, that's yours."

He drew a small circle overlapping both lines, like a bead sliding on two strings. "You can keep living here," he said, "and pretend the other line doesn't exist. You'll be better at it than most. Or you can keep listening and risk becoming useful."

"That's not how people sell life choices."

"I don't sell," he said. "I invite."

The bell blared. A tin crown pretending to be a king. The hallway noise shoved its way under the door. He opened a drawer, pulled out a folded note, and set it on my notebook.

When the silence hums again, follow it after school.

"It's dramatic," I said.

"It's clear," he said.

"Where?"

"You'll know. That's the point of listening."

I slid the note into my hoodie pocket. "If I'm wrong?"

"You'll walk a hallway twice. There are worse sins."

"You ever wish it wasn't you?"

"Often," he said. "Then I stop wishing and do my work."

"What's mine?"

"Today? Learn the difference between echoes and hums. One convinces by volume; the other endures by truth."

"Truth hums. Lies echo."

"Careful," he said, half-laughing. "You're starting to like the tidy version."

"It helps me carry the messy one."

"That's fair."

He moved aside as students flooded in. "Go," he said, not dismissal, but release.

The hallway met me with its old bravado. Lockers clanged like percussion. Someone argued about nothing. The vending machine held a bag of chips, hostage by one corner, warning about hope.

Cody slid up beside me, grin installed. "You owe me the gossip."

"After school," I said, and the words carried more weight than they should have. Mr. Sterling's note warmed faintly against my side.

"Oh? A secret meeting?"

"Something like that," I said. "You're invited, if you want extra credit."

He laughed. "Since when do we get graded on weird?"

"Since today," I said. But the joke didn't stop the hum from answering.

We split for class. As I turned toward the science wing, the building's noise folded and unfolded, the crease visible only if you knew to check for it. Under the chatter and clatter, a single clean note threaded through, steady and certain.

The hum brushed my ribs like a shy hello.

I didn't smile. I didn't pretend to hear it. I let now take its place in the day. Now.

Not a command. A compass. I walked into the noise with my hands out of my pockets and my head up, because it felt like an honest way to go to class.

Outside, the sky was blue again, undecided about clouds. I looked through the small square window at the end of the hall and watched a bird fail to make a straight line. Good. Straight lines lie more often than they tell the truth.

By lunch, I'd learned three new facts in Biology and one in English about metaphors chewing their leash. Between periods, I mapped three exits that felt friendlier than the others. I didn't call that paranoia. I called it reading the room.

The note in my pocket waited.

When the final bell threw a net over the school, calling for escape, I stood without hurrying. The hall thinned. The hum didn't, though. It found a pitch I remembered, rising with a note of resolve, tugging at my clothes, at my attention. I followed it past the main office, past the gym doors, past the spot where the tile crack spider-webbed like a map to a place I hadn't earned. I followed it all the way outside. Kids ran like they'd been threatened by the concept of time. Cody shouted something about pizza and being spiritually allergic to homework.

I didn't know what waited. I knew what I'd said already. And now it was time to hear whether Cody would say yes. Or if he says no, I'll have my answer.

CHAPTER FOUR

THE COST OF SAYING YES

"Tell me the mystery homework wasn't actually homework," he said.

"Not the kind you can copy," I said.

He squinted. "You've got that look again. The one where your brain's already in another zip code."

"Mr. Sterling asked me to meet him tomorrow," I said.

He tilted his head. "Why does it sound like he wanted your blood type, too?"

I hesitated because part of me desperately wanted to ignore the whole thing. But the note in my hoodie pocket pressed against me, far heavier than simple paper, reminding me I couldn't just wish this away. The words inside waited, silent but pounding, pulling at my curiosity and the guilt tightening in my chest. I finally pulled it out. The front still showed Mr. Sterling's instruction.

Resonance Notes, Intro.

Notice: Where does the cold sit?

Name: Which lie is asking for rent?

Breathe: Count until the first answer stops shouting.

Repeat: Out loud, the truth that doesn't move.

Refuse: "Later" is a lie's favorite word.

For the first time, I actually turned the note over in my hands, checking both sides.

I discovered a fourth line written in smaller ink on the back, nearly hidden until I looked closely.

Ending the note's instructions with just one more thing: Sunrise Church, 10am. The thought of what might happen if I were late made me anxious; curiosity burned under my skin, and I worried I'd lose a chance Mr. Sterling believed was important for me, even if I didn't understand why yet. If I missed it, I might never know why he singled me out.

I stared at it until the air around the words seemed to still.

"So that's what he meant. He wants me there tomorrow," I said quietly.

"Where's that?" Cody asked.

"The old church near downtown."

He blinked. "You're not actually going, are you?"

"I think I already said yes."

He leaned against the brick wall, eyes narrowing like he was trying to read the weather.

"You realize every good horror movie starts like this."

"This isn't horror," I said. "It's something else."

"Something else is usually worse."

I almost smiled. "You don't have to come."

"Yeah, and you don't have to chase invisible noises, but here we are."

The bell tower over the gym shattered the quiet, ringing loud enough to jolt me. We froze, hearts thumping, the world hushed all around while the sound faded.

"You really believe this guy?" he asked.

"I don't know if it's belief," I said. "It's just... when he talks, it's like the air listens, and I feel like I have to find out what he wants. Ignoring this doesn't feel possible."

He shrugged. "If this is a cult, I'm driving your car."

"I don't have a car."

"Exactly. First sacrifice."

He grinned, but worry tugged his mouth down, and his eyes clouded. The smile wobbled, not quite masking what churned beneath.

I carefully folded the note along its crease, slid it back into my pocket, and felt the residual warmth from my grip against my hand.

"I'll meet you there," I said. "Tomorrow."

Cody kicked a pebble across the parking lot. "Ever notice how normal days collapse before something big?"

"Yeah," I said. "That's how they trick you into thinking you're safe."

The wind shifted, crisp, carrying the faint scent of rain and candle wax.

Somewhere ahead, a church bell rang once. Not a call, just a reminder.

Cody exhaled. "Lead the way, divine one."

"Not divine," I said. "Just paying attention."

We walked until the hum returned.

One of the best things about where we lived was how walkable everything in town was. The high school, food, the corner store, even the church, everything.

You could cross half the neighborhood in fifteen minutes if your legs were fresh and your mind wasn't full.

My mind stormed, nerves buzzing, thoughts crashing into each other. Every step pressed with the heaviness I couldn't shake.

Sunrise Church wasn't far. Just past the old downtown strip, tucked between a shuttered florist and a furniture store that hadn't changed its display since the year I was born. Normally, I liked the walk: the way the city bled from crisp concrete into crooked brick. The sidewalks dipped and buckled, like they were tired of pretending they were flat. It was familiar. Predictable.

Today, every step carried a strange foreboding. The sidewalks seemed to tilt, old streets glowering back, and with each breath, unease crawled higher up my spine.

The rain had stopped. But everything clung to its memory. The pavement glistened and shimmered with oil rainbows. The air tasted pure, eager. Puddles rippled at the street's edge, and the sky stretched wide overhead. Pale and streaked with silver.

Cody walked beside me, hands stuffed in his jacket pockets. His hood was up even though the cold wasn't biting yet. Our footsteps crunched through the damp leaves littering the sidewalk. Red, gold, and brown pieces of a season shedding its skin.

Neither of us said much. I kept replaying last night's conversation in my mind, trying to figure out if I was chasing answers for myself or just because someone finally noticed me, and now I couldn't back down.

Even with all the talking, silence was easier.

It pressed in, thick and weighted, uncomfortable as a wound left open.

It was the kind that holds its breath.

After a few blocks, Cody finally spoke. "You think he'll actually be there?"

"I think he wouldn't have told us to come if he wasn't serious."

"Yeah, but how?" He eyed me. "Are we getting a sermon or an exorcism?"

"Not sure," I said. "But Mr. Sterling doesn't strike me as a 'youth-group-pizza-party' guy."

Cody gave a breath of a laugh, but it died quickly. The tension in the air was real now. Not imagined. Not leftover from dreams or whispered warnings.

We passed crumbling houses and wild lawns, each one sagging, watching. The further we walked, the more I felt seen, my nerves taut and exposed, as if the whole street waited to pounce.

A cat darted across the street, tail high.

Then it started.

The cold hit suddenly, squeezing my gut. It clawed at my thoughts, dredging up memories of long dark nights and fear settling in my bones.

This chill crept from behind my ears, lacing frost through my nerves as if carried in by phantom earbuds. My whole body tensed as I walked, crossing an unseen threshold.

This was different. It was slower. It didn't bite; it crept. A crawling chill started just behind my ears and sank like a thread of ice down my spine. Every part of me tensed as I walked through a threshold I couldn't see.

Notice, I thought. Where does the cold sit?

Cody shifted beside me. He didn't say anything, but I could tell he felt it too.

We slowed without meaning to. The road narrowed here. The streetlamps were too far apart. One of them flickered, then buzzed, and went out.

"Something's wrong," I muttered, too low for anyone but Cody to hear.

He didn't ask what.

Because he already knew.

The air was too still, like the neighborhood's controller had died. No birds. No rustling. Even the breeze had vanished.

My pulse stuttered. That's when I saw him.

At first, I thought it was a mannequin. Or a bad Halloween setup someone set up too early. But no.

He was real.

He waited in the alley, motionless in a pool of shadow and icy light. The sight of him sent a chill through me.

He was tall and thin. If motionless, he could vanish against the streetlamps. Dressed in a trench coat, black fedora, and dark sunglasses, he concealed everything. Hands buried deep, he seemed sculpted from shadow, unmoving, not even shifting his weight.

But the thing that really hit?

It wasn't his outfit. It wasn't even his face, what little I could see of it.

Stillness, like a held scream. Something in the way the air congealed around him. It made my heart hammer, each beat an urge to run.

The kind of stillness your brain tries to ignore because it doesn't make sense. Because nothing alive should be that still. No sway. Not even a fidget.

It was like the world had frozen just around him.

Even though I couldn't see his eyes, I felt them locked on me.

Not curious. Not confused. Just ... focused.

I froze mid-stride. My legs locked, terror rooting me to the cracked pavement. Breathing quickly and shallow, I stared at the figure, unable to move.

Cody saw me stop. He turned his head toward where I was staring. He didn't speak, but I noticed him straighten, as if bracing for trouble.

The man still didn't move. Still didn't flinch.

But I knew, we both knew, he was watching me. Only me.

His gaze paralyzed me, calling up a deep, childish terror. The memory of being small, invisible in a roaring world, utterly alone. Now, I was that frightened child again, certain that something impossible had found me and would never let me go.

For a heartbeat, I thought he might step forward.

A delivery truck turned the corner behind us, engine low, tires splashing through puddles. I blinked.

And he was gone.

There wasn't footfall. Not even a coat flap. Just … gone.

Like a tape had been paused, erased, and then resumed.

"What the …" Cody whispered.

My mouth was dry. "Did you see him vanish?"

"No," he said, voice hoarse. "That's the freakiest part. He didn't move. Not once. And then … nothing."

We stood there for a second longer, listening. Trying to decide whether to check the alley or pretend none of it happened.

I glanced toward the church. The steeple was just barely visible above the rooftops.

"Let's go," I said.

Cody didn't argue.

The hum had gone quiet, but the air still remembered it.

Neither of us looked back.

The silence followed us.

Not the empty kind, more like something walking close enough to keep count.

Cody's shoes scuffed against the sidewalk in uneven rhythm, nerves showing. I tried not to check over my shoulder, but every window felt like it might blink.

"The alley's empty," I said, mostly to prove it.

He didn't look. "Still feels like it isn't."

The chill lingered, crawling up my spine, whispering that whatever we'd passed wasn't finished with us. Maybe it never would be.

"We both saw him?" I asked.

Cody nodded once. "The guy in the alley? Yeah. Real sketch. He was just… standing there."

"Like he wasn't part of the scene."

"Exactly."Cody frowned. "You think he's what's been causing all this?"

I didn't answer right away. Because I didn't know. And even if I did, saying it aloud would've made it feel too real.

"I don't think he's just some guy," I said finally. "But I have to see what this is about. Let's just get to the Church first."

The wind picked up as we walked, rustling the trees like they were warning each other. Above us, the sky was a quilt of light grays, stitched with streaks of cloud that looked too still. A single bird circled overhead, alone and silent.

We kept moving.

Each step toward Sunrise Church felt like it peeled a layer of tension off my chest. Not all at once. But gradually, as if coming up for air after being underwater too long.

"Is it just me," Cody said after a few blocks, "or does it feel lighter here?"

I nodded. "Like we're walking into a clearing."

"Or out of something."

The streets grew quieter, older. The houses took on that timeless look of wooden siding faded by sun and storms. Porches sagging under their own history. We passed a barber shop with its blinds still drawn. A laundromat that smelled faintly of soap and dust, and a corner store where a dog lay curled in the doorway, unmoving except for one ear that flicked lazily as we passed.

And then, there it was.

Sunrise Church.

It stood at the end of the block, as if waiting. Not tall like a cathedral, or ornate like the churches you see in postcards. But strong and steady. Quiet in a way that made everything around it hush just a little more.

The paint was white, though much of it had surrendered to time, peeling around the base, cracking along the edges. Ivy crept up one side. Even nature couldn't help but be drawn to it. The roof sloped like a frozen wave mid-crash. The twin doors out front stood beneath a weathered wooden arch, carved with symbols I didn't recognize. Circles, slashes, a sunburst at the center.

But what struck me most was the people.

They came in quiet groups. There were families, students, and even a few older folks with canes and careful steps. All funneling through the doors like they knew exactly where they were going. Not a word passed between most of them. Not even chatter. Just a shared sense of purpose.

"I didn't think there'd be this many," Cody murmured.

"Me neither," I said. "This doesn't look like what I imagined as Mr. Sterling meant"

We slowed as we reached the steps.

The closer we got, the more I noticed it, the atmosphere. Not like pressure this time. Just... still. In that deep way. The kind of stillness that wasn't empty. It was watchful. Waiting and listening.

We paused at the base of the steps.

I glanced back one last time, just to be sure.

No sign of the man in the alley. No shadow stretching down the sidewalk. Just leaves brushing against the curb, and the wind tugging at tree branches like it wanted to speak.

Cody looked at me, then at the doors. "You think this is really where it all starts?"

I took a breath. The kind that felt it might stick halfway down my throat. "Mr. Sterling said we'd understand more once we came."

"Yeah, but..." He hesitated. "What if we don't like what we find?"

I looked at the twin doors again.

They weren't grand. Just wood. Hinged. Painted the same tired white as the rest of the building. But they felt important. Like stepping through them meant you were crossing something more than a threshold.

"I'd rather not like what we find," I said. "Then face something like the alley again with no understanding."

Cody exhaled slowly, lips pressed thin. Then he nodded. "Guess there's only one way to find out."

A soft breeze blew behind us, nudging leaves across the pavement. Even the wind was encouraging us forward.

I put one foot on the first step. It wobbled slightly, the creak breaking the soft silence around us. My heart skipped a beat, and a flicker of doubt brushed the edge of my thoughts. What was I really stepping into? But the pull of the unknown was stronger. Then another.

Cody followed.

Each step felt deeper than it should have. Like the ground had thickened. Like the air was paying attention.

We reached the doors.

A man in a dark vest stood beside them, tall and pale. With a calm face and eyes that looked older than the rest of him. He didn't ask our names. Didn't check a list.

He just opened one door slowly.

And nodded once.

A gesture that said: Welcome.

Or maybe: You've arrived.

Cody looked at me.

"You ready?" I asked.

He let out a small, nervous laugh. "No. But let's go anyway."

And together, we stepped inside.

Toward whatever waited next.

The inside of Sunrise Church felt bigger than it had any right to.

From the street, it looked small, humble, even tired. But once we stepped through the doors, space unfolded around us like a secret that had been waiting for permission to breathe.

The lobby spread wide under soft light. Worn gray carpet swallowed our footsteps; white walls curved into an arched ceiling where wood beams stretched like ribs. A couple of fake plants huddled in the corners, too dusty to fool anyone, the kind that stayed only because leaving felt impolite.

The air smelled faintly of brewed coffee, old hymnals, and lemon cleaner. Otherwise, the scent of every church and every childhood Sunday blurred into one.

To the right, a folding table sagged beneath the last of the donuts and Styrofoam cups. The coffee looked criminal; the donuts looked like survivors.

To the left, a hallway vanished into a wing labeled Preschool & Youth Classes in cheerful block letters. A cartoon lamb leaned against the wall, its eyes a little too enthusiastic to trust.

Straight ahead, tall wooden sanctuary doors stood slightly ajar. Light spilled through the crack, as if something inside were stirring.

We were late. That much was obvious.

Only a handful of parents lingered, corralling toddlers and finishing soft-spoken goodbyes. A teenager in a jean jacket scrolled on her phone, oblivious or pretending to be.

Cody and I hovered near the donut table, stalling. I claimed the lone maple bar just before another guy reached for it. He gave me a look; I gave him apathy.

"I'm not sure what I expected," I said around a cautious bite.

"What, torches and chanting?" Cody asked.

"Something less... fluorescent."

It looked ordinary enough. The fluorescent lights above flickered briefly, then settled into a buzz that faded mid-note, leaving a sharp silence hanging in the air. It was the kind of silence that made the ceiling feel too low, the walls a bit too tight, as if the room were holding its breath along with us.

The calm carried a weight. An invisible tension hung in the air, as if the walls were acting as a holy barrier.

Then the sanctuary doors opened. Out came a teal sweater and faded jeans. Sneakers that squeaked on the tile. Her hair was pulled into a loose bun that looked accidental in the most intentional way.

My brain didn't have to supply the name this time. Sarah Storm had stepped out.

Her eyes found mine, bright and knowing. The same look she'd given me at school.

"Kayson." Her smile widened when she spotted Cody beside me. "And you must be Cody. I've heard a thing or two about you."

Cody gave a short nod, half-grin. "All good things, I hope."

She laughed. "Mostly. Supposedly, you forget to bring your soul."

Cody put on his usual performance.

I raised a brow. "Didn't expect to see you here."

"Neither did I," she said. "My uncle asked me to meet you guys here."

"Your uncle?"

"Mr. Sterling," she said, like it should have been obvious. "He's in the sanctuary. Come on, no point wasting more time. I'll take you to him."

She turned before we could answer, moving with the easy certainty of someone who'd already made the decision for us.

Cody leaned close. "So that's Sarah?"

I nodded. "Yep."

"Figures," he muttered, falling in step behind her.

The sanctuary unfolded before us, unexpected and inviting, like a gift revealed ahead of its time.

High ceilings, soft white walls, padded chairs fanned in a semi-circle beneath warm stage lights. Everything whispered instead of shouting. There was no stained glass, no smoke machines. Just quiet expectancy.

A man in a gray shirt stood onstage with a Bible in his hand, speaking to a sea of listeners caught between breathing and believing.

Behind him, the screen glowed with an image of sunrise over still water.

It didn't feel religious.

It felt watchful.

Sarah didn't slow to find a seat. She guided us along the far-left aisle toward a narrow wooden door tucked behind the stage.

The pastor's gentle voice floated over the room, conversational, but edged with something sharp enough to cut:

"Temptation starts in the cracks," he continued. "That's where the enemy strikes first and hardest. So, we stay attentive, because the fight never sends invitations. It simply presents itself with a decision."

It hit harder than I expected.

It didn't sound scripted. It felt unknowingly directed towards me.

Part of me wondered if he knew I was coming.

From somewhere deeper, I knew he didn't. And still it was a reminder that the decision from yesterday wasn't the last I had to make.

Images flickered: Back to my dream, the pressure in the air, the underwater sensation of silent movement.

And Principal Kartikak's assembly at the field.

Her calm hadn't felt administrative; it had felt orchestrated.

Cody leaned close. "You feel that?"

"Yeah." My voice came out thin.

The corridor behind the stage was narrow and dim, lined with old posters and a carpet that had survived too many shoes.

A flyer read: *"Family Game Night — Canceled Until Further Notice."*

Another bore a verse from Hebrews: Faith is the substance of things hoped for, the evidence of things not seen.

Again, a poke at something my gut tells me I should already know.

We reached the end of the hall.

A plain wooden door waited with no sign, no window. Just an old metal handle that looked like it would fall off before the door would open.

Something about the room radiated restraint, as if it were holding something back.

Sarah paused, then knocked with two quick taps, a pause, one deliberate strike.

The rhythm echoed down the corridor like a code from another lifetime.

A moment passed.

Then the handle turned with a soft, precise click.

The door opened.

The room beyond the door felt older than the church hiding it.

Off-white paint dulled by time, with a wooden cross on the far wall, and a landscape painting whose colors had nearly given up. Dust rimmed the windowsills as if the place were an unpopular exhibit.

No hum of lights. Just the kind of silence that waits for truth to be spoken.

A long table filled the center, scarred by rings and knife marks from years of use. It looked less like furniture and more like a survivor of decisions that mattered.

Two men waited at the far end.

One was lean, dark-haired, streaked with silver. He watched with patient clarity. His calm wasn't softness; it was control.

The other sat broad, bearded, with flannel sleeves rolled. Radiating grounded warmth while keeping a soldier's readiness beneath it.

Mr. Sterling stood near the head of the table.

"You made it," he said. "Thank you, Sarah."

She nodded and took the seat beside me. Cody dropped into the one across, his nerves pretending to be posture.

"These are friends of mine," Mr. Sterling said. "They've seen what most people never even sense."

The silver-haired man inclined his head. "Solomon."

The other gave a small grin. "David. Glad you came."

Cody muttered, "Still not sure what we came to."

David's grin held. "Understanding, if we do this right."

Mr. Sterling gestured to me. "Start from the beginning, Kayson."

I hesitated before I began to recount my experiences. The air in the room seemed to thicken as I spoke, each word sinking like a stone into a deep well of silence. I told them about the hum that followed me, the colorless school, the figure of smoke and armor, and the light that felt alive and deliberate. But when I reached the moment with the mirror, my voice faltered slightly.

"It was like staring into the surface of a pond," I said slowly, reliving the strange pull of that glass. "Except instead of seeing my reflection, I saw something else. A flicker of movement that wasn't mine. I could feel it trying to reach through, the air in front of it bending as if it was pushing against a thin layer of reality."

As I described this, the room listened, the quiet confirming that I was not alone in what I had witnessed. When I finished, the silence in the room didn't question. It confirmed I had woken up.

Solomon leaned forward. "And you, Cody?"

"Nothing that extreme," Cody said. "But that same bone-chilling cold, like the air forgot what warmth is. It was hit again by an alley on the way here. Then it stopped once we reached this place."

Solomon's expression hardened. "That chill isn't weather or nerves. It's resonance."

"Resonance?" Cody asked.

"It's what happens when the Soulless Zones press the physical," Solomon said. "Not a doorway, just proximity. Think of thunder without lightning: you feel the vibration, but the storm itself hasn't touched you."

Mr. Sterling nodded. "The hum you've been hearing, Kayson. It's truth and corruption brushing close enough for the sensitive to notice."

I hesitated. "Then the thing in the alley we saw…"

Solomon met my eyes. "That wasn't imagination. What you saw was a human, more specifically, someone being influenced. The Fallen Angels can't enter our world, but their whispers can. When a spirit loses its footing to fear or anger, it becomes a doorway for suggestion. They speak through that weakness."

Mr. Sterling added, "Influence doesn't need a face to reach you. Sometimes it borrows one. That's why the stillness felt wrong. It wasn't his silence; it was something else using it."

David leaned forward, voice low. "The moment you recognized it, it recognized you. That's how influence works. It notices resistance."

The words settled heavily between us.

Whatever had stood in that alley hadn't just been watching. It had been listening.

David broke the silence first. "The Fallen Angels thrive wherever people trade what's real for what's easy. That grayness you saw in your dream, the drained version of the school. That's the mark they leave when enough people stop caring to see."

Mr. Sterling added quietly, "That vision was an echo, a warning. As you intuitively guessed, a Soulless Impression. If it spreads, the area collapses into, as you said, a Soulless Zone corrupted by silence, color drained. The spirit emptied."

The explanation fit with a cold precision I didn't want to accept.

"So why here?" I asked. "Why meet in this church?"

"Because this ground is still sound," Mr. Sterling said. "Consecrated long before us. Resonance can gather near it but not enter. It's neutral. Safe for us to speak in."

Solomon stood, his presence filling the room. "You've both been touched by resonance in a way most never are. The In-Between hasn't opened to you yet. You've only felt its echo. But that alone means you're worthy of being recognized. The Order we serve exists to guide those who sense that call before it consumes them."

Cody frowned. "Order?"

Mr. Sterling met his gaze. "An old brotherhood sworn to guard humanity's eternity from spiritual collapse. To keep what lives and what devours life in their rightful places."

He turned to me. "You weren't meant to face this alone, Kayson. But something in you answered when others couldn't hear."

The hum beneath the floor stirred again, low and alive.

Mr. Sterling's tone softened. "What happens next is yet again, choice. We can teach you how to quiet this. Attempt to return to ordinary life. Or we can teach you how to bear it and fight for those who can't."

Cody swallowed. "Can really turn it off?"

David nodded. "Awareness is mercy and burden both. Once you've felt it, pretending you haven't gets harder every day."

The air thickened; dust lifted from the tabletop, swirling as the room took a slow breath.

Solomon placed his hand on the wood. "If you continue, don't think about what you'll see. Think about why you need to see it."

Sarah's voice was a whisper of remembrance: "You won't want to look away once you do."

I stepped forward. The hum shifted inside my ribs more pulse than sound.

Mr. Sterling's words carried across the stillness.

"You find yourself at the edge of what waits to be revealed."

And the world seemed to hold its breath to listen.

David rose first.

His chair scraped across the wooden floor with a sound that felt final.

"This part isn't ceremonial," he said. "Nothing crazy like robes or incense. What happens now isn't about appearance."

He looked at me, then Cody. "It's about choice."

Mr. Sterling moved to the far wall, where a plain black chest rested beneath the faded painting of the countryside. He knelt, unlatched it, and opened the lid. Inside lay three bundles. Three colors: white, gray, and crimson.

Without a word, he set them on the table.

David unwrapped the crimson cloth. Beneath it lay a small iron blade dulled with age but heavy with memory.

"Long before there were Knights," David said, "there were people who refused to lie to themselves. Conviction came before weapons. Obedience before armor. What made them who they were wasn't steel. It was a surrender."

Solomon stepped beside him, hands folded behind his back.

"Before you can stand for light," he said quietly, "you must bow to submission."

The silence deepened until I could hear my heartbeat. Not from fear, from anticipation.

Mr. Sterling's voice dropped low.

"If you take this vow, you have accepted an opportunity. Your life stops belonging only to you. You'll carry what others can't see and guard what most don't believe exists. You'll be tested where you're weakest. And when doubt feels louder than faith, that's when the enemy whispers loudest."

Solomon added, "But you will not stand alone. None of us do."

David raised a hand, palm open.

"If you're ready, come forward."

I didn't move at first. My legs felt locked, my chest pounding like it was spelling out something I didn't yet speak. I looked at Cody.

He met my eyes, equal parts. Both fear and defiance radiated.

"If I die," he muttered, "I'm haunting you."

"Deal," I said, and we stepped forward. Solomon gently gestured for us to take a knee.

The carpet pressed into my knee, grounding me in the moment.

"Repeat after me," Solomon said, stepping between us.

"I vow to carry the light."

"I vow to carry the light."

"To speak truth when the world silences it."

"To speak truth when the world silences it."

"To guard those who cannot guard themselves."

"To guard those who cannot guard themselves."

"To remember that I serve a King no army can see."

"To remember that I serve a King no army can see."

"And to fight, not with pride. But with purpose."

"And to fight, not with pride. But with purpose."

David lifted the iron blade slightly, its edge catching the yellow light. He held it between us like a line drawn in faith rather than metal.

"Rise," he said.

Sarah stepped forward then, quiet, steady, carrying two small leather-bound journals. She placed one before each of us.

"For what follows," she said. "Write what you see, what you dream, what you can't explain yet. It helps you recognize what's real."

The cover felt warm against my palm, as if it already carried weight.

"You've taken the first step," Mr. Sterling said. "The path won't get easier. But now..."

He glanced toward Solomon and David.

"...you don't walk it alone."

David clapped Cody on the shoulder.

"Training starts soon. Tonight was just the oath to get a shot."

He gave a half-smile, more weary than proud. "The moment you said yes, your old life ended."

Cody blinked. "Ended?"

David nodded once. "Every calling begins with a funeral."

The air shifted. Not colder, just clearer. Like the dust in the room had decided to listen.

Then Mr. Sterling reached into his coat and drew a small book bound in blue that looked like a sunny day. The faintest glow along its edges. Solomon and David each did the same; theirs were deep green and maroon.

The light from their books wasn't bright; it was alive. It pulsed, steady and quiet, like three heartbeats remembering the same song.

Solomon looked at us. "What comes next can't happen in this world. Only those who've already walked may open the way."

He opened his book, pages fluttering though no wind moved them. Script not written in ink shimmered across the paper in a language older than breath.

"Don't be afraid," Mr. Sterling said. "This isn't leaving. It's being invited."

The hum under the floor grew louder. Rising into the walls, through the air, through us. My chest vibrated with it.

Sarah stepped back, eyes lifted. "They'll be safe," she whispered.

David pressed his palm over his open book. Maroon light unfurled outward like mist.

It spread across the floor, threading beneath our feet, circling the table in a slow, deliberate pattern.

Solomon's voice was steady. "Focus on what is true. That's what keeps you tethered."

Mr. Sterling laid his hand on my shoulder; the world tilted. Once, twice, then folded inward like a page turning.

The air thickened, sound fell away, and every color bled into white.

For a moment, I thought we'd been swallowed.

Then the silence breathed.

When sight returned, the church was gone. The air around us shimmered faintly, as if made of light remembering form.

Beyond us stood towers of silver and stone rising from a horizon that wasn't sky or ground. In the distance, a great citadel shone. Part fortress, part cathedral. The heart of something ancient and alive.

Cody exhaled beside me. "We're not in D.C. anymore."

Mr. Sterling's voice carried softly behind us.

"Welcome to the Crossguard."

CHAPTER FIVE

I WAS CHOSEN IN SILENCE

"This is Crossguard?" Cody and I said at the same time.

Our voices came out hushed, uncertain, a sharp contrast to the magnitude before us. I caught Cody glancing at me, eyes wide, his brow furrowed in disbelief.

The castle wasn't a gleaming fairy-tale fortress. It was solid, weathered. Immense stone stacked with a precision that felt divine, not human. Its towers rose like sentinels. Sunlight brushed their edges, half-shadowed by slow-moving, otherworldly clouds. Yet, a sudden chill ran down my spine. A visceral shiver that broke through the awe. It was as if the stones themselves whispered.

Behind us, hills rolled into fields of gold. The tall grass moved as if it had breath. No cars. No birds. No hum of cities. Only wind. A faint vibration lay beneath, like a hymn the world itself remembered.

"What happened to the church?" I asked. "Are we even in Washington anymore?"

David stepped beside us, his hand heavy on my shoulder, his other gripping Cody's with rare gravity. The easy grin he wore in ordinary life had vanished, replaced by solemnity. His eyes searched the horizon with the haunted look of one who recognizes an old, unwelcome truth.

"You're not in the church," he said. "And you're definitely not anywhere that fits on a map."

He turned toward the horizon. "This is Crossguard. Not Heaven. Not Earth. Not the In-Between. A sanctum was built between them. A fortress where truth is preserved."

Cody frowned. "So where are we, really?"

Mr. Sterling moved forward, his long coat catching the wind. "You've entered a stronghold beyond the boundary. Crossguard exists where reality folds. But doesn't break. It's the one place the war can't reach without cost."

The word surfaced again in my mind, quiet, stubborn.

"The In-Between," I said.

David nodded. "You brushed it once already. The dream of silence and gray. That was the In-Between, where the Fallen Angels feed. It's what happens when their influence corrodes a place from the inside out."

The memory hit hard. A crushing weight pressed on my chest; the voices clawed inside me; reason vanished. That world wasn't dead. It had been starving.

I looked around. The sky here wasn't perfect, but it breathed. Clouds drifted like slow thoughts. Light shifted, purposeful. Even the ground, alive underfoot, hummed faintly.

"Why does it feel safe?"

Mr. Sterling answered. "Because it is. This soil is consecrated. It's outside their reach. The Fallen can't enter Crossguard without forfeiting what they are. Their lies lose volume here."

Then Solomon spoke.

His tone didn't rise; it deepened. The air seemed to align with it.

"The In-Between is only one layer," he said. "But it isn't the whole design. Earth, the In-Between, and Crossguard all exist at once, like pages bound to the same book. Most souls read only one page their entire lives. You've been permitted to see more. And you will never unsee it." Cody glanced at me, a wrinkle of skepticism shadowing his features. "Sounds like a way to complicate things," he said. "If most only need one page, why read more?" His challenge hung in the air, not quite confrontational, but curious enough to tip the conversation into uncharted territory. Solomon studied him, a trace of a smile pulling at his lips, inviting exploration rather than retreat.

Cody exhaled. "So Fallen Angels are real? Aren't they demons?"

Solomon's gaze held steady. "No. Demons only exist in fairy tales. Fallen Angels have fallen out of grace and are countless. But not all wear armor. Some speak softly. Some comfort you while they steal from you. Some twist the truth until it sounds compassionate. You won't always recognize them."

My stomach clenched. Principal Kartikak's voice flickered through my memory, each syllable slicing with dread. The calm finality, the hollow certainty. My hands balled tight at my sides, nails digging in as the memory invaded.

"What do they want?"

"They want dominion," Solomon said. "Not through violence, through apathy. By convincing the world that truth is optional. That light is a preference and faith is fiction."

David's voice followed, rougher. "And the cruel part? They don't need to storm gates. They just need people to stop noticing they're corrupting themselves. This battle exists within just as much as it does inside the In-Between."

Cody ran both hands through his hair. "Why us? Why bring us here?"

David glanced at Solomon, then at Mr. Sterling.

Solomon stepped closer. The wind seemed to lean toward him.

"Because truth is under siege," he said. "And sometimes, when the world trembles, a few are called to hold the line. To stand where others run." In the distance, a bell's resonant chime echoed low and mournful, threading through the air. A summons only courage ever heeds. The sound curled around us, both promise and warning, as if this place demanded resilience at the core of the soul.

The wind rose, carrying warmth instead of cold. It lifted the edges of my hoodie, moved through the field like the word itself had stirred the air.

"You weren't brought here because you were ready," Solomon continued. "You were brought because time ran short. Because someone had to see. Someone had to remember what's real."

He turned toward the castle. The gates towered above us, sealed. But not closed in spirit.

"Your lives won't be simple again," he said. "But they'll finally be honest."

I stared at the stone path winding ahead, felt the quiet strength of the walls, the faint shimmer of the air. My heart thudded, nerves tight. The place didn't just exist; it waited.

Cody placed a hand on my shoulder. His grip was firm, not joking. Just steady. I met his gaze and found concern, not sarcasm.

"You good?"

"No," I said truthfully. "But I think I'm supposed to be here."

"Yeah," he murmured. "Same."

Mr. Sterling adjusted his cuff, the ghost of a smile returning.

"Come. There's someone you should meet."

The others—Solomon, David, and Sarah, were already moving toward the gate. Light shimmered faintly around them. It was the mark of resonance. As they walked, Sarah glanced back. She caught my eye with a look of gentle reassurance. Solomon touched David's shoulder. Their shared nod conveyed a silent pact of mutual trust.

I looked back one last time. At the fields, the sky, the echo of the life we'd left behind.

Then I faced forward.

Something waited. An ache of anticipation, heavy with fear and hope.

And the time for answers had arrived.

Without another word, Cody and I followed.

Still wordless, still trying to breathe in a world that felt too immense for the shaky lungs we'd brought.

We started down the hill toward the castle.

The air shifted as we neared the stone path. Grass behind us swayed, waving goodbye to the world we'd left. Wind moved more slowly here. More breath than breeze. Measured. Deliberate. As if even the air knew this ground was sacred.

Up close, Crossguard was staggering.

The walls stretched higher than reason, built from pale stone shot through with veins of silver. The metal seemed to grow from the stone itself, as if the earth bled truth. When sunlight touched the facade, it shimmered with life, propelling us forward, drawn irresistibly toward the entrance.

Two towers flanked the front.

At first, they seemed identical, twin sentinels keeping watch.

But they weren't.

The left tower was alive with carvings: vines, flowers, curling leaves so detailed they seemed to sway when you looked away. Birds hid in branches; a fox crouched at the base, caught mid-pounce, all that life entwined in stone. Yet there was something more, an elusive essence just beyond sight. This beauty served a purpose, perhaps guarding secrets or unveiling forgotten tales.

The right tower pulsed with shifting runes. They weren't decorations; they moved. Blue and violet flickers flow like starlight through water. Sometimes they looked like letters. Sometimes constellations. Every so often, one burned gold before fading.

But there was no door.

No hinges or grand gate. Just smooth stone.

Solomon stepped forward without hesitation. From his coat, he drew a small leather-bound book. The same one I'd seen in the church. It looked ordinary. Used. The kind of thing that could open hearts, not walls.

He pressed it gently against the stone.

The wall pulsed.

A green light radiated outward from the book, deep and vibrant, as if breath exhaled from an ancient forest. Silver veins in the wall brightened, then unraveled like threads pulled from fabric.

The stone didn't break.

It yielded.

Light folded back, silent and clean, until an archway opened before us. No machinery. Just permission.

"Stay close," Solomon said.

We stepped through.

And everything changed.

The air inside was warmer. Faintly scented with parchment, lavender, and something like cedar smoke. The floor beneath us was dark-stained wood, polished to a mirror's calm. Above, ribbed arches of brass and stone curved, each line purposeful. Every surface whispered order.

Tall portraits lined the hall, narrow and reverent.

Knights and scholars were scattered throughout the room.

Some faces were fierce, and others calm.

All marked by the same light in their eyes.

At the far end, a stained-glass window poured crimson and gold across the floor. An abstract sunrise spilling over a mountain ridge. Beneath it sat a desk of polished oak. Behind it, a woman looked up from a big book. It reminded me of walking up to check in for a hotel.

She was tall, composed, and elegant. Dark hair twisted into a bun, glasses perched low on her nose. Her fingers turned parchment pages with the precision of someone who didn't waste motion. She looked more like a headmistress than a gatekeeper. But the stillness around her told a different story.

"Inductees?" she asked, voice calm and melodic.

"Indeed," Solomon replied. "These two. Tour and induction request."

Only then did she lift her gaze.

And smile, the kind that wasn't surprise, but recognition mixed with an unreadable depth.

"Right on time," she said, closing the ledger. "Another joined this morning. But you should be prepared. The path ahead is never without shadows, even in the warmest welcome."

Her eyes met ours steadily and knowingly. "Kayson and Cody."

I froze. "How? No one said our names."

Cody frowned. "Yeah. What, do you have security cameras here?"

She tapped a heavy, leather-bound tome on her desk. Its pages shimmered faintly, the gilded edges catching light that didn't belong to the window. "I don't read minds," she said.

"I read names."

The air seemed to hush around the word.

Not a metaphor. Simply stating a fact.

"I'm Melinda," she added, standing. "Head scribe of Crossguard."

She nodded toward the towers above. "You'll be staying in the Northwest Wing, third floor. It's quiet, and the sunsets reach it first. You'll need the silence for what comes next."

Cody opened his mouth. Probably to ask if the book had told her that too, but thought better of it.

Melinda handed Mr. Sterling two sealed envelopes stamped with a silver emblem: a sword crossed with a quill. "Their assignments," she said.

Mr. Sterling accepted them and turned to us. His expression was serious but not heavy. More like a teacher on the edge of a difficult lesson.

"Ready to see what this is really about?" he asked.

I wanted to nod. To sound brave.

But the truth was simpler and heavier.

"I don't know what this is," I said. "But yeah... I'm ready."

Solomon walked to the back wall and repeated the gesture. Bible to stone, green pulse, the wall dissolving.

Even though I'd seen it once, it hit the second time. Like watching lightning strike close enough to feel the air change. The wall yielded again. It was like watching a locked heart open at the sound of its name.

Beyond it stretched a narrow corridor lit by torches in wrought-iron sconces.

The flames didn't flicker; more of a steady hum, focused. Even the fire here obeyed order.

We followed in silence.

Portraits lined the passage. Some showed knights in radiant armor beneath gilded skies. Others... not human at all.

One was of a figure made entirely of crystal, mid-turn, light fracturing across its body. Another with wings of black ink, eyes like burning parchment. None of them felt malevolent. Only watchful.

Guardians of another kind.

Solomon's voice carried easily. "Until you're issued your own access, my Bible will grant you entry."

I frowned. "Your Bible does all this?"

David chuckled behind us, low and warm. 'You'll learn quickly. The Word isn't just scripture here. It's authority. Every action here answers to it.'

As he spoke, a small, forgotten pebble on the ground began to shimmer, catching our attention. It lifted gently, suspended at chest height for a moment, then softly settled back to the ground. We exchanged glances, realization dawning on us.

'You mean... literally?' Cody asked.

'Literally,' Mr. Sterling said with a faint grin. 'This place responds to faith the way gravity responds to mass. The more grounded you are, the stronger the pull.'

The hallway narrowed. Torches dimmed to a cool blue glow.

Solomon pressed his Bible against a stone panel near the end, and once again, the wall breathed and vanished.

Behind it stood something out of place: an elevator.

Sleek. Stainless steel. A small panel of glowing letters. It looked like a fragment of modern Earth grafted onto eternity.

Cody gawked. "Okay... that's new."

Mr. Sterling smiled. "Crossguard mixes form and function. Faith doesn't cancel progress; it refines it."

We stepped inside. The floor vibrated faintly beneath our feet. Solomon tapped a button labeled *NW3*.

The elevator didn't lurch. It surged.

Upward. Sideways. Maybe both. The world blurred, folded, spun. My stomach dropped and rose again in the same second. Then it all softly stopped, like time exhaling.

When the doors opened, golden light rushed in.

"Sir Thomas. Sir David," Solomon said, stepping aside. "You'll handle the rest."

He gave us one last nod before the doors closed.

The corridor beyond was warm, lined with marble that reflected faint halos of light. Floating orbs hung in the air like captured stars, illuminating each step with quiet precision.

"So... your name's really Thomas?" I asked.

He laughed. "It's easier than 'Mr. Sterling."

"How long have you been doing this?" Cody asked, studying a painting of a knight clasping hands with a woman made of mist.

Sir Thomas and Sir David exchanged a look.

"Since we were about your age," Sir David said. "Feels like yesterday. And about a century ago."

Our footsteps echoed as we passed more portraits, each one heavier than the last.

A lion made of light.

A warrior kneeling before a scroll in flames, sword shattered, tears cutting through ash.

History wasn't written here; it breathed.

"This floor feels... different," I said quietly.

Sir David nodded. "It's shielded. Not just from an attack. But from noise. From distraction. You'll learn why that matters."

At the corridor's end, Sir Thomas pressed his Bible to the wall.

The stone softened, then released a warm light, unfolding like a sigh.

The room beyond was calm and sunlit.

A wide window looked out over glowing fields and silver trees.

To the left, a bunk bed dressed in navy. To the right, a single bed with thick pillows and a golden lantern pulsing faintly, like a heartbeat. Between them sat a small desk etched with a copper map of Crossguard's grounds. Above it hung a simple sword, waiting.

"This is yours," Sir David said. "For now."

Cody dropped onto the lower bunk with a grin. "Okay, yeah. I could survive here."

I moved to the window. Beyond it stretched rolling light over fields alive, clouds drifting in rhythms slower than time. It felt like breathing after years underwater.

Still, something pulled at me.

"What about our family?" I asked. "Don't they think we're missing?"

Sir Thomas met my eyes, calm but unflinching. "When you're here, or in the In-Between, they're gently shielded. No fear or grief. Just peace. A small nudge in their memory that you're safe."

"So, they think we're still at school?" Cody asked.

Sir David nodded. "Something like that. Time doesn't pass here the same way. You'll go back, and it'll be right in their memories."

I didn't fully understand it. But somehow, it made sense. Like hearing a familiar song from a dream.

Sir Thomas clapped his hands once. "Alright. Before you overthink all that. Mess hall."

Cody perked up. "You have a cafeteria?"

Sir David grinned. "Not *a* cafeteria. *The* cafeteria."

Before we could ask, they each opened their Bibles and rested a hand on our shoulders.

Light burst outward, sky blue this time.

Not royal blue. Not ocean. Something gentler. Bright and endless. It didn't blind; it revealed. Every heartbeat aligned to it, like rhythm and breath became the same thing.

We didn't walk.

We *moved,* not through distance, but through word.

And then, light receded.

We stood in a chamber the size of a football field.

Hundreds of chandeliers cast crystal firelight above long rows of tables. The scent of bread and spice filled the air. Rich laughter echoed. bringing the room to life. Apprentices, knights, and mentors sat shoulder to shoulder, trading stories like family.

It was loud. It was alive.

For the first time since being here, I didn't question it.

There had to be hundreds of knights. Each sat at a long wooden table stretching the length of the chamber. A wide center aisle cut through them like a river through stone. Light poured down from the chandeliers above, splintering into fire-colored fragments that danced across their armor. Silence. Held breaths, anticipated what would come next.

At the far end of the hall, beneath banners of silver and gold, Solomon stepped onto the raised platform. His white cloak caught the light and softened it. With one hand lifted, he spoke, not loudly, but with the kind of voice that didn't need volume to command a room.

"Be still," he said.

The noise died. Even the torches seemed to listen.

"Welcome," Solomon continued, "today we recognize four souls brought for judgment. They are not yet apprentices. They are candidates. And before this assembly, we will see who among them is chosen."

Four?

My stomach dropped. I thought it was just Cody and me.

Then the light came. Soft at first, then absolute.

In the next blink, I wasn't sitting anymore. I was standing on the dais.

Cody stood to my left, trying to look calm and failing just enough to look human. To my right stood two other guys I didn't know. One solid and sure, with gray eyes that looked like they'd already seen war. The other wiry, restless, lips moving as if whispering a prayer to himself.

Solomon turned first to the taller one.

"Johnathan McKraken," he said. "You've been seen by Sir Ivan. He believes you have seen through the resonance. This path brings pain and purpose. The light you carry must be greater than the dark that will chase you. Do you accept?"

Johnathan nodded, one hand in his hoodie pocket. "I do."

Solomon placed his Bible against the boy's chest. The room stilled, air thick with waiting.

Then the glow came, orange, bright but not blinding. Pulsing through his body like flame, breathing through him. When it faded, a leather-bound Bible rested in John's hands, the color of live embers.

"The color of Johnathan McKraken's spirit is tangerine," Solomon declared. "Weapon: Warhammer. His talent: force-field generation."

Applause thundered through the hall, boots against the floor, voices sharp with approval. Johnathan stepped back, eyes glassy but proud.

Solomon turned again.

"Cody Miles. Seen by Sir Thomas and Sir David. They believe you have seen through the resonance. The light you carry must be greater than the dark that will chase you. Do you accept?"

Cody's jaw locked, shoulders squared. "I do."

Solomon put the Bible to his chest.

The light that came was deep red. Rich and alive. It rolled like thunder across his body before condensing into a crimson Bible.

"The color of Cody Miles's spirit is crimson," Solomon said. "Weapon: spear. His talent: energy release."

More applause. Whistles from the apprentices. Cody looked dazed but standing, gripping the Bible like it might float away if he didn't.

Then Solomon turned to the third boy.

"Jonas Creed. Seen by Lady Eliott."

Jonas stepped forward, fingers twitching, courage trembling beneath the surface.

"She believes you have seen through the resonance. The light you carry must be greater than the dark that will chase you. Do you accept?"

Jonas, twitchy, shook his head yes.

Solomon pressed his Bible to his chest.

Nothing happened.

The hall waited.

Solomon whispered again.

Still nothing. Not even a flicker.

Finally, he stepped back. His voice was soft but final. "Your spirit is not meant to breach the echo."

Jonas's mouth fell open. His hand lifted slightly, as if to protest. But before he could speak, a soft light rose around him. In a heartbeat, he was gone. Not violently. Just... gone.

The silence that followed felt louder than the cheers before it.

I stepped forward before Solomon even said my name.

Something in me already knew.

He looked at me, and the world exploded.

Blinding white light swallowed the hall. I couldn't tell if I was breathing or floating. The air thickened, brimming with energy so dense it felt sentient.

Then a voice. Not Solomon's.

"Do not fear."

The light parted.

A tall man stepped forward, bronze-skinned, with eyes that seemed older than time. His robes were white; wings folded behind him like living flame. The knights around us didn't bow. They didn't move at all. Fear and reverence had frozen them solid.

"Kayson Cavalier," he said, his voice reverberating through my bones. "You have been chosen for a rarer path. The road ahead will break you. Nevertheless, the light within you has already shaken what lies beyond your world within the unseen."

He placed his hand over my heart.

Heat rushed through me. A flood of something that wasn't pain but wasn't comfort either.

When I looked down, a Bible was forming under his hand, burning like sunrise. He didn't step back immediately. His expression changed. A flash of surprise, then something heavier. He turned his palm slightly, like testing the weight of it.

"The color of Kayson Cavalier's spirit is white.... and gold," he said at last.

"His weapon: twin broadswords. His gift: the embodiment and manipulation of light."

Then his tone softened.

"Serve faithfully, Kayson. The fate of many rests on your obedience."

And he was gone.

No flare, just absence as sudden as he appeared, and the memory of power too large for the room it had filled.

The hall erupted.

Applause. Shouts. The clang of boots. But under it all... Whispers.

Not everyone was cheering. Some simply stared, unsure whether what they'd witnessed was a blessing or an omen.

Solomon raised his hand, restoring quiet. "Let us welcome our newest apprentices of Crossguard."

The noise returned in a wave of laughter, the scrape of chairs, the relief of normality flooding back in.

But my mind stayed somewhere else.

Even whatever he was hadn't expected what he saw.

And that, more than anything, terrified me.

Because this didn't feel like a beginning.

It felt like a warning.

CHAPTER SIX

HEART OF THE CROSSGUARD

The smell of sizzling rosemary and thyme filled the air, mingling with the rich aroma of roasting meat. This sensory feast drew out a profound yearning in me. A mix of nostalgia and ease. Platters of roasted meat glistened under warm light. Fruits shone like gems. Bread steamed when torn open. With each bite, a bittersweet truth unfolded, tasting like a memory from a less complicated world.

But it wasn't the food that made it surreal.

It was the air. A persistent radiance left by what had just happened, thick and electric.

The Angel's presence hadn't faded; it lingered like the scent of lightning, too bright to forget. Conversations resumed in fragments, but the hall never truly returned to normal. Every clink of metal, every scrape of a chair, carried a charge beneath it. The torches along the walls flickered with an unsteady glow, as if the room itself was still trying to hold onto something beyond our understanding. No one spoke of it, yet everyone felt the lingering tension.

And then there were the glances.

Some curious. Some wary. A few were reverent in the wrong way, as if they were watching a ghost rather than a person. Their eyes always found the white-and-gold Bible at my side.

Solomon hadn't stayed after the ceremony. When the applause faded, he'd simply said,

"When the feast concludes, you'll be shown the grounds. Training begins immediately. For now, enjoy the feast."

Then he vanished. No mention of the Angel, no explanation for the twin colors. Only silence where answers should have been.

Just three rookies left standing beneath the weight of a hundred unspoken expectations.

Johnathan scratched his neck. "We just grab a plate and hope nobody throws us out?"

"Pretty much," I said.

Cody smirked. "Welcome to the misfit knights."

Johnathan grinned. "As long as there's dessert, I'll survive."

We stepped off the platform into the current of knights. This was a river of color and intent swirling around us. Armor and robes flashed every hue: burgundy, emerald, cobalt, silver. Some knights kept their Bibles beside their plates, as if they were sacred tools. Long tables filled the hall, marked by carved sigils and color-tinted candles. Their presence felt heavy, like the air had condensed around us, tuning to the uneasy rhythm of my heartbeat. Everyone pretended not to watch, but I felt their eyes, whispering with their gaze. As their voices dipped and rose, I couldn't shake the sense that their glances hid questions I wouldn't know how to confront. The air felt stretched, too thin to breathe, filled with my hopes of belonging and with a sharp fear of inadequacy. These dual burdens were pressing against my ribs.

No one stopped us, but the attention didn't waver. It wasn't hostility; it was a heavy, palpable weight of unease. The weight hovered like dense fog, tangible yet elusive. Mistrust hung in the air with its own flavor. Yet somewhere inside, something else lingered: a quiet note of reverence. Unearned. Unasked for. This reverence felt like a distant echo, a whisper of ancient tales brushing against the edges of their uncertainty.

Cody leaned close. "Either you've got food in your teeth, or they think you're dialing the Angel."

I tried to laugh. "Maybe both."

From the far end of the hall, a hand lifted above the crowd. Sir Thomas, seated with Sir David, Sarah, and a few others. His usual mystery had softened into a faint smile, though the storm-gray in his eyes still held everything he hadn't said.

We made our way over. The farther we walked, the lighter the air felt. The stares softened, curiosity replacing judgment.

Sir Thomas shifted to make room. "Congratulations," he said evenly. "You all did well."

Johnathan slid beside Sarah. "Call me Johnny. Only 'Johnathan' when I'm in trouble."

Sir David laughed, tearing a piece of bread. "You'll get used to the eyes. First day's always a circus. Especially when an archangel crashes orientation."

Johnny asked, mouth full, "What was with the Angel? Miracle or scorecard?"

Sir Thomas smirked but said nothing.

Cody dropped across from me. "So, 'training', that gonna be push-ups or pyrokinesis?"

Sir David shrugged. "Maybe both. But in order. First, you'll learn to summon your armor. Once that bond stabilizes, your weapon follows. After that, your talent. It's not something added, it's something uncovered."

Johnny leaned forward. "So, it's already there? We're not given powers?"

Sir Thomas nodded. "Exactly. They are Soul Bibles. They don't fill an empty vessel; they draw out what's been there since the beginning."

Sarah, until now had been quiet. She set down her cup. "And it's not just combat. You'll study the Fallen; their patterns, disguises, and influence."

Johnny licked jam from his finger. "They target weakness, right?"

"Not weakness," Sir Thomas said. "Purpose. Anything that threatens their control. Especially those who carry light into shadow. They aim to fracture unity by exploiting our fears and insecurities, making many question loyalties."

The line landed heavier than expected. I felt Cody stiffen beside me.

I asked, "What if we don't unlock all three?"

Sir Thomas folded his arms. "Then you're not ready for the trial."

Sarah's tone turned solemn. "I've done everything but the test. It's not about what you can do. It's about who you are when everything safe is stripped away."

Johnny exhaled. "Then we pass it together."

"Yeah," Cody said, tapping the table once. "Let's make it official."

Sir Thomas and Sir David exchanged a brief glance of approval.

"The next trial's Wednesday," Sir Thomas said. "Two days."

Johnny stretched. "Plenty more than I thought we were getting."

Sir David raised a brow. "If you clear your pre-checks of armor, weapon, talent, and knowledge."

Johnny blinked. "Knowledge. Right. My strong suit."

Sarah smiled. "They won't expect sermons, but they'll expect awareness. You can't fight what you don't understand."

Cody murmured, "Like chess."

Sir David grinned. "If chess were full-contact and the board kept changing shape."

I took another bite, keeping my hands busy. "Eat fast, start faster."

Sir Thomas lifted his cup. "Spoken like a knight. But remember, Crossguard doesn't need heroes. It needs keepers. Guardians who don't flinch when the dark presses in."

The words were rooted deep. I didn't feel like a guardian. I barely felt like myself. Around me, the hall echoed with a whisper of doubt. A draft slipped beneath the heavy banners, as if even the ancient stones questioned my presence here. The laughter distorted in corners, stretching into shadows where light struggled to reach.

Under the noise, beneath the stares and lingering heat of the Angel's light, unease gradually shifted to anticipation. Beneath it all, something new began to stir in me. A cautious hope woven into my anxiety.

Not burning. Just steady warmth behind my ribs, as if his hand was still glowing on my chest.

I didn't know what the trial would bring. I didn't know if I'd pass.

But the part of me that had stood in vision of colorless Sonorah and still moved forward was already leaning toward whatever came next.

Johnny caught my silence. "You're eating like the table's about to vanish."

He added, "Didn't cross a cosmic doorway to starve politely."

I smiled, picking at my plate. My stomach hadn't decided which feeling was stronger: hunger or disbelief.

Johnny leaned forward. "They looked scared when the Angel showed up. Like they'd seen him before. Just not here, or not for you."

He didn't mean it cruelly, but the words still hit.

Why me?

Why that pause when he said my name?

Why did it feel like he'd seen something he hadn't expected?

Johnny grabbed another roll. "This food's unreal. I expected rations, not angelic catering."

Cody raised an eyebrow. "For a draftee in a holy war, you're handling it well."

Johnny shrugged. "I panic better with carbs."

We laughed, really this time. The tension cracked just enough for three strangers to feel almost like a team.

Johnny admitted, "Didn't think I'd be chosen. I believed in all this, just not in me."

"You're not alone," I said. "I still don't know if I'm supposed to be here."

Cody said quietly, "Maybe that's the point."

Maybe it was. Maybe being chosen wasn't about readiness or strength. Just willingness. The courage to say yes when everything in you wants to say no.

As I pondered this, a sudden, inexplicable taste of ash touched the feast's rich flavors in my mouth. My stomach twisted, caught between hunger and disbelief. It was as if my doubts had found a way to taint the present moment. The taste lingered. A whisper of something ominous. Fleeting but profound, it turned my unease into a shadow of what was coming. It left me with a sense of foreboding that clung to my thoughts.

A bell rang overhead, low and resonant, a bronze heartbeat through stone.

Sir David stood up, burgundy robe flaring in the light. "Alright, recruits," he said, clapping once. "Wrap it up. Tour time."

Johnny groaned and shoved one last roll into his mouth. "Can we take snacks?"

Sir David grinned. "You're not in high school anymore, kid. No snack passes."

Cody and I stood, setting down our half-eaten plates. Knights were already clearing tables, drifting toward the exits, all under that same quiet hum that hadn't quite gone away.

I looked one last time at the feast. The warmth and laughter felt distant now, replaced by a growing apprehension as the illusion of safety faded from my mind.

Then I followed Cody, Johnny, Sir Thomas and Sir David into the corridor.

Whatever waited next, I could already feel it, the real beginning.

Sarah hadn't spoken much after the feast, yet her smile lingered. It was soft, intentional, the kind that says more than words ever could.

A secret tether she wasn't ready to name but didn't bother hiding.

Each time our eyes met, color touched her cheeks, faint but certain. She didn't look away.

Her gaze wasn't shy or bold. It was known.

The kind of look that makes you feel seen before you've even decided who you are.

Something about her steadiness anchored me.

Sarah looked like someone Crossguard hadn't just trained but expected.

As if the Order had written her into its story before she'd ever walked its halls.

And yet, even as we walked, my mind drifted backward, to the induction, to the brilliance of the Angel's descent, to the way his voice had trembled when he said my name.

Solomon's silence afterward had felt heavier than speech.

Answers left hanging in the air, sharp and deliberate, like a truth waiting for courage to meet it.

I wanted to understand what this meant: why I was chosen, what these colors signified. I couldn't remain the guy who stumbled into miracles by accident.

I needed control.

Conviction that didn't waver when the light did.

We followed Sir Thomas and Sir David toward the back of the hall. The weight of the castle changed the farther we went. The air grew stiller. The echoes grew sharper.

Whatever lay ahead wasn't another introduction.

It was a threshold.

Behind the dais, banners draped from the rafters: Red, gold, silver, blue, and shades I hadn't earned the right to know. Each shimmered in torchlight as though it pulsed with its own heart. The fabric was alive with breath.

Retracing our path through the mess hall meant walking past rows of knights still getting up to leave their tables. Some conversed quietly. Others simply watched.

Their glances passed over us like water over stone. The air pressed in, but not with hostility.

Expectation carried its own kind of gravity.

And through it all, one question followed me: the twin colors of my Bible. White and gold.

I hadn't asked. Not Cody. Not Sir Thomas. Not anyone.

Something in my chest told me it wasn't just rare.

It was unspoken.

The kind of rarity that didn't need a warning label because the silence surrounding it said enough.

The hallway behind the stage narrowed, the stone veined with faintly glowing runes that seemed to read me as I passed. Their hum deepened at my presence, echoing somewhere inside my ribs. Then the passage opened into a high archway carved from stone so smooth it reflected the torchlight like water. Symbols traced along its curve with veins of living silver, humming softly. As though the castle itself were conscious of my uncertainty.

Then I stepped through.

Into the Courtyard.

And the air changed.

The difference wasn't temperature. It was awareness.

It was the shift between standing in sunlight and standing in the memory of sunlight, where light itself seems to remember being divine.

The courtyard wasn't vast, yet it felt endless. It seemed to pulse, as if holding secrets in its stillness. Grass dark as pine rippled underfoot in measured rhythm. Each blade shimmered with dew, reflecting something older and hinting at the timelessness of the setting. The air seemed to carry the whispers of those who had walked here before, yet it urged us forward, inviting us to uncover what lay beyond.

The vines that climbed the surrounding walls weren't wild. They grew in deliberate spirals, following patterns predating geometry. Their blossoms shifted color with the wind's pulse, crimson melting to violet, indigo blooming into gold. Every petal carried its own awareness.

And at the center...

A fountain. But it didn't flow. It sang.

No melody or rhythm you could count. Just a vibration that settled somewhere between your bones and your memory.

"Some say this fountain was born in the seven days of creation," Sarah murmured, watching the droplets rise with awe. "A piece of the world's birth suspended in time." As her words lingered, Sarah glanced at me with a soft, distant smile. "My grandmother used to tell me stories about it when I was a child. She believed that if you listened closely enough, you could hear the heartbeats of the first stars in its song. It was always her favorite place." Her memories wove into the ancient lore, lending the fountain an intimacy as personal as it was profound.

"This is the Courtyard," Sir David said. "The heart of Crossguard's grounds. Every path leads here."

He gestured left. "The Living quarters for those who've passed the trial."

Then right. "The Chapel."

Finally, his gaze met mine as he pointed toward the last archway ahead. Its stone is pale and smooth, shaped like the ribs of a giant creature long asleep.

"And straight ahead..." He paused. A smile crept at the edges of his mouth, "The training grounds."

Sir David folded his arms. "You've seen two of the three. Time to finish the tour."

Before we could move on, Sarah adjusted her gloves and turned toward the corridor. Her movements were measured, every step graceful by nature, not effort.

"I should head out," she said. "Need to grab a few things before morning drills."

That same quiet smile surfaced again, impossible to ignore.

"Catch you later."

"See you," Cody called after her.

Her footsteps faded into the soft hush of stone until only the fountain's resonance remained. Yet even gone, she lingered. A calm thread woven through the space, holding it together.

I glanced at a flower near the wall. Violet streaked with gold, its light pulsing faintly in rhythm with my breath.

I couldn't tell if it was reacting to her leaving. Or to something stirring awake in me.

Sir Thomas turned toward the final archway. The place where excuses ended. The place where potential stopped being theory and started demanding proof.

Even the courtyard seemed to hold its breath.

Johnny's grin faltered into something quieter. "You ready for this?"

I didn't answer.

Not because I wasn't.

Because part of me had already decided.

We stepped beneath the arch.

The courtyard dimmed behind us.

Warmth retreated back to the Heart of Crossguard.

Light folded inward, as though choosing to wait.

And as the air thickened around us, the song of the fountain faded.

Until only the purpose remained.

The archway shimmered as we approached, like water holding on to sunlight.

It wasn't a flicker or a glitch. It was deliberate. Alive. Something beyond the threshold was watching, deciding if we were meant to pass.

Then, with a low hum, the first note of a hymn. The wall simply ceased to exist.

Just light folding away to reveal three tall doors.

They stood identical in shape and height, forged from a dark metal that didn't reflect light so much as drink it.

Each bore a sigil glowing faintly from within:

A shield quartered in four,

a flame encircled in iron,

and a sun bound within a blacksmith's anvil.

Sir Thomas stepped between us and the doors, cloak stirring in the faint current from the arch behind.

"This," he said, his voice echoing as if the room itself listened,

"is the Threshold."

"From here," he continued, "your training begins."

He gestured left. "The Hall of Doctrine. Where you'll gain knowledge of spiritual defense: how to guard your spirit from deception."

Then right. "The Crucible. Your eventual Trial of Endurance."

Finally, he faced the center door. His tone softened.

"But today," he said, "we begin in the Forge."

The middle door opened on its own, followed by a quiet invitation.

We stepped through.

The air dropped. It was heavy. Charged. The kind of weight that precedes lightning.

My skin prickled as if anticipating a storm.

The chamber stretched wide and warm, its vaulted ceiling ribbed with silver beams and floating rings of crystal fire. The floor pulsed faintly beneath our boots.

Sir Thomas walked ahead. "Welcome to initial training," he said. "Here you begin becoming Crossguardians."

Sir David joined him. "First lesson. Draw your Bibles."

I lifted mine. It was still warm. Still feeling as though it was alive.

The white-and-gold cover glowed softly, twin swords at its center in sync with my heartbeat.

"This may look like a book," Sir Thomas said, holding his own high, "but don't mistake form for purpose. It doesn't contain power; it reveals it.

Your Bible mirrors your unfiltered soul."

Sir David added, voice crisp, "The closer you walk in truth, the stronger it answers."

Sir Thomas nodded. "Everything begins here. But to unlock it, you'll need the key."

He raised his Bible overhead.

"Armor first."

He spoke the verse slowly so we could follow:

"Put on all of God's armor, so that you may stand firm."

We echoed him, the words vibrating in the air, giving the sound breath.

Light stirred inside the Bible. Soft at first, then brighter. The cover rippled, pages rustling though no wind touched them.

The gold lining flared. The book felt alive.

Sir Thomas said quietly, "Now, crown your spirit."

Instinct moved before thought.

I lifted the Bible above my head. The moment it crossed my crown, the light cascaded downward. Liquid radiance flowed over my shoulders, chest, and arms.

In one breath, it was no longer a book.

It was armor.

The white and gold light settled against my skin, solidifying into plates that gleamed like forged dawn. It was warm to the touch, wrapping around me like a second skin, more protective than ordinary armor yet lighter, almost buoyant in its bearing. A cross of twin swords glowed across my chest. The gauntlets moved with me, etched runes that shimmered faintly with purpose.

Cody and Johnny followed, each crown of light taking its own form. Crimson steel and tangerine flame, unique yet unified.

We stood there; breath caught somewhere between awe and disbelief.

"Now," Sir David said, "Draw your weapons."

Sir Thomas tapped the glowing crest at the center of my armor. "Your emblem—take hold."

I gripped it. The badge detached like a breath released, unraveling in my hands; two bone-white hilts forming, blades of gold extending from light.

They fit as if they'd been waiting for me all along.

Cody's spear ignited, with a black shaft, crimson-crystal blade humming like controlled lightning.

Johnny's hammer materialized midair, dropping clean into his grasp, carved with spirals that glowed like constellations.

"Final step," Sir Thomas said. "Your talent."

Sir David's tone deepened, resonant as stone struck by thunder.

"As each has received a gift, use it to serve one another as stewards of His varied grace."

I breathed the verse, not to command but to agree.

Light built within, not around. The swords trembled with restrained brilliance. Gold flared through the seams of my armor.

My chest filled with heat that didn't burn. Illumination made physical.

Johnny's hammer blazed orange, energy circling his arms like orbiting suns.

Cody's spear pulsed crimson, sparks lifting from his shoulders.

"That's it," Sir Thomas said, pride edging his calm. "Talents active."

Sir David pulled a lever on the wall.

Panels in the floor slid open.

Four featureless dummies rose, waiting.

"Show me what talent looks like in motion."

One lunged at Johnny.

He grinned. "Perfect."

An orange barrier burst to life. The dummy struck and rebounded skyward. Johnny swung once. The crash echoed like thunder through stained glass.

Another charged Cody.

He rolled left, pivoted, thrusting upward, crimson light detonated from his spear, and the dummy collapsed in sparks.

Then two came for me.

Time folded. Light moved first.

I stepped, and I was already behind them.

Twin arcs of gold cut through the air.

Then both shattered into light.

Cody gawked. "Dude, you blinked."

Johnny shook his head. "No, you disappeared."

I looked down at the fading glow along my blades. The light wasn't rage or heat. It was direction. Purpose with form. My hands, acting before thought, tightened around the hilts, pulling them closer, as if drawing strength from the very essence of the glow.

Sir Thomas exhaled slowly. "Then it's confirmed."

Sir David nodded. "Strong start. Tomorrow, we prepare for the Trial. For now, rest."

Sir Thomas added, "To dismiss your armor, lift your helm. The Word will return to rest."

I obeyed. The metal dissolved into radiance and re-shaped into the Bible in my hands, still flickering with faint gold.

We regrouped in the courtyard. Evening had softened the sky to rose and amber. The fountain still sang, quieter now, like a prayer closing itself.

None of us spoke.

But for the first time since this began, I felt something stronger than fear. I clutched the Bible closer to my chest, feeling its warmth radiate through me. Cody caught my eye, and we shared a silent nod: an unspoken agreement that pointed toward the path ahead. Faith thickened around us, and so did purpose.

What would faith demand of us next in the coming trial? A question that lingered as we prepared to step forward into the unknown.

CHAPTER SEVEN

THE POWER OF KNOWLEDGE

C ody and I had barely set our gear down after the forge when Sir Thomas appeared in the doorway with his usual calm finality.

"You've got a third."

No preamble. No explanation. Just a fact, dropped like weather.

Moments later, Johnny strolled in, duffel over his shoulder, whistling off-key and already grinning. Radiating a reckless, infectious energy that shifted the air in the room.

"Hope you two don't snore," he said, tossing the bag onto the lower bunk. "Cause I do. But it's charming."

He said it with a confident spark, as if utterly certain his flaws would win us over, his eyes daring us to challenge the charm of his snore.

Johnny was from Tennessee. He never really talked about it. But you could hear it in the easy drawl of his laugh and see it in the way he moved: unhurried, grounded, like someone raised under porchlight skies. Even here, in a fortress between realms, he carried the calm of wide fields. The creak of an old porch swing seemed to travel with him, anchoring him to a place where the air smelled of honeysuckle and fresh earth.

And somehow, he'd been given prep time before arrival. We never figured out my vision, or even the sketchy guy in the alley. But he'd shown up with things Cody and I hadn't even thought to want.

Like a record player.

He unpacked it that first night, humming as he set it on the stone shelf near the window. The wood was scratched; the brass knobs, crooked. He paused and wiped the dust from a knob with his thumb. A fleeting gesture that suggested the care of handling a keepsake. When the needle met vinyl, static sighed and woke the room itself.

Frank Sinatra singing "Fly Me to the Moon."

Smooth. Timeless. A song that sounded like a retired star, reminiscing about its former shine.

The lights were out. The window spilled faint silver onto the floor. Cody took the top bunk; Johnny claimed the bottom. I had a single bed near the wall, cold compared to the warmth of Cody and Johnny's laughter. My Bible rested on the shelf beside me, its warmth lingering like a touch in the dark.

For a while, none of us spoke. The music filled the silence.

My heart twisted as my thoughts drifted back.

That blinding moment on the stage when the Order had bowed to something greater than sound, lingered in my mind. It remained a reminder of the choice that still lay ahead. A decision unmade would test my faith and resolve. Something pivotal, still hidden, waiting to challenge the essence of what I stood for.

Even now, the white-and-gold Bible pulsed quietly, as if the memory still lived inside it.

Was this really who I was now?

No more classrooms. No more half-written essays and lunch-period sarcasm.

Now it was stone halls, living scripture, and the echo of angels.

And somehow. It didn't feel wrong.

My arms ached from the Forge. My skin still buzzed where the armor touched it. The ache pulsed. A deep, lingering reminder that I was alive, forging something real. I flexed my fingers. The tremor in them stung with pride and exhaustion, as if the day's work tingled under my skin. A deep breath stirred gratitude in my chest, a fierce warmth that reminded me why I kept getting back up, purpose now etched in bone.

The record shifted.

The Way You Look Tonight.

Sinatra's voice drifted like nostalgia made of smoke.

From above, Cody whispered, "You think we'll ever go back to normal?"

"Define normal," Johnny mumbled, already halfway to a snore.

Cody chuckled. "You know. Homework. Bad school dances. The world before all this."

I stared at the ceiling, tension flickering in my chest as the vinyl crackled, unsure if I could find any answer in the static.

"I don't think we're supposed to."

Silence again, gentle but humming with questions.

The music filled it easily.

I turned toward the window. Beyond the glass, petals from the courtyard shimmered faintly in the dark. They caught moonlight like embers refusing to die. The sound of the fountain's distant song folded into Sinatra's melody.

It didn't feel like we were guests here anymore; it settled in my bones. A hesitant sense of belonging, edged with disbelief and hope.

It felt like the world had finally decided to include us.

Johnny laughed quietly. "Well, if we're gonna fight darkness, at least we've got a killer soundtrack."

He flipped through the crate of vinyls. "Got some Ella, a little Miles Davis, and Elvis 'cause balance is holy."

Cody snorted. "You're really planning to fight evil with jazz?"

Johnny stretched, yawning. "Jazz, soul, and pancakes if we can find a skillet."

I smiled, letting the memory of Mrs. Miles' pancakes tug at something hopeful in my chest, the ache of missing home blurring for just a moment.

This moment. This room. This fragile peace balanced on laughter and music.

It reminded me that faith didn't always sound like sermons. Sometimes, it sounded like friends finding calm after chaos.

The record hissed. The song changed again.

The light in my Bible pulsed once, slow and sure, as if it were breathing with me.

The warmth of the melody sank through the stone walls, through my ribs, down into the hum still flickering beneath my skin.

As I drifted off, I fell into a dream.

Not in straight lines. More like fragments of memory stitched with music.

The Forge. Training dummies. Light swirling like silk.

Sinatra is still playing somewhere unseen.

"Let me see what spring is like on Jupiter and Mars..."

Cody spun a pencil through the air. Johnny sat ringside in a velvet chair, bowl of popcorn in his lap, shouting, "Loosen up, man! You gotta swing like jazz, offbeat, but on time!"

I laughed mid-fight, actually laughed, and the sound broke something open inside me.

Because even here, in dream or reality, the world didn't feel foreign anymore.

It felt like ours.

The dream faded as morning arrived, and the castle felt different. We woke early, the halls echoing with a new energy. Something had changed overnight, and we moved from the comfort of our room into the opening of a new day.

It didn't shake so much as breathe. By the time we dressed and stepped into the atrium, Sir Thomas and Sir David were already waiting, their silence a simple nod. We followed them, descending a narrow, winding stairwell that seemed to spiral into shadow, its tight coils urging haste. The air shifted cool as we moved lower, thick with dust and candle smoke.

At the bottom, the iron-bound doors opened. Light flooded through.

The Crossguard Library.

It wasn't a room. It was a cathedral of knowledge. Golden beams poured through slanted skylights, falling across the floor in fan-shaped patterns. The shelves towered in spirals, winding toward a central dais. Each shelf was packed with scrolls and leather tomes. A visual feast of wisdom crowded on every surface. The air smelled richly of parchment, cedar, and time itself. Silence didn't just live here; it ruled, cloaked in an aura of reverent quiet.

Sir David walked ahead, unfurling a scroll. "Today," he said, "we cover the Fallen."

He glanced over his shoulder. "And we're not using the fairytale version."

He spread the parchment across a long table. The inked figure staring back at us was anything but myth. Tall, armored in obsidian plates that swallowed light. Wings spread behind it, not feathered but torn, shaped from living shadow. From a slit in its left wristplate, a black trident curved outward like smoke from a serpent's mouth.

Johnny leaned forward. "They all look like that?"

"Every Fallen wear black armor. Every one bears the trident drawn from the serpent mark. Their faces are gone, replaced by a void. They are what happens when grace is willingly traded for temporary power," Sir David explained, his tone grave.

He moved to another scroll and unrolled it with care. This one appeared more intricate. It showed a diagram of seven rings, each inscribed with a word in crimson ink.

"Now, their hierarchy is built on corruption. Six ranks, each named for the sin that defines it," Sir David continued, emphasizing the word 'corruption' with a slight raise of his hand: as if catching a pesky fly in mid-air. It was his little quirk, a consistent part of his teaching style.

His finger circled the outer ring.

"Sloth. The weakest, but never harmless. They move in packs, confined to Soulless Zones. The territory the Fallen Angels have already drained. If you're inside one, they'll sense you immediately. They don't strategize. They swarm.

Their presence is a chilling reminder. Even the weakest threat can get under your skin."

Cody muttered, "Spiritual hyenas."

Sir David smiled faintly. "Exactly." He tapped the next ring.

"Envy Fallen Angels are stronger, but solitary. Still bound to Soulless Zones, but far more aware. They're drawn to comparison. They ache of wanting what others have. They feed on it until a spirit forgets gratitude entirely."

I swallowed hard. It felt too close to something I'd already felt in that gray vision of Sonorah.

"The next tier is where corruption learns language."

He pointed to the third ring.

"Gluttony. The first Fallen able to tempt. Their whispers don't sound foreign. They sound familiar. A nudge, always what you want to hear. A thought that feels like your own. Every time someone obeys it, the Fallen grows stronger. The person grows smaller."

Johnny shook his head. "That's... brutal, ya know."

"It's efficient," Sir David said. "Most battles are lost long before anyone draws a blade."

He tapped the fourth ring.

"Lust are commanders. They can leave Soulless Zones to create new ones. They lead Sloth swarms. They gather where secrecy thrives. Whether it's addiction, obsession, or isolation. They twist those places until color drains and sound dies. That's how new Zones form."

"Spiritual colonization," Cody said quietly.

Sir David nodded. "Exactly that."

The fifth ring was darker, etched deeper.

"Greed. Their influence can walk among those residing outside the In-Between. They can't possess, but they can speak clear, sharp sentences. They use fear and guilt as currency. If you ever hear a voice that sounds like your own but preaches hopelessness, tell someone immediately. It means one is already progressing."

My fingers tightened around the edge of the table.

"And they control everything beneath them?" I asked.

"Every rank below except Envy," Sir David confirmed. "Their influence threads through entire cities if left unchecked."

He moved to the center. The ink here wasn't red. It was black edged in gold, as if scorched by both heaven and hell.

"Pride. The highest and oldest. The ones who wanted to rule instead of serve."

His voice lowered. "They can possess. Only the empty. Only those who've forgotten what light feels like. When that happens, you don't just lose control. You cease to exist."

Cody's eyes widened. "So... you're saying people like...?"

Sir David didn't flinch. "Influenced. Perhaps possessed. Not every evil act is possession. But every possession brings evil acts."

The room went silent except for the faint rustle of old paper.

Johnny cleared his throat. "So how do we fight something like that?"

Sir David looked up, eyes steady. "You don't. All you can do is the same thing that made them fall from grace, only reversed. The Word that never bends. A Pride Fallen can't touch a soul anchored in grace."

He rolled the scroll closed and let the dust settle between his words.

"The one you saw in that gray reflection, Kayson," he said at last. "Most likely Sloth or Envy. Just enough to notice its presence. Nowhere near strong enough to influence you."

I felt the answer before he said the rest.

"But if someone keeps feeding the Zone..."

Sir David met my eyes. "Then someone stronger will approach."

The words lodged in my chest like stone.

Because deep down, I already knew what that meant.

Whatever was festering beneath Sonorah High hadn't ended.

It had only begun.

The next morning was Hebrew I.

Same instructor, Sir David. Same easy half-grin.

Completely different atmosphere.

This time, the lesson wasn't about the enemy.

It was about the origin of language.

We gathered in a smaller chamber just off by the forge. A hexagonal room carved from pale stone; the walls etched with softly glowing runes. Glass lanterns hung above us, their blue fire flickering like living breath. The air hummed faintly, as if the words waiting to be spoken already knew their power.

Sir David set a scroll on the table and turned with his usual warmth, chalk in one hand, coffee in the other.

"Welcome to Hebrew I," he said. "Or as everyone else likes to call it, Don't Blow Out Your Voice 101."

A few of us nervously gave him the courtesy of laughing. The runes under our boots pulsed once, like they'd been listening.

Sir David grinned wider. "The words I'm teaching you today aren't for show. They're phonetic power lines. Speak to them with truth, and they'll move the air itself. Calm storms within the In-Between. Hold back the shadow. Maybe even knock a Fallen Angel flat on its wings if you pronounce it right."

Johnny leaned toward me. "Or summon a holy hairball."

Cody coughed into his sleeve to hide a laugh. I failed.

Sir David's eyes flicked toward us, amused. "Good. Laughter means you're not terrified yet. Repeat after me: (□□□□ □□□□□ □□□□ha'amet tischrer otech)"

We echoed, poorly.

Johnny butchered it. "Helmet teacher tech, what now?"

Sir David chuckled. "Try again. And maybe stop squinting like the letters are on the other side of the room."

I closed my eyes this time and let it settle deeper. This wasn't language. It was the resonance Solomon mentioned. Something living. When we spoke together again, the air shifted. Just a flicker, but it listened.

Sir David nodded. "Better. Again."

We spent over an hour repeating that one verse. Adjusting tone, rhythm, and breath. It was like teaching your body to sing truth instead of saying it. The sound vibrated in my ribs, as if the words wanted to live with my lungs.

When Johnny finally nailed the last syllable, he grinned. "Tell me that didn't sound majestic."

Cody smirked. "Sounded like a sneeze with good intentions."

Sir David laughed. "Progress is progress. I'll take it."

Then his voice sobered.

"These words aren't spells," he said. "Faith is the voltage. Without it, you're just making noise. But when belief drives the sound and your heart's aligned: these phrases can anchor reality itself. Remember, let your light shine before others, that they may see your good deeds. Your grace is your spirit. If it wavers, no armor in the world will save you."

The room fell silent. Even Johnny stopped smiling.

And for a heartbeat, I understood why angels spoke with fire.

The afternoon was combat.

Different instructor this time. It was a different tempo entirely.

Sir Thomas waited for us at the edge of the training field. No cloak or even armor. All he had was a sleeveless tunic, dark trousers, and a side sword strapped across his back. The sun caught on his silver wristband as he folded his arms.

"Armor off," he said. "Weapons away. You learn your body before you learn your blade."

No one argued.

We trained barefoot on smooth stone that glimmered faintly in the light. The courtyard stretched wide, ringed by banners that moved like quiet witnesses.

I expected drills or maybe a lecture.

What we got instead was demolition.

Sir Thomas moved like a precision-made human. Each strike was exact. Every pivot was silent. He didn't hit hard. He didn't need to. His balance alone did the damage. One turn. A swift sidestep. A single effortless motion, and you were on the ground before your brain caught up.

"Movement first," he said, gesturing us into pairs. "Rotate every five minutes. No strikes to the throat. No whining. You'll learn more from the mistakes that hurt."

Cody and I started first, clumsy at best. Johnny joined the next rotation. By the tenth minute, we were bruised and sweating, trying not to look like we were drowning.

At one point, Johnny lunged too far, tripped on his heel, and I instinctively went to catch his arm, but it was too late.

He landed flat on his back with a grunt. "Witchcraft footwork," he groaned.

Cody grinned. "Pretty sure I saw your soul leave for a second."

Johnny sat up, winded. "No worries. I'll find it at lunch."

By the second hour, the rhythm began to click. The patterns stopped feeling foreign. My body started to remember.

Sir Thomas wove between us, correcting posture, adjusting wrists, grounding feet. "Your grace is your spirit," he said quietly near my ear. "If it wavers, no armor in the world will save you."

He was right. Every movement was balanced. Grace made physical.

By sunset, our arms shook from exhaustion. Our knuckles were raw, and dust streaked our faces. But when the last whistle blew, no one wanted to stop.

Sir Thomas had thrown Cody twice and flipped Johnny more times than I could count. When he faced me, I moved first with a feint into a step. For a moment, I almost had him. Then a single shift of his weight, and I hit the dust hard.

Still, when he reached down to pull me up, something in his expression softened.

"You've got something," he said. "It's rough. But it's there."

We collapsed along the field's edge as the sky turned gold. None of us spoke for a while. Just the sound of our breathing, the distant life of the castle, and the faint shimmer of the courtyard petals drifting on the breeze.

Cody finally wheezed, "So that was... subtle."

Johnny groaned. "I think my spine ascended without me."

I closed my eyes and let the air settle inside my lungs. For the first time since everything began with the mirror, I wasn't thinking about becoming anything.

I just was.

Not perfect or invincible.

But present.

Besides friends who didn't flinch when I failed.

Who laughed even when it hurt.

And for the first time, Crossguard didn't feel like another world.

It felt like home.

Trial day arrived like a whispered warning. The courtyard fountain's burble had stilled the noise, an unbroken promise. Anticipation hung heavy in the air. Dim light crept through tall stone windows. It didn't feel like morning. More like the world holding its breath. Torches along the corridor burned quietly, flames bending inward, reverent. Even the castle seemed to pray.

No one spoke. Not even Johnny.

Johnny dressed in silence, humming something slow and bluesy, almost like a lullaby, under his breath. He fumbled his fingers while buttoning his shirt, missing a note he tried to whistle, showing a hint of nervousness beneath his calm. Meanwhile, Cody stood by the narrow window, watching the fog intently as if searching for omens in its shifting patterns.

We met up with Sir Thomas and Sarah in the courtyard. Sarah carried herself with the dual presence of nerves and determination; she had prepared more thoroughly than any of us. As we gathered, I could feel doubt curling in my chest, a shadow of hesitation nagging at me. I questioned whether I truly belonged among these confident companions, wondering if the armor I wore was merely a mask for my courage. My uncertainty lingered, whispering that I might falter. Still, I stood with them, determined to move forward through the fear.

We followed Sir Thomas down the same halls as on our first day. The corridors shouted history, carved before language, light, or even us.

We stopped at an iron door marked by three words in an unknown tongue that resonated to my core. Their rhythm pulsed with every heartbeat, charging the air as if promising power.

Sir Thomas turned. His voice came soft but sure. "I'm proud of you."

He didn't pace or posture. He just stood there. A man cut from conviction but carrying the gentleness of a teacher who's watched his students outgrow fear. "You've come far. Today, focus not on speed or strength, but on clarity. Know yourself."

He looked at each of us.

Sarah met his eyes, unflinching.

Cody nodded once, jaw set.

Johnny, for the first time, said nothing, just lifted his chin.

Then Sir Thomas looked at me.

I didn't nod. I just breathed.

"Victory or failure," he said, "it isn't yours alone. Cast it to your King."

He pressed his Bible to the iron. The metal shimmered, then dissolved like heat haze, leaving a threshold of light. We stepped through.

It wasn't a room.

It was a world.

Grass stretched underfoot, uneven and wild. Mist rolled across low hills and broken stone. The sky arched impossibly high, trapped inside a ceiling of carved rock masquerading as clouds. Every inch of ground felt both sanctified and scarred.

The air pushed down with pressure, as if it remembered every battle fought here.

Fifty or so initiates had already gathered near a line of glowing obelisks. Each was etched with scripture that pulsed like veins of light. The air around them carried the sharp tang of hot metal. The scent seared itself into the skin. None of them spoke. Some prayed under their breath. Others stared ahead, their armor waiting.

Then I saw him. My jaw dropped.

Judah Walker.

Same unfocused eyes and uneven grin. This time, no joke. He seemed heavier. Our stares met; his smile cracked. I was wrong.

Even Cody blinked. "Is that...?"

"Yup."

"Doesn't he only eat lunch if he steals it?"

"Yup."

We watched him approach.

"Well, well, well. Can't believe you runts actually passed the induction."

Cody clicked his tongue, "Can't believe you think you can pass."

Judah's smile twisted with malice. "Think you can pass under a worthless mentor? Shut up, and I'll cut you some slack," he sneered.

Johnny braced to snap back, but I cut in first.

I replied evenly, "Our worth will be shown during the trial. Try calling us worthless once we're done."

A vein bulged on Judah's forehead. He stomped away.

Thunder cracked, though not from the sky. From a voice.

"Aye! Quit actin' like stunned maggots and listen up!"

The voice rolled across the field like an avalanche.

A figure appeared through the fog, striding forward with the force of war itself. Broad and scarred, his hair was a mane of crimson braids, and his beard looked battered yet victorious, as if he'd survived and won a bar fight. The sheer weight of his presence rooted everyone in place, commanding attention.

"I'm Sir Finley," he barked, pacing with the slow threat of a lion. "I run this test. You listen, or you bleed. And aye, I'm Irish. Get over it."

Not even Johnny dared speak.

Sir Finley's eyes swept the semicircle. Not glancing but measuring. You could feel him weighing each soul.

"Lads and lasses. Armor on."

The order hit like a chord.

Light flared across the field as Bibles lifted. My own in my hand. The verses ignited. I drew it over my head like a helmet. Light wrapped around me. As the armor sealed to my skin, it surged warm. White and gold. Alive with quiet fire. It hummed with power. A vibration down to the marrow. This spectacle became a visceral embrace.

Cody's armor burned crimson beside me.

Johnny's blazed tangerine.

Sarah's, we saw for the first time. It shimmered a delicate teal, like water under moonlight.

Sir Finley's Bible vanished back into his coat. "Welcome to the Trial of Endurance," he announced.

His tone dropped low, slicing through the silence. "This isn't about polish or power. It's about survival. Obedience under pressure. You'll learn what breaks first. Your body or your will," he intoned.

Sir Finley's voice rumbled again. "Some of you will pass. Most won't. That's the way of it. Don't make you less," he declared, jabbing a finger at the dirt. "But every one of you will learn."

He paused, letting the weight of that truth settle.

Then, calm as judgment:

"Gear up. Wave hits in sixty seconds."

The crowd broke into motion, pairs forming, armor fidgeting, lips moving in prayer. Even the air braced.

I stayed still.

Let the fear rise.

Let it pass.

Then I pulled off my emblem. Twin streaks of gold light beamed, my twin blades steady in my grip.

Cody exhaled beside me. "You ready?"

I nodded, not because I was, but because this is what faith looked like when the clock is already ticking.

The world held its breath with us. What would the wave demand of us?

CHAPTER EIGHT
THE TRIAL OF
ENDURANCE

A second figure stepped out from beside Sir Finley.

He was taller, leaner, nothing wasted in his frame.

If Sir Finley were a war hammer. Heavy and loud. This man was a dagger.

His stride had no swagger, no thunder. Instead, a faint iron scent, sharp and lingering. The kind before violence fills the air.

He moved like every kill still lived in him.

Buzz-cut. Steel-gray eyes. A diagonal scar bisects his cheek, as if someone tried carving the truth and failed.

He didn't need to raise his voice.

When he spoke, the quiet obeyed.

"The test is simple," he said. "Survive your match. Still standing. You pass."

That was it. No more. Final.

The air tightened, the way it does when lightning chooses its mark.

Beside me, Johnny shifted, a joke stuck in his throat.

Cody's arms tensed, eyes tracking the man to the rusted lever at the far wall.

Sarah didn't blink. Her calm wasn't forced; it was trained. She'd prepared for this longer than any of us.

Sir Finley clapped once, sharp as a rifle crack.

"Aye! Sir Levi's got the right of it. Partnered free-for-all. Last one standin' moves on."

The word tasted like iron.

He didn't elaborate. He didn't have to. Whatever this was, it wasn't about instruction.

Sir Finley and Sir Levi scanned the crowd, pacing like twin wolves hunting. Some recruits straightened, meeting their eyes; others tried to shrink out of sight.

Sir Levi didn't stop for anyone; he walked through them.

Each time, he pointed: You. Partnered with you. No words, just a gesture sealing a sentence.

When he reached our row, my pulse climbed behind my ribs.

Please let it be Cody. Or Johnny. Someone I know. Someone I trust.

He didn't even glance at them.

He stopped in front of me.

The air condensed. Frigid. Weighty. Like drifting beside an ocean trench.

He studied me. One breath. Two. Then raised his hand.

First at me.

Then at Sarah.

My stomach dropped.

Sarah's gaze met mine. No fear, no apology. Just awareness. She already knew: this wasn't about us, but about truth under pressure. My worry was sharp and specific. What if I wasn't strong or skilled enough to survive this pairing? Dread gnawed at my resolve.

We hadn't trained together. I didn't know her weapon, talent, or fighting style. But I knew she saw, and that she listened. Now, she'd been asked to stand against me.

Johnny groaned from behind me. "Of course, I get Cody."

Cody cracked his neck. "Try not to cry when we win."

Once every pair was chosen, Sir Finley strolled to the ancient lever. Moss clung to its base, the scorched stone beneath remembering a fire that never cooled.

He rested his hand on the lever, fingers tightening around it, but waited before pulling.

"This ground," he said, voice suddenly softer, almost fond, "is old."

The chatter died instantly. Even Sir Levi turned.

Sir Finley's grin widened, teeth catching the light.

"Older than the castle. Older than the wars you read about. This chamber's stood since the Order began—before swords, before armor, before language named fear."

He tapped the lever with two fingers.

"She's held pain and victory. Failure and hope."

"And stories. More than all your Bibles combined."

His eyes flared with joy and madness braided together.

"And she's *hungry* for more."

He yanked the lever.

The world paused.

No movement. No breath.

Just the heartbeat between creation and command. One impossible instant where the stone itself seemed to listen for God's permission.

Then the floor screamed.

Not a creak. A howl.

Stone ground against stone in a roar through my chest. The earth convulsed, dust rising as the ground split like glass. Cracks wove between Johnny and Cody, mirroring our fragile alliances. Johnny surfed the sound, hands out. Cody laughed. Sarah never flinched.

Cracks raced outward, glowing faintly, and from them, life erupted.

They didn't *grow; they erupted, shattering the ground's silence.*

Roots clawed through the floor, anchoring trunks wider than cars. Bark split as branches speared upward. Leaves burst, green and gold, edges burning with slow light.

Vines, thick as serpents, curled around boulders. Some moved too deliberately to be natural. Fog bled from the soil, breathing like something alive.

In seconds, the arena became a forest.

Sir Finley laughed a booming, thunder-and-whiskey laugh.

"Hope you kissed your breakfasts goodbye!"

Then he vanished into the mist as the forest had claimed him.

Sir Levi stayed by the lever.

Arms crossed and unmoving, Sir Levi's eyes scanned every branch and recruit. His face stayed blank, but when his gaze met mine, the silence sharpened.

He shifted his attention from me to Sarah, eyes settling on her for a long moment.

Something flickered in his gaze. Recognition, perhaps. Or regret.

It wasn't a sparring match anymore.

It wasn't even training.

This was elimination.

And the forest had just drawn its breath.

"Does that mean we started?" I murmured.

And the horn answered.

It didn't sound like metal or air.

It sounded like the forest's lungs exhaling for the first time in centuries.

The note rolled through the mist, low and vast, shaking bark and marrow alike.

"I guess we did,"

Something screamed far away. No shape, no throat, just the sound of existence protesting its own awakening.

Then the world broke open.

Voices and steel.

The stampede of boots on living earth.

Order evaporated. Instinct took over; each of us left to our own desperate choices.

Sarah and I moved as one.

No words. Just purpose.

She ran as calculation embodied, every step landing where chaos couldn't touch her. It reminded me of the way Sir Thomas moved.

I followed, my breath turning to heat in my chest.

The forest twisted beneath us. Roots shifted, hills reshaped.

Every tree bent closer, listening. The air itself seemed to test who deserved to breathe it.

She had a bow in hand, silver-blue light threading from her chest emblem.

She loosened an arrow into the canopy without even looking; a black-armored knight fell through the branches before the sound arrived.

Precision wasn't something Sarah practiced; it was who she *was*.

My armor burned faintly, light chasing the seams like veins of molten glass.

The twin swords at my hips vibrated, impatient.

Not for blood. For release.

The first attacker came from above with no warning, just movement without sound.

A shadow breaking from the canopy, blade first, gravity choosing sides.

Instinct pulled my arm up with no thought, no angle, just survival wired into light.

Steel met steel...

...But the sound never came.

Contact happened, but the world forgot how to react.

The echo that should've followed didn't. Air held its breath. Through the stillness, one sound echoed: the light rhythm of a heartbeat, soft but unyielding.

The leaves above froze mid-flutter, caught between what had been and what refused to come next. Sparks lingered in front of my visor. Even my heartbeat hesitated, unsure whether to continue.

I moved first.

Every motion felt endless and instant, with the distance stretching to make room for me.

First step. Light pooled around my heel.

Second step. The air folded like cloth.

The knight was still falling, suspended mid-swing. His armor quivered with pent-up force, desperate to finish a moment he no longer controlled.

I pivoted, both swords whispering arcs of gold through the stillness.

No resistance. Just release.

For a heartbeat, I could see every vein of metal splitting apart, every particle surrendering to radiance.

Then I was behind him.

The universe remembered what it had forgotten.

Sound rushed back like a flood. Leaves crashed, the clash echoed, and my chest caught up with my heartbeat.

Light flared once clean, absolute...

And he was gone.

Sarah never turned. She already knew.

"Flash for a reason?" she asked, voice steady as she scanned the tree line, bow still drawn.

"There was one," I said. "Not anymore."

No answer. Just the rhythm of her breath.

That's when I understood.

I hadn't stopped time.

I'd outrun it.

The realization didn't thrill me.

We pushed on. The forest thickened, branches crossing like veins over an arm.

The roar of battle swelled ahead. A storm made of scripture and metal.

We burst into the clearing.

The air was electric.

Dozens fought in blinding arcs.

Clashes turned to shouts.

Sarah lifted her bow. Her shots weren't arrows—they were sentences.

Every arrow Sarah shot felt final. Each draw closed a chapter forever.

Then a hush filled the air. The crowd seemed to hold its breath, suspended in that one singular moment like the pause before a storm unleashes its fury. Across the clearing, I saw him.

Judah.

He stood over a boy who couldn't have been more than fifteen, armor still shimmering faintly with its first light.

Judah's crooked grin slashed through the chaos. Still sure. Still wrong.

He raised his mace slowly, savoring the motion the way a cruel man savors silence before the scream.

Impact followed by light.

The boy vanished in a pulse of gold that looked too thin to be holy.

Judah laughed.

Not in triumph.

In satisfaction.

Like he'd just fed something that had been starving in him for years.

Something inside me tore.

It wasn't recognition.

It was an impulse.

A current shot through my chest, sharp and clean.

The air thickened, bending around me as if the forest itself braced for what it already knew was coming. I didn't *decide* to move. I became movement. The current shot through me, sharp and clean, its presence as striking as the charge itself.

One blink and distance collapsed.

The light in my armor flared, chasing up my shoulders like breath returning to lungs that had forgotten air.

My blades weren't drawn. They were *there,* gold erupting along the edges, alive and waiting.

I felt something else under it all. The Angel's touch, faint but pulsing.

A memory of holiness twisting through fury, refusing to choose between them.

The forest dimmed.

Sound bled out.

And somewhere between my heartbeat and his next breath, I was already upon him.

The swords had heat licking at the edges.

Every step blurred.

A knight lunged, gone.

Another swung, I deflected, they erased.

The world narrowed to gold and rage.

Judah turned just in time to see me.

He smiled like sin had taught him manners.

"Well, well," he said. "Didn't expect the miracle boy to crawl this far."

I said nothing.

"I don't care which choir boy dropped you here," He tilted his head. "You're still just a rumor with legs."

Still nothing.

That bothered him. He stepped closer.

"Come on. Say something holy."

My grip tightened.

"Sir Thomas brought me here."

He barked a laugh. "Figures. The failure recruits saints now? What's next, baptism with soup?"

He slipped into Sir Thomas's voice.

" 'You don't...' "

The light inside me detonated, a blinding burst that felt like a sun exploding within my chest. No warning. No build. Just ignition. A halo shimmered at the edges of my vision, hinting at the cost of wielding such raw power. My armor screamed, the seams blazing open like lightning veins. The air warped, bending away from me.

Even Sarah's glow dimmed against it.

"Sarah. Down."

She dropped without hesitation.

I stepped forward. The earth cracked beneath my boot.

Heat pulsed out of me, rhythmic, alive.

The swords blazed white-gold, blinding, trembling as if holding back something vaster than metal could contain.

I sank both blades into the ground, sweeping my legs around.

The world forgot to breathe.

A blinding ring of radiance tore outward, ripping light from the base of my legs.

It wasn't fire. It was *the light,* raw and merciless.

It judged everything it touched.

The trees folded.

The shadows burned away.

Sound inverted, howling inside itself.

Then the blast faded, leaving only the aftermath.

The clearing was gone.

The forest was a crater.

Ash drifted like snowfall over what used to be ground.

Sarah rose slowly behind me, eyes wide, armor dimmed to silver fog.

Only one sound remained. The slow crackle of cooling stone.

Judah was gone.

Not a scorch mark. Not a body.

Just *absence.*

Sarah's voice shook. "What did you do?"

I looked at my hands, cracked light crawling across the armor like molten scripture.

"I think..." My throat tightened. "...I didn't hold back."

The horn sounded again, deep, final.

The crater dissolved into light.

We were back at the entrance.

Smoke curled from the edges of my armor.

The world around me was whole again.

But something in me wasn't.

Because for the first time, I realized the light didn't just *answer* me.

It obeyed.

And absolute power is never safe.

A handful of initiates—sixteen maybe- were still standing.

Out of fifty.

The battlefield stretched around us like the aftermath of a storm that hadn't decided whether it was finished.

Ash drifted where grass had been.

The air smelled of scorched bark and ozone.

Every breath felt like breathing in thunder.

The smoke was still settling when Johnny finally spoke.

"Wow," he breathed, hands braced on his knees, half-laughing through the ache. "What a test."

No one disagreed.

Cody leaned on his spear like a crutch, armor dimming from crimson to dull iron.

Johnny grinned through the sweat, somehow still managing to look victorious.

Sarah stood a few yards away, her bow lowered, expression unreadable.

The rest were gone. Vanished mid-fight, their absence marked by faint outlines of light and the smell of burned air.

A stone platform jutted from the far edge of the clearing, carved from the bones of the earth itself.

Sir Finley stood atop it. Massive, unmoving, the kind of presence that makes even silence stand straighter.

When he finally stepped forward, the ground seemed to adjust to his weight.

"Congratulations, boyos and lasses."

His voice rolled through the air like thunder, finding new ground.

"If you're still standin', you passed."

Scattered cheers followed, too tired to rise higher than disbelief.

Sir Finley let the noise fade. Then his tone lowered, more measured.

"Now comes the part that sticks."

He extended a scarred hand. "Your branch will now be decided."

Murmurs spread. Armor shifted.

A few glanced upward, hopeful. Others braced for judgment.

I just listened.

Sir Levi silently joined him at the platform's edge, posture knife-straight.

Where Sir Finley radiated heat, Sir Levi drew it in.

Sir Levi said, "The Order holds four branches." His voice didn't need volume. It carried like precision.

"Michael. The front line. Warriors of the Order. Strength and guardianship lead their path."

Sir Finley grinned. "The brawlers. The best ones."

"Raphael," Sir Levi continued, "Healing and recovery. The medics of Crossguard. They mend more than bones; they restore hope."

He gestured briefly. "The life behind every sword."

"Uriel," Sir Finley said, his grin fading into respect. "Strategy. The Advisors everyone depends on. They see the battle before it begins, wisdom in every breath."

Then a pause.

It gave everyone time to notice the silence.

Sir Levi's eyes flicked toward Sir Finley.

Sir Finley exhaled through his nose, beard rustling like dry leaves.

"And Gabriel..." His voice dropped.

The wind seemed to stop listening.

"Gabriel's branch isn't about muscle or mind. It's about the message. About carrying light where it doesn't belong, and surviving what it burns on the way. They always lead within our Order. Light in darkness, truth in adversity."

He scanned us slowly, the humor gone. "You don't apply for it. You're chosen. And sometimes..."

He tapped his chest once. "You break before you're chosen."

No one moved.

Even Sir Levi looked down.

Then Sir Finley unfurled a scroll.

The parchment glowed faintly, ink shifting like liquid shadow.

He began to read.

"Johnny McKraken. You've been chosen by Michael."

Johnny punched the air. "Let's go!"

"Harley Hudson. You've been chosen by Raphael."

"Sarah Storm. You've been chosen by Uriel."

Sarah gave a small, knowing nod, already composed.

"Donte Lorenzo. You've been chosen by Michael."

"Demarcus Okoye. You've been chosen by Uriel."

"Cody Miles. You've been chosen by Raphael."

Cody exhaled. "Guess I'm the medic."

And then, again, the pause.

Longer this time.

Sir Finley's gaze lingered on the final line.

He looked up.

"Kayson Cavalier."

My stomach tightened.

"You've been selected..."

He hesitated, not for effect, but because the air had changed around the word.

"...by Gabriel."

Everything stilled.

Just the low hum of something unseen, recognizing what had just been named.

Even the torches flickered lower, their flames bowing for a breath.

Sir Levi rattled through the final few. The hanging tension froze the remaining names.

Sir Finley stepped down from the platform, boots echoing across the cracked earth.

He stopped in front of me and placed one enormous hand on my shoulder.

"Rare air, lad," he said quietly.

His grip was steady, grounding.

But behind his eyes lived a warning: *You don't walk this path. It walks you.*

Then he turned back to the crowd.

"Each branch is your foundation," he said. "Your home until the day the light recalls you. Train, learn. Fail and rise again."

Sir Levi added, "Your first assignments begin soon. Not simulations. Real execution. Crossguard doesn't exist for sport."

Sir Finley's grin returned, faint but fierce. "This ain't summer camp. People's souls are in the balance. Treat it like it."

The platform sank back into the earth with a deep groan. The test was over.

But I wasn't sure the weight had lifted.

The crowd dispersed. Johnny jogged up beside me, grinning.

"Gabriel, huh? That's like the elite. Didn't think you were that special, man."

I smirked weakly. "Neither did I."

Sarah approached next, calm as always.

"Gabriel's branch doesn't choose lightly," she said. "It's prophecy. Intercession. You don't get that without reason."

Her eyes lingered on me a moment longer, curious. But not afraid. Then she turned away.

Cody clapped me on the back. "No pressure, right?"

We found Sir Thomas and Sir David waiting near the gate, both wearing the kind of smiles you earn through exhaustion and faith.

"You all did wonderfully," Sir Thomas said. "You stood when it mattered."

Sir David raised an eyebrow at me. "And you, Cavalier, nice light show. We'll be replanting trees for weeks."

I managed a laugh. "Still figuring that part out."

As we walked, Johnny told the story of his fight. How his opponent mirrored every move he made until Cody's energy blast sent both flying.

"Looked like interpretive dance gone nuclear," he said.

Cody grinned. "Poetic justice."

We laughed, tired. Raw laughter that felt like the echo of victory.

But as the others talked, a quiet thought pressed behind my ribs.

Michael was strong.

Raphael, mercy.

Uriel, wisdom.

Gabriel...

I didn't know yet.

Only that when the air shifted, and my name had been spoken, something ancient had stirred inside me.

Something that felt less like destiny...

and more like a debt.

CHAPTER NINE

EPHESIANS WAS BORN

A week had passed since I'd arrived at the Gabriel Branch, though the term 'training' felt painfully inadequate. The experience gnawed at me. An unsettling, constant pressure, as if the core of my being was carved into something unrecognizable. That first morning, a lonely, smokeless flame from a solitary lantern flickered across the stone walls. Its light stretched and distorted my shadow, promising transformation but also darkness. I felt fear knot in my stomach.

Not just the body. Our minds. Our will.

This wasn't about hitting harder or faster. Instead, we learned to truly understand ourselves. What made up our deepest thoughts and feelings. How to act from that place without hesitation.

Gabriel was the smallest branch. Fourteen apprentices, total. We met each morning in the Stone Hall.

It was a hexagonal chamber high in the eastern tower, lit by lanterns that burned without smoke. The walls were etched with glyphs. They pulsed faintly when you passed near them and were warm to the touch, like veins under skin. No one explained what they meant. The air itself vibrated, soft but constant, as if the place remembered every word ever spoken inside it.

Most of us kept to ourselves. Words were spent carefully here, as if each one might shatter something brittle between us.

No one shouted; even joy arrived quietly. We bowed before and after sparring, searching each other's faces for approval or regret. Our eyes confessed what our mouths refused. Even our footsteps softened with time, our silences growing thick with unspoken feeling. Silence became less a discipline, more a fragile sanctuary we shared.

Lady Zalika was one of our two representatives, though the word felt too sterile for her presence. She didn't command the room. By merely entering, she changed it. She made silence feel heavier, more sacred. She never raised her voice. She didn't need to.

Lady Zalika moved like a shadow and stood like stone. Her skin was the deep brown of desert clay. Her hair was streaked silver near the temples, her eyes forged from memory. Across her face, from her temple to her jaw, ran a single diagonal scar. It was never discussed. It didn't need to be. It felt like punctuation, an ending written so that beginnings could exist.

Every day began the same way. With Foundation Hour. We entered the Pondering Sanctuary, formed a circle, and waited. Lady Zalika would stand at the center. One hand rested on her Bible, the other palm up, as if holding something unseen. Then she would pose a question.

Never more than one. Never repeated. Just a question, as if dropping ink into still water.

That first Monday: "What do you guard when no one's watching?" Then she would leave. Without a lecture. No discussion. We sat with the question. Let it ripple through everything that followed. That was the rhythm. Some days, the question hovered like a star. Other days it stabbed. But every lesson that followed bent toward its meaning, whether we saw it or not.

One morning, during Foundation Hour, Lady Zalika asked, "What have you been given that you deemed you haven't earned?" The words pierced, refusing to leave. They needled under my armor as I sparred, as I prayed, as I lay awake blinking at the shadows. The Bible. The swords. The light. All freely given, pressing upon me with guilt and gratitude, heavy as a second heart that throbbed painfully but alive.

We didn't train with armor. Only our Bibles, our breath, and each other.

Lady Zalika believed power was a consequence, not a goal. "Speed fades. Power fluctuates. But purpose," she said once, walking between us as we practiced channeling light through our palms.

"That's what makes an apprentice unbreakable." Her presence carried weight in ways words couldn't. You didn't memorize what she said. You absorbed it.

Yet in the quiet moments, I thought back to my fight with Judah. I craved raw strength, a temptation to seize power for its own sake. But as quickly as the memory surfaced, it was swallowed by a hunger for purpose. It was a conflict that carved itself into my soul, underscoring the lesson that power should follow, never lead.

As the week ended, I realized I was changing. My questions hadn't gone away; they became quieter and went deeper. I found that answers weren't obvious or loud; sometimes, you had to find them in the pauses between actions, like between heartbeats, before you strike, or between verses. Training at Gabriel's branch didn't simply make me stronger; it taught me to wait and listen. Only then did I begin to notice the answers that had always been there.

"Every soul leaves a mark," she said. "In the In-Between. On others. On yourself. Most people live unaware of it. You won't have that luxury." We learned to feel that imprint. We traced how energy moved when we breathed, when we doubted, when we lied to ourselves. It was exhausting learning to hear beneath your heartbeat. But it revealed how easily falsehood distorts light. Misuse it, and the light dims, becomes erratic, reflecting unintended truths. My own glow began to respond more cleanly now. I could hold it longer without burning out, redirect it mid-motion, and shape it with thought rather than effort. It wasn't brute energy anymore. It was being sculpted with intention.

The swords reflected that. They didn't burst forth. They answered. When I reached for them, they unfolded like memory finding its way home. Light and thought danced together in a delicate balance. Restraint was the silent commandment. Each duel grew faster, sharper, but still quiet. Lady Zalika called that silence "The Still." "Words leave ripples," she told us. "And the deeper the water, the more damage a ripple can do." So we learned to fight in silence. We spoke through rhythm, breath, and proximity. We listened to the tension between strikes. We understood that restraint could be deadlier than aggression. In silence-driven combat, the cost of misuse was high; control dictated the clarity of light and intention.

Yet even in that stillness, I wavered. There were moments when the silence pressed too close. When I swung too soon or lost my focus, the light would sputter against my palms. Each failure hit like static under the ribs. For a second, I'd hear Solomon's voice. Steady, patient. He reminded me that truth wasn't perfection. It was endurance. I'd see Sir Thomas's calm half-smile, the way he met every setback like it was proof you were still alive. Those echoes steadied me more than any command. When the light returned, it burned steadier, like fire learning how to breathe.

Evenings in Gabriel's spire were spent alone. We didn't eat together or talk much. My room looked out over a ridge where the sun rose. I often sat by the window at night with my Bible, feeling the cold air and counting my breaths. I traced the carved symbols on the window, reminding myself to stay present and calm. Letting the quiet surround me, I felt my thoughts settle, and solitude became a real comfort, grounding me each night.

One night, I found a new page in my Bible, glowing faintly, as if lit by sunrise. It read: *He who walks into shadow with truth in his breath shall not be undone by darkness.* I touched the words, and the page pulsed once like a heartbeat before going still. The meaning wasn't immediately clear, but I trusted the feeling that mattered most was learning to see the truth for myself. That was Gabriel's teaching: discovering lessons through personal insight instead of being given direct answers.

The other branches had manuals and drills. We had silence. Questions and revelation. Among the fourteen, fractures were shown. Some trained alone, haunted. Others paired off and mirrored each other's rhythm. A guy named Noa fought beside me often. His movements were deliberate, fluid. Each strike was an act of listening.

We never spoke, yet I understood him perfectly. The more we fought, the clearer our rhythm became, until we could predict each other's motion by breath alone. Once, after a long duel that drew quiet onlookers, Lady Zalika passed me and said simply, "You're no longer hearing. You've begun listening. Continue to do so." It was the first praise she'd ever given me. It shocked me that she said something other than a question.

Johnny and Cody joined the other branches, Michael and Raphael. I hadn't seen them since the Trial of Endurance. I often wondered whether their days were as silent as ours, or whether the noise made their training different. I doubted Johnny thrived in so much silence. Gabriel's branch didn't value noise or winning for its own sake. It was about removing everything but what was true, until only honesty remained.

Week three arrived before I could prepare or step back, at a moment when everything felt paused between two breaths.

The days that followed settled into a pattern of practicing with light and learning self-control.

We fought, bled, listened. Lady Zalika observed without commentary. Sometimes she stood. Other times circling the ring like a tide tracing a new shoreline. She never crowned a victor. She never needed to.

The victory itself kept score.

Some matches were clean, crystalline.

Others devolved into beautiful chaos pretending to be choreography.

Each attack felt like revealing something personal; every defensive move was like holding back a private prayer.

"In battle," Lady Zalika said, as we sat along the ring's edge, armor cracked and steaming with effort, "your soul speaks louder than your steel."

No one spoke.

I didn't understand her then.

Not until a match where my opponent never made a sound.

No grunt, no curse, no breath out of place.

He fought like a memory fighting to be remembered.

When my sword hit his wrist, and the light reset the match, his reaction wasn't physical. It felt as if his deepest feelings spilled out, even in total silence.

Not in rage or pain.

It was the feeling of someone confronted with their own true self, unable to avoid it any longer.

That's when I realized: Lady Zalika wasn't teaching us to defeat people. She was teaching us to hear them.

To notice what people's silence held back, even if all their defenses looked perfect from the outside.

The quiet rhythms of the Gabriel Branch had begun to settle inside me: mornings steeped in soul work, afternoons spent unraveling silence until it revealed what sound never could. Those questions that hung in the air, '*What do you guard when no one's watching?*' had started to echo longer than sleep. It wasn't discipline anymore. It was a transformation. The kind that didn't announce itself; it just changed the gravity of your breath.

And then Lady Zalika broke the pattern with eight quiet words.

"Tomorrow," she said, voice calm as a dropped stone in still water, "you will spar. Show completion through listening."

No philosophy to chase before breakfast.

Just an invitation that sounded too much like judgment.

Disarm or eject was the only rule.

The next morning, the training floor looked reborn.

Benches gone. Scripture boards cleared. The smell of incense was replaced by the smell of iron and cold stone.

Even the light had changed. The lanterns were burning whiter, sharper. This wasn't a match we were preparing for, but one we'd been reenacting since time learned how to echo.

Lady Zalika waited in the center. Her robes the color of storm-ash, unarmed, unflinching.

Her scar caught the light, that diagonal mark read less like a wound and more like a verse written in flesh.

She didn't move often. She didn't have to.

"Every movement speaks," she said, and the whisper reached all of us, as though the stone itself carried her breath.

"Make sure yours tells the truth."

That was all.

No stance corrections or form.

Just moving with truth, apparently.

"Abel, step forward."

He was taller by a head, in olive armor, shoulders like the promise of impact. His breathing was steady, calculated, the rhythm of someone who had already memorized his own defeat and refused to accept it. There was nothing false about him. Just refinement sharpened to the point of silence.

My name came second. Exactly where it was meant to land.

She gestured to the circle. "Bow to your opponent."

The instant Lady Zalika's hand dropped, the world condensed to motion. A resounding clash of steel and the hiss of light filled the space, marking the beginning of our dance. He lunged low, fast, and merciless. His blade came up like a rising tide, ready to tear through ribs and hesitation alike.

But the moment stretched. I didn't think. I didn't flinch. I felt. With each strike, the sonic motif played out like a rhythm in a symphony. A clang here, a hiss there, guiding the match's pulse.

My swords found the cross instinctively in two streaks of gold, catching the upward strike in mid-breath. The impact rang like a bell. I pivoted, stepping through the rhythm instead of against it, twisting my shoulder, letting his momentum betray him. The familiar clang signaled a turning point, grounding me in the flow of combat.

My elbow grazed his armor; my blade kissed air just above his flank.

He rolled, armor clattering. As he fell away, I sheathed my twin blades back into their emblem and bowed as I always did at the end of a match. The hit would've ended a real fight, but the match wasn't about physicality... We were to present an undeniable victor.

And then he was over the line.

Out.

Lady Zalika raised her hand.

"Match three. Win three."

No applause or excessive validation.

Just her nod.

Later that night, I passed her study.

She sat by lamplight, writing on parchment.

Not scores or ranks. Summarizing each of us.

A single word beneath each name.

Mine read: Clarity.

At first, I thought it meant precision. Clean edges, steady hands.

But clarity isn't sharpness. It's exposure.

It's when the fog lifts, and you realize how much you'd been hiding inside it.

That terrified me.

Because clarity leaves no shadows to stand in the way.

But it also frees you, like a wound finally clean enough to heal.

Her last lesson returned: *Every movement speaks.*

Maybe clarity was just the moment when the lie stopped speaking for you.

When truth finally learned your name and spoke it back.

The final day arrived without warning with three bells, low and measured.

They echoed through the halls like the sound of ribs remembering breath.

Every apprentice froze mid-motion. We knew what it meant.

Book Assignment Day.

We filed out in silence without fear, not uncertain.

Just steady.

Because every soul in Gabriel knew something was coming.

We just didn't yet know what shape it had.

All the branches gathered in the Mess Hall. It had changed since our first days here.

It didn't feel like a place for meals anymore.

No more wide-eyed stares at banners or the architecture of faith.

Over a hundred of us were packed shoulder to shoulder. Michael apprentices still buzzing with adrenaline, Raphael pages sitting calm but sharp-eyed, Uriel representatives murmuring in quiet chains of strategy, and then... Gabriel.

We didn't speak. We used the silence to listen.

I sat near the back with the rest of Gabriel, Bible in hand. The leather was warm against my palm, almost alive, as if it knew the day carried weight.

The light through the tall stained-glass windows wasn't golden.

Not this morning.

It was silver. Dim.

A kind of reverence that didn't shine. It waited.

Solomon stood on the stage.

Sir Finley and Sir Levi flanked him like twin walls of judgment. One grinning with mischief barely contained under his beard, the other unreadable, jaw locked, posture straight enough to make the air seem crooked.

But Solomon? He didn't look at us like a teacher.

He looked at us like a cartographer. Mapping futures. Scanning fault lines.

The room fell silent.

His gaze moved slowly, deliberately, across the rows of apprentices, and you could feel it when it landed on you.

"Good morning, branch apprentices of Crossguard," Solomon said, his voice crisp and clean as a drawn blade. "These last three weeks have tested your discipline, your patience, and your spirit. You've trained within your branches, endured trials of body and soul. Today, we take the next step."

His words were precise.

Not a syllable wasted.

The hush wasn't just reverence.

It was readiness.

"We now enter the Book Phase," Solomon said. "The path to Knighthood unfolds in four phases. Beginning with induction into the Order. Then, getting assigned to your book as a page, and finally getting knighted as a Chapter. Each stage shapes more than your skill; it refines your spirit. From this day forward, you will serve within a Book. Four apprentices, each a page bound as one book. Each is drawn from the four branches of the Order: Michael, Raphael, Uriel, and Gabriel."

His voice echoed through the domed hall, as if chasing down the memory of centuries.

"Four roles. One mission."

I straightened. Around me, heads lifted. Bibles clutched tighter. Breath pulled in and held like a prayer.

"There are sixty-six books," Solomon said, lifting a thick scroll from the podium. "Named after the sixty-six books of Scripture. Your team is more than a training group. It is your shelter. Your battlefield family. And your calling. While you are all here, not all will hear there calling today."

The word *calling* carried differently in his mouth.

Not dramatic.

Certain.

I scanned the crowd.

Judah Walker stood off-center, arms crossed, feet wide.

That same crooked smirk, the same air of someone who thought destiny owed him a handshake.

He radiated confidence like heat off asphalt.

He must've already re-attempted the Trial of Endurance. My memory briefly flashed to the helpless kid he had tormented in our Trial.

I couldn't help but feel annoyed that he made it.

He probably already knew where he'd end up and how soon he'd start leading it.

Johnny and Cody were a few rows off to my left.

Cody looked calm, but it was the kind of calm that hid current beneath the surface.

Johnny was stone still, jaw tight, one knee bouncing like a trapped engine.

Not nerves. Just containment.

And Sarah...

She sat two rows ahead. Still. Straight. Her fingers locked around her Bible like a mast in stormlight. She didn't blink much. She didn't need to.

The naming began.

Solomon opened the scroll and started reading.

One by one, names rolled through the air. Each a spark, a thread stitching strangers together into destiny.

A Michael. A Raphael. A Uriel. A Gabriel. A warrior. A healer. A mind. A vision.

They'd rise, receive their book assignment, and vanish through the eastern doors toward the dormitory towers.

Some smiled, bumping fists.

Some looked lost.

Some looked like they'd been waiting lifetimes for this moment.

"Judah Walker of the Michael Branch, Noa of the Gabriel Branch, Ian of the Raphael Branch, and Theo of the Uriel Branch," Solomon announced, "You form Matthew." Judah rocked back on his heels with a hint of impatience, a swagger that spread through his stance. Noa tapped his finger lightly against his thigh, a subtle rhythm only he seemed to hear, grounding him amidst the announcement. Ian glanced around with a small, assured nod, while Theo instinctively adjusted his glasses, his focus sharp and attentive.

He probably dreamed his name into the scroll himself.

More squads passed.

Luke. James. Proverbs. Exodus. Esther. Genesis.

Each name chipped away at the noise.

The room thinned. Silence thickened. And I was still waiting. Still listening.

Then Solomon paused.

Only one scroll remained in his hand now. He unrolled it. And looked up.

"The final book…"

My pulse skipped, leaving an echo in my bones.

"Cody Miles of the Raphael Branch."

Cody blinked once, then stood.

No grin or theatrics. Just quiet certainty.

"Johnathan McKraken of the Michael Branch."

Johnny exhaled sharply through his nose and rose like he'd been waiting for his name since birth.

He had a grin that could light a battlefield.

"Sarah Storm of the Uriel Branch."

She moved before the words finished leaving his lips.

Like the moment had been rehearsed.

She took her place beside them, calm and grounded as sunrise.

And then Solomon said the last name.

He didn't raise his voice. He didn't need to.

"And finally…"

His eyes found mine. "Kayson Cavalier of the Gabriel Branch."

For a second, my body didn't respond. Legs locked. My heart stumbling.

Then I stood. The stone beneath my boots felt heavier as if it was acknowledging something.

Solomon's faint smile wasn't a victory.

It was recognition.

"You four," he said, "form Ephesians."

The name landed like a chord struck across the soul. Familiar and foreign all at once.

He glanced at the scroll again.

"You are assigned to the New Testament dormitory. Floor Ten."

Then, softer, "Report there immediately."

The room moved, but I barely felt it.

Cody gave me a brief nod.

Johnny whispered, "Let's go, Ephesians," like it was already a creed.

Sarah didn't speak, but the small tilt of her head said everything words couldn't.

I looked at the three of them. Different branches, different temperaments.

And yet it fit.

Like the name had summoned us, not the other way around.

As we walked toward the eastern door, I felt the weight settle.

This wasn't a squad made by paperwork.

It was a squad forged by purpose.

Unseen but undeniable.

The kind of gravity you don't notice until it starts pulling everything toward it.

And deep down, beneath the noise of boots and breath and moving crowds, one truth stirred like thunder waiting its cue.

Whatever came next. We wouldn't just face it together.

We'd *become* it.

We filed out of the Mess Hall with the other newly formed Books. A stream of armor plates, all hushed beneath the tension of beginnings. I walked in step beside Johnny, the corridor alive with footsteps and low-voiced prayers. Sarah moved ahead, Cody behind.

As we walked, I opened my Bible.

The name burned gold across the first page, clear:

Ephesians.

Kayson Cavalier | Sarah Storm | Johnny McKraken | Cody Miles.

The names weren't printed.

They were seared.

Like fire had kissed the parchment, like the Word itself had written what Heaven already knew.

Something we'd have to live up to.

The towers rose ahead of us.

Twin sentinels.

The Old Testament Tower was roughly forty stories of weathered stone and stained-glass echoes. Beside it, the New Testament Tower, around thirty levels of silver and steel. One anchored in history; the other, in revelation.

Johnny whistled low. "No pressure, right?"

We entered through the polished glass doors. Inside, the light changed into a softer hue. Four elevator doors lined the atrium, each inscribed with scripture.

Above the third door, gold letters shimmered faintly:

"Be strong in the Lord and in the power of His might."

Beside each door, a narrow slot gleamed like a keyhole made of light.

"For the Bible," Cody muttered. "Of course. They would."

He slid his Bible into the third slot with a grin. "Let's see what faith unlocks."

I followed, breath steadying as I pressed mine forward.

Orange surged through the frame.

The word *EPHESIANS* ignited in living light, washing the hallway in warmth.

Cody gave a soft whistle. "Okay... dramatic. I respect it."

Sarah said nothing, but her eyes traced the runes like she was memorizing them.

The doors parted.

What waited inside wasn't a barracks.

It was *home reimagined.*

A panoramic window stretched across the far wall, overlooking the training fields below, where sunlight spilled like molten glass. Plush seating circled a crystal table. A kitchenette hummed quietly under hidden lights. Even a pool table waited in the corner. It felt unblemished, untouched.

Against the back wall were four doors.

Each was carved with one of our names.

Johnny dropped his bag onto the couch. "I was expecting steel bunks and a verse-a-day wall calendar. This? This is divine hospitality."

Cody opened the fridge. "Apples, protein packs, Raphael-grade smoothies. Either we're blessed or baited."

Sarah stood at the window, arms folded, gaze pinned to the horizon like she was timing the heartbeat of the sun.

Me?

I walked to my door.

It shimmered faintly, my name etched *into* it.

I pushed it open and froze.

My lungs forgot how to work.

Because this wasn't a dorm.

It was my room. Not recreated. *Retrieved.*

The warped floorboard under my desk. The dent in the headboard from a reckless backpack swing. The torn poster above the desk. Even the smell of cedar dust clinging to the air. I sat on the bed, hands trembling against the sheets. This wasn't built. It was remembered. *How is that even possible?*

My Bible buzzed against my thigh.

A message appeared.

Sir Thomas:

Report to your floor's common room immediately. Your first assignment begins now.

I exhaled slowly, stretching my arms above my head until they moved on their own as if possessed.

The past faded as duty reclaimed me.

Back in the common room, the others were waiting.

Johnny was stretching his shoulders like the mission might start mid-sentence.

Cody leaned against the pool table, eyes sharp.

Sarah stood near the couch, Bible in hand, the calm before the storm.

Sir Thomas faced us by the window, cloak lowered, armor gleaming like forged dawn.

"Congratulations, Ephesians," he said. "You're officially active."

The words settled like a seal breaking open.

We were no longer simply apprentices.

"As some of you have potentially guessed," Sir Thomas continued, "your first assignment takes you back to where this began."

"Sonorah High School is under active spiritual influence."

The name hit like gravity.

Every sound dulled.

"A Fallen Angel has been confirmed to have rooted itself within the school's culture and likely through its leadership. Principal Kartikak's behavior aligns with the early stages of Fallen influence. Fear policies. Speech suppression. Distorted authority. Unexplained readings on our trackers."

The void. The weight I'd felt in the field.

It hadn't left.

It had just gone underground.

"Your objective," Sir Thomas said, "is not destruction. It's restoration."

He met each of our eyes one by one.

"Find the source. And if confirmed, confront it."

Then the atmosphere shifted again. Cooler, more deliberate.

A voice joined from behind us.

Solomon.

"To confront," he said, stepping forward, "you must cross into the In-Between."

His Bible rested in one hand, faint light pulsing beneath his thumb.

"This is the only way to perceive the true condition of a place. Think of the In-Between as a reflection. Not shaped by time, but by truth. You won't just see what *is*. You'll see what it *means*."

He stopped at the center of the room.

"To enter," he said, "hold your Bible. Focus on your destination. Think these words:

"Keep me safe on my way, and my feet will not stumble."

The sentence hung like a key suspended in the air.

"The Word will glow," he finished. "When it does, follow."

He stepped back.

I looked at the others.

Johnny's stance tightened, that fearless grin gone serious.

Cody's knuckles whitened on his Bible, breath steady.

Sarah's eyes burned with the quiet resolve of belief.

I swallowed, then nodded once.

We were ready.

Together, we drew our Bibles. The air thickened with pressure. With Expectation.

I closed my eyes. Focused on what waited to be redeemed.

The halls that once echoed with laughter are now hollowed by silence.

"Keep me safe on my way, and my feet will not stumble."

Light fractured beneath me. Then, silence.

The echo of our arrival faded like the tail of a hymn.

When my vision cleared, we were standing on dulled grass, the kind that suffered the weight of students' footsteps.

The reflection of what it truly was.

The world had been leeched of color.

Even the clouds above seemed hesitant to move, held in some half-motion between storm and surrender.

A low static filled the air. More like a pressure.

A resonance beneath the ribs.

The In-Between spoke, with the cost of corruption.

This was worse than Sir Thomas had said. It wasn't becoming Fallen territory.

It had already fallen into a Soulless Zone.

CHAPTER TEN
TABLETS OF THE TEN COMMANDMENTS

T he field stretched beneath a sky without a pulse—cold and lifeless, as if no energy remained above.

The ghost-cold scent of bleach lingered in the air. Grass lay flat and bone-pale, brittle under our boots like frost that forgot how to melt. The faded memory of a stadium accordion emerged as scattered, crumbling ticket stubs beneath the stands. Every step threatened to erase them from existence, leaving only the shadow of their purpose.

The In-Between wasn't a place.

It was awareness, stripped of all warmth, as if consciousness existed alone, without comfort or sensation.

It simply stopped being alive.

The bleachers hunched forward, ribs of concrete bending under invisible weight, as if burdened by forgotten crowds.

The scoreboard hung in the distance, blank and still, its numbers faint like ghosts—faded memories barely remembered.

Beyond the far fence, Sonorah High stood colorless and hollow.

The windows were black mirrors, dark and reflective, swallowing anything that tried to look inside.

Every brick looked dulled of warmth, like the world had tried to scrub its own memory clean.

Silence here wasn't simply the absence of sound; it felt aware, pressing in as though it had presence.

It was a type of silence that seemed to watch back...

The kind that looked back at you when you listened too long.

Even our breathing sounded wrong.

Our breathing felt too heavy, as if the air itself was missing, leaving us struggling to fill our lungs.

The old resonance, once aligned with my heartbeat, now trembled off-key—grief between notes. My chest tightened; my pulse skipped at the dissonance. Instinctively, I touched the cold earth—it murmured back, promising silent connection. Upright now, my fingers closing into a fist, I shaped grief into quiet resolve and let it drive me forward.

Sarah scanned the horizon, one hand resting near her emblem.

"This was where we had the assembly?"

"Yeah," I said. "Or what's left of the field's reflection."

Johnny shifted his hammer onto his shoulder. His breath came out white, even though there was no cold.

"Even the ghosts left early."

Cody's armor pulsed faint red, the light dulling as it left him.

"Nothing seems to be left. It's drained clean."

Sarah nodded once, studying the horizon. As she did, she noticed the subtle quiver in the horizon, hinting at the instability. "That's how the Fallen hold ground," she murmured, her voice barely above a whisper. "Consume the echo, then hollow the memory." Her hand moved to check her emblem, ensuring it was ready, as the realization struck her, adding urgency to her tone. "For every eternity they devour, the Zone gains strength. Once the sound dies, the spirit is dead with it." She keyed into Cody's silent signal, recognizing they had little time left to stabilize. "But this level of drain..." Her words trailed off as she gestured to Cody to secure the area, "It shouldn't be possible this early into Fallen influence."

We moved forward; each step landed too softly, as if the soil no longer trusted gravity.

The white lines that once divided the field twisted faintly, coiling inward as if trying to hide from sight.

Goalposts leaned together—not broken, but seeming tired, like sentinels exhausted from standing too long.

Then came the sound.

Metal slowly scraped the wood. Deliberate. Wanting us to cringe, like nails dragging across a chalkboard.

The kind of sound that didn't just exist. It announced itself.

Sarah raised her hand.

Stillness swept through us with the force of an unspoken order, freezing us in place as if commanded.

The scraping stopped.

The silence leaned closer.

It wasn't just the absence of noise anymore.

It was as if the silence itself was paying close attention, focusing on us alone.

I touched the emblem at my collar.

It pulsed once, alive and aware.

A single heartbeat pulsed in a world now emptied of all life.

Gold light crawled under my fingers, and twin blades folded from air into form.

Beside me, Cody's spear shimmered along its crimson edge, heat without warmth rippling up its length.

Johnny's warhammer glowed a dim, smoldering orange, as thunder locked inside silence, waiting for release.

Sarah's bow curved in her hand, drawn smooth, her arrow burning soft blue. A single streak of color in a place that seemed to reject any brightness or hue.

Four breaths.

Then we moved.

The tunnel beneath the bleachers waited, dark and soundless.

Its walls looked solid from afar, but up close, they flexed and moved slightly, like thin lungs taking shallow breaths.

Light bent around the frame.

The air pressed inward.

Every sound we thought we made: every step, every breath, was swallowed. It vanished before it had a chance to be made aware.

The field stretched open before us, unchanged, as if untouched by all we had experienced.

And that was the worst part.

Still perfect. Still silent. Still wrong.

Shadows stretched where they shouldn't.

They didn't move, but they didn't stay still either.

Our armor dimmed against the pressure. Each glimmer of light fought for its place against the void.

The field exhaled.

Mist curled from the far fence, thin and pulsing, peeling back to reveal what had been waiting there all along.

It hadn't appeared.

It had always been here. Part of the stillness, pretending to be air.

It faced away from us.

Half-shrouded in the gray vapor, the creature stood at the far end of the field. Tall, deliberate, still.

Its armor didn't cast a shadow; it devoured it.

Light touched the surface and disappeared, swallowed whole like memory through a hole in thought.

The noise that had followed us since crossing the Zone deepened, pressing into the ribs instead of the ears.

The kind of sound that wasn't meant to be heard, only *endured*.

Then it began muttering.

Or maybe something older.

Almost like the Hebrew David had taught us. But broken, reversed.

The vibration crawled through the ground first, then the bones. Through the thin space between breath and spirit.

The soul heard it; the mind refused it.

A language built for unmaking.

Its trident dragged behind it, tip cutting shallow grooves through the colorless grass.

Every mark shimmered with inverted light, twisting when my eyes tried to hold them.

Meaning buckled on contact.

Sarah's whisper broke the rhythm, sharp but quiet.

"That's casting. It's feeding on the field."

She was right.

The Soulless Zone wasn't fixed anymore.

It was bending to him.

"Now."

Our formation broke clean.

Cody and Sarah split, fading against the bleachers.

Johnny and I pressed forward, weapons low, breath tight, feet gliding over soil that felt soft as ash.

Then it turned slow. Certain. That hollow where a face should be tilted toward me. No eyes. No mouth. Just serrated absence, a wound in the shape of recognition. The trident rose, and as the screech came, it wasn't just sound; it was the echo of my own doubt. I hesitated.

"Move!" Cody's voice cut through my hesitation, sharp and urgent. "Flank it, don't wait!"

Johnny's shout overlapped, strong and commanding. The void fed on my uncertainty, widening with each passing second. Unable to dodge fast enough, the pressure slammed through me, cracking across my armor like thunder with nowhere to go.

"Stay together!" Sarah's words were quick and decisive, bringing cohesion to chaos.

The world folded.

Pressure slammed through the Zone, cracking across my armor like thunder with nowhere to go.

Vision burst white; balance collapsed.

The ground trembled once, then steadied, humming with the residue of its will.

The Fallen hadn't moved.

The right side of the field cracked open like a doorway, air rippling. The field peeled into the unknown, metallic tang on my tongue. My ears rang—an echo of thunder, grounding the scene.

Four Fallen Angels fell out of the impact.

Their armor jittered between metal and smoke, tridents burning with infected light.

Their wings were corroded. Just folds of blackness twitching behind them, as if trying to recall flight.

"Break!" I shouted.

My voice cut the tension. "Ephesians two-four, pivot!" We snapped into formation, muscle memory taking over.

Johnny roared forward, hammer blazing.

The first of the new Fallen met it head-on and vanished in a burst of gray ash.

Sarah's arrows followed: three blurs of blue that split the air.

Each hit center-mass, dissolving its target into light.

The air brightened around her shots, color flickering back for half a heartbeat before dying again.

Then it was us.

Cody and I.

And the Fallen Angel.

The pressure inside my chest wasn't fear.

It was alignment.

I moved.

Light gathered under my skin. It flowed through my ribs, down into the hilts of my blades.

I listened for the Fallen Angel.

Moving faster, Gold overtook the field. And I was behind it.

My twin arcs fell fast, trident intercepting both. Impact rippled like rings on glass. I skidded back, boots carving pale dust.

It hadn't reacted. *It... It anticipated me.*

Cody lunged beside me, spear alive with red kinetic fire.

He struck low, with clean form and a flawless angle.

The Fallen pivoted, swiping its trident.

Thunder echoed off their blades. Sparks burst out.

Cody slid backward, boots carving deep gouges.

"How is it adapting!"

I stepped beside him, blades still drawn.

"It's not supposed to be learning us."

The Fallen advanced.

Each movement is an equation already solved.

Not a monster. A tactician.

Across the field, Johnny's voice cut the silence.

"CLEAR!"

I turned as he slammed the last one into the stands.

"Johnny, Sarah—create an exit! Cody, with me!"

Sarah's arrow found it mid-impact. One final burst of blue that left the air trembling clean again.

"Fall back!"

The trident struck down.

I caught it; gold sparked against black.

Cody slammed his spear into the ground, releasing a red shockwave that split the dust and opened our path. We moved with urgency, the stakes too high to falter. In that moment, a vow anchored itself in my mind: *We cannot fail again, for the cost of failure is more than defeat.*

The Fallen Angel didn't follow.

Didn't raise its weapon.

It simply watched, with a faceless tilt... Radiating satisfaction.

It had gotten exactly what it wanted.

We crossed the fence line together, the stillness behind us folding closed like a held breath. I pressed my emblem. My blades dissolved into light.

The world folded.

Stone returned beneath our boots.

Crossguard air filled my nose. Clean, bright, sharp enough to remind us we were alive.

But the silence followed.

Johnny paced, hammer dimming.

"That wasn't combat," he said. "That was a test."

"It saw me," I said. "At full speed. It read everything."

Sarah's bow faded from her hand.

"It didn't just read. It learned."

Cody sat hard against the wall, armor cracked but intact.

"And it let us go."

No one spoke.

The silence that came wasn't confusion.

It was recognition.

Johnny looked up, voice steady.

"We're not waiting this one out."

He didn't need to raise his tone.

Conviction carried it.

"We're finding Sir Thomas, now."

Light from the recall still glimmered faintly along the floor, fading in uneven pulses beneath our boots.

There was no air for relief, no space for words. Only the echo of a single, unanswered question drove our steps forward: *Was survival enough to unravel the mystery of that day? Stopping meant confronting the raw edges of that doubt, of the decision lingering in the corners of our thoughts, because stopping means feeling.*

The silence from the field hadn't broken; it had only changed shape.

Crossguard's brightness felt thinner now, like light stretched too far across too much weight. The marble corridors echoed as if they *knew* what we'd brought back.

Cody and Johnny stayed close, weapons sealed but shoulders tight, armor heat still radiating like trapped stormlight.

Sarah walked a pace behind. Eyes cutting corners even here, scanning for threats that shouldn't exist in holy ground.

I led, but it didn't feel like leading.

It felt like falling forward, dragged by gravity. By what we'd seen, by what it meant, by the certainty that something had looked through me and decided to wait.

The dissatisfaction still lived somewhere in my chest.

I couldn't silence it.

None of us could.

We crossed the bridgeway above the western courtyard. Wind slipped through the arches, carrying the soft ring of ward-bells below. The sound should've been comforting. Instead, it reminded me of alarm clocks. Things that start moments you're not ready for.

The Entrance Hall rose ahead. Flame-shaped columns silvered in moonlight, ivy climbing like veins trying to reach a heart.

Two figures waited there.

Solomon and Sir Thomas.

They stood mid-conversation, Bibles under their arms, posture balanced between exhaustion and duty. Even from a distance, I could feel their attention. Steady, surgical.

Sir Thomas saw us first.

His gaze swept across us, across the burn marks, the dust, the exhaustion we didn't bother to hide.

"Well then," he said, stepping forward. "Judging by the state of you, I take it the mission was... instructive."

I didn't answer.

Didn't smile.

"I failed."

The word hit the air like a weight on glass.

No one moved until the echo faded.

Sir Thomas's expression stiffened.

Solomon didn't speak, but his focus narrowed as he'd just located a fault line under the floor.

"Go on," he said. Calm. Absolute.

So I did.

I told them how the field collapsed inward, obliterating any sense of reality while the trident carved light that twisted into distorted memories. The scene replayed in my mind. The trident's hum still jamming my teeth, as if silence itself had fractured. The Fallen Angel, feeling less formidable yet haunting, emerged from the void, their essence pulsing with the Zone's unnatural rhythm. But when I reached the part about *knowing*, my throat caught.

How it had read me. How every movement had been answered before it began.

How it hadn't fought to kill, but to *understand, manipulate.*

To taunt.

When I stopped, the hall held still, listening for something else I hadn't said.

Solomon nodded once.

"While you had been sent to defeat it," he said. "You were also sent to survive. And you did."

I shook my head. "If I'd been stronger, we—"

Sir Thomas's tone cut clean, gentle only in volume.

"This wasn't a test of power, Kayson. Even if there wasn't an outcome of defeating him. It was still reconnaissance."

He scanned the team. His eyes were sharp, his voice lower.

"And it confirmed what we feared. The In-Between at Sonorah is compromised. The people residing in that territory's physical realm will follow."

The words landed heavy, rippling through bone.

For a moment, I couldn't tell if the tremor in my hands was from battle or from what I understood too late. That surviving wasn't victory. It was a warning.

Without another word, Sir Thomas turned toward the hall.

Solomon followed.

We moved automatically, the four of us falling in step like reflex more than obedience.

The Hall should have been alive, Melinda humming over parchment.

Now it was hollow.

Her mug still steamed on the counter.

No owner.

Our footsteps filled the absence; each strike louder than it should have been.

Before us stood the mural of the First Judge. His armor was ancient, one hand holding scales, the other a sword of flame.

Solomon approached and placed his Bible into the carved palm.

The stone accepted it.

A pulse of green light crawled through the cracks, spreading like veins through waking skin.

The wall groaned to life and parted.

A corridor waited beyond; torches burning green and slow, air thick with old breath.

Johnny exhaled. "That's new."

Sir Thomas's gaze stayed forward.

"This isn't a hallway," he said.

His eyes met ours.

"This is the *Judgment Path*. Called only when *they* convene."

The word *Judgment* hollowed something in my chest.

Even the hum inside me faltered once. Then doubled back, louder.

The air changed as we entered. Not cold. Heavy.

Every step felt like it left fingerprints on time.

Portraits lined the walls. Knights from forgotten centuries, eyes following, expressions unreadable.

Among them, a few bore silver sigils over their hearts.

I looked at Sarah; she didn't meet my gaze, fingers brushing her Bible instead.

Johnny slowed, pointing. "That one—looks like—"

"Solomon," Sarah finished.

And it did.

Younger, sharper. Same weight in the stare.

"I thought you were Michael Branch," Johnny said.

"I was," Solomon replied, never slowing. "Before I was anointed."

No one asked what that meant.

At the corridor's end stood twin doors. Dark wood, wing-shaped handles, age soaked into every grain.

Solomon stopped before them.

"This Fallen wasn't merely strong," he said. "It listened. It watched. It let you leave. But letting you go wasn't an act of mercy. It's a message, a warning that Crossguard cannot ignore. If we turn away, if we dismiss what we learned, we risk creating something beyond our control," Solomon paused. His eyes lowering for a brief moment, as if contemplating his own words. His fingers brushed over a small, hidden emblem on his robe, a subtle gesture that betrayed a hint of uncertainty. Even he, in his wisdom, recognized the gravity of what we faced.

Light burst through in green and gold, alive, too bright after so much gray.

The hum we'd carried from Sonorah rose within it, as if recognizing its source.

The doors closed behind us.

And the air thickened.

Like sound itself had decided to kneel.

We stepped into a chamber that felt older than the castle surrounding it.

A perfect circle carved into the mountain's heart.

The stone glowed with faint gold veins, spiraling inward toward a Living Cross inlaid at the center.

It didn't shine; it *breathed.*

Every pulse underfoot felt like the echo of a vow made before the world had language.

Not history. Inheritance.

Solomon and Sir Thomas stopped at the circle's edge.

We stayed close behind, blades silent at our sides, hearts loud enough to hear.

Sarah whispered, "What is this place?"

Solomon's voice answered before any of us could exhale.

"This chamber," he said quietly, "is the Tablets of the Ten Commandments."

The words hit like gravity.

He continued, his tone steady, reverent.

"The Ten Commandments are the living pillars of Crossguard. The ten who embody the divine order of our faith. Each originated within a branch of heaven's virtue and bears the responsibility of leadership within the In-Between."

I felt my breath shorten.

I'd trained under representatives, learned from knights, and met a literal angel.

But this... this was another level entirely.

Something between mortal and eternal.

"They rarely convene," Solomon said. "And only when the balance itself trembles."

As he spoke, light stirred across the chamber.

Nine figures sat in high-backed chairs arranged in a wide ring. Each seat forged from a different sanctified substance: polished olivewood, volcanic obsidian, translucent crystal, gold-veined marble.

The air around them vibrated, each presence distinct yet woven into a single rhythm, like the chords of a single song.

Nine.

One seat is empty.

Sir Thomas bowed deeply.

Solomon stepped forward, his robes brushing the glowing veins.

The figures rose. Not with ceremony, but inevitability.

"Welcome, Judge Solomon," all nine said. The voice was layered, echoing as it had come through centuries.

"Thank you," Solomon replied.

We stood frozen inside the circle of light, four apprentices in armor still stained from battle, too small for the scale of what looked back at us.

"These pages," Solomon began, "have returned from direct contact with a Fallen Angel to be greater than the suspected Sloth rank, capable of anchoring and feeding on the Soulless Zone."

A low vibration rippled through the room, as if the chamber itself had taken a collective breath, the Light Cross at the center pulsing like the sacred space's heartbeat. The feeling spread outward, linking every presence in the room.

A sense of recognition filled the room, each of us in awe of the living, breathing chamber that carried them within its orbit of reverence.

"Worse," he continued, "the encounter anchored directly to Sonorah High."

One of the Commandments leaned forward, the air around them bending slightly.

"It's awake," a woman said. Her armor, liquid light, showed a near-white-yellow scar along her temple, glowing faintly.

Lady Zalika.

Solomon nodded.

"Which is why I believe the time has come to open their path toward the untraditional pace—toward the Armor of God."

The chamber responded.

Light deepened, the air trembled.

Even Johnny gasped without having a clue what was said.

"They are not yet knighted," another voice objected.

"They survived," Solomon said simply.

"They weren't meant to," Sir Thomas added. "And yet they returned. That alone demands attention."

Lady Zalika's gaze slid to me, steady and measuring. "I wonder, did you simply hear... Or did you listen?"

No warmth in her tone. Only recognition.

Sir Thomas gestured toward her and two others.

"To bear commandment rank, one must awaken at least three Armors of God. Lady Zalika. Sir David. Lady Melinda. Each has done so."

The name jolted me.

Melinda?

The woman who poured coffee and greeted us every morning.

She met my eyes across the chamber, and for the first time, I saw the light behind hers.

A gentle radiance that made the air bend.

"Why hide it?" Cody asked, voice cracking.

"It was never hidden," Lady Melinda said. "You simply didn't listen because you never asked."

Sir Thomas nodded to Solomon, "To achieve the sole rank of Judge of Crossguard like Solomon, it requires not only 4 of the armors. You must be anointed by the King of Crossguard , who sits not on the throne-"

Solomon lifted his hand.

He looked around the ring.

"But these Armors, they are not a metaphor. They are manifestations."

His tone deepened, and with each word, the chamber seemed to breathe.

"The Belt of Truth. Breastplate of Righteousness. Boots of Peace. Shield of Faith. Helmet of Salvation. Sword of the Spirit."

Each name pulsed through the stone.

Conviction rendered visible.

Solomon turned to me.

"Your enemy," Solomon said quietly, "was no ordinary Fallen. It was a Gluttony-class."

The voice carried the weight of someone who had seen each tier first-hand.

"What you faced. It doesn't simply devour; it convinces. It feeds through words, through want, through the places inside people that are already starving."

"The one you met stands at the threshold," he continued. "Where hunger learns to think. Where temptation starts to speak."

I swallowed. The voice of uncertainty echoed back to me, recalling a moment on the field: my whispered doubt about whether we should retreat rather than face the Fallen. That seed of doubt I'd ignored, the lie I'd told myself about our readiness.

"The one you met stands at the threshold," he continued. "Where hunger learns to think. Where temptation starts to speak."

I swallowed. "It tracked me. Mid-flash. It is anticipated."

Sir Thomas stepped forward, his tone low. "Because it remembers. The higher they climb, the more of their old structure they keep. Heaven's order doesn't vanish. It inverts."

Lady Zalika's voice cut through the silence, crisp as drawn steel. "You fought divine combat that has become perverse. To stand against it, you'll have to reclaim the original design."

Solomon's eyes were fixed on mine.

"To face it again, Kayson... you must awaken the first Armor of God."

Something drew tight inside my chest.

"The Belt of Truth."

The name struck deeper than thought.

I felt it vibrate in the place where my fear lived.

For a heartbeat, I tried to picture it. A real belt, forged of light, hidden somewhere.

Something I could find.

Because ideals wouldn't stop that Fallen.

"How do I find it?"

Solomon stepped closer, voice low and steady.

"You don't." The words pressed against the inside of my ribs. "The Belt of Truth reveals itself when the truth you carry is revealed."

In that still moment, beneath the weight of the chamber's silence, a memory flickered. A fleeting yet raw thought I'd buried since childhood. The silence masked by every brave face I'd ever worn. For a moment, it felt as if the breath of truth lay just beneath my skin, waiting to rise.

Lady Zalika's voice followed, softer but sharper.

"The first Armor manifests not in battle, but in confrontation."

"Some find it in the field," Solomon said. "Others in memory. Most, in a moment of choice."

Choice.

That word again.

It settled like a blade in my chest.

Because I already knew the moment was waiting for me.

Solomon's voice softened.

"This privilege is unheard of for the unknighted," he said. "But you've been marked. And time is short."

The Commandments fell silent, their light dimming back to stillness.

"We ask you to cast down your understanding and pursue the unprecedented. You are dismissed."

My throat was stuck with so many questions. Still choking on the frustration of having just been defeated, now being presented with riddles from ranks I didn't even know existed. We ascended the stairs in silence.

No one looked back.

The air's weight ascended.

At the landing, I stopped.

The others kept walking.

They didn't ask.

I sat in the Entrance Hall, hands trembling against my knees.

My room waited. Untouched, too ordinary for the weight in my chest; with no clues, no resolution to accept this defeat. To *face the unprecedented.* My head dropped back as I sighed.

The Belt of Truth.

Was it a weapon? A relic?

Something hidden in Crossguard's depths? What did they mean by manifestation?

If I could find it, hold it. Maybe I could fight *it* again.

But deep down, the smaller voice still whispered what I didn't want to believe.

I clenched my fists until the light bled out of my knuckles.

Whatever it was. I would find it. I won't run away from defeat again.

And I won't settle for anything less than the unprecedented.

CHAPTER ELEVEN

A FORGOTTEN STORY

D ays passed as I battled with the questions Solomon explained my failure with.

"Explained" makes it sound tidy. It wasn't. It wasn't a map. Not a path. Not even a name you could chase without bleeding.

It was a mirror you weren't ready to meet. It reflected back a version of me, not as I wished to be seen, but in stark, unvarnished truth. A detail that cut deep, the slight stoop of his shoulders, the creases of uncertainty traced across his brow, marks of battles both won and lost. The more I stared, the harder it became to deny what lay before him.

Waiting made the mirror itch beneath my skin. I checked it, found nothing.

We hadn't started a search. Not because we weren't willing. Because we had no idea where the world hid something that wasn't a thing.

Not knowing felt like hunger. Not for food, but for certainty and answers. It gnawed slowly at the edges of everything: my sleep, my drills, and my conversations. The whole squad felt it too, each of us restless with the same unfulfilled need. My thumbnail was chewed ragged, as if it could scratch away the intangible hunger that thoughts brought. This metaphorical hunger echoed the demands of a mind starved for understanding.

I sat in the commons, Bible open and mute. Printed words blurred. My mind replayed the fight, the trident's marks, the Fallen's pause, and Solomon's voice: *You will need your first Armor. The Belt of Truth.*

What if I'd moved faster?

What if I'd hit it first? Would I still need the Belt?

What if I wasn't just faster? What if I hadn't hesitated, and so didn't have a chance to learn?

"Kayson." Sarah's voice cut through the loop. She sat across from me; fingers laced around a steaming cup. Calm in shape; worried in the edges, where she never let worry show. If she was asking, I was visibly fraying.

"Yeah. Can't get it out of my head."

She gave a dry half-smile, knowing. "You're not the only one."

The bench scraped.

Two figures slid into the empty seats. They were out of place and older than us. Their softened Crossguard robes, were patched, showing they were lived in. It set them apart. The air shifted, ancient parchment and iron cut through the library scent.

They didn't look like instructors. They didn't look like students. They looked like people who had been somewhere most people only mention in hushed voices.

"Chasing the Armor already?" The narrow one grinned, but his eyes weren't smiling. His voice had an old-world cadence, each word clipped yet resonant, like echoes from a forgotten time.

Before I could place him, he stuck a hand out. "Judas Pilot. This is Herod." His introduction carried a formal tilt, an echo of false authority, every syllable weighted, as if names alone could conjure legacies long lost.

Their names felt like a coin dropped in water, rings going everywhere. For a second, I measured whether it was a joke. My skin didn't like his handshake. Too quick and too slick.

"New names, huh?"

"Old ones," Judas said, amusement in his voice. "If you believe stories." He sat back, grin still working, but his hands were steady, fingers scarred like a man who'd held more than tools. Herod was wide-shouldered, jaw like a slab of rock, watched us with eyes that had seen long seasons.

Sarah folded her arms. She doesn't waste emotion on strangers. If she's watching, they're on thin ice.

"You kids chasing the Armor awfully early," Judas continued, not missing her look. "Most pages can't. You're flipping ahead, aye?"

"The problem is, we don't even know what we're after."

Herod tapped the table's wood, as if testing for hollowness. "Nobody pointed you to a trail Judge Washington left?"

My mind jerked. *Trail? Washington? There wasn't such a convenient breadcrumb line. Not from anyone who'd been in the meeting.*

"A trail?" I echoed, not bothering to mask disbelief.

Judas leaned in, voice lowering the way people do when they hand you a dangerous truth. "George Washington. Once a Crossguardian, a Judge at that. He didn't stumble into an Armor. He left markers. Patterns. Not guarantees, but a place to start."

My mouth went dry. I'd skimmed history. He was a figure crowned later, not a literal Crossguard lineage in lectures.

Sarah cocked her head sarcastically, "So you're saying he hacked the Belt?"

"Not hacked," Judas said. "Learned the grammar. Left a rough dialect behind. Mount Vernon hums with echoes. Old houses keep truth better than men do." He let the idea hang there, like a coin you cast into a fountain and then it got offered back to you.

"Washington's markers were more than breadcrumbs; they were signposts in a heroic journey, whispering of a path tread by legendary figures. Each clue he left was a step echoing an age-old narrative. A quest not just for an object but for a timeless truth."

Herod shrugged. "If you're hungry enough, it's a start."

Why us? Did they just happen to hear us talking?

"You're the first foolish enough to chase the Armor early. Hunger like that gets a shot."

Herod stood, smoothing his robe. Judas pushed himself up at the same time. "Good luck, Ephesians." He walked like he owned every corridor he crossed. Herod followed. They folded into the hallway shadows and were gone, their black robes flapping in a trail. Two pages ripped out of some older book.

We sat in the quiet. A fluorescent light flickered in the hall, echoing our uncertainty. It was too easy: their timing, and Judge Washington's name. Still, it was the only path we had.

"That felt..." I started.

"Too tidy," Sarah finished. She'd already catalogued the gaps, always had that way. "Still Mount Vernon's in the physical world. Close to where you grew up, right?"

I felt the tug of home like a cord pulled tight. "Yeah. It's close. We've got nothing else to go on."

We went hunting for the others.

Cody and Johnny were drilling in the training room. Cody moved with precision, eyes flicking for threats. Johnny flowed, shadow striking in silent rhythm, all instinct and poise. Their unspoken readiness filled the space.

"We met a Judas and Herod." Sarah didn't even flavor the words. She laid the names on the table like a test.

Cody perched his eyebrows, "Judas? Herod? That's not suspicious at all. You're sure they're Crossguard?"

"They talked like us. Used Chapter protocols. Robes looked right. They walked as if they owned it."

"Or maybe they just wanted us to think so. Rogue archivists. Renegade wannabes in costumes." I met Cody's eyes. "I don't trust them. But it's our only lead." Desperation tasted like brass. I swallowed it down hard.

Johnny shrugged, towel over his shoulder. "If it's a trap, we'll find out fast."

Sarah slid a map over. "Prep tonight. We'll nail access, plan evac. Go tight." Her voice gave nothing away, jaw clamped hard.

Cody nodded. "Second it. One pull, and we get out."

"We move first thing in the morning," I said. The words felt like a cliff step.

"We go light. We go clean. And if anything smells off..." I let the sentence hang.

"Pull." Johnny finished. "Deal."

We packed quietly. Each checked piece of gear is like checking a piece of ourselves. I folded maps and stowed familiar photos. Not for help, just to steady my hand.

That night, I lay awake staring at the ceiling, thinking of Solomon's words and of a belt that might not be a literal object at all. The idea of something tangible, something I could hold, felt like a promise that could fill the emptiness inside me. But tonight was not just for thinking; it was for deciding: if the belt was a metaphor for truth, then I'd have to face and use that truth as the foundation for what came next. If it truly existed, I would begin searching for it. The decision pressed on me like unseen armor, turning my night into a quiet vow. I should have realized the metaphor mattered as much as the thing itself.

But hunger, this time, was the longing for answers and meaning. It doesn't care if the thing you seek is personal insight or a real artifact. Hunger is satisfied only by finding something real to hold onto, whether that thing is a new understanding or an actual relic.

At dawn, we would go find out whether Mount Vernon kept the truth, or whether we were walking straight into a trap.

We didn't use the In-Between to get there.

The Mount Vernon clue was part of the physical world. The fact that it was so public made it feel wrong.

No Soulless distortion. No flicker of resonance humming through the air. Just a place printed on every classroom poster and eighth-grade itinerary.

So, we took the train.

A commuter rail, with metal wheels groaning south out of D.C. and the smell of ten years of spilled orange juice baked into plastic.

We boarded early, passing for students on a field project.

Cody buried his training gear under a gray hoodie.

Johnny looked like he could belong anywhere; denim jacket, sleeves rolled, posture built for defiance. His head bobbing to probably Frank Sinatra.

Sarah tied her hair back and tucked her Bible deep into a side pocket.

I kept my Bible zipped in my backpack where I could feel its weight but not its pulse.

The train rolled on.

Suburbs blurred into trees. City concrete softened to river light and green. The rhythm of the rails filled the silence we didn't bother to break.

Sarah sat by the window, eyes fixed on the outside, as if she were reading for patterns.

Her reflection in the glass looked sharper than the world behind it.

Johnny sprawled opposite her, boots in the aisle, tapping a rhythm that didn't match the tracks.

Cody sat beside me, flipping through a glossy brochure that looked painfully mortal.

"According to this," he said, "we enter from the east gate, pass through the gardens, and the mansion dead center. Gift shop's real. Probably haunted by overpriced George stuffed animals."

I managed a smile that didn't reach all the way. "Good to know."

The landscape changed. The trees thinned, paths manicured, fences arranged with the kind of precision that pretends at freedom. History didn't vanish here; it rehearsed.

Something under that polish prickled against my awareness.

Not danger.

Just a distance that shouldn't exist in daylight. Like two worlds had been laid over each other, and one had forgotten the other was still breathing. If they collided now, the fragile peace could shatter, leaving us vulnerable to an uncharted reality, and the threat of being trapped between worlds forever would become very real.

"There's no reason this place should be hard to track," Cody said quietly. "It's public land. Cameras. Tours. But Crossguard's archives show static beyond the property line. Even the satellite scans were cut short."

Sarah's voice was almost a whisper. "That's what's wrong. It isn't off-grid. It's *on*-grid. Just filtered. Like the world edits what it can't explain."

Johnny cracked his knuckles, his gaze on the window. "So, what're we lookin' for? A secret basement under the cherry tree?"

"Maybe it isn't hidden," I said. "Maybe just disguised as normal."

"Or protected," Cody muttered. "People don't look for miracles in daylight."

The train slowed.

A bright voice came through the speakers, automated, too human.

"Next stop, Mount Vernon Historical Station. Please gather your belongings."

The train car came alive: tourists rising, bags shifting, a toddler crying over a dropped juice box.

We stayed still until the doors hissed open.

The platform glowed red brick in the sun. A white sign arched overhead: *Mount Vernon Station – Welcome to the Home of Washington.*

No fog. No omen. Just warmth, trimmed hedges, and a clear sky that felt like it was trying too hard.

We stepped off, merging with the slow stream of visitors: families, photographers, students, the hum of a hundred lives that didn't know how close they walked to heaven's leftovers.

Johnny leaned close. "This is surreal."

"Yeah," I said. "Like someone put a lock on a battlefield and called it a museum."

A guide greeted us at the gate with a memorized script about Washington's legacy and revolutionary virtue.

The words washed over me.

Because beneath the history lesson, the ground itself was listening.

The air didn't hum, but it *remembered*.

Not corruption. Residue. Like a prayer carved into the soil and forgotten by the one who said it.

We passed under the archway and onto the path.

The white siding of the mansion rose ahead.

Sarah drifted ahead, scanning not the people but the patterns.

The hedge lines, fence angles, and the rhythm between each brick.

Her eyes weren't searching for movement. They were measuring.

Cody held the pamphlet open between us, the paper crinkling under his thumb.

"Private Quarters," he said quietly. "East wing. Closed for restoration."

He tapped it once, eyes still on the building. "If I were a Judge trying to hide something in plain sight, that's where I'd leave it."

Johnny leaned over the rope barrier stretched across the gravel path, his grin small and restless.

"You think anyone would notice if we restored ourselves right through it?"

I exhaled through my nose. "We blend until we don't have to."

We moved with the crowd again, letting the flow carry us up the main path.

Kids laughed near the stables.

A re-enactor fixed his tricorn hat and posed for a photo with a family.

The illusion of peace was perfect. So practiced it felt rehearsed.

Every sound around us was too alive, too coordinated, as if someone had written the script for a normal afternoon and forced the world to stick to it.

But something else was breathing beneath the chatter: the brass plaques, the sunlight off glass, hiding just below the surface and waiting for discovery.

A quieter rhythm pulsed below the surface, faint as a heartbeat behind stone.

The kind of hum you only hear when you stop pretending not to.

The kind that lingers under polished marble when something sacred was buried beneath it, and the earth never forgot the name.

This estate hadn't just belonged to a president.

It had once housed a man who fought a war the world never recorded.

A Judge who carved scripture into history so deep the nation mistook it for revolution.

And somewhere between the walls, beneath the garden soil, behind a door painted to look unimportant, was a pattern. Listening.

The moment we stepped off the tourist path and into the upper grounds, the air changed.

Heat closed around my chest like a damp hand.

Not summer warmth, something thicker, patient, deliberate.

A breath that didn't belong to the weather.

The light was too golden. Too still.

The kind of light that didn't illuminate, it *preserved.*

No wind through the trees.

The sky looked painted and then forgotten by its painter.

We crossed the gravel loop toward a warped wooden sign:

WASHINGTON'S ESTATE — TOURS DAILY.

The paint had peeled, but the words refused to fade.

"Looks like this is it," I said, though my voice came out distant, as if sound itself were glitching.

Gravel became flagstone.

The path tunneled beneath interlocking oaks and elms, branches bowing inward like ribs protecting something sacred.

Light filtered through in thin ribbons, gilding dust that drifted but never landed.

We walked single file.

Boots on stone.

Breath shallow.

The deeper we went, the quieter it became.

At first, it felt like a weekday lull, the usual break in a routine day. But then, a shifting wind brought a foreboding reminder of the hours tilting away, pressing urgency into the still air.

The quiet turned sharp, carrying a scent of change, as if the world beyond the trees held its breath against an approaching storm.

No chirping. No buzz of insects.

Even our footsteps hit and vanished, swallowed by something that didn't want to carry them.

"Is it just me," Cody said, scanning the trees, "or did everyone else... vanish?"

He was right.

A minute ago, the path behind us had been alive. Families with strollers, a tour guide reciting patriotic lines by memory, the hum of laughter floating between the hedges.

Now there was nothing.

The gravel loop was empty.

The parking lot beyond shimmered in heat haze,

But there were no cars, no voices, no trace of movement.

Johnny turned a slow circle. "We didn't miss the tour schedule, right?"

Sarah checked her phone. "Still two fifteen."

No warning or static. Just a screen that suddenly meant nothing.

The silence wasn't an absence.

It was *an expectation*.

Like the world had taken one long breath and refused to exhale until we made the next mistake.

We rounded the final bend.

It rose out of the trees like a memory that didn't realize it had been forgotten.

Red roof. White columns. Symmetry so perfect it looks rehearsed.

Every detail was familiar, and yet the familiarity itself felt wrong.

From a distance, the white siding looked alive.

Up close, it looked preserved, defiant of decay.

The paint had no weathering.

The shutters cast shadows that are too crisp, to be honest.

The windows reflected the world, but nothing inside them. Despite the strange quiet, a single objective crystalized in my mind as I approached the mansion: *I needed confirmation of what Judas had hinted at. The Belt of Truth, that it was hidden somewhere in this place.* Clarity in purpose would guide me through the layers of history and secrets that threatened to overwhelm.

Sarah's voice lowered to a near whisper. "The clue's supposed to be... in there?"

"That's what Judas said," I answered. "We blend, find what Crossguard buried under the noise."

Johnny squinted at the porch. "Then where's the noise? Where's anybody?"

Cody's tone was barely a breath. "No staff. No security. No tourists. Not even footprints."

He was right again.

Moments ago, laughter had filled the air.

Now even the bugs were gone.

It wasn't just soundless. It was *selective.*

Everything that wasn't meant to witness this moment had been removed.

Sarah's eyes tracked the mansion's upper windows. "The whole crowd didn't just leave. They were..."

"Filtered out," I finished.

I climbed the steps first.

Each footfall landed too heavily, echoing against the air like a heartbeat in a sleeping body.

The handle was cold.

Not forgotten-cold. Memory-cold.

A chill that said someone had touched it recently and left the echo for us to find.

I hesitated, the weight of the moment pressing between my ribs.

Not danger. Recognition.

Then I pushed.

The door opened easily. No lock to resist, just permission.

Inside, sunlight pooled across the floor in slow, trembling waves.

The air smelled of cedar polish and something faintly electrical, like static trapped in the seams of time.

The house gleamed. Not preserved by caretakers, but by remembrance.

As though the building itself refused to forget what it once held.

Shadows stretched long across antique furniture.

Portraits stared down with eyes that looked wet, like paint still drying after centuries.

A staircase divided the room like an altar, and hallways on either side breathed in rhythm with the walls.

"I feel like we're trespassing," Cody whispered.

Johnny's reply came softer. "We are. But something wanted us here."

"Fan out," I said quietly. "If Washington left a pattern or a piece of the Belt, it's somewhere in this house."

We moved apart.

I drifted toward a writing desk beneath a portrait. Inks, quills, and parchment were arranged with surgical precision.

I touched the drawer handle; wood pulsed faintly beneath my fingers.

Not electric.

Alive.

Sarah examined the fireplace, fingertips tracing seams hidden by ornament.

Johnny knelt before a glass case, the saber inside untouched by time or dust.

Cody swept the wall with the edge of his light; the panel seams glowed faintly back, too exact to be random.

Everything felt poised.

Not abandoned.

Anticipating.

Then...

Thud.

A low, distant impact from above, a foreboding echo that thrummed like the tense vibrating of piano wires. Muffled. Heavy. Like something dropping through memory instead of wood. The air carried a hint of copper, foreshadowing the metallic tang of an imminent breach.

We froze.

No echo.

No draft.

Just the silence reshaping itself around the sound, tightening.

Johnny's voice dropped low. "That wasn't one of us."

Sarah was already moving. "Here. Panel seam."

Her hand found a notch along the right wall.

Click.

The wood breathed inward, revealing a narrow stairway climbing into shadow.

The ceiling pressed low.

The temperature shifted, denser.

Each step we took sounded like it was being written down.

It wasn't dust pressing on our lungs.

It was a memory.

Heavy. Unspoken.

Each board moaned underfoot like it remembered names it had sworn not to.

I realized the silence hadn't stayed behind.

It had gone ahead of us, waiting, breathing. Ready to explain where the world had gone, and why it had chosen to leave us here, to hear it.

The stairway ended in a narrow hall barely wide enough for breath.

At its end waited a single door: white paint cracked with age, hinges blackened, the brass knob dulled by fingerprints that had long since forgotten their names.

A thin seam of light leaked through the frame, gold bleeding into the dark.

It wasn't warm.

It was *intentional*.

The kind of light that watches to see who notices.

Something in my chest tightened.

Not a warning. *An Invitation.*

"I'll check this one," I said, my voice quieter than I meant. "You guys take the others."

They nodded. Sarah lingered half a second longer, her gaze fixed on the door like it had teeth. Then she turned away.

I stepped through.

The world didn't change all at once...

It *exhaled*.

The temperature dropped. Sound warped. The air thickened until motion felt like wading through thought.

The room looked ordinary, historic, and staged. But every detail *listened*.

Dust hung unmoving in the golden air, glittering like frozen breath.

A narrow bed stood to my left, the quilt tucked with corners sharp enough to slice.

At the far end, a desk waited beneath a tall window, afternoon light spilling across it like honey through glass.

On the desk lay a single book.

Open.

Unmarked by dust.

Its pages rose and fell in the faintest rhythm.

The ink jar beside it gleamed. The quill rested at a deliberate angle, not abandoned but *paused*.

I didn't notice myself moving until my hand closed around my Bible.

The book wasn't glowing. Not exactly.

It shimmered; light trapped between heartbeat and breath.

Alive in the quiet.

Listening back.

Each step I took landed softer, as if the wood beneath my boots was trying not to interrupt.

The handwriting wasn't Hebrew, Latin, or any angelic script I knew.

But it *knew me.*

Every line seemed to pivot slightly toward my gaze, curving like words tilting their heads to see who was reading them.

My pulse climbed into my ears.

Not panic but clarity.

That still moment before the storm, where your spirit braces for what it already understands.

I stopped a foot away.

The air between us felt thick enough to taste iron.

It hummed against my skin like heat remembered.

I reached out without deciding to.

The letters rippled, shadows bending beneath them.

"Yo," Johnny called from the hall, voice sharp but human. "You find anything in there?"

I flinched, heart hammering once like a struck drum.

"Just... this book," I said, steadying my breath. "It feels alive."

Footsteps approached. Sarah stepped into the doorway, eyes narrowing on the desk.

"You sure it's not a trap?"

"I don't think so." My words came out in a whisper. "It doesn't feel hostile. It feels like it's been waiting."

Sarah's brow knitted tighter. "That's what worries me."

Cody entered behind her, gaze fixed on the page. "That script, look at it. It's not like anything Sir David has shown us."

He was right. The letters were moving now.

Slow at first, then deliberately rearranging themselves. It was rewriting thought into order, like the page was searching for a memory it had almost recovered.

They pulsed faster.

Watching.

Studying.

Johnny leaned around Cody's shoulder. "Looks like cursed homework."

No one laughed.

The hum deepened too low for ears, resonating straight through the ribs.

The desk trembled, faint but steady, like something ancient stretching after sleep.

"Kayson." Sarah's voice sharpened. "Don't."

I didn't want to touch it.

But I was already moving.

My fingers hovered inches above the parchment.

The script froze.

Everything; light, sound, air... paused, as if the room were holding its breath with me.

"Kayson—" Cody started.

Too late.

My fingertips brushed the page.

A surge tore through me. Not pain, *recognition*.

Like pressing your hand against the skin of time and feeling it breathe back.

The room contracted inward.

Walls bowed.

The floor sighed.

Reality cracked not in noise, but in *meaning*.

Gravity folded.

My stomach turned inside out as color collapsed, light inverting into shadow.

The air compressed, then detonated, flinging every ounce of breath from my lungs.

And then came the laughter.

It coiled through the dark like a thought that had waited too long to speak.

Low. Mocking. Knowing what I had done.

Then, impact.

I hit dirt hard enough to rattle bones. Rolled once. Landed flat.

The air punched out of me in a gasp.

When I opened my eyes, the ceiling was gone.

Gray sky.

Still air.

A silence so complete it hummed.

I sat up slowly, fingers sinking into cold soil that felt too real to belong here.

Mount Vernon still stood ahead.

But drained.

Roof the color of ash, columns pale as bone.

Every detail intact, every hue erased.

The world wasn't moving.

We were back in the In-Between.

But not through verse. Not through permission.

We were dragged in.

Or triggered.

The book had been a key.

And I'd turned it.

Behind me, the others staggered to their feet, coughing against the still air.

Johnny rubbed his neck. "That sucked."

Cody winced, hand to his ribs. "Did we just... fall through reality again?"

Sarah's face had gone bloodless, her eyes scanning the grayed horizon. "We didn't open this gate. Someone unsealed it."

Her gaze cut to me.

"You touched it."

"I know."

"Why?"

"I don't know," I said, though the lie tasted honest. "It felt like it called me."

Cody exhaled, half-laugh, half-swear. "Fantastic. We're trapped in a colonial ghost dimension because you accepted a telepathic invitation from George Washington's diary."

No one argued.

Because he wasn't wrong.

And still. Beneath the silence, something stirred.

An unshakeable *presence.*

Ancient. Patient.

Watching to see if I'd turn the next key.

The silence after the fall wasn't empty.

It listened.

Every heartbeat felt borrowed.

Then.

Something beneath the soil stirred.

A hum. Low, distant, resonant through my chest. The same note that had pulsed from the book upstairs, now magnified until the air itself quivered. The ground flexed once, light sliding under the dirt like breath beneath skin.

I reached instinctively for my Bible.

My fingers found the spine, and the world answered.

Light flared through my hands, clean, absolute.

It threaded up my arms, chasing veins like rivers finding the sea.

My armor formed around me in one unbroken motion, gold threading across my chestplate, around my shoulders, down to the edges of my boots.

The hum deepened into a slow-rolling chord, shaking the horizon.

The In-Between reacted. It's air-bending, its color recoiling against the sudden presence of truth.

But my hands trembled.

Not from fear of the Fallen.

Not from the cold of this lifeless world.

From the weight of what I'd awakened.

That book, the thing upstairs, it hadn't just dragged us here.

It had answered.

It had recognized something in me and unlatched a memory buried older than any Crossguard's archives.

I felt it under my skin, like a second heartbeat, steady and patient.

A rhythm that didn't belong to flesh or fear.

Each pulse carried memory, not blood.

Something vast had stirred awake inside the walls of my soul.

Nothing evil.

Just awareness, as if truth itself had opened an eye.

And I had been the key that turned it.

The air shuddered.

A low growl uncoiled across the field, thunder dragging chains through stone.

The soil vibrated under our boots.

Mist pulled back in ribbons, peeling away the horizon like torn cloth.

Then shapes emerged.

Dozens.

Maybe more.

Fallen Angels.

They didn't spill from the fog; they marched out of it.

Not with the chaos I saw at Sonorah.

It was a perverse reflection of our own discipline.

Their black armor gleamed like shattered glass forged into uneven metal, jagged with guilt.

Each edge looked cut from vows broken and reforged into weaponry.

Smoke clung to their limbs like wet scripture, whispering verses in reverse. Praise collapsing into hunger, mercy twisting back into appetite. Their tridents burned with inverted flame. Light turned inside-out, feeding on its own glow. Every movement sent small motes of ash swirling through the colorless air, sparks of stolen illumination. They moved as one, an army of silence beneath a sky that refused to breathe. Every synchronized step hit the dirt like a verdict. Their purpose mirrored ours. Divine intent rewritten in defiance.

For a heartbeat, my legs wouldn't obey.

It wasn't panic.

It was pressure. Gravity folding inward. The world narrowing to pulse and consequence.

This wasn't a mistake.

It wasn't an accident.

It was *a revelation made tangible.*

Something buried in time had just remembered its name.

And now it was walking toward us to make sure we remembered ours.

The air thickened until it felt like moving through stone.

Each breath scraped.

Then...

A voice surfaced. Not from the air. From my memory.

Sir Thomas.

"For your talent to work, you need peace of mind," Even the memory of his voice was steady. The kind that could still a storm simply by naming it.

"Take a breath," he'd said once, the day I first lost control of my light.

"Then go for it."

I inhaled. Slow. Full.

And the sound of it broke the spell.

The tremor in my hands eased.

The glow along my arms steadied, then surged, scripture burning through gold, like veins of molten dawn. Focus locked into place, not found but *remembered.*

The Fallen moved.

No roar, or declaration.

Just momentum.

Like an idea deciding to erase everything that contradicted it.

But I wasn't frozen anymore. I opened my eyes, really opened them.

Cody rose at my left. His spear snapped into being with a crimson flash that bent the air around it.

Johnny strode forward. His warhammer bloomed from light to iron, orange fire crawling across the cracks in the earth.

Sarah stood poised, bow drawn, a silver arrow of living radiance notched and waiting.

The Ephesians. My book. My responsibility.

The silence fractured under the hum of purpose.

Heat returned to my chest. Not panic, not rage. The truth finding space to breathe again.

And in that moment, the understanding came whole and sharp as sunlight through glass. This was where the Belt of Truth began.

Not with a relic. Not with ritual. With a decision.

I wasn't hiding anymore. Not from fear, or leadership. Not from what the confrontation demanded of me.

The pressure didn't vanish. It transformed. It became momentum and command.

My feet rooted like pillars.

The breath in my lungs turned to language.

The words rose, not from my throat, but from the core of the light inside me. "Attack!"

The command tore through the field.

It didn't echo. Echoes require resistance.

It was simply authority incarnate. Truth given a voice.

Light met darkness halfway, melding into a brilliant arc. Beams lanced through the air, shattering the shadowed stillness, each ray a promise of resurgence.

CHAPTER TWELVE

ANOTHER IN THE FIRE

T his battle, this moment. It had to bring us closer to the Belt of Truth.

The thought rang louder than the shrieks of the Fallen Angels. It rolled through my ribs, over the clash of metal—louder than Johnny's hammer, keener than Sarah's arrows slicing air. The air tasted of copper and smoke, a metallic tang coating my tongue and teeth. It tightened my throat and honed my senses. A rasp echoed in the background, like chains scraping stone.

I vaulted skyward, armor veined in gold, my twin blades trailing like a comet through dusk. I pushed off from the fractured lawn, rising above the gray echo of Mount Vernon and the choking stillness of the In-Between. I suspended for a breath before gravity called me back.

Time loosened its grip.

Below, the field writhed with obsidian plates. Dozens, with even more behind them, poured out from the haze like a hive ruptured. Their tridents caught the gray light like molten spite made visible.

I dropped. My boots struck earth in a burst of gold. Heatless light surged outward. The nearest attackers unraveled instantly to ash, sifted fine by scripture.

"Attack formation, Ephesians!"

My voice cracked across the field with more authority than I meant. No one questioned it.

Cody veered left. His spear devoured distance, red arcs whipping from his strikes. Sarah, a breath behind him, had her bow already drawn. Her eyes were counting futures. Johnny cut right. The ground fractured with every stride. His hammer burned orange, a small sun remembering itself.

I ran into the center.

A Fallen lunged low, trident angled at my ribs. I twisted, catching its shaft on my blade, and snapped it in one strike. Another rushed in; I sidestepped, swept its legs out, and drove my blade through its chestplate. No screech, no theatrics—just ash, dissolving as its form faded.

These weren't like the Gluttony-class at Sonorah. The remnant math of angels inverted and spent. But they didn't break the way they should. They moved like a chorus with no soloists. Just one intent passed between mouths that didn't exist.

Was this how legends fracture?

We still held. Cody fought like thunder had learned control. Each thrust detonated intentionally. Each strike wasn't sloppy. Johnny was a meteor storm, ripping tridents free, folding armor with will and weight, laughing once, as if daring the world to hold.

Sarah didn't fight. She removed.

Arrow. Shift. Arrow.

Three down before the second blink. Precision as devotion. Her calm cut infection away.

We were winning.

Then the air changed.

Not sound. Sensation, like the crawl down your spine just before lightning remembers your name. My neck bristled.

A trident screamed through the fog.

I didn't move fast enough.

It hit flat against my ribs and hurled me backward. Stone steps rose to meet me. Pain shot clean through my side. My sword spun from my hand, skidding out of reach on dead grass. My chest locked halfway. My breath stuck between try and fail.

I pushed up. I didn't make it.

Silence rippled the field. Every Fallen head snapped to me at once.

They turned. Together.

And charged.

Not at Cody. Not at Johnny. Not at Sarah.

At me.

Why?

I forced my weight under me. Armor dimmed and steadied—barely. A flicker rolled across my chestplate like doubt made visible. Something had bent inside my armor or inside me.

The book pressed against my mind as if it had weight. The script. The touch. The way the world had cracked because I said yes. This was supposed to be the moment. This battle was supposed to reveal the Belt of Truth, not bury me further from it.

Footfall pounded the cracked lawn. Tridents rose.

And then the air split.

A boom with no thunderhead. Ground stuttered. Dust leapt—then fell like it had been told to.

A figure stepped through.

Sir Thomas. He didn't run.

He *arrived*.

Sky blue steel, edges silvered by a lifetime. His saber was already drawn. Light bent around the blade's line as if reality tried not to admit what it meant. His presence cooled the air, as though it commanded the temperature.

"Apologies for the delay, Kayson," he said, mouth tilting like a joke that wasn't worth finishing. "Had to fetch a little prudence."

"How—?" I choked.

"Sarah left a trail," he said, eyes already measuring the field. "Exactly where we'd look. Good work."

The Fallen didn't break stride.

They thundered toward us—tridents raised; their hunger arranged in ranks.

Sir Thomas' smile vanished. He glanced at me once.

"Behind me."

Then he moved—

—No, he disappeared.

Three lunged. Three ended.

He reappeared mid-turn, saber slicing through a spine. A second enemy attacked from the left; Sir Thomas ducked low, reversed his grip, and drove the blade up under its jaw. The third raised its trident—

A flick of the wrist.

Gone.

No flourish. No display.

Sentences. Judgments. Answers given at the speed of obedience.

It wasn't speed. It wasn't even talent.

It was *peace with purpose.*

He wrote through them as scripture writes through doubt.

Something turned in my chest. Not envy. Not idol-fire.

Desire.

To fight like that. Not because it looked strong. Because it looked *whole*.

I looked down.

My gold flickered again. Uncertainty tried to keep its footing.

The light I wasn't watching had dimmed without asking. *What if Sir Thomas hadn't come. What if Sarah hadn't left that trail. What if the world had decided different. We would've* **lost.** *I would've* **fallen.**

My jaw tightened. Not shame.

Recognition.

And if I'm chasing the Belt of Truth, that has to mean something. It can't only be a bruise.

But I didn't feel closer to it. I felt like I'd finally been handed a real test and almost failed it.

The ridge beyond the estate shivered.

Mist moved. More shadows. Dozens. Then more. Not a crowd.

A second wave. A third forming behind it.

Sir Thomas's head tilted, listening to what the world just admitted. "This isn't over."

I still couldn't move. Not yet. Not until the thought stopped skidding across my ribs and sat down where it belonged.

The Belt isn't performance.

It's alignment.

And I wasn't aligned.

Still fractured.

Still trying to make truth behave like a weapon you can hold.

I drew a breath that didn't want to arrive, felt it land, felt it stay.

Across the lawn, Cody settled into a stance like a red star finding orbit. Johnny twirled a shield off his hammer and grinned at something only courage could see. Sarah didn't blink.

The weight that wasn't crushing.

The weight I was *meant* to carry.

The Belt will begin when I stop pretending, I'm enough.

The second wave of Fallen lowered tridents. The sky refused to breathe.

And somewhere in my chest, a quieter pulse waited—patient, exact—asking if I was ready to let truth lead before I swung.

"Long time no see, kid."

The voice slashed through smoke like a spark in drought. Too casual, too human, wrong at every register. It cut through the ruins of battle like laughter at a funeral.

I pushed upright, ribs screaming with every inch. My sword hung loose in my hand, armor flickering between glow and gray. The air stung like burnt metal.

And then I saw them.

Judas Pilot and Herod King.

The haze parted for them as if it knew better. Their black uniforms looked untouched. It was as though the battle had politely stepped aside to let them pass. Their boots didn't sink into blood or ash; they skimmed above it. The ground bent like it recognized ownership.

Herod spun his sword lazily, his grin too bright for this colorless world. "Heard you were getting your tail kicked. Figured we'd drop in, fix your legend before it gets depressing."

Judas chuckled beside him—two curved blades drawn, their edges bending light instead of reflecting it. Not the glow of command. Not the pulse of holiness. Something else. Something restless.

They strode into the fight beside Sir Thomas as if choreography had been written for them long before we arrived.

In one blink Herod ducked low, his blade cutting clean through a Fallen's knee.

Judas twisted his swords, twin arcs of metal catching two tridents mid-strike, sending them whirling off harmlessly into the fog.

And yet...

Something was off.

Their armor shimmered, but not with the sunlit radiance that wrapped Sir Thomas. It quivered, almost nervous. The light bent around it.

Sir Thomas's armor looked like conviction forged in daylight.

Theirs pulsed like something remembering how to imitate it.

Something *inside* wore it.

I pushed the thought away. Help was help, even if it made your instincts flinch.

"What am I doing?" I muttered under my breath. *Standing here while the world* **burns**?

My friends were still fighting, bleeding, believing. Sir Thomas had appeared when I couldn't hold the line. That should have been enough to quiet the guilt.

It wasn't.

Because some part of me wanted to rise again. Not for pride, not even for redemption. But for truth.

My hand shook as I lifted my sword.

A flicker in the mist.

Instinct snapped first.

I turned, steel met steel.

A trident ricocheted off my blade, sparks scattering across the dead air. My arms locked, my footing returned. No pause.

I sprinted into the fog, vaulting over a charging Fallen, twisted in mid-air, and brought my blade down as I landed.

Light exploded where I landed.

Ash scattered.

One down. Thousands waiting.

The horizon blurred, shadows swelling and ranks reforming. The second wave became a tide, and the sky shuddered under its weight. Their growls rose into a low, unbroken hum, the sound of hunger older than language.

The air went black at the edges.

Something moved behind me.

I turned too slow.

A trident slammed into my shoulder, flat, but with force enough to throw me.

I hit the ground hard. Breath left me in pieces. Pain flared into static. My sword spun away again, a streak of gold swallowed by gray.

I gasped and got nothing. My hands scraped dirt. The world blurred.

This wasn't a fight anymore. It was erosion. A brief moment of stillness intervened. A solitary exhalation through the chaos, with only the soft sigh of wind catching its breath. An instance like a heartbeat that connects before breaking again.

Every second, another piece of myself wore thinner.

No rhythm. No clean victory arc.

Then... silence.

Not a pause. An *end*.

The hum stopped. The growls stopped. The clash of weapons, gone.

I didn't rise. I couldn't.

I just laid there, my cheek against the cold soil, ribs pulsing with every attempt at breath.

No footsteps. No shouts. Nothing.

When I finally rolled over, the field was empty.

Not cleared.

Not won.

Empty.

No Fallen. No bodies.

Only ash drifting in the air like snow that had forgotten how to fall.

The silence buzzed, hollow with absence.

Cody stumbled from the fog, dragging himself upright, blood staining his temple. He was alive.

Sarah knelt nearby, one knee down, bow still drawn though there was nothing left to aim at.

Johnny limped toward me, his hammer slung low, a hand pressed to his chest.

"You good?" he asked, his voice as if it had been sanded rough.

I nodded more motion than truth.

Behind us, Sir Thomas lowered his sword, eyes scanning the horizon the way generals do when they know the next sound will be worse.

"Is it... over?" I asked, forcing the words out through grit and breath.

He didn't answer at first. He just looked upward.

The sky stayed gray.

Still. Dead.

He exhaled. "If it were, the color would've returned."

I followed his gaze. Nothing moved. Even light seemed afraid to exist.

"No," he murmured, voice sinking into the air like a warning. "This isn't over."

And I felt it then that pulse behind the ribs.

Not pain. Not wound. A question.

Like the world was waiting for me to *answer* something I hadn't learned to name.

Behind me, movement. Not from the field, from the edges of it.

It was Judas and Herod.

They were watching. Not the fog. Not the ruins.

Me.

Their eyes didn't read curiosity. They read measurement.

For a heartbeat, I felt like a coin between two fingers being spun.

Judas tilted his head, voice smooth as glass.

"You sure you're ready for what comes next, Cavalier?"

I blinked, chest still burning.

He smiled, like he'd already seen the next page and decided not to warn me.

The pressure hit before the sound.

Not a weight. Heat.

The kind that squeezes lungs flat and turns air into liquid. Every breath became a drowning.

My armor groaned. Not metaphor. Metal *mourned.* The seals whined under a pressure they were never meant to meet.

Cody dropped to one knee, teeth bared, breath coming in shallow bursts that sounded like prayer.

Johnny froze mid-step, hammer sagging at his side.

Sarah slid behind us into perfect form, shoulders low, bow half-drawn. But she didn't speak. Didn't even blink.

None of us did. We all felt it. Not only *danger.*

Presence.

A silence so loud it became its own gravity.

The kind that presses through bone before it reaches ears.

And then... Herod and Judas were gone.

No flash. No exit. Just absence, like they'd been erased from the frame.

Sir Thomas still stood a few paces ahead, sword drawn, shoulders braced against something we couldn't see.

But his stance was wrong now.

The fluid grace had vanished.

He looked like a man holding a collapsing sky on his back.

"D-don't worry, everyone!" he called, voice straining, cracking around the edges. "I—"

The next word never came.

His mouth stayed open. His eyes widened.

He'd *seen* it.

Then came the laugh.

Low. Cold.

It slid through the world like sermon smoke, ancient and exact.

It didn't try to terrify. It didn't need to.

It only wanted to remind you that you were small and that it never was.

The world agreed.

Flame erupted behind Sir Thomas.

Not orange, *scarlet.*

A wall of molten light climbed the gray sky, claws of fire dragging heaven down by its ankles.

Two silhouettes emerged through it, black against the burning: Herod and Judas.

And something else. Someone else was in the fire.

Something that made the air kneel.

Sir Thomas turned just enough for me to see his face, and for the first time since I'd met him, he looked at the oncoming threat. "Impossible," he breathed.

He whipped toward us, voice a blade cutting through the roar:

"EPHESIANS—GET OUT! NOW!"

The order cracked open the sky.

A scream of metal followed.

A massive axe, doused in flame, howling, burst through the fire like a falling star.

Sir Thomas met it mid-swing, saber colliding with an impact that split the air into thunder and ash.

The axe spun back, caught neatly by its master.

He didn't walk out.

He *descended*.

A judgment given shape.

One half of him burned. Armor of scarlet and silver, regal in its lines, precise in its ruin. Flame coiled along the pauldrons but never lost control. It was *obedient* fire. His anger was disciplined into doctrine.

The other half?

Midnight.

Black metal scarred from within, matte enough to swallow light whole.

Smoke whispered from the slit of his helm, climbing upward like a forgotten chimney.

The split ran the length of him. Scarlet and silver against void and ash.

A man divided by history.

Each step cracked the ground.

He didn't announce himself.

He didn't need to.

"How the Commandments have fallen," he murmured.

The voice was silk through broken glass. Amused, weary, and completely certain.

I didn't know his name.

But my spirit knew I needed to.

He lifted the axe and the air flinched.

"Ah…" he said, helm angling toward me. "The next light of Crossguard."

Every word landed like a fingertip against my chestplate, testing, measuring.

Sir Thomas didn't blink.

"Don't think I haven't seen through you."

The Knight's tone softened, mocking concern.

"Your talent betrays you, Commandment. All your superior learning, all your faith, revealed a single truth."

He vanished in a streak of fire.

"You will suffer from Wrath."

The name struck harder than any blow.

Wrath.

The world shuddered as though it recognized him.

Even the light dimmed, ashamed.

Steel screamed. Fire detonated.

Sir Thomas and Wrath collided.

The shockwave tore us from our feet.

Ash spiraled. Sound shattered.

They reappeared twenty yards away, mid-air, mid-swing.

Every impact sounded like cities falling.

Sir Thomas moved with everything I'd ever admired: speed, faith, precision.

But something in his rhythm had fractured.

A hesitation.

A heartbeat too slow.

Wrath's breath didn't even change.

"How unfortunate," Wrath said, almost bored. "I had only graced you all my presence to speak with Crossguard's budding talents."

Sir Thomas roared back, saber flaring.

"You'll never touch them!"

Wrath smiled beneath the helm.

"No..."

He vanished again, reappeared low. His voice dropped, losing its seductive charm.

"Know your place, Commandment. "

The axe swept wide.

Sir Thomas blocked, but Wrath flowed through the recoil, pivoted, and the second swing carved clean.

Steel met flesh.

Sir Thomas's arm hit the ground before he did.

"Sir Thomas!" I shouted.

He staggered, blood blooming down his armor. One eye closed against the pain.

"No, Kayson," he rasped. "Take the Ephesians... get out. If he reaches you—I've already lost."

Wrath's laughter rolled across the field, slow and brutal.

And then. I was there.

Before thought.

Just *there*.

Sword raised.

Voice shaking but alive.

"Don't—touch—him!"

I swung with everything left.

Wrath caught my sword with his hand. Effortless.

"Ah," he said, almost kind. "The budding light."

Then his fist met my chest.

The world broke.

The ground and sky traded places. My lungs collapsed into dust. My ribs screamed. I tasted smoke.

He advanced slowly, each step rewriting gravity.

"I was premature in calling you," Wrath said. "You're not ready."

He lifted the axe.

"To reward you for your worthless efforts, I have the truth you came to find. You're too weak for peace and not worthy of giving me war."

I rolled—barely out of his way, heat blistering my skin as the blade sank beside me. The edge of the blade cut into my face. The wound sealed shut before blood could fall. I screamed through clenched teeth, dragged my sword toward me, and forced my knees under.

He came again.

I swung too slowly.

But the strike never landed.

Because someone stepped between us.

The axe cleaved through him. Through his back, and out his chest.

He didn't cry out.

He stood.

He looked at me.

Sir Thomas smiled.

Not with accusation.

With peace.

"Kayson..."

His voice was thinner now. A prayer running out of breath.

"It's okay. Please, go back to Crossguard."

Blood soaked his side; dripping out of his mouth, his free hand removed his armor and clutched his Bible.

"If he gets you... I can't win."

He whispered into the pages.

The words burned gold across his fingers.

The ground beneath me lit—sky blue script spiraling outward into a circle of light.

A way out.

Not for him.

Wrath tilted his helm, laughing, watching.

"Let me offer a warning..."

His tone dripped with almost tenderness.

"The brightest of lights..."

He raised one hand.

"...cast the darkest shadows."

Then the light took me.
I didn't *step* into it.
I was *torn* through.
"Sir Thomas!" I screamed as the portal snapped shut...
The last thing I saw was Wrath, walking forward through smoke.
Sir Thomas still standing.
Still bracing a smile.
Still refusing to fall.

Chapter Thirteen
Ashes of Wrath

E ven unconscious, maybe especially then, my mind refused to rest.

The darkness wasn't empty. Instead, something waited, poised just outside my awareness, for my first breath. An urgency stirred within.

I dreamed.

But it wasn't a typical dream.

No drifting abstraction. No half-built memories dissolving at the edges.

This was clear. Constructed. *Deliberate.*

Like something had decided it was time to show me the tape it had kept locked away.

Stone corridors unfolded around me—Crossguard, but older. Deeper.

Far below the New Testament Tower, the air turned heavy with history. Torches burned steadier than clocks. The walls breathed scripture carved in tongues I half-knew: Hebrew bending into Greek. Each verse glowed faintly, not painted, *remembered.* Dust hung in the air, tasting like old parchment. It whispered stories only the stone remembered.

Light lived here differently.

It didn't flicker. It knelt.

Three knights stood ahead. Young. Barely older than I was now.

The space acknowledged them the way a cathedral welcomes prayer.

One I knew instantly—Sir Thomas.

Younger by a decade, energy in his stance, that crooked grin untarnished by regret. His armor unscarred, his faith untested, his eyes still wide with the kind of courage that doesn't know it will one day cost everything.

Beside him—Solomon.

Still an apprentice, robes instead of a Judge mantle, but already carrying that stillness that comes from living half a breath ahead of everyone else. He didn't just *look.* He *saw.* You could feel calculation and compassion sharing the same heartbeat behind his gaze.

And the third—

I didn't know him.

Yet as soon as I saw him, a sense of recognition or alertness tightened inside me, as if I was responding instinctively.

He stood slightly apart—no insignia, no ornament. Yet his very presence commanded respect and implied authority.

Apprentice robes pressed clean, hands clasped behind his back, posture relaxed as if the world answered to his composure.

His features were refined, his smile patient—not the self-assured calm of arrogance, but the equilibrium of a man who had already made peace with every fear and still chosen to fight.

Sir Thomas laughed first, voice young and bright.

"I still can't believe you've already awakened a piece of the Armor. How long has it been, Kaiser?"

That name struck me—sudden, electric, like being called out in my deepest place, The name vibrating with buried meaning. Lightning, but personal.

Kaiser.

Something in it resonated through my ribs—an echo without origin.

I'd never read it in any archive. Never heard a Commandment whisper it.

Yet it felt *familiar,* like a memory that wasn't mine.

Kaiser's smile deepened—gentle, humble.

"A few weeks," he said. "Still learning its weight."

Solomon tilted his head, a scholar even then.

"They say it's hidden under Mount Vernon. Judge Washington's last stronghold. Was it true?"

Kaiser chuckled softly—the laugh of someone who has already outgrown rumor.

"No," he said. "The Belt isn't found in stone or ruin."

He stepped forward—closer.

Through the dream. Through Sir Thomas and Judge Solomon.

Through *time.*

And his eyes met mine.

The corridor's air thickened, pressing against my skin like the weight of unspoken words. Each breath seemed to slow, the atmosphere charged with anticipation. Then there was a moment—sharp and crystalline, suspended in silence. And then, the dream snapped taut.

He saw me.

A current surged through the air—cold, clean, absolute.

Every part of me wanted to step back, but the gravity of his gaze pinned me in place.

Then he spoke. Calm. Clear.

" 'You will know the truth... and the truth will set you free.' "

I'd read it a hundred times—above the chapel door, etched into sword hilts, recited before battles.

But here, it wasn't scripture.

It was *a command.*

The verse burned through my thoughts, all the way to my core, revealing a lie I had avoided facing. It exposed my persistent doubt: that without the armor, I was inadequate. The Belt of Truth not only uncovered this fear—it forced me to confront the belief that my strength was an illusion, hiding vulnerability I was afraid to acknowledge.

Sir Thomas's grin faded to awe.

"So, it's not a place," he murmured. "It's a moment."

Kaiser nodded once. "It's a confrontation."

His voice carried that same weight—truth spoken by someone who'd already paid for it.

"The Belt doesn't appear where you *search*," he said, stepping between the flickering torches. "It appears when your truth becomes too loud to ignore."

Solomon's tone was quiet, reverent. "Then... it finds you."

"Only when you're ready to wear it," Kaiser answered.

The torches dimmed.

Not extinguished—withdrawn.

As if the vision itself had finished its purpose.

Shadows lengthened. Gold cooled to gray.

And the corridor began to dissolve—stone melting into smoke, scripture unraveling into light.

I tried to hold on. Tried to ask—*What truth? Whose?*—

But the dream wouldn't allow questions.

Only understanding.

Before it faded completely, Sir Thomas glanced at Kaiser, voice softer.

"How do you know when you're ready?"

Kaiser smiled.

"When the lie finally hurts more than the truth."

The words fell into me as an anchor dropped into deep water.

The dream collapsed inward: walls folding, verses scattering.

But the echo remained.

The truth will set you free.

I woke into darkness that still remembered light.

My chest rose once—steady, unfamiliar, deliberate.

And in that breath, the realization hit: *this is why the Belt of Truth comes first.*

Not because it's easiest.

Because it's the only piece you can't fake.

It isn't about knowledge.

It's about the thing you keep refusing to admit.

The fracture you pretend isn't there.

The lie you've made peace with. And the longer you hide it—

The further you drift from who you were created to be.

A name surfaced in the silence.

Not summoned—*delivered.*

Wrath.

It didn't echo.

It *arrived.*

And something inside me shifted.

Not understanding. But recognition.

Like hearing a word I wasn't meant to remember.

The name carried weight that bent the air around it.

And the Belt, whatever it was— felt closer now, but not clearer.

It wasn't a revelation.

It was the beginning of a question I didn't know how to ask.

My fingers twitched. My breath caught.

I was waking.

Light came first.

Too white. Too *still.*

Not the warm, uneven pulse of torches in Crossguard.

Not the patient rhythm of sacred air between stone.

This light had no mercy in it. It was sterile. Surgical. It was as if the brightness pierced the air with cold precision, contrasting sharply with the chaotic drum of my heartbeat, which echoed in my ears. The juxtaposition of the unyielding light and the restless rhythm within my chest heightened the tension, painting the moment with a sense of unease.

A hospital room.

Sheets crisp enough to crackle when I moved.

Machines murmured in polite, timed intervals.

The walls were so spotless they seemed to resist recalling anyone who had ever suffered within them.

A window at the far end opened to trees, asphalt, and a sky that didn't know what it owed the living.

I blinked. Once. Twice.

Still here.

A shadow crossed the glass. A nurse or a ghost maybe. I couldn't tell. I didn't care.

The only motion I trusted was my own chest trying to relearn how to rise.

How... how had I come back?

Memory didn't flood.

It bled slow, each drop a blade.

Fire.

Axe.

Sir Thomas.

The name fell through me like metal down a well and kept falling. A silence so heavy it ached, grief collecting with every echo in the endless dark.

My throat moved before thought caught up.

"So that means... he didn't make it."

The voice didn't sound like mine.

It belonged to whatever hollow space grief builds when it finally decides to speak.

The door burst open.

"Hey—hey! He's awake!"

Footsteps rushed in. Voices collided. "Oh man, we were so worried about you," Cody jumped in first, his words rushed and sincere.

"You're lucky to be here," Johnny added, voice slower and careful. Sarah followed, softer and melodic.

"Thank goodness you're awake." Humanity tripped over itself to prove we were real. They talked over one another, words tumbling like broken glass in water.

I tried to listen, but the sound blurred, too vibrant for a body that had forgotten how to belong.

Only Johnny's voice surfaced, clumsy and sincere.

"Dude, we thought— I mean, we weren't sure if—"

"—You look terrible," Cody added, forcing humor that didn't land.

The room swam.

Their voices merged into one bright, impossible noise.

My lungs hitched, not from fear, just *tired*.

A nurse entered, raised one hand, and silence obeyed.

Even the machines seemed to listen.

Sarah crossed the room carefully. Each step deliberate, as though even kindness might bruise.

She sat on the bed's edge, hands clasped, voice a whisper.

"Kayson... how do you feel?"

How did I feel?

Like my soul had been carved out and replaced with a cold ache, the emptiness echoed with questions I wasn't brave enough to ask aloud.

But leaders don't say that.

Leaders hold their ruin quietly.

"Yeah," I said. "I guess."

Barely a word. Just vapor shaped into sound.

Johnny leaned against the window, eyes bruised from sleeplessness.

"You were out for two days—maybe more."

He didn't finish the rest. None of them did.

Sarah nodded. "We made it back. All of us."

Her voice cracked once—the truth slipping through mercy.

"But if it weren't for you and..." she stopped.

Cody finished for her, no cushion, no disguise.

"Sir Thomas didn't make it."

I closed my eyes.

So, it wasn't a dream.

The pain said so—the kind that begins where flesh ends, and faith begins.

I raised my hand, touched the new scar curving from my left eye down my cheek.

It burned faintly under my fingers—not like a wound.

Like a verdict—undeniable, final. Not a wound to heal, but a truth to be carried, written into skin as an unerasable mark.

Not an accident.

A *signature*. His signature.

Silence thickened.

When Cody finally spoke again, his voice came low.

"We held the report till you were stable. Medics say you'll be cleared soon. You're gonna be okay."

Johnny tried to lift the air. "Next time, you're not going alone. We've got you."

Sarah's smile was gentle, hopeful.

I couldn't meet it. Couldn't mirror it.

There was nothing left behind my eyes to give back.

"Judge Solomon wants to see you when you're cleared," she said softly. "We'll wait for you."

They left one by one—their footsteps careful, glances lingering too long.

The door clicked shut. Silence returned—not sacred this time. *Sharp.*

I turned toward the window.

But all I saw was *fire.*

Sir Thomas's silhouette standing against it—the arc of his sword, the voice steady even as blood blackened the steel.

That look belief offered like a shield I hadn't earned.

I blinked hard. No tears.

Just the ache of absence shaped like him.

The nurse came later armed with a clipboard, a neutral smile, and compassion on autopilot.

"You're healing well," she said. "No internal damage. Mild concussion, deep facial laceration, bruised ribs. You're lucky."

Lucky.

The word cracked somewhere between my ribs and reason.

I nodded.

But I didn't hear the rest.

Because when the door closed, the methodical spiral began.

Relentless. The mind rehearsing failure like liturgy. *If I'd moved faster, no metal would've burned. If I'd acted sooner, no ashes would've fallen. If I'd held his wound, I would hold no regret.*

Maybe Sir Thomas would still breathe. Maybe the Belt wouldn't feel so impossibly distant.

Maybe I wouldn't wear a scar shaped like a consequence.

If I'd done more than freeze while he bled for me...

My hands knotted the sheets until they strained.

My jaw ached from clenching.

He died saving me.

Not because I was **worthy**. Because I wasn't **ready**.

And now I carried his silence where his guidance used to be.

I could still hear him—not in battle, but before.

That last day in the training hall, his grin after sparring.

"Help me win, Kayson."

It wasn't a command. It was a hope.

*And **I** broke it.*

I buried my face in my hands and stayed that way for a long time. Not crying. Just *empty.*

Eventually, exhaustion claimed me. Sleep arrived like an unwilling surrender.

When I opened my eyes again, it wasn't morning. It was a memory. Flame. Wrath's helm. Sir Thomas's blood.

The scar on my cheek pulsed faintly. Warm, aware.

He hadn't spared me by accident. Wrath had *chosen* to let me live.

Because I was still useful. Because the chess board wasn't out of pieces.

The war had only changed its shape. And I was now a marked piece upon it—one etched in fire, and legacy.

Four days later, they discharged me.

The nurse said it gently, as if it were supposed to mean relief. Her clipboard clicked shut with the sound of closure, pretending to be mercy.

"You've stabilized," she said. "No lingering concussion symptoms. The scar's healing well. You're clear to leave, Kayson."

Clear.

A word that didn't fit.

I nodded, murmured thanks, and walked out of the room with the stiffness of someone who'd forgotten what his body was built for.

But I didn't go back to Crossguard. Not yet.

I went home.

Cody's family lived just outside the city limits, where suburbia forgot how to end and the forest hadn't learned how to begin. Their house wasn't large, but it *breathed*. Low ceilings, soft lamplight, furniture that had survived laughter. The fridge was a collage of drawings, magnets, and hope that refused to match.

The second I stepped inside, Mrs. Miles was already there—arms out, voice trembling somewhere between mother and medic. She pulled me in until her heartbeat drowned my own.

"Oh, honey. You're here. You're safe."

I nodded into her shoulder because words would have betrayed me.

Mr. Miles looked up from the kitchen island—the quiet kind of man who'd seen enough to recognize pain without interrogating it. He didn't ask questions. Just poured coffee into a chipped mug and slid it across the counter.

"Creamer's in the fridge," he said. "Cody's upstairs. Take your time."

The house smelled like cinnamon and detergent.

It smelled like *before*. But *I* wasn't the same anymore.

The climb up the stairs felt longer than any battle.

Each step echoed like a prayer in an empty chapel.

Every creak of the wood was a reminder of armor shattering, breath breaking, an axe sinking through light.

Cody looked up from his bed the moment I entered. He'd been typing something into his computer; the screen dimmed at once.

He didn't speak.

He just stood, crossed the room, and pulled me into a soldier's embrace—shoulder to shoulder, no sentiment, no performance.

Then he stepped back, nodded once. "Room's yours."

"Thanks," I said.

That was enough.

He closed the door softly behind him.

I didn't unpack. Didn't remove my boots. Just collapsed onto the bed.

No Crossguard order here. No consecrated steel humming in the corners.

Just an ordinary mattress, a faded quilt, the faint scent of home that no longer recognized me.

I closed my eyes, hoping for rest. I got silence instead—the kind that presses until you can hear your own heart.

Something was in my jacket pocket. I reached in and pulled out my Bible.

Warm—not from heat, but from *presence*.

I held it against my chest.

And the dream came back like a tide that knew my name.

Sir Thomas. Solomon. Kaiser.

The torch-lit corridor.

Kaiser turning—not to them, but to me.

"You will know the truth," he'd said, "and the truth will set you free."

I'd read those words on church banners, on walls, on mugs.

But in that corridor, they hadn't sounded like scripture.

They'd sounded like *an assignment*.

I sat up slowly.

Sunset filtered through the trees—orange bleeding into gray. The world outside moved forward, oblivious to the man it had left behind.

Sir Thomas would've known what that verse meant.

He would've felt it instantly, found its center, named its cost.

But I wasn't, Sir Thomas.

I was a scar that happened to breathe. A weapon with no rhythm. A student pretending to lead.

My hand traced the fresh line down my face. It still throbbed—not pain, exactly, but a reminder.

A mark that refused to fade because it wasn't just from battle. It was from *belief*.

Sir Thomas had died to save me.
And what had I done since?
Recovered?
Waited?
Existed?
The Armor hadn't appeared.

The Belt of Truth hadn't come, but the implications of its absence reach far beyond just my own inner turmoil. Truth, in its absence, became a silent threat lurking in the shadows of my consciousness. It whispers fears and doubts that ripple through every bond, every allegiance. What happens when deception festers in the heart of those meant to protect and lead? The stakes are higher than just personal confrontation; they are as wide as the world itself, where truth is the only shield capable of defending against the intangible battles within.

Because truth wasn't something you summoned. It was something that cornered you when you ran out of lies.

What truth have I locked away, afraid to face its relentless whisper? What is the one lie I still serve? This question lingered like a shadow, hinting at the Belt of Truth's true challenge.

Morning arrived slowly, as if uncertain I deserved it.

Cody knocked once, then eased the door open.

"We're heading back," he said. "Sarah and I thought we'd walk together, but..."

"I'm not coming," I said.

He hesitated. "Kayson—"

"I'm going back to school. Just for a while."

As I said it, Sir Thomas's voice echoed in the back of my mind, a whisper from a memory sharp as the blade he'd wielded. "Help me win, Kayson." It was a hope, an unfulfilled promise now hanging between my decision and his sacrifice. The reminder of what I'd left behind simmered beneath this calm, coloring each word with the weight of what it meant to avoid facing what must be confronted.

His eyes flicked toward the Bible on the nightstand, then back to me.

"You sure that's the right move?"

"I don't know what the right move is," I said, rubbing my eyes. "But I need to be somewhere I'm not a knight. Just for a day."

He exhaled through his nose—acceptance disguised as disapproval.

"Alright. You know where we are."

He left quietly.

The house felt emptier without them.

I dressed in silence putting on my hoodie, jeans, and sneakers.

No armor.

No scripture in steel.

Just fabric. Just weight.

Outside, the air was too clean.

Too *normal.*

I walked to Sonorah High in the half-light.

Sidewalk stretching ahead like memory made concrete.

I remembered the first morning I'd walked this path—Sir Thomas's instructions in hand, heart half-hope, half-fear.

Wondering if Crossguard was real.

Wondering if faith could burn.

Now I knew.

And the knowing hurt more than the battle.

Students filled the courtyard, laughing and scrolling through their phones, living in moments that appeared both casual and eternal. A group gathered near the statue, buzzing with excitement about an unexpected test, with whispers,

"He said it'll be multiple choice, but who knows with these pop quizzes?" The smell of fresh-cut grass mingled with the distant aroma of cafeteria pizza, grounding the speculative stakes in a reality where toned-down myths met school day mundanity.

Their world was intact.

They hadn't seen the way reality splits when truth demands blood.

I slipped inside.

The smell of linoleum and disinfectant hit like déjà vu.

A poster by the door read:

WELCOME BACK, SENIORS! MAKE THESE MOMENTS COUNT!

Moments.

They counted, all right.

I passed familiar lockers, familiar faces.

A teacher waved.

I waved back.

No one noticed the scar.

No one noticed the way I moved—half ready for war, half hoping for none.

The world had gone back to sleep.

But I hadn't.

By lunch, I sat alone at a corner table.

Didn't try to join anyone.

Didn't try to remember how.

I set my Bible on the table, unopened, humming faintly against the noise of normal life. But then something shifted. The hum grew louder, just for a moment, cutting through the cafeteria chatter as if the pages themselves were speaking, reminding me how easily normalcy could be shattered. A few heads turned, puzzled by the sound, before dismissing it as a figment of their imagination.

The page that found me wasn't one I'd marked.

It waited like a door I'd passed before.

"You will know the truth, and the truth will set you free."

I read it once. Again. A third time.

Not for *understanding*.

For *permission*. Because deep down, I knew it was about confronting that final moment. There, I had faltered, hesitated when action was needed most. It wasn't just a lie I had told myself; it was the tangible memory of that critical lapse, a silence I carried like a scar.

If I were ever going to wear the Belt of Truth...

I needed to change.

CHAPTER FOURTEEN
THE COST OF SURVIVAL

T he morning sun poured through the window, casting a warm glow that carried the faint aroma of coffee and dew-kissed grass. Grounding me for a moment in a sense of normalcy, as if the world hadn't shifted beneath my feet.

I opened my eyes, waiting for the comfort of waking, but it didn't come.

Instead, what I felt was resurfacing—an uneasy return to consciousness.

It's the kind that happens after you've sunk too deep. Your lungs scream for air, but you're still not sure you want to breathe. Your chest rises and falls—a mechanical response. But the absence lingers, heavy and cold. Your body moves. Yet your soul hasn't caught up.

The light cut clean lines through the blinds, landing on the edge of a battle-weary rug, touched by the faint scent of smoke. It fell on the carpet, brushing past a pile of worn clothes and a sword in the corner, remnants of a world not entirely ordinary.

But something *was* wrong.

Not in the way a storm is wrong.

In the way an echo doesn't finish.

The wrongness lived in silence.

In the weight beneath my ribs.

In fact, I didn't know if it was Tuesday, when Sarah usually made us laugh with her stories, or the Friday quiz I might have missed completely. Just that it was after the last red circle on my calendar marking the day everything changed.

I rolled out of bed slowly, dragging my feet to the edge like gravity had doubled overnight. My muscles didn't ache—not in the physical sense. But every movement felt expensive. Like I was burning fuel I hadn't earned.

I pulled a shirt from the floor—gray, wrinkled, probably worn two days ago. Didn't matter. My hands moved on instinct, one sock at a time. I looked in the mirror and barely registered what I saw.

The scar was healing.

Somehow, that hurt more than I expected.

It meant the world was moving on.

Even if I wasn't.

Cody's parents were already gone.

His mom had left a note on the fridge, written in her soft, curly hand-writing:

Have a peaceful day, Kayson. There's banana bread on the counter. Don't forget to eat.

I didn't eat.

It wasn't that I wasn't hungry. I could feel it. But my hunger didn't belong to me anymore.

But hunger drummed hollow inside me, an echo of life that refused to settle. It belonged to people who didn't carry Wrath's voice in their lungs, turning breath into smoke. The memory of a silent battlefield pressed against my chest. The tight knot in my gut reminded me of a man stepping in front of an axe to give me one more breath. Sir Thomas's death wasn't something I was ready to take in.

So, food? Yeah, it can wait.

I grabbed my jacket.

My Bible was already inside.

Warm.

Like it had been waiting.

Outside, the world had the audacity to parade normalcy.

Sunlight sprawled lazily across sidewalks. A breeze lifted the edge of a neighbor's newspaper and sent it fluttering across the yard. A sprinkler hissed somewhere down the street, spitting water in rhythmic arcs.

Some kid rode by on a scooter, earbuds in, nodding along to music I couldn't hear.

I envied him.

Not because he was happy.

But because he looked *unaware*.

People who hadn't seen what I'd seen—people who didn't carry the taste of smoke in the back of their throat—could afford to live like the world made sense.

The air didn't match the light. It clung thick and wet, like the sky had been crying before I woke up. Like it hadn't gotten around to clearing the grief. A sudden honk from a nearby car shattered the momentary calm, pulling me back in my tracks and making my heart skip a beat. The world outside intruded on my thoughts, reminding me that life continued its restless march, indifferent to my inner turmoil.

My shirt stuck to my back before I made it two blocks.

I walked with my head down, not because I was trying to avoid anyone, but because I didn't trust what I'd see if I looked people in the eye.

Would they know? Could they tell? That I wasn't just a tired high school kid, dragging himself toward algebra and vending machine lunches?

Could they see the sword still buried in my chest?

Every step toward Sonorah felt heavier than it should. The school loomed ahead. Unchanged. Within its facade, the crack in the pavement seemed to widen each visit. It mirrored the unhealed wound beneath my skin. The mural watched. Cartoonish, eyes reflecting a truth too raw. Tall brick walls kept their guise of welcome. They echoed more confinement than education. Schooling felt more like a ritual of constraint than liberation. Like, I didn't belong here anymore. Or maybe like I never had.

Normally, Cody would've been beside me, slinging jokes like arrows, nudging me in the ribs until I cracked a smile.

Normally, Sarah would've said something quiet, grounded. Something that made me think.

Even Johnny, with all his loud charm, would've offered just enough noise to drown out the ache.

But today?

It was just me. And ***silence***.

And the knowledge that I wasn't the same person who'd first stepped through those school doors months ago with a borrowed Bible and a head full of questions. That Kayson was gone.

"You were so eager, weren't you, Kayson?" I whispered to the air, feeling the weight of that lost self. And I didn't know if I missed him or pitied him.

I reached the front steps.

Other students clustered around the courtyard, laughing, showing each other memes, sipping iced coffees too expensive for high schoolers. Someone shouted across the lawn. Someone else blasted music from their phone.

I walked past all of it like a ghost.

No one stopped me.

No one noticed the scar.

No one looked twice.

Somehow, being unnoticed felt even heavier.

The bell rang, and the crowd moved toward the entrance in a wave. I followed, carried by the current, steps mechanical, breath tight.

Inside, the hallways looked exactly the same.

Lockers. Posters. Classroom doors with laminated syllabi taped to the glass.

But everything was smaller.

Not physically.

Spiritually.

This place, this school—it wasn't built to hold what I now carried.

And yet, I was here. By choice.

I found my old locker.

Spun the numbers without thinking. It clicked open.

Inside: a couple of old notebooks. A jacket I didn't remember leaving. A broken pencil at the bottom, like some tiny grave marking the last lingering memory of a hurried math class, and a doodle of an elephant captured in its final use. Each stroke hints at a lost normalcy.

I closed it again.

Hard.

I needed to keep moving. If I stopped too long, I was afraid I'd disappear completely.

I reached my first class and slid into a seat near the back.

The teacher walked in, cheerful and oblivious. "Alright, class, let's get started. Pull out your books, we're continuing with *To Kill a Mockingbird*."

The irony settled over me—learning justice while feeling so apart from it.

A book about justice. About truth. About the tension between what's right and what's real. I thought of Finch's unwavering bravery—the kind that stood silently, but defiantly, against a world so ready to suppress it. It mirrored the courage I had to find. The quiet determination to face the truth.

I pulled out my Bible instead. I opened it in my lap beneath the desk.

The pages turned on their own.

Again.

"You will know the truth, and the truth will set you free."

The words burned.

Not physically.

But deep.

Sir Thomas's voice still echoed inside. A ticking sound threaded through the silence, like the classroom clock—each tick a hint of Wrath's laugh. That sound scratched even my best memories of Kaiser's dream. I didn't know the truth yet. Not fully. But I was starting to see it wasn't just about facts. It was about *reckoning*.

The truth wasn't just a thing you learned.

It was a thing you *carried*.

And maybe... maybe I was finally ready to start carrying it.

Even if it hurts.

Even if it costs me.

Outside, the sun kept shining like it had no idea.

Inside, I sat quietly with a Bible in my lap.

Not open for answers. Just open to begin.

I drew the Bible from my backpack and held it up, letting the morning light spill over its cover. It wasn't just a book anymore; it was a compass, pointing me toward where I needed to be. *No more hiding.*

Even if I was afraid.

Even if it never came.

I wasn't the same anymore.

And maybe that was the start of something.

Or maybe it was the end.

I closed my Bible softly and looked up.

My schedule had been changed. What was once first period with Mr. Sterling, was now my second class of the day.

But the part that stung the most? The school hadn't changed.

Same beige walls. Same hum of tired lights. Same motivational posters clinging by a single thumbtack over lockers that had outlived their paint.

Even the clock above the whiteboard kept the same broken rhythm—tick, pause, tick—as if nothing sacred had ever happened anywhere else.

Everything looked normal.

Maybe it was—for them.

But not for me.

The Fallen hadn't touched these halls.

No tridents. No light. No proof that heaven and hell had brushed shoulders here just nights ago.

Only gossip between bells, and another history quiz waiting to happen.

I'd stood face to face with Wrath.

Now I was back in a classroom pretending to care about the past.

A punishment disguised as routine.

Every scrape of a chair, every whisper of paper sounded like mockery.

The world had already stepped over the ashes and kept walking.

No headlines.

No memorials.

No trace of Sir Thomas, as if he had never existed.

I stared at the doorway, half-expecting his silhouette—arms crossed, that quiet patience that once held a room together.

But the door stayed empty.

The only thing watching me now was the clock.

Tick. Tick. Tick.

I sat in the same seat as always—third row from the back, by the window.

The same desk. The same scuffed tile underfoot.

But everything else was wrong.

The hum under my skin wasn't nerves anymore.

It was the echo of what was gone. It resonated with the flickering light and the skewed poster, a dissonance that seeped into the room's bones. The space, once a place of learning, now felt like a poorly tuned instrument, each detail slightly off-key.

The room itself had changed—barely, but enough.

The shield above the whiteboard was gone.

The portraits of the historical figures were gone.

Blank walls patched with posters about *Excellence* and *Believing in Yourself*—the kind of lies people print when they've never had to bleed for truth.

The space had been scrubbed clean.

Sir Thomas erased.

History rewritten in dry-erase marker.

My chest tightened.

The Bible in my jacket felt heavier, like it knew something I didn't have the courage to admit.

And then the door opened.

She walked in.

Sharp lines. Jet-black braid.

A suit jacket instead of the soft sweaters Sir Thomas used to wear.

Every step landed like punctuation. Measured. Unforgiving.

Her eyes swept the room as if she were cataloging weaknesses, not students.

"Good afternoon," she said, voice clipped and clean. "Homework was due today. Pass it forward."

No hello. No introduction. Just control.

Her gaze found me. Locked.

"Mr. Cavalier, yes?"

I nodded once.

"You didn't submit your work."

Statement. Not an accusation.

"I was—"

"Hospitalization is no excuse," she interrupted smoothly. "If anything, you had fewer distractions than the rest."

I wondered if she'd practiced that tone in a mirror—perfect symmetry between judgment and indifference.

My ribs still ached when I breathed too deeply.

The scar still pulsed like memory made flesh.

Nightmares still dripped between every blink.

But I said nothing.

Arguing would've been like shouting at a gravestone.

"After class," she said. "We'll speak privately."

I nodded again. Mechanical. Hollow.

A different kind of battlefield, fought with locker dents and bulletin-board tacks instead of tridents. The scrape of metal against metal, the forgotten notes pinned with sharp tacks, each marking its own silent war. My jaw tightened involuntarily, a small tell of the unspoken tension, while the hallway lights flickered briefly, casting long shadows that danced like poised combatants ready to strike. Subtle cues that transformed words into weapons as lethal as swords.

Halfway through the lecture, the door burst open.

"Fortunately for you all," a voice boomed, "I have arrived!"

I didn't need to look up.

Of course, it was him.

Judah Walker.

He strolled in with arms spread, grin wide enough to be a weapon.

I hadn't seen him since Branch Selection.

I'd hoped I didn't have to have another pain today.

Ms. Mallory—apparently that was her name—lit up like a switch had been thrown.

"Judah, there you are! I was worried sick."

Worried sick?

The world tilted sideways.

Had I stepped into parody—or penance?

"Hey, teach," Judah said, pointing a thumb toward me. "Mind if I borrow Kyle for a sec?"

Kyle?

I almost laughed. I didn't.

"Of course," she said brightly. "Mr. Cavalier, step into the hall."

I stood, slow and steady, half disbelieving, half detached.

Part of me wanted to resist.

Part of me wanted to see what kind of ghost I looked like in fluorescent light.

The hallway hummed its lonely hum. The kind that fills every empty building between bells.

It felt like Crossguard's silence had followed me here, only thinner, sadder.

Judah leaned against the lockers, posture all performance.

"Man, heard you suffered a big loss." His grin twitched toward my face. "That's a gnarly scar."

"Yeah," I said flatly.

He blinked—thrown off by honesty—then smirked again, eager to regain the script.

"If I'd been there, Sir Thomas would still be alive."

I turned to him fully.

Not angry.

Just hollow in a way he'd never understand.

"Maybe," I said.

The smirk cracked—just a flicker—then returned, brittle and sharp.

"Honestly? Might be for the best. This new teacher's way hotter anyway."

I didn't react. Didn't blink. Didn't give him the satisfaction.

My gaze drifted past him—past the lockers, the college flyers, the thin world he still belonged to.

"Low standards, I guess," I said quietly.

That stopped him cold.

He froze—unsure whether I'd condemned him.

The silence tilted, heavy enough to make the air hum.

For the first time since I'd known him, Judah Walker didn't know how to play out his own scene.

He waited for me to flinch. I didn't.

Color rose up his neck. His hands twitched.

Then he spun on his heel and stormed back into the classroom.

I followed at my own pace.

The scar along my cheek burned—not pain, not memory. Restraint.

The kind that tells you progress isn't a straight line.

That sometimes moving forward feels exactly like falling back.

Because some wars don't happen on battlefields.

They happen in hallways.

Between words. Between breaths.

And the quiet that followed was louder than any roar Wrath had ever given.

Class dragged on. Seconds didn't pass; they folded, stretching thin as elastic pulled too far.

The hum of the lights became a pulse I couldn't sync to.

Ms. Mallory's voice cut through it in perfect, mechanical rhythm. A cadence built for bureaucracy, not breath.

Half the class took notes.

The rest pretended.

I didn't bother pretending either way.

The scar along my cheek itched again. Like the wound had learned to heal everywhere except the place it mattered.

Every pulse beneath it whispered the same thing: *still here, still marked, still yours.*

The clock ticked, relentless.

The sun moved across the floor, cutting light into measured rectangles that marched toward my desk like time itself was hunting me.

By the time the bell rang, the sound hit like a verdict. Chairs scraped. Zippers hissed.

Voices returned to life, as if someone had turned the volume of humanity back on.

Laughter. Plans. The shuffle of people who had never buried a mentor.

The world moved. I didn't. I stayed seated.

Hands folded on a notebook I hadn't touched. Still.

Listening to silence return like a tide reclaiming its shore.

Ms. Mallory lingered by the door until the last voice disappeared down the hall.

Then—click.

The soft sound of finality.

Not a lock, but a line.

"Mr. Cavalier," she said, her shadow crossing the sunlight, splitting into stripes along the tile.

Her voice was too even, too deliberate—like control was something she couldn't afford to lose.

"Do you know why I asked you to stay?"

I lifted my eyes.

"Nope."

A flicker, offense, maybe surprise, passed over her face before she reset it.

"Try showing some respect."

I leaned back. Not rebellion. Just gravity.

"I would," I said, "if you'd introduced yourself."

Her mouth twitched—caught between smile and strike.

"It's Ms. Mallory," she said sharply. "Don't forget it."

"Thanks for clarifying, Ms. Mallory."

Her restraint creaked, visible in the stiffness of her jaw.

It reminded me of glass—clear, cold, waiting to shatter the moment it decided you didn't belong.

She started pacing.

Her steps weren't rhythmic—they stuttered, uneven.

The sound echoed sharply off the walls, as if the classroom itself didn't like her being here.

"You didn't do your homework," she said finally. "You think this school is going to hand you sympathy because you came back with a scar and a story?"

My hand tightened around the edge of the desk. Not anger. Weariness.

Her words slid through me, searching for soft places to land.

"I don't expect sympathy," I said.

"Good," she replied quickly. "Because you won't get any. You won't coast through my class—whatever personal drama you've got going on."

Personal drama. Like I'd missed a pop quiz, not a war.

"You should be more like Judah," she added, tone brightening like his name lit something pleasant in her.

"He's been consistent. Focused."

I almost laughed.

Almost.

"Understood," I said instead. "I'll improve."

She stopped pacing and studied me.

Her eyes narrowed slightly, as if adjusting to a light only she could see.

It wasn't an inspection. It was an assessment. Like she wasn't asking *if* something was wrong—just *how deep it went.*

"You think you're clever," she said.

"I think I'm ready to go."

Confusion flickered across her face. just for a moment. Before she smothered it beneath authority again.

I stood slowly and slid my notebook into my bag.

"Anything else?" I asked, voice low, level. "I'd like to get started on tonight's assignment."

Her breath hitched—quiet, sharp.

For half a heartbeat, I thought she might say something else.

Something true. Something that didn't belong to this world. But she didn't.
"Fine," she said. "Whatever. Get out."

I closed the door behind me with a sound softer than hers—but heavier.

The hallway stood empty.

Late morning light slanted through high windows in narrow gold blades, cutting across the floor with the precision of judgment.

Each footstep struck too clean, too measured.

The echoes lingered in the air, refusing to die. The building held its breath.

Still, but not calm—an expectant stillness that pressed against the lungs.

My fingers brushed the Bible inside my jacket. Breathing under the fabric.

Then came the hum. Low. Subtle. Too steady for electricity or pipes.

A tone suspended between presence and memory—resonance caught in its own hesitation.

It passed through the corridor, more vibration than sound, then thinned into silence before I could follow it.

The quiet that remained wasn't empty.

It watched. It *knew* I was there. I didn't turn back. I kept moving.

By the time I stepped outside, the day had hardened into motion.

The world resumed its routine without apology.

Students poured through the courtyard, earbuds in, shoulders colliding, laughter flaring and fading as quickly as sparks.

A whistle blew from the track field.

A teacher's voice carried through an open window, too cheerful for the weight still clinging to me.

Everything moved, but nothing felt alive.

The color of the world had texture without temperature.

I adjusted my jacket.

The scar along my cheek pulled tight with each breath—no sting or ache, only presence.

That absence of pain unsettled me more than the wound itself.

Pain means there's something left to fix. This felt finished.

Somewhere, Wrath was still working. Still building his silence into shape.

Still watching to see if I would crack in the same places, Sir Thomas did.

But not yet. The day had only begun. Four more classes.

A war still whispered behind the hum of fluorescent light.

I gripped the strap of my bag and kept walking.

The hum was gone, but the memory of it stayed—a pulse beneath the noise of ordinary life, steady and waiting.

The halls were still. Not empty—hollow.

The same amber light from second period stretched thinner now, thinning to dust against the floor tiles.

It felt older than it should have been, as if time inside this building had aged faster than the day outside.

Lockers lined both sides of the corridor, dented and dulled, their metal faces staring back in silence.

Footsteps followed me—a second echo born from my own. Too perfect. Too rehearsed.

The kind of sound that convinces you you're not alone even when you are.

Sir Thomas used to walk this hall.

Not often, but when he did, everything sharpened.

The noise settled.

Even the light seemed to straighten its posture.

He had been the anchor—the quiet axis that kept this place from tilting into chaos. The kind of man who didn't have to shout to hold gravity. He made you believe Crossguard wasn't just a mission—it was a mirror.

A way to see yourself without distortion. And now he was gone.

Not fallen in memory—*scrubbed from it.*

The shield in his classroom. Gone.

The walls were repainted until the ghosts gave up.

The ache that spread through my chest wasn't the scar's doing. It came from the emptiness. From the neatness of forgetting.

Sir Thomas hadn't simply died. He'd been erased. And the world called that progress.

If I stood still, if I swallowed this silence without protest, then it felt like facing an empty plaque mount. Its surface scrubbed of honor, or a faded paint outline on a wall where a portrait of purpose once hung. The neatness of forgetting pressed against me.

A faint aroma still clung to the air, a scent reminiscent of Sir Thomas's favorite coffee, stubbornly lingering amidst the antiseptic cleanliness. It was as if the very walls were trying to erase the man, yet failing to completely cleanse his essence.

The Fallen didn't just corrupt through darkness and claws.

They moved through normalcy—through systems, through order, through people who called it routine.

Mrs. Mallory. Ms. Kartikak. Sonorah itself.

All wearing the same smile of purpose while truth quietly suffocated beneath the paperwork.

Wrath had called it once—*corruption that wears the mask of reason.*

He hadn't been wrong about everything.

I pressed my fist against my ribs, half expecting to feel the hum return.

Instead, there was warmth.

I stopped walking. Reached into my jacket. Pulled out the Bible.

The leather felt heavier than it had that morning. It seemed to pulse with a silent understanding, each creak whispering its readiness to shoulder the weight I could no longer bear.

Its surface breathed faintly against my palms. The pages loosened, caught an unseen current, and opened. A light flared between the lines—white fire folded into language.

Words shimmered into view, letters forming slowly as sunrise:

"To all members of Crossguard— As many of you are aware, we have lost the Eighth Commandment, Sir Thomas Sterling. His memorial and Bible Retirement Ceremony will be held tomorrow evening.

Attendance is encouraged. Stand in light."

The glow lingered for a breath, then dissolved. Letters faded until only afterimage remained.

I stared at the blank page long after it had gone dark.

A memorial. Not a rescue. Not a reckoning. A ceremony to dress the wound without treating it. Grief, packaged for public use. Containment disguised as closure.

My throat tightened until words became useless.

Was I even allowed to stand in that room?

To look at his name carved in marble when I'd been the reason his blood hit the ground first.

When did my hesitation become his sentence?

Would they tell stories about his courage, or would they edit the ending for comfort?

Would they lower their heads and promise never to forget, then forget anyway once the candles dimmed?

I closed the Bible.

The leather creaked softly—one more sound swallowed by the hallway.

My body remembered the way back even when my mind didn't.

Somehow, the Miles' house found me.

Dinner might have happened. Words might have been said. I couldn't swear to either.

The only thing that stayed was the pressure beneath my ribs.
Not grief anymore. Something older.
A seed taking root in the cracks Sir Thomas left behind.
It didn't rage. Didn't burn. It waited.
And I understood what it meant.
This wasn't just mourning a mentor.
It was the beginning of a reckoning.
Tomorrow will tell me. One way or another.

CHAPTER FIFTEEN
CONFRONTING THE TRUTH

I didn't sleep. Rest was impossible. Sleep requires peace of mind.

The room was too small for pacing, but I made it an orbit anyway—round and round, circling the same poisoned gravity.

The carpet learned the map of my thoughts before I did.

Every step landed, endless. A ritual without relief.

It wasn't emotion anymore.

It was as if the clockwork of my mind was grinding mercilessly, each thought turning into an echo of guilt.

Every time I closed my eyes, the axe returned. The arc of it. The sound of steel shattering bone.

Sir Thomas's voice. His eyes. He hadn't looked afraid. He'd looked *certain.*

Even as Wrath's blade entered, he looked at me with steady belief—his gaze unwavering despite the pain. The weight of the axe made my arms tremble, grounding me in reality. The cold steel seemed to steal away Sir Thomas's breath, yet he held my gaze as if to give me his last breath of faith.

I froze. Didn't scream. Didn't rise. Didn't move.

The armor that once obeyed my heartbeat stayed silent.

My strength dissolved when I truly needed it.

All that remained was a scar I hadn't earned. And a silence that refused to fade.

By two, I'd stopped checking the clock.

By three, I sat on the bed's edge, gripping my knees. A whisper in my mind confessed, *'I am terrified of what I have to confront.* The thought lingered, daring me to face the truths I'd avoided.

By four, I was pacing again—my reflection pacing with me in the dark window like a ghost rehearsing its regrets.

The guilt soured into nausea—a physical ache replacing the spinning re-morse that ruled the night. As fear shifted into something heavier, my mind grew quieter, no longer only troubled by what had happened, but by what it meant next.

The doubt congealed into something heavier, nameless.

Each thought scraped the same wall.

What right did I have to attend his memorial?

What was I really mourning—his death, or the illusion that I could've stopped it?

Was I mourning him...

Or the version of myself he believed existed?

Knighthood wasn't a calling anymore. It was a mirror, and I couldn't look into it without bleeding.

At five, the window began to lighten.

The glass was cold against my fingertips—clean, indifferent. It made the warmth in my hands feel borrowed.

Outside, dawn stitched itself across the trees: black into indigo, indigo into gray.

The first birds broke the silence with their small, reckless courage.

The world had already resumed.

It didn't care that it had cracked open days ago.

But I did.

Sir Thomas was gone.

And I was still here.

That was the injustice no sword could balance.

I pressed my forehead to the glass until the chill reached bone.

Somewhere out there, the memorial was being prepared—quiet hymns, folded Bibles, words chosen to hide the wound they were written for.

They'd make his death a ceremony, something gentle, containable.

But I had seen the truth.

The battlefield. The breath that left him. The fire that watched. That wasn't a eulogy. It was war.

And still, I hadn't decided if I would go.

If I deserved to stand among those who hadn't seen the blood, *who could still believe the light didn't burn?*

Yet beneath the fear, below the questions tormenting me, something older had already chosen. Here, doubt shifted to resignation: an acceptance settling in beneath the surface, not in defiance, but in yielding to what waited.

It wasn't bravery.

It was surrender—to purpose, to truth, to the pulse that refused to die beneath the ruin.

I turned from the window. The Bible waited in the drawer.

Its presence filled the room louder than any noise.

When my fingers touched the leather, heat met skin.

Not burning. Living.

It thrummed faintly beneath my hand, a pulse that wasn't mine but remembered me anyway.

It hadn't left. Not when I failed. Not when I fell. Not when I let silence become my language.

It hadn't asked for an explanation or apology. It simply stayed.

I lifted it out slowly, the way one handles something that's both relic and responsibility.

The weight settled across my palms. Not heavy by mass, but from meaning.

It carried too many echoes: Sir Thomas's voice, Judge Solomon's restraint, my own cowardice folded into the seams between verses.

I sat at the edge of the bed, spine bowed, the Bible resting in my lap.

I didn't open it. I didn't know how. I just held it.

I let it hum faintly against the hollow in my chest. Let it remind me that faith doesn't always sound like courage—sometimes it sounds like breathing through guilt and still staying.

This was the last piece of Sir Thomas; I could keep nearby.

Not his sword. Not his armor.

But his belief. The fragment of light he'd placed in my hands when he chose to stand between me and death.

My eyes burned, but no tears came.

Tears are for wounds that still believe in healing.

This wasn't that.

What lived inside me now wasn't grief. Something colder, heavier, like stone shaped by intent. It filled the space where sorrow had been. Not anger. Not vengeance. Just conviction. As grief faded into determination—a slow, unyielding kind that outlives readiness.

I inhaled. The air trembled against my lungs.

And before I could second-guess it, the words left me—not shouted, not forced—just spoken as truth, finally remembering its shape.

"Take me back."

The Bible pulsed once.

The air bent inward, as if the room itself bowed in acknowledgment.

As if the world had been waiting for me to mean it this time.

A low hum filled the room.

The kind of sound prayers make before they find a voice.

Gold light bled from the Bible's edges, spreading across the floor in slow, concentric waves. The light shimmered with a gentle intensity, flowing seamlessly without harming its surroundings. It was governed by a singular rule—the Word protected what it touched, infusing the world with its glow but leaving it unharmed. The carpet didn't burn. The walls didn't tremble. But the air remembered me.

The edges of the room softened. The world dissolving at the seams.

Streetlights vanished.

The echo of distant cars folded into silence.

I didn't pack a bag.

Didn't leave a note.

Didn't even tie my shoes.

I just stepped toward the light.

One hand wrapped around the Bible.

One heartbeat still deciding if it belonged here.

The air shifted—soft, final.

And the world fell away.

And then—

I had returned to Crossguard. It was dim. Silent.

The corridor outside the command wing, scripture faintly pulsing along the stone.

The place I'd been avoiding.

The place that had never stopped waiting.

I was home—or at least, in the place that used to be.

The Ephesians' quarters.

My room.

Untouched, preserved, suspended somewhere between memory and denial.

Light leaked through the window slit, brushing the walls with faint silver. Everything sat where I'd left it: socks over a chair, my training uniform folded too precisely at the bed's foot, the half-empty water bottle on the desk, dust softening the cap. The air felt like an old soldier, rigid, awaiting a command.

It hadn't been abandoned—only paused.

Every object seemed to have practiced stillness, as though the room itself had drawn a breath the night I left and never let it go.

Stillness ran beneath the quiet, faint and unsettling—the kind that lingers after something vital has left.

I stepped forward, my boots whispering against the stone, and the sound folded almost instantly back into the silence. There should have been noise here—Cody laughing through half a sentence, Sarah's calm voice balancing the chaos, Johnny's hammer tapping against the wall because rhythm had always been easier for him than words. Instead, the air pressed against my chest like armor turned inward, heavy and cold where warmth had once lived.

No Cody.

No Sarah.

No sound of the living.

Just me—and the space that refused to move on.

I faced the mirror. The scar, once raw, had settled—a line from brow to cheek, honest and final. My eyes, calmer now, held quiet storms. A small crack in the mirror echoed my own fragility. The ceiling fan spun slowly above, casting simple, shifting shadows across the floor.

I turned away before I could start dissecting what I'd lost. The silence closed over me, deliberate and absolute. For a moment, it tempted me—to sit on the bed, to let the stillness reclaim me, to vanish into a version of peace I hadn't earned.

But the weight of my Bible in hand denied me that mercy.

Its warmth pulsed faintly through the leather, a heartbeat both foreign and intimate. It didn't accuse or command—it reminded.

The memorial was already underway. I could feel it through the walls: that collective hush that settles over sacred ground when grief becomes its own kind of prayer. Even stone absorbs mourning; even air bends to reverence.

They were all gathered there, not for me, but for him—Sir Thomas—the knight who should still have been walking these halls, the man who had taught me that truth, when worn properly, was armor, not weight. The man I had failed to save.

Still, I opened the door.

The corridor greeted me as though it were unsure whether to recognize me. The torches flickered with tired flame, their usual gold dulled to the color of old parchment. The warmth they gave off reached the walls, the floor, everything but me. Each step stretched too far, echoing longer than sound should, as if the stone itself wanted to delay my arrival.

Crossguard was holding its breath.

And maybe, so was I.

The air felt thinner now, shaped differently around the absence that haunted it. I passed the open common rooms—emptied of laughter, emptied of light. The training halls lay still, swords sheathed, benches abandoned, the faint metallic tang of oil and sweat lingering like perfume from a ghost that hadn't learned to leave.

When I reached the archway near the courtyard, I stopped. Sir Thomas's archway. He had stood there every morning before drills, steam rising from his cup, eyes narrowed with that mixture of patience and amusement that made even failure feel instructive. The memory struck with the precision of an arrow—fatal in its tenderness. I couldn't linger. Some memories are too sacred to dissect.

So I kept moving.

Past the lower quarters. Past everything that pretended the fracture hadn't happened.

The skylights above offered no color—no gold, no blue—only a slow-moving gray that clung to the air like unfallen ash. It was the color of exhaustion. It suited the day. It suited me.

At the final corner before the Mess Hall, my body froze on instinct. My breath caught somewhere between dread and duty. Yet, within that fear, a question beckoned. *What lay beyond this threshold that my heart so longed to discover but feared to confront?* Every step I'd taken since waking had been leading to this place; it was not just a memorial I approached, but an answer I sought. No one had asked for me. No one had summoned me. And none of them knew what had actually happened.

If I crossed this final stretch, I wouldn't only be walking into a memorial. I'd be walking into their eyes—their expectations, their judgment, their forgiveness. And I couldn't tell which frightened me more.

My hand curled at my side, not from anger but from the shame of lateness—of absence—of surviving. I drew in a breath and held it until it hurt, until it felt earned. The air scraped raw inside my lungs, but I refused to let it go.

Not yet.

Then, finally, I stepped forward.

No radiance followed.

No power announced my return.

No miracle softened the path.

Just a boy—scarred, exhausted, carrying the weight of what refused to be buried.

The stone floor whispered beneath my boots as I walked toward the light spilling from the Mess Hall. It wasn't divine light; it was human—dim, unsteady, trembling on the edge of remembrance. The kind of light that knows it's fading and chooses to shine anyway.

And still, I followed it.

When I stepped into the Mess Hall, silence met me like an impact.

Not the absence of sound, its presence.

It moved through the air in slow, invisible waves,

The kind of silence that presses against skin and ribs until your own heart-beat sounds too loud, until you feel like existing is an interruption.

The room was full—fuller than I'd ever seen it.

Pages in their apprentice robes, faces tilted down.

Knights in polished armor.

Commandments lined the front rows, unmoving pillars of ceremony.

Even the representatives from the branches had gathered, their presence carved into stillness along the sides like stone sentinels waiting for something worthy of reaction.

Hundreds. Maybe more.

But not a single voice among them.

The torches along the pillars burned high, their flames restless but reverent, casting stretched, trembling shadows that reached for one another across the walls.

Above, the stained-glass windows that usually caught sunlight in radiant color were darkened beneath heavy black cloth.

No daylight would enter this place.

No gold, no blue. Only the living light of fire.

Grief lived here. Not as a visitor—as a resident.

It had moved in, made a home in the walls, breathed into the mortar and stayed.

You could feel it clinging to the floor, saturating the air until every breath carried the weight of someone else's loss.

And beneath it all— beneath the mourning and the reverence and the still-ness was something quieter.

I saw them before they saw me—the Ephesians.

Seated together near the front, second row on the left.

The four seats that had once felt like belonging.

Now they felt like a shrine.

Sarah sat in the outermost seat, posture perfect, braid drawn tight down her back, armor polished to a glow that didn't quite reach her eyes.

Those eyes, normally alive with thought, were fixed somewhere far beyond the room—somewhere she could think without feeling.

Johnny sat beside her, arms folded, jaw locked, his foot motionless for the first time in memory. Even the rhythm had left him.

Cody leaned forward, both hands on his spear's shaft, forehead pressed to the hilt as if in prayer or apology—it was hard to tell which.

None of them looked up. They didn't have to.

They felt me coming.

Each step I took sounded too loud, a heavy punctuation against the sacred quiet.

The stone answered back with that hollow echo reserved for tombs,

And in a way, that's what this was. Not a hall.

A tomb dressed as a sanctuary. No one turned. No one whispered.

But I could feel the eyes behind helmets.

Their silence had shape. It filled the air around me, folding over itself until I wasn't sure whether it was judgment or mercy that kept them still. And yet, I walked.

I reached our row and stopped.

The space between Cody and Sarah was open, waiting.

Whether by accident or intention, they had left it for me.

I sat down slowly, the sound of armor shifting breaking the fragile rhythm of the room for half a heartbeat.

Then nothing. No words. No glances. Only breathing.

The air thickened, that peculiar density grief always brings, as if the building itself were exhaling through the stone.

And then—movement.

A single, steady set of footsteps advancing from the far end of the hall.

Judge Solomon.

Even before he reached the podium, I knew something in him had changed. His gait was too deliberate.

Each motion is balanced between control and pain. He didn't move like the Judge today. He moved like a man whose bones remembered carrying more than they were meant to.

His right hand clutched the edge of the podium. His left remained still at his side.

When he raised his head, the torchlight struck the silver in his hair. And for the briefest moment, he looked both infinite and mortal all at once.

"Good morning," he said.

The words barely carried. They weren't for attention—they were for composure.

"As I'm sure you all know..." He hesitated. "...we have suffered a great loss among our ranks."

The sentence fell heavily, not against stone, but against hearts.

"Our very own Sir Thomas Sterling," Judge Solomon continued.

His voice was steady but stretched thin across grief, "Eighth Commandment. A fellow knight. My friend."

Each word landed like a hammer striking not an anvil, but a grave marker.

"He fought valiantly for our Order. Without him, I would not stand here as your Judge. Without him, I would not be who I am."

He paused.

His silence was louder than any sermon.

When he spoke again, his voice had shifted quieter, more human, as though he had descended from command to memory.

"I was blessed to know him most of my life," he said.

"He didn't just teach me how to serve. He taught me how to stand when I no longer wanted to. How to hold faith when the world looked ready to burn it."

His throat caught mid-word. He swallowed hard and didn't hide it. The silence that followed was total.

Even the torches seemed to lower their breath. Somewhere behind me, armor shifted—a faint clink of gauntlet against chestplate. Someone else's breath faltered, half a sob, half a prayer.

It was real now. No longer a ceremony. No longer ritual.

Just mourning.

"But grief," Solomon continued, his tone sharpening through the sorrow, "Though sacred, it cannot hold us forever."

The stillness trembled. "We cannot let his sacrifice dissolve into silence. Not when his blood still calls us to stand."

He straightened, one hand tightening on the podium's edge.

His voice rose—not in volume, but in conviction. "We fight not for vengeance, nor for pride, nor for the false comfort of peace. We fight for truth. For mankind's eternity in this unseen world."

A murmur swept through the hall, not chaotic, but collective—a shared breath of resolve that began in whispers and built like the tide.

"So, I say to you all—" Solomon's voice deepened, the kind of tone that no longer belongs to one man, but to the fire he carries. "Take up your armor. Take up your Word. And remember who we are."

He lifted his gaze, and when he spoke next, the sound cracked through the air like scripture made thunder. "We are Crossguard!"

The cry struck stone, rebounded, rolled through the hall like an echo of creation itself. "And we will not fall!" The hall erupted. A roar of voices, metal, and conviction.

Knights rose to their feet, weapons raised, helmets lifted toward unseen heavens. It wasn't rage. It wasn't vengeance. It was faith that made noise.

A storm born from grief refuses to die quietly.

But I couldn't rise. I couldn't speak. Couldn't move.

Their unity rolled over me like water over stone, and I remained cold beneath it.

Because every shout, every oath, every word they spoke in his honor fell against a wall inside me that hadn't cracked.

The sound was static. Empty.

They were roaring over a grave I had helped dig. They were celebrating a man I had failed to save.

The torchlight blurred at the edges of my sight, bending, twisting, reshaping into the glow of fire on the battlefield— the echo of Wrath's axe, the smoke. The look in Sir Thomas's eyes as he believed in me one last time.

My chest tightened. My throat burned. The strength I needed was gone.

The hall shook with life around me, but all I could hear was the static I created—the silence where his steadiness used to live.

My heart stuttered. My mouth moved before thought could catch it.

Barely a whisper, "...Help me." The words vanished before they could reach anyone else.

A hand found my shoulder. Not forceful. Not hesitant. Just steady.

I looked up through the sting in my eyes, hiding behind my helmet.

Judge Solomon stood beside me, framed by the dying torches and the re-treating echoes of the crowd. His face looked carved from something older than grief—tempered steel lined with sorrow, yet alive with an understanding that felt almost unbearable. His cheeks were still wet. His jaw was still locked tight against emotion. But behind it all was a kind of certainty—not peace exactly, something sharper. A decision.

"Come with me," he said quietly.

We walked away. Through the hall, still trembling from the storm of voices. Through ranks of Knights, lowering weapons in reverence. Through the tide of Pages and Chapters that parted instinctively at his passing. His hand never left my shoulder. And with every step, the noise behind us fell away until it was just the sound of our boots and the long echo of silence that followed. Not their silence. Mine.

Each step made it heavier.

Guilt had gravity, and it drags everything down with it.

We moved through the arched corridors, lit by the cold flame of memorial torches. The walls were lined with relics—broken swords, ancient banners, shields cracked from battles so old their stories had been written out of time. Every relic whispered the same question beneath the flicker of blue fire: *What did you learn from loss?*

The deeper we went, the older the architecture became—scripture not painted but seared into the walls. The words didn't reflect the light; they generated it. A dim, living pulse, as though the Word itself breathed beneath the surface.

We reached the circular chamber, back to the Tablets of the Ten Commandments. The place where decisions more difficult than death were made. The air here felt alive.

Alive, but heavy.

The round table stood at the center like an altar of purpose. And waiting there, already risen from their seats—were Cody, Sarah, and Johnny.

Their presence struck harder than the silence that followed us. Sarah's eyes were red and sleepless, her hands clasped like she'd been praying before we arrived. Johnny's gaze stayed fixed on the table, unreadable, shoulders coiled as though holding something fragile inside. Cody's eyes, steel and sorrow braided together, met mine first.

And when they did, mine fell.

Shame always bows before it speaks.

"It's my fault," I whispered, before my voice could decide otherwise.

No one moved.

No one interrupted.

"It's my fault," I said again, louder this time, the words shaking out of me in uneven gasps. "Sir Thomas fought so hard—and I wasn't strong enough. I wasn't fast enough. I fell into Wrath's trap. He died because of me."

The words fractured as they left me, scattering across the floor like shards of glass. My knees gave before I realized it. The sound of armor meeting stone was almost gentle. My forehead met the cold surface. Unforgiving.

"I'm sorry," I whispered, the phrase unraveling into repetition until it became a prayer that didn't know what to aim for.

"I'm sorry. I'm sorry. I'm sorry."

I wasn't crying anymore. There was nothing left to pour out.

Just the hollow trembling that follows a storm, when even the air feels emptied.

Then—warmth.

A hand on my back. Light, but unshakable.

Sarah.

"Kayson..." Her voice quivered through the quiet, soft but strong enough to reach the part of me I'd buried. "You don't have to carry this alone."

A tear struck my shoulder.

Then another.

Not mine—hers.

"You didn't take my uncle away," she said, her voice cracking mid-syllable. "He chose to protect us. He gave everything because he believed it was worth giving. And he wouldn't want you to break for it."

Another touch. Firmer. Grounded.

Cody.

"You're not alone in this," he said, voice low and deliberate. "We were there too. We all fought. We all failed in ways that hurt to remember. But this guilt, this burden, you don't get to hoard it."

He leaned in slightly, his hand steadying my shoulder, the weight of it anchoring instead of pressing. "You're our leader, Kayson. You and Sir Thomas saved us. Now let us carry you for once."

Then came Johnny's voice, smaller than I'd ever heard it.

Almost reverent.

"I didn't know," he said, words tripping into honesty. "I didn't see what it cost you. You looked like a hero, man."

He crouched beside me.

"But even heroes need shields. That's me."

His hand joined theirs.

Three points of contact—warmth against cold armor, light against the stone.

"Let us protect you," Johnny said quietly. "You're safe now."

The weight in my chest didn't vanish. But it shifted.

For the first time since Mount Vernon, I could breathe without feeling like it hurt to exist.

Was it okay to believe them?

Was I allowed?

My doubt's ran deep.

But their hands stayed steady, grounding me where faith had slipped.

Then Judge Solomon stepped forward.

And his voice—steady, no longer soft—cut through the stillness like judgment and mercy in the same breath.

"Kayson," he said, "are you so selfish that you'd ignore your Book—and worse, your friends?"

The words snapped through me.

I lifted my head, startled. "What?"

"This isn't about you alone," Solomon said. "You lost. That's the truth. But truth isn't meant to cage you. If you stay here—if you live inside that loss—it will rot you from the inside out."

He stepped closer, his shadow falling over me, his eyes alive with that fierce, sacred authority that could make the heavens pause.

"Pain has a purpose," he said. "Shame does not. Shame is poison, and you've been drinking it willingly."

The room held its breath.

"Doubt is a seed," he said. "And faith—the real kind—is the sword that cuts it down."

He paused just long enough for the words to settle.

Then: "You are the knight of light, Kayson. And light shines brightest where darkness forgets to hide."

The words struck deep, cracking something I hadn't realized had calcified.

The static in my mind broke apart.

The fog in my lungs lifted.

And for the first time in what felt like forever— I breathed.

Not shallow. Not trembling. Fully.

My spine straightened. My fists unclenched.

The world felt heavy again, but not unbearable.

Tears still fell—but they no longer belonged to despair. They were released.

I rose.

And when I looked at them—my friends, my teacher—I found words that didn't feel rehearsed, only real.

"Thank you," I said quietly. "All of you. Thank You."

They didn't nod. Didn't speak.

They just stayed.

And for the first time, that was enough.

Then my Bible pulsed.

Once.

Twice.

A breath of light expanded from it, quiet but absolute.

It filled the chamber in smooth, rippling waves.

I staggered a step back, blinded but unafraid.

The power that moved through me wasn't wild. It wasn't violent. It was peace wearing strength.

My armor responded before I did—igniting in soft radiance, the plates forming around me in layers of disciplined light.

It didn't overtake me. It aligned with me.

And then I felt it— the warmth around my waist solidifying, threaded silver laced with scripture. It felt alive, singing faintly in rhythm with my breath.

A manifestation. Its threads shimmered with words of light, each verse breathing.

At its center rested the emblem of Crossguard—the Living Cross—burning with restrained grace.

I stared down at it, understanding what it meant—not what it gave me. But what it demanded.

Judge Solomon's expression softened, awe folding into reverence.

"Congratulations, Kayson," he said, his voice quiet but heavy with pride. "You've found it."

My breath caught.

Because in that moment, I finally understood.

Truth wasn't just something I'd spoken. *It was something I had survived.*

And now, I wore it, as the Belt of Truth.

Chapter Sixteen

The Rise of Ephesians

The first morning began before the sky lightened, when everything was colorless and new.

I stood in the courtyard, dew slicking the stone beneath my boots. My breath formed a thin, stubborn thread that rose and vanished, making it seem like the air didn't want witnesses. Dawn hadn't arrived yet; night still clung to the leaves, and only a faint light pressed at the edges. Everything was suspended in a moment between what had been and what was about to be. The quiet wasn't just silence. It was a silence so precise, it was like someone taking account of what I would bring to the day and what the day would demand in return.

Warmth pulsed at my waist; the Belt was neither glowing nor humming, simply alive—a second set of lungs keeping pace with mine. Its warmth synchronized with my breath when my thoughts and actions met truth, linking my convictions to the world.

Judge Solomon stood beside me, his cloak blending with the dim light, as if he had stepped out of a shadow and was keeping it in place. He stayed silent for a long while. His presence alone made me stand straighter. When he finally spoke, his words were clear and purposeful, like a tool on a table, meant to be used, not to threaten.

"You will run five miles," he said. "No shortcuts. No pace but your own. Go."

No bark. No sting. Just a sentence that assumed I would spend myself and find what remained.

I ran.

The southern ridge took me past the outer walls and under old arches, where scripture had been worn smooth by time and touch. Then, I traveled into the thinning fog near the testing grounds, where it brushes against something mysterious. The cold air stung the scar on my face. The hills rose and fell again and again, demanding effort without offering comfort. My lungs burned—not just from pain, but because pushing myself so hard was like metal being shaped by heat. I kept going, not because Judge Solomon was watching or out of fear of failing, but because moving forward was the only way that aligned with my new sense of responsibility.

By the time I returned, my legs were shaking, salt on my lips, shirt clinging. The courtyard had settled into a pew-like stillness. Judge Solomon sat cross-legged in the center, eyes closed, as motionless as a verdict. He lifted one hand and pointed at the stone beside him.

"Sit. Breathe."

I obeyed—not from compulsion but from relief that someone had given me a simple task. When my eyes fell shut, the quiet surged in, and with it came the old noise—static with a memory's voice.

You weren't enough.

You watched him fall.

He believed you froze.

My chest tightened, and my fingers twitched on my knees. I sensed that Judge Solomon was reflecting on his own beliefs as much as he was testing me, searching for answers in the silence between us.

"Control your breath," Judge Solomon said, his voice gentle like turning pages. "You are not the voice speaking doubts. You are the one hearing them."

I inhaled—roughly. Exhaled, steadier.

The noise in my head didn't disappear, but it lessened, like ocean tides that pull away from shore for a while even though the moon still controls them.

"I can still feel it," I said, eyes closed. "Pressure sewn under the ribs. Guilt stitched into the seams."

"That is not pressure," he answered without opening his eyes. "That is fear, shaped by lies. And what breaks lies?"

"...The truth."

A small nod—a hinge moving. "Good. Again."

So I breathed, not to run away from my pain but to ground myself. I didn't try to erase my pain, but to keep it in its proper place—outside of my most important thoughts and decisions.

The days became routine, repeating like a practiced ritual until they shaped me. Each morning, running helped clear my mind. But a particular drill marked a real change.

One late afternoon, with shadows stretching across the grounds, I was tasked with holding a single stance, unmoving and strong as if my feet were rooted like a tree. The exercise was simple but demanded all my focus and patience. Requiring the deep awareness that makes a landscape still. My muscles trembled and burned as time passed, but the world grew quieter until nothing was left but my steady determination.

That evening, during our study by lamplight, I noticed a change inside—strength in my limbs and a quieter, lasting confidence.

By the third day, my breathing settled into its own natural rhythm, and my legs responded automatically. The Belt felt almost like a second heartbeat—not as a decoration or prize, but as a connection. It didn't make me stronger, but it seemed to clear away everything that blocked my true strength.

On the fourth morning, mist lifted from the lake in slow silver ribbons as if the water were telling the sky that rising is possible.

Judge Solomon folded his arms, "Activate your light."

Doubt returned, as familiar as a pain that always comes back when the weather changes. I didn't try to ignore it; I faced it. I let memories of Mount Vernon return, seeing them as honest experiences rather than wounds. The fear and pressure from my past were still there, but so were the choices to keep going. I remembered Sir Thomas's last words—not as a burden, but as trust. I took a single deep breath, feeling the Belt's support.

The air flexed.

A controlled burst of silver-gold light shone from my palm, spreading calmly over the shore and water and settling everything it touched. It almost knocked me backwards. I was surprised not by the wildness of the power, but by how hard it was to remain steady and peaceful in the face of such strength.

Judge Solomon's eyes flicked wider—just a fraction, the only luxury he grants is surprise.

"Controlled. Intentional," he said. "That is the beginning of mastery."

I dropped to a knee, breath ragged, ribs steadying. He knelt with me, voice lowered to the register where truth lands without bruising.

"Your talent was never broken," he said. "Your foundation was." Each stagger proved my talent was sound. Only my foundation had faltered, and now, with each step, it solidified.

We read by candlelight that night. The library was thick with dust and age, much like the scent of incense that lingers long in old cathedrals—a sign that prayer, spoken or not, remained. Judge Solomon passed me a worn training log, its edges frayed and ink blurred from time or tears. The name on the first page startled me:

Sterling, T.

"Did you know," Judge Solomon said, studying me rather than the book, "that he failed a mission worse than yours?"

I frowned. "Worse? Sir Thomas?"

"He lost an entire book of knights to a misread prophecy," Judge Solomon said, a half-smile at the memory's sharpness. "Carried it like a stone for years. Until he learned what failure asks that success refuses to teach."

His eyes found mine. "You are not here to be perfect, Kayson. You are here to be transformed."

The candle's flame flickered, but the room stayed steady. Even a small flame can push back the darkness more than you expect.

By the sixth day, my light no longer trembled when it touched the world. We sparred beneath a low ceiling of cloud, sweat mixing with dust, our circles cutting clean arcs into the field. Judge Solomon's blade spoke scripture; there was no wasted motion, no volume without meaning. He wasn't measuring strength. He was testing clarity. As we moved, I sought the space between breaths, not blades. This was where belief lived, where each lungful of air aligned with purpose.

Steel kissed steel. I pivoted. He stepped off-line. I struck. He turned my momentum and showed me the space I hadn't recognized between doubt and delay.

"You're hesitating," he said.

"I don't want to fail."

He slid my blade aside with the smallest economy, stepped through the opening my fear had left, and tapped the flat of his sword against my chest. Air left me; the ground introduced itself.

"You will fail," he said, calm as a closed book. "The question is whether you will rise."

I lay there long enough for the clouds to move and the old voice to try. It did not accuse this time. It yielded.

This is your fight.

On the seventh morning, we didn't run. He led me to the overlook above the forest where the valley stretched quietly under a sun that was starting slow on purpose, as if reverence were a speed. We stood without words. Silence, when it rests, is not empty; it gives back what clamor steals. The valley answered with nothing—*was that freedom or exile?*

"You've done well," he said at last. "But the next movement is yours alone."

A knot turned somewhere under the Belt. "What do you mean?"

"You carry the Belt of Truth," he said. "Few receive it. Fewer understand it. It will not make your truth lighter to bear. It will only make it impossible to ignore."

I nodded because there was nothing else honest to do.

"It will show you what is real even when you would rather look anywhere else," he added, and the gentleness in it hurt more than warning.

Wind moved through the upper branches below us. Leaves answered with a sound that always reminds me of prayer in another language. His voice changed—no harder, just unmistakable.

"Go back to the physical world," he said. "Finish what was started."

My stomach tightened. "You're sending me back?"

"I'm not sending you," he said, and the faintest curve touched his mouth. "I'm trusting you."

The sun lifted fully over the tree line. Gold poured over stone and field and the edges of my armor, and for the first time since Wrath split our sky, I didn't flinch from standing in it.

The next morning, I woke to birdsong instead of battle.

No stone walls.

No scripture pulsing in the air.

No clang of blades in the mist.

Just sunlight leaking through curtains and the soft percussion of wings brushing the edge of dawn.

The wind stirred faintly through the open window, lifting the linen in slow waves, cool against my face. Pale light stretched across the ceiling—ordinary light, thin and forgiving. But under my ribs, the ordinary no longer existed.

I sat up.

The room hadn't changed.

My backpack slouched where I'd left it weeks ago, the zipper half-open, a textbook tilting out like a held breath. The same cracked phone charger coiled on the nightstand. The same half-empty water bottle, untouched and stale.

Yet everything felt newly awake.

The Belt's presence lingered, quiet but certain, woven into the marrow like a second pulse. Not visible. Not heavy. Just there—settled truth, no longer something I wore, but something I *was*.

I pressed a palm against my chest.

A warmth answered.

The air seemed to notice, as if the room itself had waited for confirmation that I had made it back.

No static.

No voices gnawing at the seams of thought.

No old ghosts with knives for tongues.

Only breath.

And peace—unbroken, unearned, and, for once, allowed to stay.

At school, nothing looked different, which somehow made everything sharper.

Same linoleum—scuffed, dull, remembering thousands of shoes and none of their names. Same flickering lights that hummed like tired insects. Same white-brick walls that had trapped the same air for decades.

But I walked differently.

The ground didn't drag at me anymore.

Each step had weight, but not burden.

My shoulders were back, my chin lifted. Not arrogance. Alignment.

The scar caught a few stares—faint whispers, fleeting curiosity.

I let them look.

Let them wonder.

They couldn't know what the mark meant. And they didn't need to.

In history class, Ms. Mallory's voice drifted in and out, talking about empire and oaths, the rise and collapse of nations built on half-truths. I stared at the map, but what I saw instead was the edge of a different war— Sir Thomas's silhouette framed by flame, Wrath's voice sliding through smoke.

My pulse didn't race.

I didn't spiral.

I breathed.

The Belt kept me balanced. Not as magic. As presence.

Between periods, I passed Ms. Mallory's desk again.

Her glare rose on instinct—sharp, measuring. But when our eyes met, something faltered. A blink, small but real. For the first time, she looked away first.

The hallway felt one degree warmer, as if honesty carried heat.

By lunch, I had chosen solitude.

The cafeteria buzzed with the same noise it always had—laughter, trays and gossip that meant nothing to the sky. The rhythm of a world blissfully unaware of the other one bleeding beneath it.

I sat near the windows, half in sunlight, half in shadow, listening. Not to the room. To the undercurrent.

And there it was.

A flicker.

Not sight. Not sound. A shift.

A small jolt ran through the floor. A repeating thud from the vending machine echoed slightly longer than expected, hinting at something wrong. A small hum in the center of everything. The kind of distortion that makes the air taste metallic.

I closed my eyes and reached. Not outward, but inward.

It wasn't a call to arms. It was a call to awareness.

When I opened my eyes, the world looked the same—but one corner had dimmed.

Zachary.

A quiet kid. The kind of presence that fades into the background until absence would make more noise. He always sat alone. Always seemed harmless. But today, his posture was wrong; folded inward, jaw tight.

His hands fidgeted, rubbing thumb to thumb until his skin went pale. His eyes were locked on the table. Seeing something that wasn't there.

Then a brief shimmer came.

His backpack, rippled faintly in the air, silver at the edges, the sheen of oil atop water. A lie was trying to root itself.

A whispered "They won't miss me" lingered in the air, fading mid-breath, crystallizing the danger.

I stood.

No one noticed.

The buzz in the cafeteria went on—forks, laughter, a phone ringing two tables over. I walked toward him, quiet and steady. My pulse slowing with each step.

My fingers brushed the space near my waist; where the Belt would be if I had called it forth.

Warmth met skin.

Truth answered.

The shimmer broke apart, like dust scattering in light.

Zachary blinked, confusion rippling through him. He rubbed his temples, drew a breath that sounded like it belonged to someone who'd just been forgiven. Then he looked up.

Not at me.

At the world.

His gaze met mine only for a moment.

He didn't speak.

But silent gratitude glimmered there.

I nodded once. That was enough.

Evening found me at Cody's house.

His parents opened the door with warmth that felt more like faith than politeness.

"You look taller," his dad said, trying to sound casual.

Mrs. Miles tilted her head. "You feel different," she murmured.

I smiled, small.

They didn't need an answer.

Upstairs, my bag hit the same corner it always had, and the room seemed to settle. Recognizing something familiar wearing a new shape.

After dinner, I climbed out the window and onto the roof. The night stretched wide, sky rinsed clean of clouds. The stars looked close enough to touch—distant fire arranged in order, scripture scattered in light.

I sat cross-legged, Bible resting in my lap. My palm traced the cover's worn leather, feeling not for proof, but presence.

No glow. Just warmth.

The breeze moved across the shingles, cool and steady.

I breathed it in, slow.

No static followed.

No shadows curled behind the ribs.

For the first time in weeks, the silence didn't frighten me. It comforted me.

It was not the absence of sound. It was the presence of peace.

I listened to what remained.

Not Sir Thomas's death.

His choice.

Not Wrath's power.

My survival.

My phone buzzed softly beside me.

Cody: *Back to Crossguard. Judge Solomon's ready for us to try again. Are you ready for tomorrow?*

I stared at the screen for a long moment before replying.

Me: *No.*

A pause. Then I typed again.

Me: *Ephesians is ready. What happened last time won't happen again.*

Send.

The fear was still there, quiet and patient. But it no longer led.

I stood, stepping toward the roof's edge. The stars blinked above, distant witnesses to both heaven and Earth.

I lifted my hand. Light sparked across my fingertips—soft silver-gold.

Not fire.

Faith.

"To the one who gave everything so I could live," I whispered.

"I won't waste it."

The light danced once against the dark and vanished into the wind.

I turned back toward the window, feeling the Belt's steady warmth faintly within me.

Not stepping into a battlefield this time—but into a world still fractured,

And for the first time, I didn't just believe I could fight for it.

I *was ready to.*

The portal whirred under my boots as I crossed through.

Not trembling. Not gasping.

No fight against the current this time.

I didn't fall into Crossguard.

I *arrived.*

The world met me with balance—light bending softly across the marble of the Ephesians' floor, air charged but calm. The faint pulse of scripture running through the walls like a steady heartbeat.

For the first time, it didn't feel like stepping into another world. It felt like *returning home.*

Not as a survivor.

As something new. Refined in the furnace that had nearly unmade me.

The corridor greeted me in silence, reverent rather than empty. Lines of engraved scripture shimmered as I passed, each verse flickering once, as if bowing in recognition.

By the time I reached the training grounds, the doors had opened on their own.

Judge Solomon stood in the threshold; arms crossed beneath his cloak. The torches behind him painted him half in gold, half in shadow. For a breath, his expression was unreadable—then it softened, just slightly, into something that resembled pride.

"You're late," he said.

"I'm early enough," I answered.

He huffed, the ghost of a laugh. "Confidence. Good. Let's see if it's earned."

Two silhouettes broke from the shadows before I even crossed the courtyard.

Upper-class apprentices.

No names. No greeting.

Just motion.

Steel cut the air—one blade arcing high, the other sweeping low for my legs. Their timing was perfect. Brutal. Efficient.

I didn't flinch.

My body moved before thought caught up.

Breathe in.

Breathe out.

My sword met the high strike mid-swing, sparks leaping between us. I rolled through the pivot, ducked low, and swept the first opponent's leg from beneath him. The second lunged, but my stance was already waiting.

Parry.

Step in.

Reverse grip.

Steel kissed the hollow of his throat before his breath could finish leaving it.

He froze.

I eased the blade back. No flourish. No gloating. Just completion.

Both of them stared up at me, panting. The disbelief in their eyes mirrored by something quieter, respect.

I hadn't broken a sweat.

Judge Solomon stepped forward, boots whispering against stone. His gaze swept the courtyard, then landed on me with the weight of both judgment and benediction.

"I see the belt has changed you."

"It's still changing me," I said.

He didn't nod.

Didn't smile. Just tossed another blade.

"Dual wield," he said.

I caught it mid-air, felt its balance immediately—slightly heavier at the tip, meant for precision over force.

The next half hour blurred into scripture and motion.

Judge Solomon's voice filled the courtyard, his tone, even. A teacher shaping steel with syllables.

"From your center—always your center."

"Let the offhand wake up; don't let it follow."

Sweat pooled at my collar. My shoulders burned. Every clash echoed through the marble like a percussion instrument.

Two blades flashing, each struck a verse answered by another.

I stopped thinking about form. I stopped fighting the exhaustion. I moved until exhaustion became rhythm itself.

When static whispered at the edges of focus, I exhaled it.

When fatigue pressed against the wrists, I leaned into it.

When the Belt warmed against my core, I didn't reach for its power. I aligned with it.

The Belt wasn't a tool.

It was a mirror.

A truth that didn't strengthen me. It clarified me.

Motion became meditation.

I hit the final stance without hesitation. Without fear.

At the courtyard's edge, two figures watched.

Cody and Sarah.

Cody let out a low whistle. "He's a whole different guy."

Sarah didn't speak. She didn't need to.

Her gaze carried both appraisal and something softer—something like belief.

Judge Solomon's hand raised, calling the session to a stillness. The courtyard obeyed.

By the time Johnny wandered in, his usual half-grin had returned, flanked by two first-years he'd clearly taken under his wing. He dismissed them with a nod and leaned against the wall, watching.

Judge Solomon's voice carried across the courtyard—steady as a war drum.

"You'll train together for the next two weeks. The next Branch Trial approaches. It will not forgive hesitation."

Cody cracked his knuckles, smirking. "Good. We're better when it's hard."

Sarah crossed her arms, quiet but certain. "We won't fall behind again."

Johnny slung an arm across my shoulders. "Our captain's got divine plot armor now," he said, grinning. "We're basically untouchable."

I laughed, not because it was funny. Because, for the first time, I believed him.

Belief earned in fire and fracture.

Judge Solomon's gaze swept over us, weighing, measuring. When his eyes found mine, something shifted—resolve, yes, but also release.

"Kayson's performance today proved one thing."

He stepped forward, the courtyard lights catching faint silver in his hair.

"He's ready to lead again."

The words landed cleanly.

Not heavy. Not grand.

Right.

The drills that followed were relentless—designed to erase whatever confidence hadn't yet been tempered.

Sarah moved with surgical precision. Her strikes were arcs of mathematics and instinct, no wasted effort, no falter. She swept my leg out from under me and smirked as I hit the ground.

"You've grown," I said, rising with a grin that still burned with breathlessness.

"You disappeared," she countered, blade spinning idly at her side. "We had to catch up."

She lunged again.

And this time, I barely blocked.

Yeah—she'd caught up.

Cody came next.

If Sarah was speed, he was impact incarnate.

Every strike landed with the authority of thunder. But there was control now—refined momentum, not chaos.

"You're finally fighting like a tank that thinks," I said mid-swing, ducking under his arm.

He grinned through his breath. "Only took almost dying to figure that out."

We collided again, sparks scattering across the courtyard. The sound of our laughter broke through the rhythm like sunlight through storm clouds.

Johnny didn't join in. He sat perched on the stone wall, watching us with an expression that didn't quite fit his usual ease.

"I'm good," he said when Judge Solomon beckoned. "I'm more shield than sword anyway."

Then, quieter—"You know you're glowing, right?"

I froze mid-motion. "What?"

He squinted. "Your aura. It's different. Warmer. Fuller. It doesn't look like light anymore—it looks like truth."

The words sank deeper than a compliment. They landed where transformation hides.

That night, Crossguard slept.

I didn't.

I walked its corridors in silence. The torches hummed low, their light soft against scripture-lined stone. Every step carried memory—less pain now, more reverence. Each hall whispered of who I had been, and what it had cost to return as something new.

Eventually, my path led me to the chapel.

Torchlight bent across marble walls inscribed with the names of those who had given everything.

At the far end—a new engraving.

Sir Thomas Sterling.

The grooves were still raw, the stone paler where the chisel had cut.

I stepped forward, the air thick with the weight of prayers unfinished. My hand rose and settled just beneath the name. The stone was cool, grounding.

"You were right," I said softly. "The truth did set me free."

I didn't expect an answer.

But something shifted.

Not a voice.

Not light.

Just peace—quiet, sure, unmistakable.

It moved through me, filling the places that guilt used to own.

I stood there until the torches guttered low and the room settled into breathless stillness.

Then I turned, stepping back into the dark corridors of Crossguard. Not as a wounded apprentice chasing redemption, but as a leader reborn in the truth that had once broken him.

Ahead, I could already hear the faint hum of the world waiting.

The training grounds felt ancient—part cathedral, part coliseum, the kind of place where sweat and scripture had both left ghosts behind.

Sunlight poured through the arched window. Long beams slicing the air like searching blades. Dust drifted in them—slow, suspended—particles of memory too stubborn to fall.

The scent was old leather and iron.

And beneath it all—expectation.

A ring was drawn into the floor's pale dirt, barely visible now. Its edges worn smooth by years of combat and correction. It wasn't grand. It wasn't meant to be.

This was not a place for performance.

This was the line between *learning* and *loss*.

No training dummy.

No illusions.

No safety in rehearsal.

This wasn't an instruction. This was judgment.

I rolled my shoulders, the armor settling into place—familiar weight, but different now. Heavier, because I finally knew what it cost to wear it.

The Belt of Truth at my waist, quiet but certain. Every breath I drew vibrated through it.

It wasn't fabric anymore. It was a memory made real.

Across the ring, Judge Solomon waited.

The Judge of Crossguard.

The man who had watched me break and then dared me to rebuild.

His armor was carved with vines and scripture, older than any inscription in the Archives. The markings glimmered faintly in the light, each word alive with resonance. His helmet concealed his face, but I didn't need to see it.

I could feel the smile behind it, steady and proud. The kind of smile a craftsman gives when the flame finally holds the shape it was meant to.

Behind me, Ephesians stood at the boundary—Cody, Sarah, Johnny.

Silent.

Still.

But not waiting in fear. Waiting in faith.

This wasn't a test of strength. It was proof of truth.

Judge Solomon drew a slow breath, then lifted a hand to the emblem on his chest.

Light unspooled from it—silver and green, metal and scripture interwoven.

The light condensed, reshaped and hardened—becoming a longsword nearly as tall as I was. Its surface shimmered with living roots etched into the steel. When he swung it once, the air vibrated like the weapon remembered every war it had ever ended.

"At last," Judge Solomon said, voice low as thunder behind a mountain. "Let's see the fruit of your restoration."

I reached pulled my twin blades out of the emblem. Twin flashes of light—sharp and ready. Their awakening vibrated through the room.

I smiled beneath my breath. "Careful," I said. "It might be more than you're ready for."

His chuckle was genuine. Deep. "We'll see."

Then the floor cracked.

His blade slammed into the ground. The sound shook the bones of the room. Dust leapt into the air as roots burst through the earth like the veins of something ancient, remembering how to move.

They came alive—thick, gnarled tendrils surging upward, twisting toward me with jagged hunger.

I didn't flinch.

Didn't tighten.

Inhale—control.

Exhale—clarity.

No static.

No ghosts.

Only light is beginning to form at the edge of vision.

The world slowed. Not time—*perception.* The air stretched. The dust froze in the beams of sunlight, hanging there like suspended breath.

I moved.

Not frantic. Not wild.

Intentional.

One root snapped toward my leg—I pivoted, slamming the hilt into its base. Another came from overhead—I dropped low, rolling beneath it, then sprang back upright.

Every step, every swing felt preordained—muscle and truth in synchrony.

He was testing me. Not to punish, but to *measure.*

I drove forward. Two steps. Three. Then vaulted backward, using a lunging root as footing. My boots found purchase mid-air. I stabbed both blades down, anchoring myself against the pull of gravity.

Momentum built.

Light followed.

I swung through the air in a single arc.

Gold and white streaked behind me in an X that burned through the dust. The sun caught my armor mid-turn, scattering light across the room like shattered mirrors.

I landed hard.

Blades drawn.

Directly beneath Judge Solomon's chin.

Stillness.

Pure and absolute.

For half a heartbeat, I thought I'd reached him.

Then—*clink.*

His sword was already there. Point pressed under my jaw. His counter had been waiting the entire time.

Of course it had.

I exhaled a laugh. "Closer than last time."

"Much closer," he replied, lowering his blade.

The roots sank back into the earth like waves retreating from shore. The room settled, dust drifting down again in quiet reverence.

"You didn't win," he said.

I sheathed my blades. "Didn't expect to."

He turned, looking toward the others, his voice echoing just enough to carry. "But victory was never the measure."

I frowned. "It wasn't?"

He faced me again. Beneath the mask, his eyes caught the light, sharp but kind.

"Growth was."

The words hit harder than any blow.

"You've grown more in a week than most do in a year," he said. "You've found your footing. Your truth. You've earned your place again."

My pulse thudded once, clean and centered. Not fear. Not pride. *Certainty*.

He set a hand on my shoulder, "Ephesians will return to Sonorah," he said. "This time prepared."

I nodded. "Thank you, Judge Solomon. For everything."

He shook his head. "No. I only pointed the way. You chose to walk it."

He turned then, leaving the ring—and left the echo of those words standing taller than either of us.

I drew my Bible.

The pages fluttered once, alive, and script bloomed in soft gold across the first page:

Ephesians — Meet me on our floor. It's time.

My boots were already moving. Through the hall, past the arches. Up the spiral stair etched with Crossguard's oldest prayers.

When I reached the top, the doors were open.

They were waiting.

Cody.

Johnny.

Sarah.

No words.

None needed.

They stood in quiet alignment—shoulders squared, eyes forward.

I stepped into the center of the common room.

The torches lining the walls flared to life, flames bending inward. Gold light wrapped the chamber like sunrise, finding its home again.

My armor shimmered softly—white and gold threaded through with truth.

Cody nodded once, arms crossed—solid, unshakable.

Johnny leaned against the wall, grinning that easy smile that meant *finally*.

Sarah exhaled and stepped forward. Her gaze held mine.

"Welcome back, Kayson," she said.

The words hit the floor and stayed there, real enough to stand on.

And for the first time in a long time—

I smiled.

Not because I was whole.

Because I was *becoming*.

And becoming was enough.

CHAPTER SEVENTEEN

RETURN TO SONORAH

W e stood at the edge of something final. It was neither fully victory nor complete ruin. It felt as if we were holding hands in the darkness, balanced between hope and defeat. The air was thick with the smell of damp earth, merging with a tension that almost crackled around us. The ground beneath our feet shifted uncertainly, reflecting how unsure we felt in that moment.

The world seemed frozen, caught in a moment where even creation itself hesitated. Unsure whether to move forward or stop.

The air hung heavy, pressure humming with power waiting to be named.

Every heartbeat seemed to echo in the emptiness, swallowed by fog that moved without wind.

This wasn't a return.

It was a reckoning.

The ash-colored ground trembled faintly under our boots. In the distance, the fractured skyline of Sonorah shimmered through the haze. Ruined towers clawed toward a light that never reached them. Among the remnants, a rusted street sign lay half-buried in the rubble. Its faded letters proclaimed what once was a bustling avenue. Its presence whispered stories of a city alive with movement, now silenced by time. The sign stood like a forgotten sentinel. It bore witness to the moments before the fall, making the devastation personal and haunting.

A ghost of the world we failed to save.

A graveyard wearing the shape of memory.

I glanced sideways at the team beside me. They were no longer apprentices, no longer children trying to fill armor too big for them.

They were tempered. Hardened by loss. Unified by something more powerful than survival.

Cody stood nearest, his stance coiled with restless energy.

The crimson glow that always flickered around his armor burned steadier now.

His hands sparked faintly, arcs of lightning tracing his knuckles like veins of living electricity.

His power blended with the hum of the world itself. It was as if the lightning within him was tuned to some ancient thrum beneath the earth. The source was his unique bond with the elemental forces. A connection forged through training and sacrifice. It sharpened his resolve and focus.

"One swing for every bruise I took last time," he muttered.

Not to us.

To the air.

To himself.

A promise whispered in static.

Johnny adjusted the massive warhammer testing its weight. The metal gleamed faintly beneath the pale light, marred by cracks he refused to polish out.

He exhaled through his nose, steadily and in control.

"Forget bruises," he said, voice low. "I just want to punch that freak in the teeth with this thing."

To anyone else, it might have sounded like a joke, an attempt to lighten the mood. But there was an edge to his voice, an unspoken yearning for something more—to make things right in his own way. It almost did.

The humor had teeth.

Johnny didn't talk much about Wrath or Sir Thomas. But every time he trained, he hit harder than before.

Sarah stood slightly apart, the wind catching the edge of her hood. Her teal armor reflected faint silver streaks through the gray.

Her eyes were calm but focused, fixed on the horizon where the world began to break.

"I'm not here for revenge," she said, voice steady. "I'm here to finish what my uncle started."

The silence that followed didn't feel empty. It carried weight, like the world itself bowed its head for a moment.

No one tried to answer.

No one needed to.

That sentence belonged to all of us.

I turned toward the horizon. The border of the In-Between was not a clear line but felt like a long, trembling breath—caught between two worlds. Despite the stillness, an urgent feeling built, as though time pressed us from behind. The longer we waited, the stronger the hum in the air grew, reminding us we could not stand still for long.

Beyond it, Sonorah waited. Bleachers swallowed by ash and fog.

Back then, we stumbled out of this place—bleeding and afraid.

Now we were walking back in willingly.

We hadn't come to escape.

We'd come to *reclaim*.

The ground beneath my boots darkened as I stepped to the threshold.

The space between breath and purpose. The border between memory and mission.

"This is it," I said softly. My voice didn't need to be loud to carry. It carried because it was the truth.

Behind me, the shuffle of armor followed—three sets of boots finding rhythm in unity.

Sarah's eyes found mine first.

Not hardened.

Certain.

"Welcome back, Kayson," she said quietly. "Really."

I nodded once, the word *back* meaning more than she could know.

Johnny rolled his shoulders, his expression tightening into focus.

"Lead the way, Captain."

No sarcasm.

No smirk.

Just trust—clean and unspoken.

Cody grinned as he stepped up beside me, shoulder brushing mine.

"And try not to die this time," he said.

That one actually earned a breath out of me—half laugh, half relief.

"Not planning on it," I said. "Makes the paperwork a nightmare."

I chuckled, the tension easing for just a brief moment.

Then I looked at them—really looked.

Cody.

Sarah.

Johnny.

Not the ones I met in the beginning.

They'd bled.

They'd fallen.

And still, they had *risen*.

They had stared at despair and said, *I'm not done yet.*

And so had I.

Standing there, with fog shifting and the ruined skyline ahead, I realized something new:

We weren't survivors.

We were Ephesians.

No longer just a title.

A vow made flesh.

I raised my hand toward the horizon, the world ahead glinting with both ruin and redemption.

"For mankind's eternity..."

The words carried through the mist, heavy and sacred. I let the last two fall like scripture.

"Let's fight."

The Belt of Truth burned warm against my waist—steady and approving.

The fog parted.

And together, we stepped forward.

Leaving the fog and our hesitation behind us, we entered the field where Sonorah's original shatter mixed with the strange emptiness of the In-Between.

The ground was no longer whole.

It rippled beneath our boots like glass, remembering how it shattered.

Each step left faint prints of light that faded almost instantly.

The silence here wasn't empty.

It was *watching*.

Ash drifted through the air in thin spirals, rising instead of falling.

This was the same field where we had first fallen. Where our purpose had faltered, and the Ephesians had fled.

The Gluttony-class Fallen Angel turned Sonorah's shadow into a graveyard. It felt *watchful*. As if the field itself was waiting to see if we'd finally come back to finish the story we started.

A breeze brushed past, carrying with it an eerie whisper. For a fleeting second, distant children's laughter floated through the air, a contrast so sharp it seemed to fracture the stillness, tingling along my spine.

"Eyes up," I said quietly. The Ephesians moved into formation without a word.

Cody to my left, light flickering around his gloves.

Johnny to my right, warhammer balanced against his shoulder, the head still scorched from our last mission.

Sarah, behind us, bow drawn, the teal glow of her armor radiating in time with her breath.

We'd stood here once before.

This time, we'd come to finish it.

The fog thickened around our ankles, curling higher, carrying that old metallic tang—iron and smoke.

"I feel them," Sarah murmured.

Her voice didn't waver.

It carried the weight of a soldier who'd stopped asking *why* and learned to listen for *where.*

The air shifted.

A pulse.

Then another.

The ground quaked in short, measured intervals, growing stronger with every tremor.

"The Gluttony zone's still active," Johnny said, eyes narrowing. "Residual corruption."

"Then we cut it out," I replied.

The first tremor split the earth.

Cracks spidered outward, seeping black vapor that hissed when it touched the light from our armor.

They came crawling through— Sloth Class Fallen: Twisted, half-formed bodies of shadow and bone.

They devoured the light around them but were never satisfied. Their claws dragged across the stone, leaving trails of ink that writhed like living veins.

Johnny advanced, stance low and steady, cutting off the Fallen's lunge. As the creature launched, he swung his hammer with precision. The collision cracked—the creature dissolved into vapor.

Cody darted ahead, lightning streaking behind him, each impact a heartbeat of divine rhythm.

Sarah loosed two arrows in silence; each found a mark, each burned a shadow to ash.

But the tremor didn't stop.

It deepened. The fog convulsed.

And then it stepped through. The Gluttony-Class Fallen.

It emerged from the fracture like a memory crawling out of a wound.

The air squeezed around its body, light pulling toward its chest and vanishing into darkness, as if it devoured the world's glow.

Its armor still bore the same fracture I remembered. Not from battle, but from overindulgence in stolen light.

The armor's plates shone unevenly—some sections glimmered with false light, while others had decayed where sacred words were stripped away.

Lines of false verse crawled across its chestplate, glowing faintly before collapsing back into ash.

Each movement made the words shift. Language feeding on truth until nothing pure remained.

From the faceless helm came a low, rasping breath. The sound of something that didn't hunger for flesh, but for belief.

Its trident dragged against the stone, carving glyphs that smoked where they touched the air.

Every movement whispered hunger.

Cody inhaled sharply. "It's still here."

I nodded. "And it remembers who interrupted its feast."

The creature tilted its helm, amused.

A rumbling hiss spilled from its throat. A wordless invitation.

"Form the line," I said.

Johnny's hammer struck the soil; a ring of earth flared outward, orange and trembling.

Cody's palms lit crimson, arcs of lightning leaping between his knuckles.

Sarah's bow drew itself from the mist, teal light stringing the air into tension.

The Gluttony Fallen opened its mouth.

The pull began instantly. A force that didn't drag flesh, only *light*.

It reached through our armor, prying at the glow beneath our skin, drinking the warmth from our lungs.

"Resist!" I called, teeth locked.

"Anchor yourselves!"

The Belt of Truth seared warm against my waist—its light pressing outward, forming a pulse that broke the suction.

The others staggered, caught their ground. The vacuum snapped.

The Fallen shrieked and lunged forward, trident spinning through the haze.

Its charge cracked the field in half.

I met it head-on.

Steel met corruption.

Light met appetite.

The trident's three points carved arcs through the air, warping it like glass under heat.

I parried high, pivoted low, struck for the joint along its flank.

The blow connected. But the armor did not yield.

The light only branded scripture into its plating.

Behind me, the Ephesians moved as one.

Johnny drove forward, hammer-first, scattering the first wave of Sloth Fallen.

Cody's bolts detonated through the ranks, energy snapping like judgment across the ash.

Sarah's arrows burned teal, each one leaving a trail of light in the fog before striking.

"Keep its focus on me!" I shouted.

They listened.

Not because I commanded. But because they believed.

The creature's trident came down in a sweep that split the ground.

Johnny took the hit on a forcefield around his hammer, the impact hurling dust in all directions.

"Still standing!" he barked.

"Not for long," Cody answered, energy pooling in his hands. "Move!"

I dove aside.

The blast struck, a perfect hit, and the Gluttony Fallen screamed.

But then—It inhaled.

The energy Cody had released turned back, sucked toward its chest.

It was feeding—twisting truth into power.

Sarah dropped to one knee, whispering under her breath.

Her arrow flared, shot straight, and pierced the gap in its helm.

The suction faltered.

The beast howled—wounded, not slain.

Its armor glowed, pulsing with what it had stolen.

It had consumed too much.

Only the truth could end it.

I stepped forward, breath steady. As I moved, a shadow of doubt flickered in my mind, a whisper questioning if I was truly ready for this.

What if I faltered? What if the past repeated itself?

But the warmth of the Belt of Truth reminded me of every trial we had endured, every moment that had brought us here. I couldn't give in to hesitation; I owed it to those who believed in me.

The Belt of Truth flared white-gold.

Light cascaded across my armor, tracing living scripture down my arms.

The field brightened with every breath, until even the shadows trembled.

The Fallen swung, desperate, the trident shrieking through the air.

I didn't block.

I walked through it.

The impact hit—then broke apart, scattered by the force of what I carried.

My blades crossed in one motion.

Truth moved through them.

The cut was clean.

Not savage... Final.

The Gluttony Fallen froze mid-screech, its body flickering between holy and hollow. It dissolved into ash that rose like smoke and vanished into silence.

The field exhaled.

Every Sloth Fallen crumbled, their forms unraveling into harmless mist.

Only the faint scent of ozone and rain remained.

Sarah lowered her bow, the teal fading from her armor.

"That wasn't the same Gluttony," she said softly. "It was worse."

Cody kicked through the ash, sparks of fading light scattering under his boot.

"Guess it finally met someone it couldn't eat."

Johnny let his hammer rest against the ground, breath steady.

"Or someone who stopped feeding it."

The wind shifted. The field, once dead, felt lighter. Redeemed.

I looked toward the horizon, where light finally reached the soil again.

"Thank you, Sir Thomas," I whispered. "For every truth we almost forgot."

Johnny laughed under his breath, bracing his hammer across his shoulder. "Good. Because I'm out of prayers for second rounds."

I looked at each of them—the exhaustion, the belief, the quiet fire behind their eyes.

I turned toward the fading ash where the Gluttony Fallen had stood and let the words come on instinct—soft, certain, final.

The In-Between didn't feel cursed.

It felt *cleansed*.

I couldn't help the small, tired grin that tugged at my face.

"We finished."

The words weren't dramatic. They didn't echo.

But they *settled* into the silence, into the soil, into whatever part of this world still remembered what faith felt like. And maybe that was enough.

Then the light began to change.

Not in a blinding surge. Not with divine fanfare. But softly, like a sunrise remembering its duty after a long night.

Color bled into the gray edges of the In-Between. The pallor of the mist warmed from silver to gold.

The torn horizon, once an endless expanse of ash, shimmered and reshaped—lines reforming, fragments stitching themselves into familiar geometry.

The field began to breathe again. Grass whispered through cracks in the stone, green returning where only ash had lived.

Where ruin had once choked the air, a vibration rose softly—not song, not language—just the sound of peace, remembering how to exist.

The air began to change as if whispering a secret understood only by the senses. Redemption lifted the stillness, replacing the hunger that once threatened to consume everything with an abundance that felt tangible.

This was not merely a victory. It was a restoration.

The haze thinned, the horizon stretched wide and golden, and for the first time, color bloomed here.

The sky above glowed richer than any daylight on Earth. A living amber threaded with veins of silver.

The air shimmered like breath made visible, the ground alive with soft radiance seeping from beneath the soil.

The In-Between here was redeemed, a reflection that makes its source truer.

Light met shadow. The two didn't clash this time. They balanced, as though creation itself had finally exhaled.

The Belt's glow dimmed, its heat subsiding into something gentler.

I exhaled slowly, feeling the pressure of two realities easing from my ribs.

The exhaustion hit all at once. An avalanche of weight my body had been too busy surviving to notice.

Then my knees buckled. My vision blurred, the vibrant colors of the field around me fading into muted hues. A tremor ran through my fingers, a quiet, unmistakable sign of vulnerability beneath the veneer of triumph. In that moment, the weight of what we had endured pressed down, and I felt a whisper of fear that the past could reclaim its hold. But alongside it, determination burned brighter, refusing to yield to doubt.

"Whoa—got you," Cody said, catching me just before I hit the ground. His shoulder took the weight easily, steadying me without needing thanks.

Johnny moved in on the other side, his hammer dragging faint lines in the dust.

"Dude," he muttered, half-relieved, half-grinning, "you drop a Gluttony, and then *you're* the one who almost face-plants?"

A shaky laugh broke from my chest. "Guess I'm dramatic like that."

"Guess?" Johnny smirked. "Confirmed."

Then Sarah stepped forward.

No words at first. Just that quiet presence, like still water in a place that had forgotten how to reflect.

Her bow faded into her emblem as she approached, the teal glow dissolving into the air.

She knelt in front of me, eyes clear.

"My uncle would be proud of you, Kayson."

The words hit deeper than any wound ever had.

They didn't hurt.

They *healed*.

Her voice shook—but not with grief, with completion.

There was no pity in her tone, no weight of mourning left to carry. Only truth.

I drew in a breath that trembled through my chest. "Thank you. For staying. For not letting me fall when I deserved to."

She gave a slow nod, a ghost of a smile threading through exhaustion.

"You never gave us a reason to."

Silence followed—full, not hollow.

Cody turned away slightly, eyes scanning the horizon where the last trails of shadow vanished into the fog. "We've got a lot to fix here."

Then, softer, steadier: "We will."

Johnny slammed his hammer into the earth beside him. The sound rang out like a bell calling faith to stand again.

"Together," he said simply.

The word echoed—not in sound, but in conviction.

And the world *agreed*.

The golden light swelled once more, washing over the field.

It didn't erase the scars.

It revealed them, clean and honest.

The place where we had fallen was now the origin of our rise.

I looked toward the far end of the clearing—the spot where the first Gluttony had nearly consumed us, where doubt had been born.

Now the soil there glowed faintly with scripture etched by the fight itself—lines of living verse written in ash and memory.

We had not cleansed this place. We had *redeemed* it.

Cody dusted off his gloves, cracking a grin that still carried a hint of adrenaline. "Ephesians really doesn't lose twice, huh?"

Johnny chuckled, leaning on his hammer. "Nah. We just take intermissions."

Sarah shook her head but smiled anyway. The kind that said, "We're *still here.*"

I turned my gaze skyward.

The last of the mist broke apart, unveiling fractured light pouring through invisible clouds.

The beams caught the drifting dust, turning it gold—like heaven, remembering the way home.

I whispered into the quiet:

"We did it, Sir Thomas."

The name didn't echo.

It belonged here.

A soft hum filled the air behind us.

When we turned, my portal was already open—not cold, not demanding.

Warm. Familiar. It pulsed like a heartbeat leading home.

I looked back once more at the restored field.

Then at them.

"Let's go home," I said, feeling the weight of the promise of what we carried forward. Our return was not just survival; it was about bringing back the strength and wisdom forged in darkness. The insight and unity we discovered here transcended victory.

We were no longer broken.

Ephesians had overcome.

CHAPTER EIGHTEEN
DAWN OF THE IN-BETWEEN

The chill of the stone pillow against my cheek was the first betrayal—a cold reminder that comfort and rest had escaped me. Waking was a deception; sleep abandoned me, leaving an emptiness that was neither nightmare nor solace. Before true awareness settled, I hovered in an uneasy grayness, blurred by sleep's unexpected betrayal.

My thoughts sloshed in my mind, slow and uncertain, refusing to settle. I lay there breathing, waiting for my name to return. For the world to remember who I was.

The ceiling above me wasn't familiar. Soft gray tile, dusted with specks of blue paint. Not my dorm. Not the infirmary. Definitely not my bed.

My back ached as if I'd lost a fight. Someone had thrown a thin, scratchy blanket over me—more utility than comfort—but it carried the faint scent of sandalwood and metal polish. Crossguard's version of compassion.

The air was too quiet. The kind of quiet that didn't feel earned yet—like silence holding its breath, waiting to see if peace was real this time.

Memory returned in fractured reels. The field. The Belt. The scream. Gluttony turning to ash. Ephesians standing where faith had once fallen.

We'd won, but no one would celebrate. There were no banners or cheers—only a victory that humbled, echoing in my chest with guilt and a desperate wish to finally belong within Crossguard and myself.

I let my head sink into the cushion, every muscle reminding me that divine purpose still had a human cost.

"Thank you," I whispered. To no one. To everyone. But really—to him. Sir Thomas.

The first man who showed me that "Knight" wasn't a title—it was a posture. He wasn't perfect. He didn't need to be. He was constant. Unmovable faith disguised as gentleness.

Without him, none of this would've held together. Without his sacrifice, I wouldn't have learned what truth actually means.

I smiled. Immediately regretted it. My jaw ached. Everything ached. Still, I moved. Eventually.

The floor bit cold against my bare feet. At each step, I hoped for warmth to ease my muscles' pain, but the stone remained indifferent. The fortress itself demanded resilience.

The shower hissed. Steam rose, cloaking the room in mist. The water ran hot enough to sting my old cut, a single pain scrubbing away the last bit of battle. It didn't heal. It soothed.

For the first time since I found the belt, my shoulders dropped. The battle was over. Now, I needed to find allies and food—regroup and prepare for what lay ahead. The shower's warmth marked a beginning, not just an end.

I dried off and pulled on the first things I could find—old jeans and a gray shirt that hung loose, faded letters spelling *Crossguard Invitational 2016.* Classy. Didn't care.

By the time I reached the common room, I felt ancient. Like a veteran trapped in borrowed youth. The couch was waiting, as loyal as ever. I collapsed into it and exhaled everything I hadn't realized I was still holding.

Silence. Too much of it.

No laughter. No chatter from the training rings. No clatter of armor or Cody's movie quotes. No hum of Sarah's pages turning.

It felt like the entire stronghold was holding its breath.

Then— Heat.

My Bible.

I sat up, wincing, and pulled it free. Golden letters flared across the first page, each stroke unfolding like breath on glass:

Calling all members to the Mess Hall for an urgent meeting.

I groaned softly. "Of course."

You crawl out of hell, barely stitched together, and before your ribs stop aching, the universe sends a calendar reminder.

Still sore, I zipped my jacket and pushed myself upright.

The walk to the Mess Hall wasn't far, but each step was heavy. Torches flickered lazily, shadows stretched. Silence felt thick, making every movement echo through history.

Each step echoed too long, as if time thickened. It wasn't fear trailing me—just awareness. This was recalibration: a world catching its breath after nearly unraveling.

By the time I reached the Mess Hall doors, my pulse had steadied—not calm, not fearless, just... ready. The shift from the heavy silence of the hallways to this gleaming threshold sharpened the anticipation.

The scripture carved along the frame glowed faintly. *Perseverance. Unity. Hope.* Words I'd once memorized for a test. Now they carried weight.

I caught my reflection in the brass. Same face. Same scar. Different eyes.

Maybe this was what restoration really looked like. Not serenity. But clarity.

The Bible in my hand still pulsed, soft and rhythmic.

"Let's see what you've got," I whispered.

And I pushed the doors open, not because I wasn't afraid, but because courage takes the lead before fear decides.

Readiness isn't silence. It's movement.

Whatever waited beyond those doors—it wasn't another debrief. It was the next test. The next truth.

And whether I was ready or not didn't matter. I went anyway.

By the time I reached the Mess Hall doors, I was already questioning every decision that led me upright.

The Bible pulsed in my grip—warm and alive, throbbing with its steady, familiar rhythm.

It wasn't just light.

It was *awareness*.

The same pulse that had guided me through ruin and revelation, through ash and faith.

Now, it simply waited.

I exhaled once. Rolled my shoulders back. Straightened my spine.

After the In-Between, after the Belt, after watching faith and fire trade places inside me—I'd come to expect the serious kind of summons.

Dark corridors. Stoic faces.

Judge Solomon stood at the front of the hall like a carved judgment, ready to deliver another lesson written in consequence.

Sound hit me like light breaking the dark before the doors even fully opened. A wave of cheers, laughter, metal cups clanging in toasts, and voices raised in life.

I froze.

Then blinked twice.

Inside, Crossguard was *alive*. The sharp contrast from the silent corridors to the bustling Mess Hall stunned me for a moment.

Every table, every torch seemed to vibrate with life. Knights from every Branch filled the room shoulder to shoulder, the air thick with celebration. Banners hung from the rafters, woven gold and crimson forming the Crossguard crest, shimmering above the crowd. Yet under the noise, the scent of oil and sweat lingered, weaving through the feast as a reminder of the recent battle. Steam rose from food fit for a king; spices and the earthiness of metal grounded the joy with survival's memory.

And beneath all of it—

Relief.

That unmistakable, bone-deep release of people who'd survived the storm.

I stood there at the threshold, blinking into the brightness, half-convinced I was hallucinating.

Just days ago, we'd fought for our lives in the ruins of Sonorah.

Now it looked like heaven had decided to throw a block party.

A second heartbeat joined mine, disbelief. My hand hovered near my Bible, but it was a habit, not danger. *How could joy exist when screams still echoed in my chest?* As I stepped forward, I wondered: *Did surviving mean becoming whole, or would memories always linger?*

The sound was foreign after so much silence. It felt too loud to be real, too sacred to be casual.

And yet—it belonged.

I stepped forward. The crowd rippled.

A few knights turned, and before I could brace, the shouting began.

"Kayson!"

"Cavalier!"

"The Lightbringer!"

That one caught me off guard.

Lightbringer? Really?

It sounded like something out of a ballad, not a boy still sore from battle.

Hands reached out, delivering slaps on the back and handshakes with enough force to dislocate a shoulder. Armor plates tapped against mine in salute.

Cody's voice pierced through the clamor with a quick, "Guess they really like you, Kayson."

As the cheers rose around us, Johnny jumped in with his typical long-winded style. "Man, look at this parade! No pressure, just the whole realm deciding you're the best thing since sliced bread. Hope you're ready for the knighthood talent show next!"

Though their styles differed, both voices wrapped around me in unity.

By the time I wove through the maze of knights, my legs were jelly.

But there it was—the Ephesians' table.

Front and center, directly under the floating Crossguard emblem.

The sigil glowed faintly above us, as if aware that something sacred had transpired and was choosing humility over grandeur.

I collapsed into the nearest seat between Cody and a pitcher of water that looked like it had descended from heaven itself.

Cody didn't even look up.

"Bro, how come light *always* arrives last?"

I grunted. Fluent.

Cody snorted. "Man's out here speaking in Second Language: Exhaustion."

Across from us, Johnny was already a crime against fabric.

Neon shorts. A Nirvana shirt older than civilization.

My eyes considered quitting.

Sarah leaned forward, her hood down, a rare smirk ghosting across her face.

"So you're alive," she said. "We were taking bets."

I mumbled into the table, "Still thinking about me then?"

She sighed in fluent *disdain*. Then smacked my shoulder hard enough to remind me I still had nerves.

Before I could retaliate, wind.

A sudden, holy gust ripped through the room, and in an instant, our entire table lurched forward.

Space folded, reality blinked, and I was standing forty feet closer to the front.

Oh no.

Only one person did that kind of theatrical teleportation.

"Solomon," I muttered.

Silence dropped like a curtain.

Every head turned.

Every suit of armor gleamed.

I stood center stage, wearing sweats, bed hair, and an expression that probably screamed *accidental protagonist.*

The dream of showing up to class in your underwear?

Yeah. This was worse.

More swords.

I summoned my armor.

Gold light cascaded over me, the Belt of Truth sealing across my waist in perfect rhythm with my pulse.

The room chuckled—soft, human laughter. Not mockery.

Relief disguised as joy.

Then came the voice that silenced even breath.

"Everyone. Be still."

He stepped forward through the glow of torches, emerald armor whispering with age and battle.

The Judge of Crossguard.

His presence didn't need a crown.

"Not long ago," he began, "we stood in this hall in mourning. Today, we stand in celebration."

The roar that followed was thunder incarnate.

Chapters and pages alike raised blades.

Some pounded fists to their chests.

A tidal wave of faith rippled across the hall.

Solomon raised a single hand. Silence returned.

"The page behind me," he said, "has achieved what our history determines as unprecedented."

His gaze found me. "Kayson Cavalier led his Book into battle without losing a single member. He faced the enemy that moved a Soulless Zone and prevailed."

"He faced his own darkness," Solomon continued, "and found truth within it. And now... he stands as the youngest in our history to awaken the Belt of Truth."

The hush that followed wasn't empty. It was reverent.

I turned toward my book.

My family.

Cody smirked. Johnny gave a mock salute.

Sarah's eyes caught mine bright, and certain. The calm after every storm.

"Kayson Cavalier," Judge Solomon said, his voice a steady flame. "Please step forward."

I did. Slowly. Every bruise in agreement.

Judge Solomon's greatsword manifested in his hands. A sound like creation inhaling.

Light crawled along its edge, scripture alive in the steel.

"In the eyes of the Almighty," he said, "the Council of Commandments declares you worthy of Chapterhood. Do you accept this honor?"

I should have said *yes*. Every instinct told me to. Acceptance would ensure my place among the esteemed, a chance to rise without question. But turning it down put me at risk of being seen as insolent or ungrateful, challenging the very traditions that held Crossguard together. Eyes from across the room weighed in with silent judgment, the air thick with anticipation and potential fallout.

But I looked at them—Cody, Johnny, Sarah—and the word changed in my throat. "Of the accomplishments listed," I said quietly, "none were mine alone. Ephesians as a whole carried every battle together. They carried me."

Sarah's lips parted. Johnny blinked. Cody just smiled, shaking his head.

"I'll accept when I've earned it fully," I said. "When I've claimed the Breast-plate of Righteousness. Until then, I will remain only a page of Ephesians."

The hall froze.

Then Cody exaggerated a point, "Man, look at him trying to be poetic."

Laughter broke. Loud, free, rolling through the room like the sound of walls crumbling in reverse.

Solomon's smile was small but radiant.

"Thomas would be proud, Kayson."

I breathed in slowly. "I think so too."

Solomon lifted his hand, and a wind swept through the hall again.

I blinked, and I was back at our table. Plates appeared as if summoned by some unseen hand. Cups filled themselves.

The air hummed with harp strings and soft percussion.

The celebration had begun.

For the first time in weeks, I let myself feel it—not the pride, not the atten-tion, just the peace that comes when light finally outweighs the dark. In that moment, I allowed myself to *belong*.

The smell found me before the noise did. Roasted meats and warm bread tearing under fingers. Coffee deep enough to pass for confession. It didn't land all at once; it layered, familiarity stacking until my body remembered a language older than fear. You are safe; you can eat.

Comfort had a temperature. It soaked the room. Not numbness—whole-ness. Plates clinked. Someone laughed too loudly, and no one shushed them. Music thrummed under the stone like a steady heart finally refusing to flatline.

Our table looked like a penance and a reward.

Johnny had already declared open season on the menu. Three burgers in—one wrapped in a pancake, which I suspected wasn't an accident—he chewed with the gravity of a man negotiating a peace treaty. Cody dismantled a fried chicken leg with surgeon's calm, barbecue in one hand, eyes tracking mashed potatoes like a tactician considering supply lines. Sarah sat cross-legged, a bowl of creamy pasta sending up soft clouds between her and the world; braid over one shoulder, armor gone, gray layers and scuffed boots grounding her back.

My coffee waited—black with a whisper of cinnamon, hot enough to anchor my palms. I didn't ask how the cup knew. Some blessings don't require explanation. I sipped. It spread through the ribs and marrow. I'd tasted water in Crossguard and light on my tongue.

But this? This tasted like healing. Ordinary and holy in the same breath.

Johnny leaned back, grease-shiny and satisfied. "Best fight ever. Best food ever. Motion to never do that again."

Cody raised a fizzing amber glass. "To being alive."

We clinked. The sound rang clean.

Sarah lifted her tea, steam weaving up past her cheek. "We earned this."

Steel beneath the softness. Fire banked, not gone.

"Yeah," I said, setting the mug down. "We really did."

No speeches. No armor. No shadow poised behind us. Just the room's noise of chairs scraping, cutlery whispering, relief stitching itself into the ordinary.

For a span of breaths, we weren't Crossguard, weren't Ephesians, weren't even knights. Just tired kids whose vocabulary hadn't caught up to what they'd survived—so we let the silence speak for us.

Sarah nudged me, gently. "Sore?"

"Manageable," I lied politely.

Johnny snorted into burger four. "Manageable? Our captain stood up this morning, sounding like a haunted staircase."

"Did not."

"Did too. Thought it was thunder."

Cody wiped his hands; the napkin vanished the second he set it down. "He groaned so hard the universe filed a complaint."

My mouth betrayed me with a smile. "Glad my suffering is a team sport."

Sarah smirked over her rim. "It's familiar. Comforting."

"You're all terrible."

"We're all here," Johnny said. "I'll take terrible over dead."

Beneath the teasing, there it was again—the reverent weight that kept us honest.

Cody's voice dropped, the grin thinning into something true. "No jokes—" he laced his fingers—"I'm proud of you, Kayson. Wouldn't have followed anyone else into that mess."

He meant it. No wink, no punchline. Just the truth placed quietly on the table.

"Wouldn't have made it without you," I said.

Around us, knights danced in scuffed armor. Others leaned shoulder to shoulder, sharing food and stories and sometimes nothing at all. There's a language you only learn after battle; it moves in glances, in the way people breathe when they finally can.

Sarah set her fork down and tilted her face toward the vaulted ceiling. Her eyes closed for half a heartbeat; the exhale that followed sounded like a door unlocking. "Feels like we finally exhaled."

"It does," I said. And it did. Not because the world was fixed. Because rest had been permitted.

Johnny popped the last bite, sat back with the look of a man preparing to keynote joy. "Do you think the cafeteria, I mean Mess Hall, can just... stay like this? You know—manifest feast whenever we don't die?"

Cody tapped his chin. "Divine catering is a respectable theology."

Sarah laughed—not the small, guarded sound from before, but open and clean. I wanted to bottle it, stash it with the relics, something to unstopper when the dark pressed in again.

Johnny leaned in, eyes brighter than he let people see. "Confession. Remember when I couldn't summon a shield to save my life?"

"I remember a shield coming in sideways and assassinating two chairs."

He grinned. "Back then, I figured I was the comic relief. Backup. Distraction."

"Still true," Cody murmured, deadpan.

Johnny flipped him a look without breaking stride. "Anyway—last fight? I wasn't a backup. I was part of it. Felt like a knight."

"You are a knight," Sarah said. No pity. Reverence.

I nodded. "We've changed."

Cody bumped my shoulder. "You especially, Mr. I'll-solo-a-Gluttony-because-I-have-a-feeling.'"

"You trusted me," I said. "That changed everything."

He shrugged. "Not hard. We've seen you come back from worse."

Johnny raised his cup. "To still being here."

Sarah lifted hers. "To Crossguard."

Cody raised water, unabashed. "To winning ugly."

I lifted my coffee. "To Ephesians."

We all lifted our drinks high. The sound carried farther than it should, truer than earlier, as if the room itself cosigned it.

Pieces of us were still scattered out there, like fragments of cracked glass on stone, in smoke, in memory. Some wounds hadn't gotten around to closing. But we weren't running, we weren't bracing for the next hit, and we weren't afraid.

We were standing. Whole enough. Here. The warmth from my mug lingered in my hand, a reminder of the comfort found in this moment and a silent promise of the trials that awaited. I let my gaze drift across the hall. A pair of veteran Chapters laughed until one wiped his eyes with the heel of his hand. Two pages dozed at a corner table, heads together on a folded cloak. A Commandment walked slowly along the wall of portraits, fingers brushing names like prayers.

Heat seeped back into the world in ordinary ways: in stew and steam, in music that made no promises, in gold light skimming armor and catching dust midair like held breath finally let go.

Sarah's attention flicked to my face and stayed. "You look lighter," she said.

"I feel... clearer." I touched the Belt unconsciously; even unsummoned, its certainty lingered. "Truth doesn't make it easier. It just makes lying to yourself impossible."

"Useful," Cody said. "Annoying, but useful."

"Ask my knees," Johnny added. "They're currently telling me the truth about stairs."

We laughed. It landed like a blessing.

Across the room, Judge Solomon spoke quietly with a trio of knights. He didn't look our way, but I felt the thread—the way he watched without hovering, the way permission radiated from him without words: *Rest. You've earned it. There will be more, but not in this breath.*

I wrapped both hands around the cup again, drawing in the last of its heat. The scar on my cheek pulled when I smiled—less a wound, more a line drawn under a paragraph. Not finished. Just honest.

"Hey," Johnny said, softer now. "For what it's worth—if the next fight is worse, if the next step is darker—"

"It will be," Sarah said, not unkindly.

"—then we'll do what we did today," Johnny finished. "We'll stay."

"Together," Cody added.

I looked at them—Johnny who learned to think like a shield, Sarah whose quiet carried storms, Cody who finally believed he belonged in the line, and the gratitude had nowhere to go but out through breath.

"Together," I said.

We ate until hunger stopped being the point. We let the noise fold around us and didn't push back. We let peace sit at the table without questioning whether it would stay.

For now, it was enough. And for the first time in a long time, "enough" didn't sound like surrender. It sounded like a foundation.

Chapter Nineteen
Eye of the Storm

The morning light struck a familiar street corner where a warped stop sign stood, its rays cutting through the fog. It was as if the sky remembered how to breathe.

The air was sharp with dew, asphalt, and the faint sound of distant traffic — ordinary things that, somehow, felt miraculous.

And beneath it all was a scent I hadn't known I'd missed: Life that wasn't burning.

I tugged my hoodie tighter, burying my hands in the pockets, and lifted my face to the light.

It didn't sting this time. It was just clean.

For the first time since I found the belt, I could inhale fully, my chest rising without hesitation. As the static that once clawed at my ribs faded, a hitch in my breath remained—a single tremor that surfaced, echoing battles past and emotions long buried. I noticed my fingers unclenching from fists I hadn't realized I'd formed. Tension released, my shoulders dropped. With that, a quiet relief settled, like dust returning to rest after a storm, signaling the shift from survival to fragile safety.

The weight that used to anchor me wasn't gone — it had changed shape.

It had settled into something quieter, steadier.

The tiredness that comes *after* a storm, not during it.

No armor. Just jeans, sneakers, and a gray hoodie.

But the protection ran deeper now.

Cody walked beside me, hoodie half-zipped, energy drink in hand. His fingers twitched, nearly dropping the can before catching it, a small sign of his tension.

His stride was lazy, but his gaze kept darting toward the sky, as if he half-expected it to tear open again.

I didn't blame him.

The silence between us wasn't uneasy anymore. It was the quiet that comes from healing, from both of us having survived more than anyone can see.

We'd survived the kind of noise that rewires a person.

Now, quiet was the reward.

"You think it'll feel different?" Cody asked, kicking a pebble that rattled across the cracked pavement. His voice carried the unspoken weight of the past month, as if searching for an answer he couldn't quite name.

I hesitated, letting the silence stretch. "Feels like the world might think so," I replied, but left the rest unsaid. Maybe it wasn't just about us.

He grunted, thoughtful. "Guess we'll find out."

The school emerged through the morning haze — its brick facade washed pale by sunlight, windows blinking back streaks of gold.

Same cracked sidewalks.

Same bent fence from freshman-year rebellion attempts.

The same half-dead oak slouching in the courtyard caught my eye as I moved forward. The familiar presence echoed all around, weaving a tapestry of who we were with who we are now.

Not vanity — verification.

Proof that I was still here.

Still me. Mostly.

But the posture was new.

The eyes no longer flickered away.

The shoulders carried weight without apology.

The first-period bell echoed across the courtyard.

I was early on purpose.

Cody slowed beside me. "You sure you wanna start the day that way?"

"Yeah." I adjusted my hood. "Feels right."

We stepped through the doors, school noise rising up to meet us.

The hallway yawned awake around us — a mix of chatter and the burnt smell of coffee from teachers faking alertness.

Lockers clanged, paper shuffled, sneakers squeaked across linoleum.

Ordinary noise.

For once, it didn't grate. It sounded *human*.

His voice surfaced in my mind:

"History doesn't end, Cavalier. It waits for the brave to be remembered by it."

That gentle-warm laugh.

That steady conviction that truth wasn't fragile — it was alive.

I stopped at the doorway.

The brass handle was cool beneath my palm — too cool for morning sun.

It pulsed faintly, or maybe that was my pulse, caught between grief and gratitude.

I hadn't set foot in here since right after the battle. My hand brushed against the cool brass handle, and a pulse of memory rippled through me, mixing with the rapid heartbeat in my throat.

Cody lingered at my shoulder, his eyes flickering with an unspoken question. I could feel his concern like a soft nudge, urging me to take a moment.

"I do," I said quietly. "If he could face Wrath, I can face a classroom."

The air steadied in my lungs.

Then I pushed the door open. Light and memory collided as I entered.

The hinges creaked — familiar, almost welcoming.

Inside, sunlight fractured through the blinds, painting slow-moving bars of gold across the walls.

A young substitute — navy blazer, tired kindness in her eyes.

She smiled, small and unsure, as if she could sense that the school had changed.

The desks were the same — initials carved deep, gum fossils beneath.

Maps still curled at the corners.

And at the far edge of the whiteboard, faint and stubborn, was a ghost of chalk. A smudged line, barely visible, drew the eye, whispering of permanence despite all attempts to erase it.

Students murmured, half-asleep.

They didn't feel it, I did. The weight was reverent, not heavy. Instead of pressing down, it lifted me, turning memory into something sacred and letting me breathe.

I took my old seat by the window.

Same view.

Same slow crawl of sunlight across the tiles.

Only now, I could see it for what it was — not just light, but continuity.

I set my notebook down. The same one that had survived battles, training halls, and the Between. Its edges were worn, pages warped from travel between worlds.

The bell rang clean, and final.

I didn't flinch.

Outside, the day continued; cars, voices, laughter. All of it ordinary again.

But inside, something sacred stirred.

For the first time, I didn't feel like a survivor walking through ruins.

I felt like a student stepping into an inheritance.

A continuation, not a ghost.

And that was enough.

Then I saw the plaque.

Room 103 – History / Mr. Sterling.

Even the letters seemed heavier now, etched with memory.

My pace slowed before I could stop it.

The smell of chalk dust, old ink, and worn leather met me first.

Impossible that it still lingered, but it did, like the room itself refused to forget the man who had filled it with light.

I stepped into the classroom and time forgot how to move.

The air stayed still, like the room itself remembered what it used to be and what it had lost.

Everything had shifted back into place.

Sir Thomas's desk still anchored the front row, edges worn smooth by years of elbows and conviction.

The corner lacquer had peeled into soft ridges—a mark of a man who believed the present was never finished.

The chair beside it leaned slightly to one side, one leg shorter than the rest—forever tilting with him mid-rant about Rome or faith or both.

Even the faint coffee ring beside his lamp remained, dried into permanence.

Above row three, the ceiling stain, shaped vaguely like Australia, lingered like a ghost map.

A yellowed watermark. The invisible coil that had once cinched around my ribs in this room was nothing more than a memory now. Where a persistent inner voice used to whisper, 'You don't belong here,' I had now found acceptance. As I sat in my familiar seat, the air felt lighter. The unwelcome tension was gone, replaced by a quiet sense of belonging. What was once static beneath my skin felt different, too—quiet strength that surprised me with a new comfort.

The static that used to live beneath my skin had dissolved into something gentler.

At the front, Ms. Mallory stood.

Not slumped behind her fortress of coffee mugs and ungraded papers.

Not drowning behind sarcasm. She stood upright. focused and present.

The exhaustion that once haunted her eyes was gone.

Even her movements felt deliberate, as if she'd chosen to return to herself.

She turned, uncapped a marker, and wrote three words across the whiteboard in slow, measured strokes:

No textbook. No agenda. No quiz.

Just those words.

And the silence they demanded.

The air shifted. Not with excitement, but with awareness.

Something *real* was about to happen.

The chair groaned in greeting, same loose bolt under the right armrest, same faint "J + T 4EVER" scratched into the laminate.

Even that graffiti felt different now—like the room's history was finally something to honor, not escape.

This used to be just another checkpoint between storms.

A place I survived until the next bell. Now it felt like a monument.

A sanctuary made new.

Ms. Mallory turned back to face us.

Her expression wasn't soft or severe. Just anchored, like she'd stopped pretending to float.

"For today," she said, her voice calm but clear, "no lecture. No notes." The clock on the classroom wall ticked steadily, each second stretching the silence, setting the scene for something more. The hallway outside seemed to pause. Students' movements slowed, as if even time were preparing for what was to come.

A few students exchanged curious glances. Even the usual chatter stilled.

"Instead," she continued, tapping the board with the cap of her marker, "I want you to think about these."

Legacy. Sacrifice. Impact.

A hush settled over the room. Students held their breath, eyes focused and pens hovering above paper, as if capturing the moment required an unspoken permission. The atmosphere thickened, reverence palpable without needing to be declared.

"Someone," she said, "who changed how you see the world doesn't have to be famous. Doesn't even have to be alive. Just someone whose presence stayed."

Then she set down the marker and without pretense—sat among us.

Not above. Not apart.

Just there.

The hush that followed wasn't bored. It was *focused,* like the moment before a blade meets truth.

My fingers hovered over my pen, and the image came before the thought.

Mr. Sterling.

Not the Eighth Commandment. Not the knight Sir Thomas.

Just the man. *Just Mr. Sterling*

The one who turned lessons into lanterns.

Who refused to let me stay invisible.

Who saw my edges and still expected light to come from them.

Someone whose presence stuck.

I hadn't written yet.

I just sat with it.

Let it hum through me like the aftershock of something holy.

Then—a voice, quiet but surgical.

"So..." Judah drawled from behind me, that familiar arrogance curling through each syllable.

"All this confidence just because you almost got knighted?"

Not loud—just enough.

A few students snickered, the uneasy kind that doesn't mean funny—just confused.

That middle ground between curiosity and fear.

I didn't turn right away.

I let silence stretch long enough to make him wonder if I'd heard him.

Silence, I had learned, was its own kind of blade. The pause stretched, expanding in the room like a held breath poised between heartbeats. Classmates began to shift in their seats, eyes flickering between Judah and me, unease creeping in like a shadow. It was a moment that demanded acknowledgment. A confrontation with something raw and unresolved. Then I turned, breaking the tension not sharply, not angrily, but simply done.

"Didn't know you were still keeping score," I said evenly.

He blinked, caught off guard.

"Some of us don't need special treatment to walk in confidently."

I didn't take the bait.

Didn't even blink.

"Some of us," I said softly, "don't need to borrow our confidence from someone else."

The smirk cracked—only slightly, but enough.

He looked away first.

The sound of pens scratching resumed like a tide returning after interruption.

From the corner of my eye, I saw Ms. Mallory glance up mid-stride.

She didn't say anything—

But the ghost of a smile brushed her lips, almost imperceptible.

The silence that followed was no longer fragile.

It had purpose.

Every student wrote, even the ones who never did. Even Judah.

Pens moved. Eyes dropped.

The room breathed together.

I didn't write much. Just one sentence: *He taught me how to fight with truth.*
That was enough. Minutes slipped by.
Ms. Mallory didn't grade. Didn't scroll. Didn't fill the air.
She watched. Listening with her eyes.
Still and intentional, like Judge Solomon before a sparring match.
Like Sarah in the second between inhale and strike.
When the bell rang, the sound felt almost sacrilegious.
No one rushed for the door.
They moved slowly, reverently, as if leaving a place that had blessed them.
I rose, slinging my bag over my shoulder.
"Mr. Cavalier," Ms. Mallory said as I passed.
I stopped. "Yeah?"
Her gaze met mine, unflinching.
"Keep showing up like this."
I blinked. Unsure how to reply. Unsure what *this* even was.
But I nodded, the only kind of honesty I had left.
Then—
BZZZZZT.
The intercom crackled through thin speakers.
Every head turned.
Principal Kartikak's voice followed, distant, too composed: *"All students, please report to the auditorium for a mandatory assembly. Teachers, accompany your classes. Attendance will be taken."*
Groans rippled through the halls outside—teenage noise, predictable, harmless.
Backpacks zipped, chairs scraped, someone cursed about losing lunch.
But beneath it all—I heard something else.
Not *what* was said.
How.
The cadence was off.
Too perfect. Too rehearsed.
Principal Kartikak was strict, but never stern.
This voice?
It didn't sound *human* in the way it should.
A prickle crawled up the back of my neck.
I glanced toward the hallway.
The lockers. The stairwell leading toward the auditorium.
Everything looked ordinary.
But ordinary had a sound, and this wasn't it.
My Bible pulsed faintly through the fabric of my backpack.

Just a warning heartbeat.

But the air around me shifted—ever so slightly—like the world had inhaled and forgotten how to exhale.

This wasn't a pep rally.

This wasn't another slideshow about school spirit.

This was a ripple. A subtle, invisible fracture in the calm. A faint metallic echo trailed in the silence after the intercom announcement. The kind of sound that didn't quite belong, like a distant warning bell in an ordinary morning. It was slight, barely noticeable, but enough to make the hairs on the back of my neck rise. It seemed to foreshadow more than was said.

And even without the armor, I could feel it.

The next storm had already started brewing.

CHAPTER TWENTY
IN MEMORY OF...

T he hallway buzzed with bodies. But my mind was somewhere else.

My feet were on autopilot. Shoulders set in invisible focus. Alert enough to look normal, distant enough to stay unbothered. My skin prickled. It was an echo of the uncertainty in my thoughts—a sensation neither painful nor soothing, simply waiting to break the calm. It mirrored the doubt inside me, circling my awareness without ever settling.

Lockers slammed. Voices rose and fell. Laughter bounced, thin and forced, off the concrete walls.

On the outside, I was just another sophomore drifting toward a "mandatory assembly."

But inside?

Inside, I felt separated and untethered, a growing sense of disconnection with each step, as if the hallway stretched the space between me and reality.

My thoughts dragged behind me like anchors, each one chained to the same question that refused to drown:

What if it didn't work?

We'd won.

We had closed the breach.

We had driven a Gluttony-Class back into the dark.

The Belt still pulsed faintly at my core — a living rhythm under my ribs — proof of victory, proof of grace, proof of something beyond us.

And yet...

That same pulse whispered that something unfinished remained.

Not fear.

Not failure.

Just an image on the wall—a reminder that something is out of place, hovering at the edge of sight—a flaw you can't unsee.

It felt like turning in a test too early—confident in every answer, but haunted by a page left unseen.

You know you missed something.

Something small.

Something final.

And once the test is gone, there's no getting it back.

That's what this felt like.

A conclusion that hadn't exhaled yet.

Days had passed, but the tension hadn't released. The world resumed its routine: bells, lockers, caffeine, life. I hadn't. Silence wrapped around me, intense and deliberate. You didn't realize its weight until you stepped into it—like the quiet before a string snaps.

The static in my chest was gone, but the silence it left behind was louder.

My lungs drew easy breaths, but my chest still tightened, as if my body resisted relaxation and waited for a danger only I could sense.

The Belt wasn't on me — not physically — but I still felt it.

Like a phantom heartbeat.

Thrum. Thrum.

Buried deep. Not as a burden. Not as power.

As presence.

A ribbon of unseen light coiled along my spine, humming—waiting for me to remember.

It never left.

I just watched.

And still...

Something deep inside remained unsettled, a subtle wrongness that I couldn't quiet, no matter how much I tried to blend in.

Not loud. Not obvious.

Just *true enough to notice.*

So I kept my hands buried in my hoodie pockets — not to hide, not to fight.

Just to *wait.*

We rounded a corner. The crowd thickened—a tide of backpacks and earbuds, moving like a river toward a drop. Someone bumped my shoulder. It snapped me back to the present moment. A locker scraped open, its echo blending into the corridor's buzz.

Someone laughed too loudly.

Someone swore.

Teachers barked half-hearted orders.

Life played its usual noise.

The world had moved on.

But I remembered.

Every footstep toward the gym landed like a countdown.

Same smell of waxed linoleum and burned-out fluorescents.

But beneath it all—silence.

Not the kind you can hear.

The kind that *listens back*.

The last time I'd been summoned for an assembly, a vision tore open.

The world cracked.

And I woke up.

That day, the air turned holy and hostile at once.

Crossguard had revealed itself.

Wrath's shadow had stretched over us all.

And something inside me split just wide enough for light to enter.

I became who I was meant to be.

Now, as those doors drew closer again, I didn't feel fear.

I felt sharpened awareness—an alertness frayed with tension and anticipation. Not fear, but a readiness for whatever was coming.

The crowd pressed around me — laughing, careless, human.

But I wasn't one of them anymore. I was simply among them, not of them; moving in rhythm with a world I could no longer fully belong to.

Each step narrowed the hallway — not physically, but spiritually.

The air thinned, sharp and glass-like; the kind that hadn't broken yet...

But *could*.

A chill slipped down my neck—a wordless whisper threading my spine.

Not panic.

Instinct. Reflex.

The truth speaks in silence.

I turned my head slightly, scanning faces as the flow carried us.

Dozens of classmates; familiar and ordinary.

But one light overhead flickered—a tremor too precise to be electrical. A faint chill swept the air, as though the light lost a breath of warmth in its flicker.

Because this was the problem.

It was *too normal.*

No scorch marks on the gym walls. No cracks in the floor from the clash of light and ruin. No residual hum of a breach. Not even a shimmer in the air where the Between used to bleed through.

It was *perfect.* Too perfect. And that's what made it wrong.

Peace wasn't meant to look this clean. It was like walking a battlefield scrubbed of scars, the air stripped of smoke and echoes.

This wasn't calm — it was choreography.

Every sound. Every smile.

Too aligned. Too intentional.

It felt like a dream, trying too hard to convince me it was real, like walking through a photograph frozen in time.

We neared the double doors. The metal was cold beneath my palm—not winter cold. Memory cold. The kind that holds echo instead of temperature.

Through the narrow pane of glass, I saw the gym.

Students packed the bleachers. Teachers pacing. Phones glowing.

Every bit of it screamed *ordinary.*

But I'd seen what ordinary looked like before the veil split.

And this wasn't it.

It was the wrong kind of normal. The one that pretends to be perfect.

It reminded me of those dreams where your house looks right—but the pictures are off, clocks tick backward, and the air hums just below hearing. You know something's waiting just out of frame.

You just don't know *where.*

My fingers tightened on the handle.

I looked once to my left — the bulletin board plastered with club flyers and spirit-week posters.

Then, to my right, the old fire extinguisher box. Empty since before we were born.

Then forward, where the battlefield waited.

Because that's what this was.

Not a gym. Not an assembly.

A battlefield in disguise.

I looked over my shoulder, scanning the faces behind me.

Sarah, a few rows back, her brow slightly furrowed — she felt it too.

Cody, pretending to scroll but watching the crowd through the reflection of his phone screen.

They knew.

Not fully.

But enough.

Everyone else?

Unaware that they were already standing in the next chapter of a war that refused to stay buried.

I closed my eyes.

Not to escape. To *listen.*

Solomon's voice rose from memory, quiet and unyielding: "Clarity isn't peace unless you choose to trust it."

I hadn't understood it then. But I did now.

The truth was clear.

The peace was counterfeit. The war wasn't over. Just paused.

Clarity doesn't promise comfort — it demands choice.

And mine was simple: trust what I felt, not what I saw.

I exhaled slowly. The kind of breath that's not relief—it's readiness.

"All right," I whispered.

My hand pressed forward.

The hinges groaned.

And the gym doors opened—spilling light, laughter, and something underneath it all.

Something *waiting*.

The noise was already waiting for us.

Not chaos—rhythm. A thousand conversations overlapping like static, pretending to be normal.

The gym vibrated with it.

Metal bleachers. A fluorescent hum. That faint smell of varnish and sweat that never quite left the floorboards. Light pooled harshly on the court below, bending off polished wood where blood and faith had once mixed.

Cody nudged me before I'd even found my footing. "You planning to stand there all day, or what?"

He shifted aside, tapping the empty space beside him.

I slid into the seat.

The instant I did, an invisible pressure settled over the room, an almost imperceptible shift of weight.

It was as if the air held its breath. Teachers lined the walls, islands of forced calm. Some stared through the noise, coffee growing cold. Others gripped clipboards. One mouthed words like prayer.

Principal Kartikak was nowhere in sight.

That absence carried weight.

Cody leaned in, voice low. "So, your bet?"

"On what?"

"Why are we here. Victory lap or round two?"

I tried to laugh. It didn't stick.

"You're not the only one thinking that."

Around us, students filled every row—phones out, heads together, all pretending everything was normal. But I could feel the tension in the air, the emotional dissonance that set me apart from the others.

Cody drummed his fingers on his knee. "If it's really over, shouldn't there be something? Headlines? Celestial press releases? A divine newsletter?"

"Would've settled for a push alert," I said.

He nodded, eyes narrowing. "That thing we fought wasn't small. Not local."

He scanned the corners, voice quieter now. "You feel anything?"

My gaze lifted.

Then down to the court that had held Mr. Sterling's stand. The polish couldn't erase what the soul remembered.

"Peace still feels temporary," I said.

"Yes, but it holds something more," Cody interjected, "Persist beyond fear."

We sat in that pause that isn't silence but suspension—the kind that comes right before glass decides to break.

Then the lights flickered once. Quick.

Cody's knee bounced. "Tell me that's just old wiring."

The lamps steadied. The hum returned. But the air had already changed.

A door opened along the side wall.

Heads turned.

Principal Kartikak stepped through first; pressed blazer, graying curls, shoulders straight. Same woman, different presence.

Her eyes weren't cold anymore. They were *awake*.

And behind her, Sir David. Just jeans, a button-down, and boots that looked too mortal for who he was.

Cody's breath caught. "Is that—"

"Sir David," I said. The word came out more reverent than surprised.

He moved with the quiet assurance of someone who'd seen endings and decided to walk back anyway. Calm. Human. And that was what made it unnerving.

The Belt inside me stirred once—one slow pulse, like a heartbeat answering another.

Cody leaned in. "Why does he look like he's about to hand out raffle tickets?"

I didn't answer. Light bent faintly around Sir David, not enough to reveal, just enough to *remember*.

Principle Kartikak reached the microphone.

Her smile was small, unguarded—something I'd never seen survive on her face for more than a second.

"Good morning, everyone," she began, voice steady, carrying that faint resonance that brushed the edge of the Between.

Sir David stood beside her, still as stone, gaze sweeping the crowd.

"They're... in a good mood," Cody whispered.

I stayed quiet.

Because underneath their calm, the air was already vibrating—a heartbeat shared by the room itself.

Principle Kartikak's eyes moved over us like she was counting souls.

"What we're about to discuss will change our path," she said.

The bleachers shifted with a ripple of murmurs.

Cody went still.

This wasn't routine.

It wasn't closure.

It was the start of something waiting to breathe again.

Principal Kartikak waited until every whisper fell away.

It didn't take long.

Whatever sound the gym had left—the rustle of jackets, the coughs, the restless tapping of shoes—disappeared the moment Sir David stepped beside her.

Not from command. From gravity.

Something about the space changed direction, as if the air itself remembered who was standing there.

Not celestial light. Not spectacle. Just a quiet shift—like truth had re-entered the room.

She stepped to the podium. Both palms rested open on either side, grounded but unguarded. Her shoulders didn't brace; her face didn't harden.

She wasn't performing.

She was *present*.

When she spoke, her voice carried like linen over steel.

"Before we begin, I want to thank you all for being here."

No microphone crackle. No fidgeting. Just that single tone—clear enough to steady a thousand hearts at once.

"Today's assembly wasn't called for grades or sports or policy," she continued. "It was called because this school—like many of us—has endured something we still don't have words for." She paused, letting silence stretch as everyone absorbed the meaning behind her words.

Around me, the bleachers groaned softly as students adjusted, but no one dared speak. Even the lights seemed to dim their hum.

Principle Kartikak looked across us then—not scanning, not counting. Seeing.

"We've lost someone important to the school."

Her voice softened. "Mr. Thomas Sterling, our history teacher and longtime faculty member, passed away recently."

The words didn't shatter; they *settled,* like thunder that doesn't announce a storm—it ends one.

Gasps rippled through the crowd. A few muffled sobs, a curse caught halfway before regret.

But no laughter. No disbelief.

Even those who'd never had his class straightened, as if the room itself demanded posture.

Because everyone in Sonorah had heard the stories—about the teacher who made history feel alive, who turned lectures into crusades, who looked at you like he could already see the version of yourself you were afraid to become.

Then she added, "There was a day — maybe a Tuesday like this one — when Mr. Sterling stopped an entire lesson just to walk us outside. We stood there in the autumn breeze, and he asked us to close our eyes and feel the world turning. 'History,' he said, 'is what happens when you let life in. Don't miss it.' He made history something you could hold in your hands."

She paused. Let silence do the work.

The kind of silence that listens.

I didn't blink. I didn't move. I just breathed—slow, even—while the ground inside me tilted.

Principle Kartikak's voice didn't waver.

"I won't pretend to know every detail," she said. "I won't bury truth beneath comfort. What I can tell you is this—Mr. Sterling was more than a teacher. He was a mentor to many of you. And though he's no longer with us, his impact remains."

Something caught in my throat.

Sir David stepped forward then. His hands stayed folded, expression quiet but resolute—the face of someone who had seen loss so often that faith had learned to breathe through it.

Principle Kartikak looked toward him, then back to us.

"When I first came to Sonorah High School," she said, "I made choices out of fear. Out of control. I stripped away the values that once gave this school its roots. I silenced the things that made it sacred."

She exhaled, eyes bright.

"I was wrong."

The hush that followed wasn't shock.

It was relief.

Collective honesty found air for the first time.

For a moment, she looked smaller—human in the best way.

Then she set her notes aside. Didn't glance down, didn't shuffle them. She simply let them go.

"No formal announcement," she said softly. "We wanted to invite you here to remember someone who mattered to Sonorah."

Nothing rehearsed.

No cadence of administration.

Just truth wearing its own skin.

The gym turned still—so still I could hear the soft buzz of the lights bend against it.

Then, with a faint nod, she whispered, "While it may be too late to say it face-to-face... thank you, Thomas Sterling."

She stepped back.

Sir David approached the small table waiting at the center of the court.

On it—only three things: a navy sweater; frayed at the elbows, a worn paperback, edges curled and marked with the years, and an unlit candle.

He struck a match. Flame touched wick—steady and unwavering with no flicker.

Then he stepped away. That was it. No choir. No applause.

Just the sound of breathing.

Silence expanded until it felt like a living thing; gentle, sacred, and alive. For a moment, I let my hand hover above the navy sweater — the frayed elbows, a silent testament to years of wear. The pause held a heartbeat longer than it should, a soft throbbing that carried grief deeper than any narration could capture. A quiet nod to all the things left unsaid and all the farewells whispered into empty rooms.

Some students bowed their heads. Some linked hands. Others simply stared, eyes glazed with the unfamiliar weight of reverence.

Mr. Sterling had always seemed too large to leave. Too rooted to vanish.

Cody leaned toward me after a while, his voice barely above a whisper.

"You holding up?"

I nodded once. "Yeah. Just... strange. Seeing everyone quiet for the right reasons."

He smiled faintly. Not with pity but understanding. The kind of smile that knows how rare peace is, and how much it costs.

After a moment, I rose.

The movement felt heavier than it should've—each step like walking through memory instead of air.

No one stopped me. No one had to.

I crossed the court and stopped at the table.

The candlelight brushed my hands, warm against skin that remembered too much cold.

I touched the edge of the book. His book. The one he once made me write ten pages on because I "looked like I needed discipline."

Typical Mr. Sterling.

Demanding in all the ways that built you without asking permission.

I let my eyes close.

His voice echoed—dry humor, that thunder-warm conviction.

I whispered back,

"Thank you... for finding me."

Then I stepped away.

No tears.

No collapse.

Just the ache turned steady—no longer wound, but weight.

Something carried instead of endured.

Behind me, a chair creaked.

Someone sniffled.

Somewhere in the rafters, a light buzzed and steadied again.

I walked back toward the bleachers—toward Cody and Sarah—toward the people who'd learned, same as me, that silence can be holy when it's honest.

When we stepped outside, the air was cool and thin.

The clouds were still there, but lighter now—edges frayed by sunlight trying its way through.

It didn't break all at once. It never does.

But it broke enough. And in that half-lit morning, I understood.

This wasn't an ending.

It was a threshold. A promise held by every sunrise, whispering of tomorrow's relentless march.

Chapter Twenty-One
APOCALYPSE

J udge Solomon paused at the top step. A cool draft brushed against his skin, anchoring him with its chill as he began his descent. Each step echoed through the stone beneath the sanctuary, resonating with deliberate rhythm.

Each strike of leather on granite was a heartbeat measured in conviction.

The stairwell breathed with him.

Torches guttered as he passed, their flames bending toward his shadow like they recognized the one who had carried too many wars. Scripture lined both walls in fractured etchings—verses carved by hands that had known both revelation and ruin. The words shimmered faintly, old light trapped in older stone.

He didn't rush.

He hadn't rushed in years.

When you've buried other-worldly knights, time stops threatening you.

The chill at the base of the stairs rose to meet him, a cold that lived in the marrow of the Crossguard itself. It was the kind of air that remembered blood.

He exhaled once, steady.

He's back.

The thought came not as panic, but recognition. An echo that had been circling since the moment he felt the veil shudder.

Not a rumor. Not a dream. Not a whisper of fear.

Truth.

Wrath had returned. He had come for something only Crossguard could protect.

Judge Solomon's jaw tightened. The torches trembled.

At the final step, the corridor widened into the war chamber's threshold—iron-bound doors marked with the emblem of the first sanctuary. He placed one hand on the cold metal. It didn't resist him. It never did.

The door swung inward.

No banners. No marble. No indulgence.

Only flame, stone, and the heavy stillness of consequence.

Three torches burned equidistant around the circular chamber, their light moving like breath through ribs. The table at the center was carved from the gates of the first stronghold. Its surface was scarred and blackened, alive with memory. The texture of ancient ash and cold iron seemed to cling to it, filling the air with the scent of lingering smoke and history. Every Commandment had once stood here to decide the world's direction. Every scar was a decision someone hadn't come back from.

Sir David was already there.

Of course, he was.

No armor, no robe. Just black boots, dark jeans, and a button-down tucked with surgical precision. A knife glinted at his belt—the mundane shape that disguised the sharp edge of his beliefs. He saw the world as a series of calculated moves, each element fitting into a pattern of precision and inevitability. Sir David knew faith wasn't just something you wore; it was a blade you kept honed, ready to strike when certainty demanded action.

He didn't nod. Didn't greet.

Just watched.

Judge Solomon crossed the threshold and laid both hands on the table. His knuckles were pale against the charred wood.

"He's back."

Sir David's gaze didn't flinch. "How certain?" Judge Solomon paused, a momentary hesitation before his reply, as if weighing the cost of certainty against a hidden dread. His voice, though steady, betrayed a flicker of unease, adding a layer of complexity to his assertion.

"He laid a trap."

"For who?"

"Ephesians," Judge Solomon said. "After they reclaimed the school. He didn't strike. He observed. Let himself be seen."

Sir David frowned. "That isn't Wrath's way."

"Exactly."

The air thickened around the table.

From the far wall came the quiet slide of armor—Lady Melinda stepping out of the torchlight. Her presence was blade and scripture at once: polished steel tempered by experience. The scar along her neck caught the light like lightning frozen in flesh.

"Wrath doesn't let survivors walk out," she said.

"This time he did," Judge Solomon answered.

Sir David's arms crossed. "You're saying he planned the whole encounter?"

Judge Solomon's voice lowered as he leaned in slightly, his eyes taking on a deep solemnity. "He planned everything," he said, allowing his words to hang in the air, charged with the weight of their implication. A pause followed, tension wrapping around them as the team exchanged glances, each silently willing Judge Solomon to confirm their worst fears.

Lady Melinda's eyes narrowed further. "So the question isn't why now. It's why *them.*"

Judge Solomon nodded. "Yes. Why Ephesians?"

Silence. The torches hissed softly.

Sir David leaned forward. "He's studying them."

"Not them," Judge Solomon said. "*Him.*"

Lady Melinda's gaze flicked toward the flame. "Kayson."

Judge Solomon didn't need to confirm it.

Sir David's voice hardened. "Wrath doesn't test. He corrupts."

"He used to test," Judge Solomon murmured. "When he was still one of us."

That stilled even the fire.

Lady Zalika spoke first, careful and quiet. "What are you implying?"

"That this isn't simply an ambush. It's an evaluation." Judge Solomon began pacing the perimeter, each torch igniting a faint shimmer in his armor's engraved scripture. "He's measuring the boy. Pressure testing faith. Like a craftsman tapping the blade he forged before he turned it against its maker."

Sir David exhaled, slow and sharp. "You think Wrath remembers?"

"He remembers *everything.*"

Lady Melinda stepped closer. "Then what's his plan?"

Judge Solomon's gaze rose to the vaulted ceiling where shadows writhed like unspoken words.

"I think he's done residing in the shadows."

That landed like lightning behind clouds.

Sir David's voice was nearly a whisper. "Do we warn the kid?"

Judge Solomon hesitated. Shadows of doubt flickered within his mind, a fleeting thought surfacing momentarily before he dismissed it.

"Perhaps..." He silenced the possibility before it could take root.

"No."

Lady Melinda's head snapped up. "He deserves to know. He deserves to *be ready,* not afraid."

Judge Solomon's tone remained calm, yet firm. "The Belt of Truth awakened in him only weeks ago. Revealing this now would direct his path rather than allowing him to find it himself."

"And if Wrath reaches him first?" Sir David asked.

"Then we'll know which truth the boy serves."

The words sat between them like a loaded weapon.

Lady Melinda broke the silence, voice low. "If we wait too long, Judge Solomon, we may not get another chance to tip the scale."

He met her eyes, the weight of command older than either of them could bear. Judge Solomon felt the familiar pull of duty clashing with the whispering doubt that lingered just beneath the armor of his resolve. He hesitated briefly, as the burden of past decisions flickered in his memory—choices that had reshaped battles and claimed lives in their wake.

"Then we won't wait long."

Sir David moved closer to the table. "Tell me straight—do you think Wrath means to destroy him?"

Judge Solomon's reply came softly, almost reverent. "No."

A pause.

"I think he means to *use* him."

The room exhaled.

Torches hissed.

Lady Melinda's shoulders stiffened. Sir David's jaw set like stone.

Judge Solomon looked back at the flames. His voice dropped to the cadence of scripture and prophecy.

"He isn't a Fallen. He isn't even a traitor."

He drew a long breath, the kind that feels like remembering a nightmare you once survived.

"He is the **Knight of Calamity.**"

The title spread through the chamber like frost—slow, invasive, and absolute.

No one moved.

The flames leaned inward, drawn by something unseen.

They all knew the story.

Once the greatest among the Crossguard. The one blessed by both Gabriel and Michael.

The knight who'd built a kingdom of faith—and then set it ablaze.

Sir David's voice was almost a prayer. "He vanished for years. Not a trace. Now he returns, not to strike... but to *watch*."

Lady Melinda glanced toward the torches. Their fire wavered, thin and nervous.

"That's worse than any battle."

Judge Solomon didn't answer.

He simply stared into the flame, watching its heart bend and breathe.

Because deep down, he already knew.

The war they thought they'd survived wasn't finished.

It hadn't even begun.

Only the light on the walls moved, trembling under the weight of something vast and patient.

And somewhere, beyond Crossguard's borders, beyond mortal comprehension, a shadow smiled—waiting for the blade it forged to decide which truth it would serve.

The fortress rose from the horizon's wound—a black geometry of refusal, all edges and absence.

Not merely old. Older than memory.

Not built by hands. Built by decisions.

Cowardice mortared with fury.

Stone layered over the bones of vows.

Obsidian walls held fractures that never healed, each fissure a testament to unrest. Suddenly, a gust of wind tugged at the parapets, dislodging thin flakes of ash that danced and spiraled away, carried by currents too subtle to see. No stars watched this place. Not for want of sky, but because something darker occupied it. No banners. No torches. No welcome. This architecture wasn't made to shelter. It existed to erase.

An obsidian bridge, split and webbed, crossed a chasm where smoke moved downward, not up. Chains as thick as trunks throttled the iron gate. The inscriptions carved into their links—once scripture—had been scored out until the grooves bled red. Once, this threshold had been holy.

It remembered.

No guards stood at the arch. Fear kept the vigil, and fear kept hours.

Beyond the gate, murals blistered along the corridors: betrayals softened by heat, halos charred to rings, angels with wings snapped mid-hymn. Each footfall left no sound of its own; it folded into the echo that had been repeating for years.

At the center, a room that did not breathe waited.

The throne chamber.

No windows. No candelabra. Only a darkness with opinions, the presence of something that listened and then decided what to hear. In that dark stood a throne—not golden, not ceremonial—a ribcage of history assembled from conquered things: helmets caved in, crowns buckled, broken swords still rusted at the edges. A weapon repurposed into a seat. Not for comfort. For containment.

Wrath sat within it. Helmeted. Unmoving.

Time thinned around him. Heat rose, failed, rose again; gravity behaved, then reconsidered. Silence did not simply linger—it obeyed.

The helm had once been Crossguard-perfect: polished scarlet trimmed in silver. Now, a split cleaved it clean down the center. One side still bore the Order's discipline. The other had gone black and molten, metal flowing into ridges no forge would claim. The fissures pulsed with emberlight—not damage, but consequence. A faint, unsettling hum seemed to emanate from the split, like the residual echo of all it had witnessed. When one drew close, there lingered the acrid scent of molten metal, embedding its scarred history into the senses.

Smoke threaded out from the narrow visor. No eyes showed, yet the gaze pressed through stone. The room adapted to it.

Before him stood the Four.

War closest: breadth of a siege tower, jaw held by will rather than ease, armor dulled red with fresh scoring. Power present, fear confessed in the clenched hand he wouldn't name.

Famine half a pace behind: elegant in pallor, plates woven thin as silk over calculations, eyes turned sideways to weigh angles the rest had missed.

Pestilence held himself like masonry: still until breath proved otherwise, armor stitched from ruins, a green exhaustion clinging to exposed skin.

And farther back, where shadows chose to gather—

Death.

None of them knelt. None of them moved.

Wrath's gauntlet flexed once. The temperature rose in obedience. A command without language.

"He bears the Belt," Pestilence rasped, words dragged through bone-dust.

"I know," Wrath said.

The voice was not monstrous; it was correct in a way that hurt. Calm with edges. Final by nature.

Famine's whisper skimmed the stone. "You designed this?"

"I did."

War's jaw worked. "To what end?"

Wrath stood.

The room altered its opinion of distance. Shadows retreated. Weight settled upon the air until Pestilence skated a half step without deciding to. War's hand reached for his hilt, then reconsidered. Famine, though known for her cold detachment, flinched almost imperceptibly. Her eyes flickered as if betraying a moment of doubt, only to swiftly regain their calculated focus. She masked the movement as if pausing to assess the dust that seemed to have taken a life of its own.

"When a seeker reaches for truth," Wrath said, "the first confrontation is with the lie that raised him."

He paused, allowing the notion to curl through the room like a lingering shadow ready to forge its form.

"Kayson stood on the precipice of that confrontation, unaware of the turmoil gathering within him. The Belt of Truth, still unfamiliar around his form, seemed to pulse as if echoing the words spoken, binding him to a challenge he could not yet comprehend. In the shadows of Crossguard, the truth Kayson sought was not merely an answer, but a battle against the very foundations of his beliefs. It was a clash between the teachings that shaped him and the revelations demanding to be heard."

"He wears the Belt now," he continued. "We will let him."

Famine's eyes lifted a fraction. "Why have we poured into their light? Do you still judge Crossguard to be the liar?"

Wrath did not hesitate. "I bear no judgment. I remember."

War's gaze narrowed. "They'll call for your execution."

"They already did."

The visor swept the room. Each of the Horsemen stood in its path and was weighed.

"You've seen it", Wrath said. "Contradictions conducted as doctrine. The rot behind prayer. 'Submission unto the Almighty is the foundation,' yet obedience is taught as a virtue while inquiry is punished as treason. They hoard what they name 'truth,' bury their fallen without saying why, and bless peace while forging children into instruments."

Famine said nothing. Her silence carried agreement.

Wrath's hand closed. Metal creaked softly. "I have no pity for their ignorance. Their false sense of justice, they've dictated, is black and white. Yet they're blind to its gray nature. As justice is merely dictated by the champion. I will break the illusion."

Pestilence drew air through ruin. "What is the next movement?"

Wrath returned to the throne. He sat. Pressure changed again; the chamber measured the decision and held still.

"I will weaponize the apocalypse that is now complete."

Famine angled her head. "Death?"

Wrath turned toward the rear.

Death stepped forward.

Armor that had once been a light Crossguard blue was now charcoal and cleaved, script along the breast burned into illegible scars. One arm absent from the shoulder, the stump sealed in a brutal weld of metal and flesh. The cloak dragged, heavy with a soaked memory that never dried.

Beneath the ruined helm was a flicker of a face known too well.

Sir Thomas Sterling.

Not risen. Not puppeted.

Unmade and re-authored.

He stood with the posture of a man missing the part that made posture human. The eyes behind the visor held no spark—no echo of the teacher who steadied rooms, the knight who held lines. The fire that had once warmed and warned had become ash that did not accuse.

War, who did not startle, shifted.

Famine's breath caught, thin and truthful. "You turned a Commandment."

Wrath's answer carried the cadence of old vows turned inside out. "I didn't turn him."

He reclined, smoke curling. "I let him see."

Silence gathered its cloak.

"Kayson believes the battle has ended," Wrath said, voice lowering to something that could pass for prayer. "He believes victory proves truth. He has not yet learned what the Armor requires."

Wrath lifted a gauntlet. Shadow rose behind him, opening like wings that reversed the light.

"Light casts a boundary," he said. "Everything beyond it begins to speak."

The throne crackled faintly. The heat climbed.

"When the hour arrives, they will suffer from a man whose love has faded—"

Death's visor caught ember-red.

"—who now bears the power of hatred."

No feeling. No forgiveness.

"History only recalls the victorious, as it will only remember the name of Wrath." His voice did not grow louder. It grew inevitable.

"They will remember the fire I taught them to survive."

Far above, where the night should have been, the stars held their breath.

In the fortress that had chosen erasure, ash continued its patient fall.

And somewhere between those two silences, the war turned its page.

ACKNOWLEDGEMENTS

Ten years.

That's how long this story has lived with me , changing shapes, growing roots, waiting for me to grow into the person capable of finishing it.

It started as an idea, but somewhere along the way, it became a mirror — one that showed me who I was, and who I wasn't yet.

To my wife — for walking through every draft as my support and editor. Every doubt, and every late night with more patience than I deserved. You believed when this was just an idea.

To my son — you became the reason every word mattered. You reminded me that legacy isn't written; it's lived.

To my parents — for the quiet support that built the foundation I stand on.

To my brothers — who have motivated me to become someone they see as having faith, kindness, and leadership, both in writing and in life.

To my friends — the ones who spoke truth instead of comfort, who challenged me to refine, not retreat.

To Micah and Tyler Millard, and Jackson Wiser — for capturing Crossguard's spirit and giving its face the weight it deserved.

And to everyone who carried even a fragment of belief in me over the last decade — you helped this story survive long enough to finally be seen.

This isn't just the end of a journey.

It's the beginning of everything it was preparing me for.

ABOUT THE AUTHOR

Jeremiah LaSalle is a Washington-based fantasy author, with The Belt of Truth as his debut novel. His writing blends cinematic action, emotional depth, and spiritually subtle worldbuilding designed for readers who crave character-driven adventure. He lives with his wife, their son, and two energetic dogs, who inspire much of the heart behind his stories. When he isn't writing, he's spending time with his family, exploring new ideas, and expanding the universe of House of Lore.

ALSO BY
JEREMIAH LASALLE

The Chronicles of the Crossguard
Book I: The Belt of Truth (February *2026*)
Book II: The Breastplate of Righteousness (*Coming 2027*)
A modern fantasy saga exploring truth, conviction, and the unseen war for mankind's soul.
The Tale of Kaspian the Silver Dragon *(Coming Soon)*
In a world reborn from ashes, the remnants of humanity forge a new age of steel—
And one man's name becomes legend.
Sweet Dreams *(Coming Soon)*
A quiet story of romance, a twist, and what lingers between them.
— ✦ —
Published by House of Lore Books

www.ingramcontent.com/pod-product-compliance
Lightning Source LLC
Chambersburg PA
CBHW050035120726
47903CB00006B/2053